EVERDARK

METACOSM CHRONICLES

BOOK ONE

N.A. SOLEIL

Book Cover by Lance Buckley [lancebuckley.com].
Cover symbol design by N.A. Soleil.

Dedication

To Redd, who has gotten me through more than I think she knows. I only hope I can tell her story to her satisfaction.

To my mother, Melissa Conway, for supporting me always.

Special thanks to Aimee, Sarah, and Sara. I wouldn't know what to do with myself without you wonderful humans.

Content Warning

This book contains discussions of abuse (but no detailed descriptions; characters talking about it after the fact), mental illness, swearing, violence, some gore, discussion of trafficking, a mild sex scene, and discussion of sex.

This is not a book meant for children.

Note:

No part of this book was algorithmically generated (commonly known as "AI"). What you hold in your hands is simply the result of hundreds of hours of human blood, sweat, and tears.

(I can't freaking believe I have to say this.)

The darkness of non-memory. A place of retreat, where what happened to the physical shell was rendered distant and dull.

Within the darkness, a gentle golden light, from which emanated soft singing. And, sometimes, a muffled voice, unintelligible, like another tongue heard through thick walls.

She'd turned inward through their 'treatments,' just as Survive, Resist, Escape had taught her. There, she'd found the light.

Though SRE had never made mention of such a thing being expected in the depths of one's mind, she'd embraced it unquestioningly. Certainly it was for this reason that the subversive channel had taught Specials to look inside when the 'Recruiters' and 'Specials Investigators' came knocking. Why should she doubt its origin? The song was beautiful, the warmth comforting.

Though sometimes it flared hotter than a star, and she felt she'd be seared to ash if she didn't find a way to release it. Worse, there was an undoubtable sense of anticipation, as though the star were simply biding its time before it would rise up and consume all.

Worst, it was impossible **to** *release it. Something external was smothering it, and her.*

But the more the doctors and her parents pushed her, the hotter the star grew, the more frequent its attacks, the harder it became to fight it. Some part of her wondered when it would turn its barbed fury on her.

Yet never did its heat serve to make her afraid of that light. It was a part of her; that she knew as an absolute.

The light was angry for her, for which she loved it all the more. It couldn't respond in kind, but she spoke to it often, letting the pain wash over her, shutting out the outside.

And so she watched, and waited. As SRE had taught her. As the light bid. She swallowed every pill without complaint, and allowed every injection.

They thought her a good, compliant, little girl...

But just like the light, she, too, was simply biding her time.

ONE
The Strike

"For Redd's … treatment resistance … we recommend a *specialty* institution."

The words, heard without hearing, had been scorched into her. They endlessly repeated as a backdrop to the sounds of the nightbound megacity and her own labored breathing.

The fuck could an institution do that her parents hadn't already?

No, don't think about that, she thought. *You don't want to know, and it doesn't matter, because you'll never see them again.*

In that amorphous time between 'late' and 'early,' the city formed a maze in the dark. But in her fragmented mind, the unfamiliar landscape might as well have been spawned by whatever unnamed poison clung to her soul.

She *had* been heading to the industrial complex where there would be fewer patrols, with the intent of finding her way to one of the surface access points: a series of tubes filled with ladders and catwalks. They led down, out of the raised tiers of the megacity, to the surface of a planet long abandoned.

That had been the plan.

But an inexplicable fog had risen and she'd lost what little direction she'd managed to glean under her parents' watchful eyes. Maps of the megacities weren't easily accessible by the populace, as they traveled by tube or slide-walk. No one needed to know how to navigate by foot, because the Federation so graciously provided them with the means to get from one place to another without thought.

She stumbled, a wave of dizziness stealing her breath for a moment. She rested a hand on a nearby building to let the feeling recede, but the need to *get away* drove her to push off from the wall before long.

Her uneven footsteps, slapping bare on the cold ground, echoed in that damnable fog. Her thoughts fluttered like too many birds in a too-small cage, never alighting in one place for long but always flying with one driving purpose:

Keep moving. If I stay, I'll kill them all.

Sick heat rose within her, and she battled it down. It left her gasping, vision greying at the edges. These attacks were coming on more frequently. Her anger taking on a life of its own, seeking retribution for her suffering.

The eerie wails from her nightmares rose and wove themselves seamlessly into reality. They seemed to bounce off the shifting mists, coming from everywhere at once.

— a battlefield, the dead and dying scattered over blood-soaked land like some grisly flower bed, and her hands slick with bodily detritus and gore —

She broke into a sprint with a cry of panic. She was exhausted, but the fear would accept nothing less. The spectacle of dead faces closed in, driven by too many nights of little sleep and whatever cocktail her parents had forced on her most recently. She skidded around a corner into an open space, desperate to escape it all, rushing headlong through parting mists to a sheer drop — revealed too late to stop.

As her feet hit nothing but air, something awoke within her out of pure self-preservation.

It lashed out, rent the very fabric of the universe, and made a hasty connection for her to tumble into. The portal flickered and died after her, and she landed hard on the other side. Her legs failed and the world swam.

Darkness rose to envelop her and she welcomed it, retreating to a place where the memories couldn't harm her.

***

Temperjoke hated reporting to Ichiryu — hell, he hated everything about this assignment. Striding down the obsidian hallways of her castle, he lamented the part he had to play. Despite his personal reservations, when he came to the thick, dark wood doors leading to her quarters, he knocked.

The doors swung open without indication as to what moved them — which was typical of Ichiryu: she liked passive displays of her power — revealing her private space.

While the lightless interior was spacious and well-furnished, it had neither the comforts nor the wasteful opulence one might expect from the sleeping quarters of a tyrant. The room was vaguely oval, and opened with the majority of the curve to the right instead of splitting the shape in half. Directly across from the doorway Temperjoke stood in was the balcony where Ichiryu overlooked her unwilling subjects.

Nestled in the conclave to his left was a vanity with a mirror and a low, padded stool. To the right was her bed, a large four-poster affair with such a plush mattress that it mushroomed in the middle. It looked hardly used.

On the walls were all manner of tapestries and weavings — spoils from her conquering past — each from a separate world, most of which no longer existed as more than cosmic dust. In certain cases, these tapestries, worn with age and gently flapping in the breath of wind seeping in from the open balcony door, were the only objects left of their respective civilizations.

Temperjoke's eyes settled on Ichiryu herself, a malevolent pale ghost on the balcony, wreathed in flowing cloth that flounced gravity's hold. She was a frail thing, at least compared to Temperjoke, who sported the kind of build that would rouse envy in a professional bodybuilder.

Ichiryu turned, regarding her General. Her white-grey hair — also flowing upward with no regard to gravity —

shifted with the motion. Temperjoke almost grimaced. Even with Ages under his belt, it was no dance in the posies to meet that gaze. Her white visage was narrow, emaciated, with almond-shaped eyes ringed heavily in kohl. Her irises were bloody red pinpricks, lips matching the color. The whole effect was akin to a death mask.

"Your orders?" Temperjoke asked.

"The voices whisper a name," Ichiryu rasped. "*Redd.* Watch her; then kill her. I must know how another of my kind has been born after so long."

Temperjoke bowed and exited. The door closed softly after him. As he strode down the hall, boots clicking in the dead silence of Ichiryu's austere dark castle, his thin lips pulled a humorless smile.

It has begun.

TWO
The Girl With The Golden Eyes

Lutius was on his way to see his brother.

It was just after dawn. Assisi, being an ancient planet, wasn't attached to a companion star. A wide bar of the Creator's light swept across the planet in even intervals, giving it a day-night cycle without the involvement of a 'sun.'

Dawn was Lutius' favorite time. The color of the sky was beyond compare, the air clean and cool. Truly, the world thanked the Creator for his blessing every day.

Though, this morning, his eyes were not on the thankful sky, or the cream-colored brick buildings that rose to either side of him, or the trees in perfectly-spaced intervals along the road, placed to provide a splash of color and just the right amount of shade on a warm summer day. Rather, he regarded the white sidewalk, made from a mélange of local rock. He remembered when this was still all dirt …

Something in his peripheral vision, down an alley in between buildings, caught his attention: a body. Alarmed, he darted toward it.

The body was that of a young female, seemingly unconscious, whom he identified as human from the hazy shape of her life-spark. Or *something* hominin, at least. She was just on the cusp of adulthood, with light brown skin and blood-red, shoulder-length hair. She was wearing a long, loose shirt and pants of some thin fabric.

Lutius frowned and knelt beside her. She *was* breathing, but raggedly, and her skin shone with sweat.

"Hey," he said gently. When she didn't respond, he touched her shoulder, then pinched her. Nothing.

He sighed and gathered her in his arms.

***

As Lutius climbed the hill to the front gate of his brother's mansion, the dead weight of the unconscious girl pulled at his arms and shoulders.

A human butler, more guard than servant, let him in. Lutius wondered why no one gave him a second glance as he carried the girl through the lavish halls. His suspicions crowded like unruly puppies at the back of his mind: he shushed them. Get the girl stable first.

He stopped at the bottom of a wide staircase and blew out a breath, dreading the climb. His young body had been strong before the Creator's grace left them. Now, the angels weakened by the day. The Elysian would get their victory in the end, so it seemed.

He shook his head and took the first step. Ruminations on the fate of the angels could wait. His arms and shoulders were cramped and his fingers were beginning to go numb as he reached the top.

Almost there.

He took a left. At the end of a well-decorated hallway was a set of double doors, intricately carved and made of a heavy, dark wood.

He nudged one door open with his hip and entered his niece's sanctuary.

The morning light peered through wide windows, creating slanting rectangles across dozens of bookshelves. Several sturdy, carved tables ranged about, on which were stacked old tomes, grimoires, rune-bound spellbooks, scrolls, and parchment tied with reeds or plant fibers. Bibles and canonical texts, gold-plated and gilded, rubbed spines with the few historical books remaining on Haven, dusty and damaged.

At the far end, in a large lounge chair worn and comfortable with great use, sat his niece, Ara. On her lap was a thick tome, open. Her alabaster skin shone like moonstone in the light, an effect compounded by her choice of clothing: a sleeveless white dress held at her throat with a blue oval jewel. White-blonde hair cascaded in such thick waves it almost seemed there was more hair than girl, ending finally in a pile on the floor over the edge of the chair. When she stood, it trailed behind her. How she kept it clean was a mystery. Her face was round, with delicate features. The three opalescent horns of an archangel arced back from her temples and forehead.

How Lucifer could mistreat such a sweet little girl (which was still how Lutius saw her, although she was almost an adult), he couldn't understand.

Especially given her … unusual circumstances.

She had no wings.

Lutius felt his own twitch in unconscious sympathy. An angel without wings was like a dwarf without a beard. No one knew why she hadn't earned her birthright yet, least of all Ara herself, although she tried to hide the pain it caused.

She looked up at the sound of the door. Her eyes were so dark a blue as to be almost black. A pleased smile lit her face — but the expression was quickly replaced with confusion.

She stood, taking a moment to set aside her open book. "Uncle! What — "

"I found her on the street."

"Put her here," she ordered imperiously, suddenly all business, and gestured to her own chair.

She scooted a side-table supporting a drink and a plate of half-eaten snacks out of the way. Lutius crossed the room with difficulty, trying not to bump the unconscious girl's head or knock anything down. Some of the books seemed fragile enough to fall to dust at the turn of a page, and the library wasn't exactly neat.

He knelt awkwardly, rolled the redhead into the chair, then moved out of the way. Ara took his place, stretching her hands out to hover them over the girl's chest.

"Her life force is low … almost catatonic," Ara said, then frowned. "There is something very odd about her life-spark, but I can't place it." Ara's inspection moved down the length of the unconscious form. "Multiple lacerations, bruising on her wrists, upper arms, and neck. Clusters of pinprick marks on her arms — some swollen, possibly infected … signs of dehydration, malnutrition, broken blisters and cuts on her feet, embedded detritus ..."

She sat back on her heels. "Uncle, do you think you could find mother and bring her here, please?" she asked in a careful voice without looking back at him.

"Sure."

***

He found Persephone in the kitchen, speaking with the cook. He didn't want to interrupt, so he took a moment to study Ara's mother.

Not that he'd admit it even to himself, but he'd never shy away from a chance to watch Persephone.

In the same way Ara was intelligent and kind, her mother radiated strength and calm. Her large white wings were dusted in pale pink at the tips of each feather. The snow-white locks of her hair were pulled into an elaborate sculpture of art on the back of her head, the excess allowed to fall freely in curly waves down her back. It was almost as long as Ara's. Her horns were two on either side of her head, curled back and up. Her halo shone behind her head.

Every move was graceful. From gestures she performed with small, white hands, to the way she turned after concluding the conversation.

"Lutius, this is unexpected," she said, her voice tinged with just the right amount of surprise, concern, and warmth.

Persephone was like a queen. Polite, gracious, and more than anything, politic.

"Yeah, well … I had something to deliver to Ara." He grinned at his own ambiguity. "Speaking of your daughter, she wants to talk to you."

"Oh." Persephone smiled. "Well, you are welcome to stay as long as you like, but I should go see what she wants."

Persephone swept past him and Lutius fell in line behind her, ignoring the implied dismissal.

***

"Poor thing … " Persephone breathed as she drew a stray scarlet curl from the girl's cheek.

"Can she stay?" Ara asked.

Persephone sighed and stood, clasping her hands before her. "I agree that she is in a bad state, but you know the rules. You'll have to ask your father."

"But mother — he'll refuse!" Ara cried. "We cannot abandon her!"

"She can stay until your father comes home." Persephone pinned her daughter with that look that all mothers develop. Ara stared back in defiance for a moment, then dropped her gaze. Persephone touched Ara's cheek.

"I know how you feel, dear heart, and I will make your case to him." When Ara looked up, Persephone offered an encouraging smile. "I don't want to turn her out either, but this is your father's house, and the final decision is his."

Lutius, silent witness, had to work very hard not to make a face. Since when had the angels been so aggressively patriarchal?

Ara finally nodded.

Persephone kissed her forehead. “Stay with her for now, dear. I will deal with your father.”

She turned and, seeming to glide across the floor, made her way to the door. Lutius opened it for her, was rewarded with a smile of gratitude, and walked with Persephone down the length of the hallway.

‘“Something to deliver’, hm?” she said, amused.

He grinned impishly. “Couldn’t let the kid rot out there. Not when I happen to know the best Healer in Haven.”

“Will you stay until Lucifer returns?” she asked quietly.

Maybe it was his imagination, the restrained hope he heard.

Lutius laughed. “You kidding? I can’t *wait* to see what my dear brother does.”

She said nothing, but he didn’t miss the smile fade from her features.

***

By the time Lucifer came home, dusk had transformed the library into a place of mysterious shadows interspersed with warm lamp light.

Ara hovered like a worried hen over the girl while Lucifer inspected her. Lutius stood with his back to the wall next to the door, arms crossed over his chest, his wings spread slightly so as not to take the full brunt of his weight. Persephone stood in front of him, her hands entwined with one another, watching her husband. No one spoke.

Lucifer was a fairly short angel, pale like his daughter and wife. His platinum locks were chopped off at mid-back and always pulled into a ponytail at the nape of his neck. His horns were a dull grey-white, and spiked almost straight up, and his halo was dim and small. He was a terminally thin man with narrow shoulders, a long face, and angular features. His wings were grey with a gold and blue cast.

What concerned Lutius as he studied his brother was the display of wealth on Lucifer's person. He had somehow acquired a gold watch, and a thin gold chain hung around his neck. Several rings adorned one hand. The clasp holding back his hair was gold inlaid with gems.

Haven was a segregated community, the last of the angels. There was no mining, no ore to smelt, no gems to collect — and the planet below them was supposedly dead, a husk that the angels of Haven no longer had contact with. How had Lucifer gotten his hands on these fripperies?

Lucifer cleared his throat, interrupting Lutius' thoughts, and turned to Ara. "I sup*pose* she can stay." He had a tendency to over-enunciate in odd places. "When she is recovered, we will work out a payment method for time and expenses incurred. *Agreed*?"

For Lucifer, this was incredibly generous.

Ara nodded.

"Good. Now, I have *business* to attend to." He pivoted on one heel and swept out of the library without so much as a 'hello' to his brother or wife.

Lutius glanced sidelong at Persephone. Her face was an immovable mask.

Always politic.

"I should probably get going. Let me know when she wakes up?" he said.

"Of course," Persephone responded. "You know you are always welcome here."

Ara called out a distracted "Good night," and Lutius left.

***

The redhead was moved into one of the spare bedrooms nearest to Ara's room, where she would remain until recovered. Ara had taken to reading at the girl's bedside, not wanting to miss the critical moment when she awakened.

Several days later, Ara's intuition and attention paid off. Her patient became feverish, tossing and mumbling. She wasn't speaking angelic or any of the other tongues Ara was fluent in. Ara did recognize a few words, though, so deduced that the redhead was probably speaking the common trade tongue, which Ara could hold a basic conversation in. Her facial expressions and the begging tone of voice, though, only strengthened Ara's growing hypothesis.

The redhead started sweating profusely. Concerned, Ara checked her vitals through a Seeing, and was shocked at what she saw. No natural affliction 'looked' like this.

It looked like … an addiction.

The redhead went from twitching to thrashing. Ara grappled with her and was thrown on her rear end, some ten feet away.

She blinked, dumbfounded by the girl's strength.

The noise brought in two servants, who almost found themselves in similar situations. Those two servants called for help, and before Ara knew it, half the household was crowded into the little room. Ara backed into a corner to get out of the way when her mother's commanding presence swept in. Something passed across Persephone's beautiful face. Although Ara didn't know how to recognize it, it was the hollow look of determination when conscious emotion recedes — when you know you might have to do something that will haunt you forever. Persephone turned to the nearest housekeeper.

"Tie her down."

The man hastened to do her bidding.

He returned with a magically-enhanced rope used to haul large things. Luckily, the redhead seemed to run out of whatever manic urge was possessing her to fight, and she settled back down into fever sleep. The army of servants filed out, leaving one to tie her down to the heavy wooden frame of the bed.

Persephone closed the door after the last servant and turned to her daughter with a peculiar look.

"Ara…?"

"She appears to be in withdrawals," Ara said hesitantly. "Though, from what precisely, I don't know."

Persephone turned her full attention on Ara: gentle but firm. Ara resisted the urge to fidget.

"Tell me everything," Persephone said.

"I don't think she did it to herself. She has been having night terrors. I think she was tortured." She gingerly picked up a floppy hand, turned it over, and moved the loop of rope. "These bruises are from restraints, and what I saw was attacking — attacking! — her nervous system. Whoever was torturing her injected her with these chemicals. I think they were trying to change something about her brain."

After a profound silence, Persephone said, "Keep a close eye on her, Ara."

***

The next day, the redhead awoke.

Her body arched like she'd been struck by lightning.

Ara shot to her feet, alarmed, and set aside her book. The morning light through the window illuminated the girl's eyes as they flew open. They were green — no — even as Ara watched, the color shifted, turning yellow, then orange, and finally settling into metallic gold.

The girl strained against her bonds while the transformation finished, then dropped heavily to the bed.

Ara breathed again.

She chanced a few steps forward until she was at the edge of the bed. The girl stared above her without comprehension, and were it not for the ragged lift and fall of her chest, Ara would think her dead.

Suddenly the girl blinked. She tried to speak, but coughed instead. It was then that she noticed her bonds. She glanced at her hands and down to her feet, pulled feebly at the ropes, then turned blank eyes on Ara. The expression of abject acceptance rent Ara's heart.

Ara hastened to her side, resting a gentle hand on the girl's cold fingertips.

"No," she said in halting Common. She'd been practicing. "You are safe. My name is Ara Luschia Invenes."

The girl's brows furrowed in confusion. She opened her mouth, ran a bone-dry tongue across her lips and mouthed, 'water.'

Ara covered her mouth, aghast. "Oh. Oh. Of course. I apologize."

Ara had been keeping the girl's body alive through the transposition skill, which Healers who lacked Ranger or Accord technology used. Transposition's first step was the Sight, a basic Healer ability which formed a connection between Healer and patient to allow the Healer to visualize and manipulate their patient's body. Using the Sight as a conduit, transposition allowed the Healer to transfer fluids, nutrients, and cells from their own body into their patient.

Ara was lucky she was an angel: angelic blood was less physical and more Weave and quantum, which made it incredibly malleable. She had been taking her own plasma in small amounts and using transposition to keep her patient's body from falling into lethal dehydration, and providing necessary nutrients in the same way. Her Sight allowed her to take a snapshot, giving her access to the state of a body's systems, which she could then tweak through various methods.

It was exhausting work, though. Not just the mental toll of constantly checking, but the physical toll of eating and drinking more (and things she wouldn't necessarily consume, so as to have the right kinds of nutrients), in order to give it away.

She couldn't possibly transfer enough to keep the girl from becoming at least moderately dehydrated, though.

"Don't try to talk," Ara advised as she gave the redhead small sips from a glass, "or sit up; you are still too weak. You have been in a catatonic state for three days."

Insofar as Ara could tell, the girl took this in stride. Ara raised the water glass to check its level, then set it on the table next to the bed.

"That's enough. Don't want you getting sick."

The girl nodded and leaned against the pillows, closing her eyes.

As Ara expected, her mother came in, escorted by several servants. Persephone somehow knew everything that went on in the house. By this time, the girl had fallen into an uneasy doze. Surprisingly, her father followed, but remained by the door, his eyes guarded.

"How is she doing?" Persephone asked.

"As well as can be expected."

Persephone watched the sleeping girl. "Well, when she wakes again, make sure to call us immediately," she said. "Will you stay with her?"

"Yes."

Persephone shot Ara a little encouraging smile and left. Lucifer remained to give the redhead a strangely cold look — or was that Ara's imagination? — then followed his wife.

Ara went back to reading her book, despite the questions that spun in her mind like a disturbed flock of birds. After a while, she napped in the chair.

When she awoke, a soft glow from the lights outside illuminated the room just enough to see by. She shifted, and the noise brought sudden motion from the girl in the bed.

The girl watched her solemnly. Ara moved her book to the table, lit the lamp, and offered a smile. The girl flinched. Dark, dark circles were under her eyes. Her lips were chapped and cracked. Ara felt a sudden, sharp pang of sympathy.

"Hi," the girl said, her voice rough. She *was* speaking a dialect of Common.

Ara was flooded with relief that she'd guessed correctly. "Hello."

"Your hair is really, really long," the girl commented, then paused a moment and added, "It's pretty."

Ara self-consciously tucked a white-blonde strand behind her ear. "Thank you."

"What's on your head?"

Ara touched one of her horns. "These are … something my species has."

The girl's face screwed up in confusion. She still looked like she wasn't thinking clearly. "You're not human?"

"Ah, we can talk about that later. How are you feeling?"

The girl shrugged and grimaced. "Like shit."

Ara helped her drink more water, then sat back down.

The girl surveyed the room, then asked, "Where am I?"

Ara sensed a wealth of meaning behind the words. "You are safe. We are in my family's house and well protected." Ara hesitated, unsure of what the reaction to her next question would be. "What happened to you?"

"I'm not sure. The last few months have been bad."

"Tell me as much as you feel comfortable."

Golden eyes lifted, calculating. Ara blinked, feeling inexplicably exposed. Then the girl looked down and the sensation faded. She fidgeted, fingers playing with the blanket.

"A couple years back, I … things started happening. I sometimes heard voices, uh, things moved when I got angry … ugh, I sound unhinged."

"Go on," Ara urged.

The girl took a deep breath, steadied herself. "My parents sent me to … doctors, ran tests … they called me psychotic, behind the white walls they assumed I couldn't hear through … but I could. They — started therapies, what they called therapies … but it got worse; nothing was helping."

The words tumbled out, as though she'd been holding them back for an eternity. "The medication, the treatments … none of it worked. I kept getting worse. A lot of it I don't remember … but the dreams … " Her voice lost its strength. She cleared her throat to continue. "Um, and then last night — or, the last night I remember — I heard them talking about sending me somewhere for, uh, 'full-time care' … so I ran away. I couldn't — I'd kill them."

She was a picture of horror — staring emotionless eyes, pallid skin pulled taut to her bones with dehydration and malnutrition, words emerging through barely open lips.

"So many times I thought of murdering them all ... imagined it down to the last detail — something in my mind begging me to let go — every day, harder to resist ... "

She trailed off and blinked, coming back to reality. "I'm sorry," she whispered, shrinking into herself.

Ara shushed her. "Let me get mother; she will want to talk to you before you go back to sleep," she said, and stood.

"Wait — you're going to keep me here? A murderous psycho? Aren't you afraid?"

Ara shook her head. "You're not either of those things, and I'm not afraid. If I'm right, what those … *people* did to you was reprehensible." Ara didn't bother to hide the scorn in her voice and hoped she'd used the right words.

The girl stared at her. Whatever was going through her mind, it didn't show on her face.

"My name is Redd," she said at last.

"A pleasure to meet you, Redd," Ara said with relief. "Give me a moment to fetch my mother. Try to drink a little more water, if you can."

***

The door opened again. Redd didn't know whether to flinch or be glad — being alone made the things that weren't real clamor for her attention, but having to deal with people was almost as bad.

She looked up as Persephone entered, and felt the world spin.

Wings ...

"Could you leave us for a minute, dear? I think perhaps Redd should be hungry by now." Persephone's voice had a peculiar tone.

"Mother?" Ara questioned.

"Soup should be fine, but she will need something solid, too, so perhaps some bread."

THREE
Trust and Deception

"You're the only one who ever understood me … " Ichiryu murmured, her voice a soft caress. "No one else understands what it's like, to have to live *this way,*" her voice cracked, on the brink of hysteria.

"Don't let it affect you!" The other voice echoed despite its soft, sibilant hiss.

"I know, I know." She calmed, and smiled.

"Remember: no one else sees the things you do. You are only doing what must be done … you were denied the help you deserved! It all went horribly wrong."

Ichiryu nodded slightly, her fingers running across a cold, smooth face. "It isn't my fault," she whispered.

"It's the only way to quiet the voices," the other responded.

"It's the only way to be free," Ichiryu affirmed vehemently. "They will understand in time ... "

"They will … but what about Temperjoke?"

Ichiryu's lips twisted. "What *about* him?" she hissed, paranoid suspicion rising like bile.

"Are you sure you can trust him?"

There was silence for a long, long time.

"He has been with me for so long," she finally replied. "The only one … is that wrong? Is he a danger?"

The other voice paused to consider. "He is so weak," it said confidently. "How could he be a threat to *you*?"

"He is a tool to be used, nothing more. He calms the voices." Ichiryu nodded, the long, upswept silver strands of her hair shifting like grain in the wind. "He cannot disobey me."

She closed her eyes as a stab of pain lanced through her temples.

... I am Daystar ...

Ichiryu leapt away from her vanity mirror with such violence that the stool skidded onto its side. The words that echoed through her head woke the spirits dormant within, and set them to ricocheting around in her skull like a hurricane.

"We are all mistakes! Cosmic accidents — none of us deserve to exist! We are wrong!" She shouted at herself in the mirror.

"*No — I won't listen...*" she whimpered, turning away. The pain increased, and despite herself, she returned to the mirror.

Her wide, bulging eyes stared back from the vanity. Behind her, in the reflected shadowy recesses of the room, the girl with the golden eyes stood, impassively watching. Ichiryu screamed and whipped around, backing up against the vanity.

There was nothing there.

She twisted to slam her fist into the mirror. It shook but did not break.

"*You LIED to me*!" she screeched over the wailing of the voices in her head.

Her accusations turned into bestial howls of fury as she tore around the room, thin arms swinging to knock down or destroy whatever she could, fueled by her mindless rage.

The door burst open and she cringed away from the light, choosing to cradle her aching head in her hands. She barely heard someone call her name.

"Temper?" she gasped pleadingly.

The presence disappeared and the door closed again. Ichiryu curled up on the floor and cried, barely aware of her own self in the thousands of voices that roared in her head for release.

One moment she felt like she would be gone forever; the next, blessedly, they receded. Opening her eyes with painful effort, she raised herself on her elbows and saw, through a bleary haze, Temper standing over her. She hadn't even heard the door open.

To her, the look on his face as he was backlit from the doorway was pity … and hatred. All at once her grief subsided and returned to anger with such a force that she was frozen in place.

"Lady?" Temper questioned the sudden silence.

"It's your fault … " she hissed, staring up at him with venom in her eyes. He blinked. "This is all *your* fault!"

"How is your curse my fault, Lady?" he asked mildly. It only inflamed her further.

"You told him to do it, you — always behind me, always plotting! All I wanted — and you told him to do it!" She struggled to her knees and wavered back and forth, nodding her head to her own conviction. "Told him … always always pay … always, for eternity … "

Temper sighed above her. He reached down to help her to her feet. She leaned against him, unable to support her own minuscule weight. He assisted her to her bed and covered her up, placing her teddy bear within reach. She nabbed it from him and held it close, shutting out the world.

***

Persephone sat and studied Redd, who was staring at her like a cornered mouse.

"Where are you from?" Persephone asked gently, in perfect Common.

Redd's mouth worked for a good few seconds before she managed: "H-hero."

"Pardon?" Persephone asked.

"You … you're a Hero of the Revolution."

Persephone was jolted, but didn't let it show on her face. "So you're from Federated Earth. Which megacity?"

"Jewel City," Redd said weakly after a pause. "Where am I now?"

"You are on Assisi, a planet far from your home. We are the remnants of the angels."

Redd hiccuped a hysterical laugh, then abruptly quieted. She pointed over Persephone's shoulder. Obligingly, Persephone stood and turned. She wore a loose robe that dipped down in the back to make room for her wings, which she now spread slightly.

"Oh," Redd said. "You're real? Wait — the Heroes were … angels? There are different planets — other people? None of this makes sense." She sounded like she was on the verge of tears, and Persephone's heart went out to her.

But Persephone didn't have time to educate her.

"I can't answer your questions right now," Persephone said urgently. "My daughter will be back shortly, and there are things you must know. You are in serious danger here. Beware my husband. I will try to protect you, but you must leave as soon as you can."

"What? Leave? Where the hell am I supposed to go?"

Persephone ignored the question, leaning forward. "You honestly have no idea how you got here?" she asked intently.

Redd shook her head wordlessly, her eyes wide and fixed on Persephone.

The door opened and in came Ara, carrying a large bowl of soup with a piece of bread balanced on the edge. Persephone smiled slightly. Ara was doing a great job hiding how much she wanted to know what was going on. But she was a good child, and wouldn't ask.

Lutius suspected the vileness in the underground of Haven, but Persephone was neck deep in it. As soon as her husband spent any time around this girl, she'd be lucky to get away, for one reason or another. She'd either be sold or killed.

Using this girl, Persephone could finally do something to derail her husband, after all the atrocities she'd had to witness.

Even if he killed her for it.

Ara set the bowl down on the little bedside table. Redd ate slowly and not very much. Her hands began to shake and her attention was continually drawn to something across the room.

"Are you alright, dear?" Persephone asked.

Redd stammered something incomprehensible, then closed her eyes and tried to curl up in a ball. Ara went to her.

"Redd?" Ara called. The redhead was muttering and rocking and had turned ashen. Persephone looked to where Redd had been staring — an empty corner of the room.

"What's the matter?" Persephone asked. Ara had put her arms around Redd and had the distant-eyed look of a Seeing.

"She's hallucinating," Ara replied at length.

Persephone thinned her lips. Ara was quiet for long minutes; finally, Redd sighed and relaxed. Ara let out a breath as well and leaned back, her eyes opening.

"You helped her to sleep?" Persephone asked.

Ara nodded, an unusually haunted look on her young face.

"Good."

"What will happen to her, mother?"

"We will help her recover." Persephone said firmly. She stood. "I must be off, dear." She paused. "I love you, Ara."

Ara graced her with a smile. "I love you too, mother."

Knowing what she had to do, Persephone left.

***

Over the next three weeks, the withdrawals crescendoed, and then began to taper off. Hallucinations, shaking, and mood swings came and went as Redd gained strength; though the nightmares hung around tenaciously. While the dark circles under her eyes faded somewhat, it was obvious she was still not sleeping well or often.

Ara hardly left Redd's side in that time. When the girl was sleeping, which was often, Ara was researching and cramming Common. Thankfully, the language came easier and easier for her as the weeks went on, and with the real-world practice of conversing with a native speaker, Ara achieved fluency in record time. She had already had a decent familiarity because many of her books were written in Common. Redd's specific dialect was Federated Common, which wasn't covered by Ara's books, but talking with Redd helped her pick it up quickly.

Ara brought her books into Redd's room and began to slowly fill Redd in on what initiated folk already knew. The first thing was what 'initiated' meant.

Redd was uninitiated — basically, she came from a society unready to commingle with the other universal societies.

Ara's lessons included that the universe at large was kept in check by multiple organizations. A Creator artifact (known as the Obelisk of Time) with its Chosen — individuals tied to the Obelisk — made political decrees from the elven home city of Terelath. They, and the Obelisk, were protected by the elven Council and a sort of intergalactic military known as the Rangers. The final major group was the Universal Accord — commonly shortened to 'the Accord' — a group made up of representatives from all initiated societies. They were mediators primarily.

Though Ara didn't tell Redd this, Lucifer had always said that the Rangers had abandoned Haven. Ara had never truly believed him, and she believed him even less as time went on.

Being a part of the Accord meant acquiescing to certain rules meant to keep peace. If a species hadn't reached certain milestones, there was no way they could be expected to follow those rules, and therefore were ordered to be left alone.

The final decision on initiation was made by an informal council of the Rangers, Accord, and various other organizations. For those left uninitiated, it was for a reason.

Redd emphatically agreed with Ara about that. If any kind of alien came down from the sky — even ones that looked human and spoke Federated Common — on her Earth, it would cause worldwide panic and unrest. The only reason she believed she was talking to someone who wasn't a human was because it was *happening*.

And even then, sometimes it was too much.

Redd also learned that angels once had an illustrious society. Three centuries prior, the angels' home planet, Assisi (Haven floated over its wasteland of a surface), was attacked by false gods known as Elysian, a space-faring species legendary for their cruelty and power. As far as Ara was aware, the survivors on Haven were the only angels left, and they had barely made it.

Redd had asked about the 'Heroes of the Revolution' and how they were related to the angels, but Ara had never even heard the term. She didn't know much about Federated Earth.

Redd's basic education happened over many days. She had a hard time accepting it, still struggling against the reality her head was trying to assert, which mostly manifested as hallucinations.

Redd's grasp on shared reality was tentative at best; Ara knew that completely upending everything she'd ever known had to be done excruciatingly carefully.

***

About a month and a half after Redd's arrival, Lutius came to visit, announcing that Lucifer's mansion was far too stuffy for two youngsters and that he was going to take them out to breakfast. Lucifer was out on business again, so it was Persephone who gave the blessing for the outing.

Lutius led the two girls down onto the street with easy strides of his long legs. He smiled over his shoulder. His features mimicked Lucifer's only in the baldest sense of being siblings. While Lucifer was all narrow angles and harshness, Lutius had the weight of muscle on his slim frame, broadening his shoulders, chest, and waist. His sandy hair was cut short, and he shared his brother's blue eyes. His horns were short, curled close to his ears, and a shiny dark brown. His halo was grey and almost disappeared in certain lighting. His wings were tan-colored, darkening to a chocolate brown toward the tips.

"This is City Center," Lutius said. "It's become rather large recently, so I'm afraid I can't show you the whole of it, but I will take you girls to the market. Ara, you've been there, right?"

Ara smiled slightly, a little sadly. "Not lately."

Redd wished she could stop seeing. If she weren't afraid of tripping, she would squeeze her eyes shut — not that it would help. Inside his mind, Lutius wanted to be more to Ara and her mother ... much more, in the case of the latter. Redd felt dirty, being privy to such private knowledge. If she spent too much time focused on it, she almost felt like *she* was the one in love with Persephone, and she started to panic that she was losing herself.

She tried to focus on her outer surroundings, lest the inner world overwhelm her.

They moved into a fairly empty street lined with little buildings that seemed to be places that sold things.

Redd had never been shopping. Her parents hadn't let her out of the house, with the exception of when the 'specialists' took over her 'care.'

But on such a beautiful day, with the sky bright and a gentle breeze blowing, she didn't want to think about that.

Lutius led them to something called a bakery, where people made sweets and other edible things out of ground grains. Redd, who had eaten from a replicator her whole life, didn't know that food could even be made by people. She wished she were in a better mental state to enjoy the new experience.

The bakery was small and homey, made out of sandy-colored bricks, with a counter displaying goods on the far end from the door. The rest of the space was a dedicated seating area where a few angels already sat drinking tea and eating from the counter.

The trio sat in a corner by the window and had light pastries drizzled in honey with fruit paste and tea. Then Redd watched people pass by as Lutius talked about City Center, and Ara interjected a few things here and there; but in general, Redd wasn't really able to pay attention.

The withdrawals had been hell. As bad as Redd's hallucinations must have been for Ara, her mother, and the servants who had often had to tie her down, they were a hundred times worse for the owner of the mind trying to vomit up its sickness.

Ara had told her a little bit about the state they'd found her in. Redd didn't remember much from her frantic nighttime escape, other than the desperate need to *get away*. Even thinking about it made her feet twitch.

They tortured me, she thought with piercing clarity, and the bite in her mouth turned to ash. She swallowed it with an effort and took a sip of water to suppress a sudden urge to gag.

Ara, with the detachment of a professional, had once listed the general terms for the chemicals found in Redd's system: the things she was detoxing from. Psychotropics, stimulators, and psychic blockers laced with addictive chemicals. Ara had remarked with some bland curiosity that it seemed like they were *trying* to drive Redd out of her mind.

Redd had spent almost that whole night over a bucket, but didn't have the heart to tell Ara it was her bold-faced discussion of what Redd had survived that had triggered it. Even so, Ara seemed to pick up on it and had staunchly avoided the subject since.

Now that the suppressive drugs were out of her system completely, she was gaining her power back … which she straight-up rejected.

She didn't want it. She didn't want to throw things without touching them when she got mad, or to listen to people's thoughts. She *was* finding that she could tune them out, but it took a monumental effort. She just didn't have that much control yet. It was like trying to flex a muscle you knew you had but had never used before. It was exhausting.

As she had while actively being tortured, during the worst of the withdrawals, she often slipped into her own mind to listen to the golden music and bask in the warmth of the light.

She hadn't told Ara about it, but she would take a bet that the little angel already suspected something else was going on in the tangled depths of Redd's mind.

She hadn't necessarily wanted to leave the mansion that day, but she had to admit that the change was nice. Perhaps she had been suffering from a little bit of stagnation — but Persephone's urgent warning almost a month ago had never left her, and she'd always been very careful around Lucifer.

While Redd was recovering, he had been checking in on her occasionally — more frequently than she'd have liked — and asking the kinds of benign questions that, with the way he phrased them and the way he looked at her, came across as predatory. The status of her health, how her mental recovery was going … always just that line of inquiry, nothing to learn about her as a person. His visits sparked panic attacks that Ara had to help her through: his cold, assessing gaze reminded her too much of the 'doctors' who were supposedly trying to fix her.

Maybe now was her chance to take Persephone's advice and run. Her eyes darted to the edges of City Center. She'd seen from the windows of the mansion that they were surrounded by forest.

Her heart started racing.

She could ask to go somewhere near the woodline, lose Ara and Lutius in the crowd, make a run for it.

She'd been camping, so she knew the very basics about moving through a forested area. But she wasn't familiar with this terrain, and they were. They'd find her. If she tried to escape, what would they do to her? Did it even matter? If Lucifer had some nebulous nefarious plan for her, was there any point in trying to rebel against it? Better to —

"Redd?"

Redd looked up, startled, to meet Ara's worried dark eyes.

Her half-formed plans to flee dissipated in an instant. If she left, she'd be abandoning Ara, who had been so kind.

"Sorry," Redd said. "Guess I spaced out."

Ara gave her a confused smile.

Redd smiled slightly in return and dropped her spoon into her tea. "You were saying something about bees?"

Ara looked down shyly. "The honey … under normal circumstances, insects and other animals could not survive at this altitude, but the ancient angels that raised Haven to the sky created a sort of bubble of magic around it that neutralizes the effects of the upper atmosphere, like gas composition dispersion and cold."

Redd took a bite of her pastry, taking a moment to consider the honey. "It is very good," she agreed, then sighed. "I'm sorry. Everything tastes like rainbows and sunshine, honest ... it's just — " She lifted her hands to indicate the other people in the bakery, and made a face. "It's hard to shut them all out."

Ara looked stricken.

Lutius snorted a laugh under his breath and stood. "Come on, let's pay and we'll head out to do some shopping."

"I don't have any money," Redd said after a moment.

"Oh, don't worry about that. I'm buying."

"That's very kind of you, but you don't — "

Lutius shook his head. “You’ve had a rough time. Just pick out something you like and try to relax.”

Redd looked down to blink away tears. Why were they being so nice to her? After all she’d been through, the last thing she wanted to do was open up to somebody, but Lutius and Ara … her uncontrolled mental scanning, guided by emotions running a little high, told her they were genuine.

Lutius paid, and the three of them headed out into the open market. Past the neat little buildings, all the same size and shape like interlocking child’s play blocks, the street widened into a huge courtyard with a statue in the center surrounded by a small garden of beautiful white flowers. Redd was somewhat surprised to see dozens of angels already perusing the wares of the merchants.

Something about being in the market put Lutius on edge, but Redd was trying to ignore his stream of consciousness and focus on winding down.

She felt like a damn spring, she was coiled so tightly. Like she was expecting an attack at any second.

Luckily, relaxing became easier as the morning advanced. Redd and Ara got to chatting, and Redd was able to mostly ignore the strange looks from passersby and Lutius’ underlying uneasiness. She was the only human in the market — and, seeing this many angels in one place, Redd was struck by how *all* of them had horns and wings and halos of varying colors and shapes. The only angel present who didn’t have wings or a halo was … Ara.

Redd lingered over stalls with intricately-crafted jewelry (made of what looked like twine and crystallized flowers and plants), bright scarves, stone knives of delicate craftsmanship, small animals in cages, and fragrant and exotic plants in little pots that seemed to be made out of pressed earth and nothing more. She stopped entirely as she came to a stall with clothing in rainbow piles. She looked down at herself. Persephone had given her some clothes, but they were ill-fitting.

As Ara talked animatedly with the proprietor of the stall next door about the herbal remedies for sale there, Redd picked over the selection of clothing with great care. While there were some beautiful dresses made of soft fabric unlike anything she'd ever felt, she found herself drawn more to the sturdy pieces meant for traveling. Their material was a mystery; thick and rough.

She could grab it and run … or, no, maybe it would be better to just slip behind the stall, right now, when no one was looking … this was her last chance —

There was someone else at the stall. She'd been ignoring them, but just at that moment, they sidled a little too close for comfort and broke her train of thought. She turned her head quickly, intending to rebuke, but was cut off before the words left her lips.

"Don't look at me," a deep voice hissed in a language Redd understood. Nobody else in the market spoke anything but that sing-songy shit that seemed to be angelic in origin — one of the reasons Redd hadn't asked to buy anything. The shopkeepers also looked uneasy when she came to their stall.

"Just … keep your eyes forward," he continued.

Redd scowled, but slowly picked up a shirt and pretended to consider it. "Why?"

"You shouldn't be here."

She went cold inside. Persephone's insistent questioning about how she had arrived in Haven came back to her. "You are the second person to say something to that effect. Why?" Her voice sounded harsh to her own ears.

Suddenly the warm light from overhead, the smells of cooking food, the sweet scent of flowers, and the casual buzz of conversation around her all seemed very wrong.

"Lucifer brings in humans, yeah?"

Redd hesitated, then ventured, "Okay ... "

"Well, suddenly, a human he didn't bring in shows up. How long do you think it will be before he does something about it?"

"Does something about what? I'm not causing any trouble."

"But you don't belong to him."

She turned to ask him what he meant, and he hid his face.

"Everything okay, Redd?" Lutius asked from behind her.

She about-faced and put on a false smile. "Yeah, fine." She couldn't bring herself to tell Lutius the truth. She was barely able to comprehend what she'd just been told.

Her head was swimming. Who could she trust?

Lutius and Ara had been kind, but if Lucifer *was* involved in bad shit, how far did it go? Was his family involved? *Were they just setting her up for something?*

She reined in her spiraling paranoia roughly.

She'd read Ara and Lutius, to the best of her abilities. They weren't play-acting. If there was one thing she trusted she could sense with accuracy, it was deception.

The man in the market hadn't been lying, either.

Lutius gave her a smile, but it didn't reach the suspicion in his eyes as they flicked to the figure hurrying away through the crowds.

"I think I found what I want," she said, maybe a little too loudly, to bring his attention back. Something made her want to protect the man who had tried to warn her.

"Oh, yeah?"

Redd pointed out the traveling outfit she'd looked at earlier: a light, loose shirt; thick, tight pants; boots; and a jacket. Lutius quietly paid for it all, and he and Redd went to get Ara. Ara had her own money — allowance from her parents — and she had bought several pots of herbs, which she was having trouble juggling. Lutius laughed and took two of the plants from her.

They wandered around the rest of the market, got some snacks, people-watched, and talked, but Redd's concentration was permanently shattered. The whole thing felt like a charade, like everyone was pretending to be happy to keep the oppressive forces off their backs.

Which felt awfully fucking familiar.

As the dusk crept in, they headed out, and Redd finally got close enough to see the statue at the center of the plaza in detail.

She was not surprised to see it was of Lucifer, one fist raised to the sky and the other across his chest.

FOUR
The Pomegranate Seed

Redd was absorbed in her own thoughts on the way back to the mansion. She must have said good-bye, or thank you, or something to allay suspicion, because Lutius left with a smile.

Inside, Ara left to go to her room, and Redd went back to hers.

It was in the dark hallway just outside her room that they caught her — an arm across her throat, hands pulling at her limbs. She fought blindly, coherency chased away by panic.

Her power began to rise in response to the fear, a heat prickling under her skin, but a sharp pain in her neck stole it. To her horror, the power bled away, leaving her numb and sightless.

She knew a needle-stick when she felt one.

Her mind fragmented, and Lucifer swam into her view.

"You will learn to *mind* me, you worthless *animal.*"

What's going on? Redd thought in panic.

He looked over her shoulder at someone she couldn't see. Her body was tingling; she couldn't move a muscle.

"Lock her in. I *won't* have her escaping again. Prepare a place for her in the pens."

They threw her in her room. She heard the door slam and the lock engage. Eventually, the feeling returned enough that she managed to crawl toward the bed, but she sensed nothing. The world around her was dead.

And eventually, she surrendered to sleep.

43

Lutius made his way up the hill to his brother's mansion, Persephone's emergency message still ringing in his ears. Long ago, she had given him one of the very few communication crystals remaining on Haven. Since he traveled a lot, she had reasoned with Lutius that he should carry it for his safety, and he'd taken it at face value as a smart idea. He'd never expected that she had ulterior motives.

He crept like a shadow, sticking to the trees. The last thing he needed was to run afoul of one of Lucifer's 'staff.' He almost allowed himself a tight smile. *Never thought my old training would come in handy again,* he thought.

So it was true, then. Lucifer was trafficking in sapients. And he'd set his sights on Redd.

Lutius had been trying to piece it together since his brother's abrupt change in temperament. Lucifer hadn't dealt very well with the losses incurred by the Elysian attack. While it had affected them all, he'd gone distant, cold. There was an obsessive look in Lucifer's eyes that Lutius didn't like — no, it was more than that. That look terrified him.

Lutius' trips to the other islands of Haven had yielded nothing — no other angels. That meant he was without the outside support he'd need to make any serious moves against his brother, even to confirm his own suspicions.

Who knew what kind of people Lucifer had allied himself with? The fact that he was not working alone was obvious. What kind of technology and magic did he have access to? One wrong move, and Lutius would be finished. Up until now, he was fairly sure that his brother had dismissed him as not being a threat, and he wanted to keep it that way until he had some firepower as backup.

If only the Rangers had arrived sooner.

Their camp was camouflaged using technology, not that such a thing posed much of a deterrent to someone with Blackwing training. He'd sensed the distortion while flying over during one of his routine patrols and made contact just that afternoon. The Field Commander he'd spoken to, a Sergeant Beowulf, had told him they'd been set up for only thirty-two hours and briefed him that they were there to investigate the planet beneath the cloud layer. Though, that had come off as a flimsy excuse. Lutius knew about the five-hundred-year quarantine for Elysian-touched planets and that it hadn't passed.

They must be there for his brother.

Beowulf was too professional to give any of that away, though. She did advise him that they weren't fully set up — including their leadership still being en route. So when he got the emergency call from Persephone while still in camp, he made the decision to leave on his own rather than ask the Rangers for help. He had the skills to sneak a few people out from under his brother's nose, but if he waited for the Rangers to be ready to assault the manor in earnest, he'd lose his window and probably the girls with it.

Getting into the mansion wouldn't be easy under normal circumstances, but he had an inside agent. He waited in the treeline until a door opened and one of the guards was called in. Just as Persephone had said. Luckily, Lucifer was arrogant and that made him careless — he let the forest almost brush right against the fence. Hopping over it silently from a high tree branch was literal child's play.

Persephone had described the window to one of the mansion's many unused rooms that she would leave unlocked; Lutius hurried to it. Creeping through the darkened hallways was an unnerving experience; most of the household staff had bedded down for the night, but Lucifer did have patrols. He'd have to trust that Persephone knew their rounds as well as, if not better than, they did.

His first objective was to free Redd. They'd shot her up with something and locked her in her room with a guard posted outside. Lutius fingered one dagger out of its hidden sheath as he rounded the corner, his heart thudding a loud accompaniment to his silent footsteps. Lucifer kept the house dark after the night cycle started, probably to hide his misdeeds from outside eyes; Lutius was free to move about as long as he kept low and made no noise.

He was on the guard outside Redd's door before the man even saw Lutius' shadow.

Lutius wrapped one arm across the guard's throat, keeping the air from escaping his lips, and plunged the dagger into his back. It wasn't a fatal wound, but the mixture of poisons coating the blade would keep him from waking for as long as it took the girls to get to safety.

Most of his species would say angels did not kill *at all*, but Lutius knew better. The harsh reality he'd witnessed and experienced would ill-suit those feathered prayer-bell-clutchers.

If any even still lived.

The guard slumped against him. He braced awkwardly and slid the dagger back into its hiding spot (which re-applied the poison), then quietly laid him prone.

He opened the door after retrieving the key from the unconscious and paralyzed guard, then dragged the body inside, dumping it in a corner. Redd was asleep on the floor in a pool of starlight. Lutius' heart hurt; she hadn't even made it to the bed.

"Hey," he called quietly. "Redd, wake up."

He flinched inwardly at the panic that crossed the girl's face as her eyes fluttered open. Her gaze focused, and she mumbled his name questioningly, reaching out a hand. He helped her up, letting her lean on his shoulder. Her muscles were still twitchy and not responding well, which made the flight down the hall all the more nerve-wracking.

He tapped ever-so-lightly on Ara's door, and it opened after a moment, revealing Persephone's drawn, worried face. His heart hurt anew.

She moved to one side and he came into the room. Ara stood in the middle of her reading nook/foyer, already dressed in traveling clothes. Redd fell into Ara's arms and the two girls clung to one another and cried.

Lutius had to close his eyes against the anger that surged up. He put on a brave smile as he opened his eyes again.

"Hey. We'll get you out of this, yeah?" he said quietly.

A noise outside the room made all four of its occupants freeze. Persephone stepped close to the door and listened; after a moment, she shook her head and pressed a hand to her chest.

"Mother, what is happening?" Ara pleaded as Redd stumbled into Ara's sleeping room to change her clothing.

Persephone gathered Ara against her chest instead of answering, squeezing her. Ara grimaced but didn't protest.

"I cannot explain now, dear," Persephone finally said. "Just go with your uncle. Be silent, and be safe."

"Can't you come with us?" Ara begged.

Persephone smiled tightly. "No, dear."

Lutius clenched his jaw at the hollowness in the denial.

Lucifer would be furious. An opportunity like Redd — an uninitiated, untrained, already-mentally-unstable young woman with psionic powers who could be conditioned to serve evil in any number of ways — would probably have netted him a small fortune. The blame for letting it be lost would fall on Persephone's shoulders as the one running his household. Undoubtedly, her orders were to keep an eye on the girl.

And while he *could* secret the two girls out and it would be a while before they were missed, if Persephone wasn't there to cover their tracks, their absence would be noted immediately.

He vowed he would come back for her and take her away from this place, no matter the cost.

But for now …

Lutius placed a hand on Persephone's shoulder. She jumped and looked at him with wide eyes, then nodded. Redd emerged from the other room, wearing the clothes Lutius had bought for her at the market. Her gaze was clearer, her movements more sure. But her brows were knitted, fists clenched and trembling.

"Come, follow me, girls." Lutius made for the door. "Be as quiet as you can."

Persephone reached for him. He offered her a slight smile.

I'll be fine, it said.

Lucifer may have had the guards, the weapons, and the money … but Lutius had one advantage. Before the Elysian came and ruined everything, Lutius had been in Blackwing training — an elite group of angels who practiced the ways of secrecy and reconnaissance. They were the closest thing the angels — a species that cherished life above all else — had to assassins. It had been centuries since his training, but it was in his blood.

Persephone had done her job admirably, and they ran into no one as they made their way — quiet as mice and jumping at every tiny sound — to another window left unlocked. Lutius held it open for the girls and climbed out after, gesturing for them to stay put while he scouted ahead.

Again true to Persephone's word, there was no guard. This time, Lutius had to pull from his bag of tricks. He doubted either Ara or Redd could climb the wall, so with one arm of each girl over his shoulders, he cloaked himself in darkness and unseeing, and spread his wings.

With three strong beats and buoyed by his innate magic, he was up at the height of the wall. He stretched his wings to the limit and dropped lightly on the other side. A wave of dizziness staggered him. *I'm out of practice,* he thought wryly. Redd shot him a panicked look — he shook his head and gestured her forward.

They escaped into the treeline.

Lutius sent a silent prayer to the Creator that Persephone would survive the night.

***

When they were far enough into the woods, Lutius stopped and made the girls rest, eat, and drink. Lutius saw the look of pain cross Redd's face and figured her stomach would rebel against the process, but they'd need the nutrients if they were going to push through out of danger.

"Can we talk now?" Redd asked, hushed. The forest was hardly quiet — the chirruping of insects and the rustling of brush from the wind came from all directions — but he understood why *she* felt the need to be.

Lutius went to respond, but something alerted him. He whipped around, drawing his daggers from their hidden sheaths in the same smooth motion.

A fourth figure loomed out of the darkness nearby, a blade in each hand. One crackled with lightning, the other burned red.

Lutius heard the girls cry in fear from behind him, but had to focus all his attention on the figure in front of him. He had no idea who or what Lucifer had access to — any unknown entity was a threat.

But the figure didn't attack.

And after Lutius' initial startle reflex faded, strength flooded his limbs and a sense of certainty bolstered his frayed mental state. Sensations that emanated from … this figure.

Justice has returned? he thought wonderingly.

He slid his daggers back into their sheaths slowly. The figure that felt like Justice released his weapons, which disappeared into nothing. He raised one hand, snapped two fingers, and the clearing lit up with a metallic click, probably as a courtesy for the girls still cowering behind Lutius. Lutius didn't sense anything behind him, so it was unlikely the noise was of other assailants flanking them.

The light revealed details of the figure: an extremely tall, armored warrior whose skin tone was darker than Redd's by several shades. Long, blue-black hair was tied into a complicated loop attached to the shoulder of his breastplate.

He had pointed ears, a big jaw, and dark, serious eyes. But he also had huge wings held tight to his back — dark brown/black, with tattered feathers and leathery spots. They didn't look like they worked. Someone with varied genetic ancestry, perhaps.

He had unnaturally wide shoulders and unnaturally long arms, a broad chest, but a narrow waist and hips. He wore elven Legionnaire armor, which was a sleek metallic plate set that allowed for the agile movement the elves were known for. Spiraea's crest was emblazoned on his breastplate.

"You're not one of Lucifer's men," Lutius said in lower angelic.

"No," the warrior responded in high angelic. His teeth were sharp. Definitely varied genetics. "My name is Pheonix Barandor, Executioner and General of the Phoenix Legions under Lord Tyyrulriathula."

What are you? Lutius thought, mystified. *A genetic oddity who feels like Justice, with a Ranger clan name, a high position in the elven Host, and an Executioner to boot? Are you lying or have I missed something major in three hundred years?*

"Lucifer. That means I'm on Haven, right?" Pheonix asked, bringing Lutius back around to the present.

"Right," Lutius responded, switching to middle angelic. He wasn't fluent in high angelic as it had mostly been used by the stuffy upper echelon. He waited for confirmation that Pheonix understood: at the warrior's slight nod, Lutius continued: "My name is Lutius Invenes; this is my niece, Ara Luschia."

He doubted Ara could understand middle angelic — it wasn't spoken much these days — and was positive she didn't know high angelic. (He wasn't going to even start on how this 'Pheonix' was fluent in it — too many questions for what was already a very exhausting night). The language spoken in City Center was lower angelic, and the cadence of both higher and middle angelic was rapid enough that even if she'd picked up some words, she was unlikely to be able to follow them with much accuracy. And he was doubly positive Redd didn't know a single word of the song that was all of the angelic dialects.

"Related to Lucifer?"

"Yes; unfortunately, he is my brother."

"You were aware the Rangers have been trying to contact your family?"

"Not until I ran across the camp just a few hours past, no. There were previous attempts?"

"Over the span of a year, many."

Lutius swore. He figured he could be blunt.

"So the goblin-fucker knew," he said. "Yes, he's been trafficking from his home base, keeping the last of our people hostage in some sick mercantile fantasy. His most recent acquisition is behind me — the one with the red hair. She's an uninitiated human from Chaos Earth with psionic powers. Lucifer's wife, Persephone, smuggled us out. She has been forced to run the public face of his trafficking, I think under threat of her life."

Lutius took a breath. "I don't know who Lucifer is working with, or how he's managing to get people here. After the Elysian, we don't have the technology or the magic left to open portals, so he's gotta have outside contacts. I'm sorry I don't know more."

Pheonix shook his head. "No need. You have just given us everything."

"I need to go back and rescue Persephone before her bedamned husband finds out the girls are missing and punishes her for it. Can you escort the girls to the Ranger camp?"

"You've just met me. Why would you entrust me with that?" Pheonix asked without inflection. Lutius smiled slightly.

"I know what you are."

Pheonix nodded and silently reached over his shoulder. Out of nowhere, he pulled out a small wooden case. He snapped it open, revealing a selection of gems in an array of colors and cut in rounded, thin rectangles.

"You may need these." Pheonix offered.

"What are they?" Lutius asked.

"Elven spell-gems," Phoenix said. "Spells bound to Ranger-made crystals by way of elven magic. When the fragile crystal shell shatters, the spell fires. Let me know what kinds of magic might be beneficial and I will help you find something that matches."

Pheonix helped Lutius pick which gems he might need.

Then Lutius turned and knelt in front of the girls, who had their arms around one another. They had been watching the exchange without understanding for long minutes.

"I'm sorry about —" Lutius said in Federated Common so they both could understand him.

"I heard," Ara said quietly, her voice strained.

Lutius' stomach dropped into a pit. Apparently Ara *could* understand middle angelic.

That's what I get for assuming, Lutius thought.

"I'm sorry," he whispered. Ara shook her head minutely, but her eyes were wide and horrified. "I need you two to go with him," Lutius said, referring to Pheonix.

"What?!" Redd exclaimed in panic. Lutius felt his brow furrow in sympathy.

"I know you don't understand, but I truly do not have time to make it any clearer. Please, trust me."

Redd glanced over his shoulder at Pheonix, back at Lutius, and seemed to come to a decision. Her lips thinned with determination and she nodded once, barely.

Lutius turned to Ara and she leapt at him. He caught her in a crushing hug.

"Be strong, my little dove," he said, his voice thick. "We will all get out of this. You'll see."

Ara nodded. Lutius turned to Redd and bumped her chin with his knuckles. She smiled wanly.

“Take care of my dove,” he said. “She has flown the only cage she has ever known, gilded though it may have been. You will be safe with Pheonix. I swear it.”

The girl swallowed hard, and nodded. He stood, turned back to Pheonix, and said in middle angelic, “I must go. If I can get back before dawn, I can probably get her out without issue. Thank you. Keep them safe.”

Pheonix nodded, and, without looking back, Lutius leapt into the trees.

FIVE
Rangers

"How long were you traveling before I arrived?" Pheonix asked after Lutius was gone.

"About a half hour," Redd supplied.

"We should keep moving for a little longer then, if you are capable of it."

Redd and Ara looked at one another, then Ara nodded.

"The Ranger encampment is several hours from the city, according to reports," Pheonix said. "I leave it up to you whether we travel all night, but I will want to stop again once we are farther away so you can explain the whole situation. Do you know where we're going?"

Redd clicked her tongue in frustration and spread her arms. "No? I don't know anything."

Pheonix nodded and stood. He pulled a small crystal from nowhere (same as he'd done with the box) and messed with it.

"Kedash, kedash," he repeated over and over.

Redd walked a little ways away and sat against a tree, putting her face in her hands.

Great ... stuck with some random guy from who-knows-where who is talking to a crystal in gibberish, she thought bitterly. *Lutius, you better not be in on this.*

A sick paranoid fear settled in the pit of her stomach and almost doubled her over.

“Is that a communicator crystal?” Ara tentatively asked, effectively distracting Redd from her sudden fit.

Pheonix nodded but held up a hand.

The crystal blinked and a ghostly voice emanated from it, speaking a language Redd didn’t understand. Pheonix responded, and a brief conversation took place. Finally he nodded and returned the crystal to wherever he’d pulled it from. Redd stood.

“I contacted the camp,” Pheonix said. “We should get moving now.”

He lifted a hand and the globe of light illuminating the clearing dropped into it. He closed his fist around it and it disappeared, returning the forest to darkness.

“This way,” he gestured.

Ara and Redd fell in line before Pheonix, and he directed them through the forest.

***

Pheonix called a halt. He didn’t seem any worse for wear; in fact, despite being ensconced in all that armor, he was better off than either of the girls as far as Redd could tell. Ara looked like she was about to drop dead. Redd realized that was probably why Pheonix had stopped them.

Ara caught Redd looking at her and offered a weak smile. “My favorite place is a library,” she whispered with a sort of ‘what did you expect’ look.

Redd reached over and squeezed her hand in sympathy.

Pheonix made them eat and drink, just as Lutius had, before he would talk, gently turning aside their inquiries.

When they were finished, he squatted across from them and fixed first Ara, then Redd with his keen gaze. Redd prickled.

“I need you to tell me everything,” he said.

“What do you mean, ‘everything’?” Redd asked, increasingly irritable.

“Let’s start with how you arrived here.”

His blunt way of putting things and lack of inflection seemed rude to Redd, but she braced herself and told the story of her flight through the portal to Haven, the withdrawals, and the aftermath of both, and her encounter with Lucifer. Pheonix watched her without expression, except for a lowering of his brows as she told of her parents.

“I see,” he said, his voice so controlled that, conversely, it gave away some fierce emotion hidden underneath. Redd didn’t need her powers to sense it.

“This needs to be dealt with,” he said. “Who are your parents?”

“Kenji and Brecca Pine.”

Pheonix’s eyes went a little blank for a moment, then he continued.

“Do you remember any defining features from the others? The ‘therapists’?”

Redd closed her eyes and searched her memories. She had a hard time recalling; anything before Haven was foggy, distorted. She swallowed and opened her eyes, looking up at the night sky to drive back the *other*-reality that threatened to overtake her again.

When she felt stable, she looked back at Pheonix, who seemed like he hadn’t moved. She described the bits she could.

“I … I don’t remember much,” she said by way of apology. “Why? I mean, why is it important?”

“I need to know if the trafficking extended onto the uninitiated planet, and if there is anything in your memory that could point to who is working with Lucifer, or if the two incidents are related at all.”

Ara spoke up, which was good, because Redd wasn’t sure if she could talk. “Master Barandor, if I may?”

Pheonix looked at her and inclined his head.

Ara twirled her fingers nervously. “If it may be of some assistance, I was there as she was going through withdrawals. I am a natural-born Healer, trained by books. I analyzed the chemical composition of the compounds in her system; they were inconsistent with psyker-conditioning attempts documented as being used by pirates involved in human cargo.”

“What, then?”

Ara described what she’d already told Redd, then: “Nothing meant to enhance sensation or aggressiveness as would be used on a gladiator, or volition inhibitors as would be used on a shock-troop. In my opinion, she was being conditioned with pain and fear, and the drugs were meant to facilitate that. Conditioned for what, I’m not sure.”

“How do you know this?”

“I have multiple pharmacological texts — likely outdated, though — which detail the composition of many types of common pharmaceuticals and their usages.”

Pheonix nodded and stood. He twitched his wings, probably an indication of irritation.

“Rest, if you can,” he told the girls. “I’ll keep watch.”

Redd looked at the ground, trying to will her tired body to lie down.

Even as she was delaying the inevitable, Pheonix reached over his shoulder and pulled a pretty sizable box, maybe two times bigger than a shoebox, out of nothing. It opened like a clamshell. He picked up what looked like two pieces of metal foil from inside and laid them next to one another on the ground. Two small cubes followed, which he set at the north and south boundaries of their camp. He pressed a series of buttons on the clamshell box and a distortion stretched over them in between the two smaller blocks. Simultaneously, the two pieces of foil popped up into small tents.

Pheonix then reached into the box once more, grabbed a handful of small packets, and unwrapped them. He shook them out, then tossed a mat, a blanket, and a cylindrical pillow into each tent.

He found himself a spot to sit away from the tents and looked expectantly at the girls.

"Where did all this come from?" Ara asked excitedly.

Pheonix, surprisingly, cracked a little roguish grin. It took a lot of the harshness away from his face.

"Fold-space. A new Ranger invention. It is a field of space in a place where nothing exists, tied to an individual's life-energy that can hold as many items as said energy can support."

Redd made a noise of disgust and climbed into the nearest tent.

Pheonix interrupted the question hovering on Ara's lips.

"Your friend has the right of it. Go; sleep. I can explain it later if you wish, or you can ask the Rangers themselves when we arrive at the camp tomorrow."

Redd, already in the tent and arranging her sleeping gear, heard Ara's sigh. Redd blew out a breath and rolled into the blanket. She set her head on the pillow and shifted to get herself as comfortable as she could. Considering, it wasn't that bad.

She'd slept in much worse places.

She hoped for no nightmares, and in her dreams, a raven perched at the edge of her vision.

***

Pheonix woke them up just after dawn. Redd crawled out of her tent, bleary-eyed and grumpy. She guessed they had gotten maybe four hours of sleep, and while the rest had helped somewhat, she was stiff and wishing for the plush bed at Ara's mansion.

Pheonix set a series of small cubes on the ground in front of Redd, and a series of small … art sculptures? … in front of Ara.

"Good morning. Did you sleep well?"

The question sounded forced — asked out of politeness.

Redd mumbled noncommittally, kneeling down to get a better look at the cubes.

Out of the corner of her eye, she saw Ara nod shyly before responding, "It took me some time to fall asleep, but I slept soundly once I did. What are these?"

"Food."

Redd regarded her cubes with some suspicion. She picked one up at random and turned it over in her fingers. She found a button on one face and pressed it — dropping it as it began to writhe in her hands, like something inside was desperately trying to get out. It unfolded several times, revealing what looked like a cafeteria tray on which was a pile of noodles, dotted with colorful vegetables and bits of meat. It actually looked appetizing. Delicious smells wafted up.

She glanced at Ara, who had picked up one of her sculptures. It gracefully opened, the motion akin to the spreading of a flower's petals in the morning sun, to reveal a pile of fruits and vegetables.

Ara dove right in, but despite Redd's food looking familiar, she was still hesitant. Her stomach made the choice for her by cramping painfully as the smell worked its magic. She sighed. Pheonix had had many opportunities to kill them up to this point; why would he give her something poisonous?

Pushing her irrational paranoia back, she dug in.

After eating, she helped pack up the tents. Pheonix instructed them to leave the blankets, pillows, and mats, claiming they were biodegradable. He tucked the small boxes back into the larger box, and then put that back into 'fold-space.'

They got underway and moved in silence for a long while. Pheonix stopped them suddenly.

A man materialized out of nowhere in squares, like a digital image loading too slowly.

Obviously a soldier, he was dressed in sleek, non-metallic black armor and held a long, scary-looking sniper rifle. She recognized the shape from vids; while there were some key differences, the long, snake-thin barrel was hard to mistake.

The soldier didn't even look at her. He spared a glance for Ara, then pointed his weapon at the ground and turned to Pheonix. "General, this way."

Pheonix gestured that the girls should precede him and brought up the rear.

The camp opened in front of them suddenly, coming into view much as the soldier had — not there and there in the span of a moment. Dome-shaped buildings were assembled in an almost grid-like pattern in the clearing, with two much larger buildings on either side. As they entered the open space, Redd felt something; above, the sky was distorted in the same way that it had been in their temporary camp.

The inhabitants of this place were all military types dressed in black armor, though theirs had lines of neon purple across it in what seemed like a calculated pattern.

Redd's little group got some curious looks as they moved among the buildings, but for the most part, everyone seemed too busy to pay them any attention.

The soldier led them to one of the bigger buildings, whose fan-shaped door opened automatically as they approached. Redd blinked as her eyes adjusted to the interior. The inside was just as austere as the outside: a flag she didn't recognize in one corner, a desk, two doors on either side of the room, and a couple of cabinets. In front of the table stood two people, an older man and a woman who looked to be in her thirties. The man was unremarkable, but the woman …

Taller than Redd by at least six inches but still shorter than the towering Pheonix, she wore a uniform similar to that of the other soldiers. Over her thick frame, she wore a strange blue half-coat that seemed to attach to the front of her armor via little metallic circles so it didn't/couldn't close in the front. Said coat still had the sweeping tail of a trench-coat or duster, whose bottom edge brushed her calves. On the outside of its sleeves were a variety of highly-technological looking armor pieces, and her legs were entirely covered by thick, armored boots.

She shifted to look at Redd and company, and the movement revealed a complicated contraption of straps attaching across her waist and thighs. Attached to the straps were two holsters, containing shiny blue guns.

Her skin was a dark beige, lighter than Redd's light brown but not by much, her hair a sandy color that fell to her hips and tied loosely at the nape of her neck. Her eyes were colorless — like a dirty mirror, they reflected the light of whatever she was looking at, and her pupils were shaped like the lens of a camera. She had green triangular marks on her cheeks. She was handsome and intimidating. Her height, the exposed guns, her natural girth amplified by her layers of armor, and her coolly inquisitive expression all screamed of a warrior not to be trifled with.

Then a wide grin spread across her face. "If it isn't Ol' Stoneface," she called jovially, her voice husky and deep.

Pheonix saluted stiffly. "Commander Abyssterilon."

The Commander made a face at him for no reason Redd could fathom. "What are you doing here?"

"I failed a slide. Got lost in the stream."

"Ah, that's what happened ... Minrathous freaked, you know."

Pheonix looked as genuinely remorseful as someone with as blank a face as his could. "It was a mistake. I will sincerely apologize as soon as I can. How long was I gone?"

"About two and a half months. You disappeared just before this whole debacle." The woman spread her arms, rolling her eyes.

Pheonix shook his head. "Bast."

Apparently it was an invective, for the woman laughed, then looked past him at Ara and Redd.

Her expression softened somewhat. "And who are your friends?"

Pheonix held up a hand. "Hold on, before introductions are made, we have a situation. I'll brief you later. Commander-at-arms, if you will?" he said.

The second man perked up; he'd had no interest in some kids, Redd sensed, and now that there was a chance to end this hurry-up-and-wait bullshit, he was all over it.

Redd frowned and shook her head. The drugs must be wearing off. That thought had most certainly not been her own.

The two men left the tent, and the woman leaned back against the table, crossing her arms over her broad chest. She smiled.

Feeling like she was expected to say something, Redd introduced herself, and Ara followed suit.

"Well, I'm Chanilinaicanau M'tyoiderit Abyssterilon," the woman said, "but you can call me Chani. I'm the Commander for the Special Projects Division for the Rangers. The man who just left was Commander-at-arms Ricchenni."

"What are you guys doing here?" Redd asked, remembering Ara's lessons. "Didn't you think the angels were extinct?"

Chani pushed off the table and walked forward, looping one arm across each girl's shoulders.

"It's complicated. Let's talk about why you're here, first. Would you be dears and enlighten me as to what's going on?"

Chani led them out and into another, smaller building that was little more than a hallway lined with doors (it turned out to be a barracks), while Redd explained what had occurred. By the end of yet another retelling of her abuse, she was shaking. Chani had much the same reaction as Pheonix, although the woman's mobile face showed her anger much more readily.

When Redd was done, Chani leaned down to look intently into each girl's eyes.

"You two are now under the Rangers' protection, alright? This is your room for now. You're free to wander around the camp, but stay within sight of the guards and don't leave this clearing. If you need anything, ask someone; they'll know where I am. We'll get this all sorted out, but for now I've got work to do. I'll send someone a little later to fill you in."

Redd nodded. Chani seemed very honest, like Persephone; Redd *wanted* to trust her. Ara was unusually quiet, her dark eyes downcast.

The door closed after Chani, and Redd turned to survey their room. Not as grand as Ara's mansion, to be sure; it was probably ten feet by ten feet, with a cot and footlocker on either side. A terminal was mounted to the wall in between the beds.

This wasn't exactly like the terminal she was familiar with from home, but it was close enough.

Redd wandered over to stand in front of it — there was no chair — while she let Ara work through whatever it was she was lost in thought over. A lot had happened; she didn't begrudge her friend a moment to process.

The terminal screen lit up as she approached. A single box sat in the middle of it — no instructions, no help button. Just an empty interface.

"What the hell …?" she muttered under her breath.

"Please input name," the console said, seemingly in response to her voice, "using holographic keys, or vocal command." A keyboard slid into existence. Redd stared at it, then carefully poked at the solid-looking keys. Though it *looked* different, it *felt* exactly like the ones she was used to. After poking it a few more times to be sure, she put in her name. The screen lit up with words, not that she was sure how to access them.

After some more prodding, she realized it was a touch screen. That, too, was familiar.

Redd swiped through the displayed options, vaguely aware that Ara had gone to lay down on one of the beds.

She tried not to think about why everything was in a language she could read. At the moment, she didn't want the answer.

The screen innocuously offered her the choice between Home Archives, X-tra Net, or Information Request.

Redd pressed her lips together, trying to dredge up memories of talking with Ara through the haze of her withdrawals to see if any of those were things they'd discussed yet. She poked at 'Home Archives' and the screen changed to populate with articles mostly from Federation sources. She quickly swiped back, her heart hammering.

She didn't want to be reminded of anything Federation just then.

She could guess what the X-tra Net was, so she skipped that in favor of 'Information Request.' That was an entire list of words she sort of recognized with the word 'request' next to it, like 'Ranger Request,' though the whole list of request lines had empty blocks that she assumed were search boxes.

She backed out to the main menu. X-tra Net was exactly what she had thought it would be: an ordinary information service window.

However, the fact that everything was so tailored to her was starting to become unbearably suspicious. So when the Federation's citizen verification briefly flashed across the screen, she wasn't surprised.

What did surprise her, though, was that, before she could input anything, the box disappeared and was replaced by the Federated Information Service Personal Access Space designated for her. Normally you had to verify your citizen I.D. and credentials, but somehow this 'terminal' had bypassed it.

She felt divorced from her body. Her heart was pounding, her mouth dry.

On autopilot and without her input, her finger tapped the Federated Message Services logo.

She had many messages: tons of official ones from the Federation itself notifying her that she'd disappeared (the ridiculous irony of that almost cut through her disabling shock), and that if she didn't show back up, she'd face harsh penalties.

Interspersed with those were the Individual Standard Messages: messages from the Federation in an official capacity that were sent out to every citizen to inform them of things like new laws, and to remind people to 'protect their Liberty, turn in any uncooperative Specials.'

Redd's eyes unfocused. A tangle of thoughts tumbled like a roiling nest of snakes. She'd see the tail of one and it'd be replaced with the head of another.

These dates — they're all wrong. This first message telling me to report, I would have been eleven. I didn't disappear until years later. That's when I started manifesting. Did they hide me? For what? Just to hurt me? And these last messages would have been years after I actually did disappear.

She strained to remember, but the memories were worse than a nest of snakes, and she found herself gripping the edges of the keyboard to force them back down.

The memories and thoughts and panic twined with her power. Her vision went dark; her senses reduced to the frantic hammering of her own heart and labored breathing.

This time, there was nothing to stop it.

A sense of calm spun out of the core of that hideous tornado, an eye of detached observation — and relief.

It'll finally be over, and I can rest.

Another voice cut through: *Is that what you want? To rest?*

The storm receded, replaced by that halcyon singing.

Do I ... want to rest? Redd asked blankly in her own head, not really processing that the golden light she'd spoken to for so long was actually *talking back*. Then, with force: *I want this to stop.*

You know better than anyone that it won't stop if you give in here, the voice said sharply, each syllable calling an answering echo from something deep inside — a pool across whose surface ripples were chased in sync with the golden words.

She wanted to shrink from it, but she *knew* the voice was right.

What does it matter if I don't want to fucking do this anymore? She asked defiantly, anger giving her strength. *What happens if I give in?*

A response to her question was not immediately forthcoming. Yet, the storm remained at bay — present, but quelled — and she was unable to retreat. She was stuck, a prisoner in the liminal space of being and nonbeing.

Coward! She yelled — or, tried to. The effort made no noise that she could tell. The utter silence was terrifying. *If you know everything, then tell me:* ***what would happen?***

A ghostly figure shimmered into her mind's eye, seemingly in answer to her taunt. The impression she got from it was a child's doodle of a human, unfinished and abandoned.

The figure said in the golden voice, a calm contrast to Redd's frenzy:

The cycle continues.

Those three words pulled such an answering horror from Redd that it jettisoned her out of the space between. She gasped and opened her eyes.

In the time she'd been lost inside herself, she'd fallen to her hands and knees. She was panting and sweating and weak, but the storm was gone.

It must have been only a second, because Ara was roused by the noise and was sitting on the edge of her cot, watching Redd with concern.

Redd waved a hand in irritable dismissal and climbed onto her own cot with effort, feeling as though she'd run a marathon. She rested her elbows on her knees, leaned over, then put her head in her hands.

Thin arms encircled her shoulders. She looked up into a worried face, haloed by the directionless white light from the ceiling. She rested her forehead on Ara's shoulder, letting the tears come that she'd held back her entire life.

Some time later, when she'd cried herself out, Ara sat next to her and there was silence for a little while, each girl involved in her own mental process.

"Everything I knew is a lie," Redd finally said, miserably. Releasing the thought aloud didn't relieve the tightness in her chest, but, perversely, she felt compelled to say it.

She didn't even want to acknowledge the words that hovered on her tongue next, let alone say them: *I never knew anything.*

"I can sympathize."

Redd looked at Ara. For the first time, the little angel wasn't smiling. She seemed exhausted. Redd abruptly realized Ara had pretty much lost her entire family in one night — as far as she knew right at that moment, she'd never see her mother or uncle again, and her father had been revealed to be an evil son of a bitch.

Redd curled her arms around Ara and gave her a squeeze. Ara remained still, except to put a few fingertips lightly on one of Redd's forearms. They stayed that way for a while.

"Hey, Ara … "

"Hmm?"

"If the angels were cut off from the rest of the universe, for as long as you say they were — centuries — then how did you have those books? How do you know all the things you told me?"

Ara was silent for a moment, studying the small hands that rested in her lap. "Father would bring them to me."

Of course.

Lucifer was trafficking — slave-trading — that much she knew … Pheonix had said they needed to find out who he was working with, and that he was dealing in uninitiated humans.

That meant that he would certainly have contacts outside of Haven.

An absolute, bottom-of-the-barrel fuckwad. He'd known all along about the Rangers and the rest of the universe. And he chose to let his people die, and stagnate, and live in fear.

What a person to have as a father. Redd vowed that if he ever got anywhere near Ara again, he'd pay.

"What were you doing, anyway?" Ara gestured at the terminal.

"Nothing. Just messing with it."

"Likely, I should try 'messing with it' as well. I may as well be uninitiated for all the things I don't know. But, right now … " Ara trailed off with a shaky sigh.

Redd swung her legs around and stretched out on the cot, folding her arms behind her head. She stared at the featureless ceiling. "It wasn't a good experience," she said, "looking at the terminal. We're probably better off resting as much as we can."

Ara hesitated, then stretched out next to Redd. The cot wasn't big enough for the both of them, but Redd didn't mind the company. They'd often slept in the same bed in Lucifer's mansion. Neither one of them, once having met the other, particularly coveted being alone.

After a while, Ara rolled towards Redd. Redd moved unconsciously to give her as much room as possible on the little cot.

"Redd?"

Redd turned her head to meet the worried face of her friend. Alerted, she asked, "What's wrong?"

"I'm not … bothering you … by being here, am I?"

"'Being here'?" Redd echoed blankly.

Ara pointed at the bed. "Our closeness."

"No? Why would I be bothered?"

Ara looked away and, shockingly, blushed. "I mean, I don't want to give you the wrong impression …"

"'The wrong impression'?" Redd echoed again, this time even more confused.

Ara glanced up in mild annoyance. "Are you content with repeating me?"

Redd sat up and turned toward Ara, who sat up as well.

"I'm repeating you because I truly don't know what the hell you're talking about," Redd said testily.

Ara blinked. "You know … attraction. Wanting to have sex? You *don't* know?"

"I was raised by a terminal. My parents didn't give two shits about me unless it was to stick me with something or make me swallow some pills. Pretty sure most of what came through the terminal was lies, too." The words came tumbling out because she was feeling attacked. She blinked away tears.

"I'm sorry," Ara whispered.

Redd sighed and wiped her eyes with shaky hands. "I didn't — you're the first person I've ever met who's about my age. I don't know anything about sex other than it's another word for breeding, which creates babies. On my planet you needed some kind of a certificate for that or something. There was a process. I don't know what 'attraction' is."

"I think, with sexual attraction, your body gets involved," Ara said hesitantly. "As in, your body … wants to be touched, or to touch someone else. It's supposed to feel good."

Redd flopped back on the bed again, arms behind her head. "Huh. I wonder why you'd need a certificate for that, then." The thought made her dizzy and she clenched her teeth. *Lies. More and more lies.* To distract herself, she continued, "Well, I don't feel that way about you, so you can rest easy. Hugs, sure. Hanging out nearby is comforting. But I don't have any particular burning urge to touch you."

After a moment, Ara laid down again. "I'm glad. I wouldn't want anything to ruin the friendship we have."

"Would me wanting to touch you ruin our friendship?" Redd asked.

"It … probably would, because I don't think I will ever want to. With anyone. And it isn't for lack of opportunity; I have gone into the market many times, and have seen many different kinds of people. But I've never felt anything the way my books describe it."

"And who cares if you can't? Sounds like a bother."

Unexpectedly, Ara laughed. "You know? That's always how I've looked at it."

After a while, Redd said: "So, wait, how old *are* you?"

"I'm one-hundred."

Redd sat up abruptly, twisting to stare incredulously at her friend. "*A hundred? Years?*"

"Yes, years."

"But — does that mean — are you an adult, or … "

Ara made a face. "I can't really tell you what is and isn't an adult, because 'maturity' isn't really something angels ascribe to. For most other species, there's a physiological component to maturity. Most mortals of a certain age will act 'immature' because parts of their bodies and brains are physically not finished developing. Angels, biologically speaking, are only tied to the physical plane by the thinnest of threads. To attempt to answer your query — I believe I am more child than not. I may have lived a hundred years, but the quality of that living was … hampered. I don't have the kind of life experience someone else of my age would."

"Huh." Slowly, lost in thought, Redd laid back down, locking her hands behind her head.

"My family is all thousands of years old. As a comparison, I would be young indeed."

"Thousands — damn."

"Angels are immortal, after all." Ara smiled somewhat. "I hope that doesn't make you uncomfortable."

"No, no … I'm still getting used to all this, that's true. But in an immortal species, one hundred does seem pretty young. I think we're more similar than we are different. Especially considering … well, you know."

"I agree."

***

Some time later, the girls agreed to try to sleep and moved to their own cots. They laid in silence, both awake, both aware the other was awake, but trying their best to do what they were told to do and 'rest.'

Then came a knock.

Redd glanced at Ara, who looked at her at the same moment, then rolled off the cot to open the door. The girl standing in the doorway was short, stocky, dark-skinned, and wore the same black ensemble Redd saw everybody in around here.

Her deep purple hair was cut into a layered bob with bangs that lengthened around the back of her neck and curled towards her cheeks, completely covering her ears. She had a heart-shaped face and piercing red eyes. The cerulean diamond markings on her cheeks — marks Redd had seen on quite a few of the soldiers around the camp, including Chani, though they varied in shape and color — danced as her jaw worked in irritation.

"Um … hi." Redd said. "Did Chani send you?"

"Yes," the girl answered bluntly, her words clipped with anger. "Imae Rivios. You need anything?"

Redd glanced back at Ara. "I'm hungry; I don't know about you." Ara nodded.

"I'll show you to the mess hall," Imae said stiffly. She was hoping they would send her away; she was pissed at having to play butler. Redd frowned at having a foreign thought insert itself into her mind, again. She still felt raw from everything that had happened.

Redd and Ara exchanged looks and followed the purple-haired youth out into the late afternoon. A domed rectangular building stood near the center of the camp. As they got close, Redd caught the scent of food and her stomach twisted in response. The plate of noodles provided by Pheonix seemed a lifetime ago now.

Inside, there were long tables, each about half-filled. A few curious diners looked up as the three girls entered, but their interest quickly returned to their food. Redd felt like she had a police escort, as Imae then led the way to a line of machines. They looked just like terminals. Before Redd could be confused, she witnessed someone walk up and type something into the holographic keyboard. A plate slid out of a hole that opened in the terminal's front. They were very different from the replicators Redd knew from Federated Earth, which had visible keyboards and a giant open hole for the food to materialize into.

Redd approached a terminal, waited for the keyboard to pop up, and entered the first thing that came to her mind: steamed rice, fish, and a carbonated beverage. She lifted the slot flap and took her tray out, putting it near her face to get a good sniff as she turned around. *Smells fresh,* she thought. *So far so good.*

She picked a spot close to the machines and watched Ara input something and also receive a tray. The little angel's meal consisted of a pile of fruit, cut up into bite-sized pieces, and water.

Redd made a face as she picked up the fish with her fingers and popped it into her mouth.

"How can you get full on that stuff? I eat fruit and I'm hungry ten seconds later."

Ara just smiled enigmatically, taking a spoonful of fruit pieces.

Redd jumped as a fist, clutching chopsticks, crashed down onto her tray. She looked up; Imae stood over her, her fist still pressed into the tray. Her lip curled in disdain. Redd found herself scowling, a familiar heat crawling under her skin that she was unable to quell.

"You forgot to ask the machine for these."

That's what Imae's mouth said. What her brain said was, *What, were you gonna eat that rice with your hands? Stupid bitch.*

Redd swallowed the fish that tasted like wet newspaper as her anger soured it in her mouth, and closed her eyes. She placed her hand over Imae's. Though her eyes were closed, she could sense the look of surprise that darted across the youth's face like a deer startled out of the woodline.

"Apparently," Redd said quietly, "nobody told you I'm psionic. Watch what fucked-up shit crosses your mind."

Imae's eyes widened in surprise, anger swelling in her. Redd looked up, her face blank.

I dare you, Redd's expression said.

Finally Redd drew her hand back, and Imae did the same.

Imae offered a tight, completely unconvincing smile. "Sorry," she grated. "Anything else?"

"No, I think that's about all I need from *you*."

Imae about-faced almost before Redd finished her statement.

Redd called after her. "Thanks for the fucking chopsticks."

She watched the youth cross the suddenly quiet mess hall until she was gone and the door closed, then turned her burning gaze on anyone who had been watching. Some met her eyes; most looked away.

As her mind swept the room, she froze. Someone rebuffed her mental 'net' and had her pinned inside her own head. She struggled, but couldn't move. Panic rose, drove her to lash out within the bubble. The stranglehold loosened. Redd couldn't pick out who had done it, and she'd had to clamp down to keep from being attacked again.

An older man stood up a few tables down, answering her question for her.

"Redd?" Ara sounded miles away. Redd zoned in on the man as he approached. Several other people stood up to follow him, one of whom was a soldier frantically whispering in his ear. The older man waved the whisperer away and made for Redd.

"Lieutenant!" One of the soldiers called to the man approaching Redd. He was faceless to Redd, who only could focus on the threat bearing down on her.

"Who are you? How dare you psyk on another soldier!" the apparent Lieutenant barked, loud enough for everyone to hear. "Where the hell is your uniform? What is your rank, soldier? For Fug's sake, I bet you are some Creator-damned private, still shitting in her diaper. Get off your ass and stand at attention!"

The faceless soldier kept trying to talk to the Lieutenant, who kept ignoring them. Other people were talking, too, and it became a storm around Redd's head that she couldn't make any sense out of. She wanted to cover her ears, to scream and run away; it was too much, too much — but her body wouldn't respond, forced her into this paralysis, forced her to endure.

She couldn't even stand up, as the man they'd called Lieutenant continued to scream in her face.

Was this the psyker power? Something inside of her begged to be let out, to kill them all, to make them shut up. She railed against it with the whole of her being as the anger tore her apart. She closed her eyes, hoping the removal of visual stimuli would give her strength.

She was a plankton trying to stop a hurricane.

Oh no, she thought with surprising clarity and calm. *It's happening again. But this time I really can't stop it.*

There was no sign of the golden being.

A familiar voice, several familiar voices — someone crying — snippets of the real world managed to break through her red haze, like beams of light through the rotted roof of an old building. None of it made sense, though, taken out of context.

A vortex of her rage and power mixed, rising and building, creating a knot of darkness inside her mind that almost seemed to have a mind of its own.

And it was swallowing her alive.

Moments before the last of her shredded will fell away and she unleashed, the pressure choking her suddenly eased and Redd gasped. The rage dragging her down into the depths receded and she was able to breathe again. She opened her eyes, and a young man stood before her, his hands out — almost, but not quite, touching her. He smiled gently.

“Better?” he whispered. It should have been lost in the noise surrounding her, but he was the only one she heard clearly.

He moved around to the side of her to let someone through. She tried to follow him with her eyes, but Chani stepped forward and filled her vision.

Losing sight of him almost caused a resurgence in the anger, but he rested a hand lightly on her shoulder and she instantly calmed. She found she could focus on Chani, and the older woman was talking to her.

“… okay? Redd, answer me. Let me know you can hear me.”

Redd blinked and nodded haltingly.

“Can you speak? Find a way to tell me you’re here with us.”

“I’m — I’m here. I’m okay, Chani.”

Chani searched Redd’s eyes for a few moments longer, then turned around like a rising stormcloud. “Who. In Fug’s name. Did. This?”

The Lieutenant found himself alone as everyone around him took at least one large step away from him, leaving him to entirely bear Chani’s searing gaze.

“I tried to … ” The once-faceless soldier (who now Redd saw was a beautiful person with pointed ears ... an elf?) spoke up. Chani merely put a hand up, and his jaw clacked shut.

Her eyes lasered into the Lieutenant, who stared over her shoulder. He could have been carved from wood.

“Did you really fuggin’ think that one of our trained psykers would just up and display in a group? Did you pay attention to the roster at all? No, I’ll answer that myself; you had your head up your fuggin’ ass for the last two and a half months. Report to the Commandant. I’ll be there in a minute.”

The Lieutenant didn’t speak. Ashen, he saluted, then turned on his heel. Chani had already moved on. She pointed at the soldier who had attempted to deflate the situation.

“You. Why the Fug is she,” apparently referring to Redd, “even here?”

“Cadet Rivios.”

Chani sighed and clenched her hand into a fist, closing her eyes.

Redd was abjectly relieved to find her head flat-lined ... as long as the young man’s hand remained on her shoulder. She couldn’t see what was going on in Chani’s mind.

The older woman dropped her hands and looked upwards pleadingly. “Creator, why? Why me?”

Chani addressed the young man at Redd’s side: “She needs to be taken to the training room. Grab a couple of psykers — level-headed ones, please; I’m sure you will know who will be best for this. We’ve got to instill some discipline in her or we’re facing a firestorm.” Her voice was shaking. “Shit, let’s be honest — we almost did.”

“Can I accompany her?” A quiet voice brought Redd’s attention around. Tears streaked Ara’s cheeks; Redd fumbled for Ara’s hand. Both her fingers and Ara’s were trembling. The little angel gave her a brave smile, but it was forced.

“I’m sorry, sweetheart, but it’s best if you go back to your room. This isn’t something visitors should attend,” Chani said.

Ara looked down, but nodded.

“I doubt you are hungry, but I’ll have some more provisions sent in a little later,” Chani continued, then straightened and faced the pointy-eared soldier. "Escort the young lady back to guest housing."

The person Redd had decided was an elf came around the table, helped Ara up, and led her away. Ara glanced over her shoulder once, the worry shining in her dark eyes.

Redd felt like the pit of her stomach was between her ankles. Chani jerked her head, and the crowd dissipated. Chani straddled the bench and took Redd by the shoulders.

"Listen, you just need some control. And you *can* learn control. This is not your fault, hear me? Psykers are just like this sometimes, especially before they are trained. You did good for resisting the firestorm. You did so good."

Redd felt tears spilling down her cheeks, but she couldn't look away. Most of her was focused on the young man's hand on her shoulder, the strength and tranquility that flowed through him and into her. The other small percentage chased itself around, trying to make sense of things in a mind still flooded with emotion. The diaspora only made the whole situation harder to take.

Chani pulled her into a hug, and after a moment of resisting, Redd leaned into it, letting herself be comforted.

When Chani pulled back, Redd actually felt calmer. When was the last time her mother had hugged her? Panic that bringing up her past would get her riled up again pushed the thought away.

"Ready?" Chani asked. Redd nodded silently. "Alright, let's go."

***

She scurried through the forest; the dark, curling limbs of dead trees ripping at her as she went. Gnarled roots breached the dry ground, but she leapt over them easily. As agile as any hunting wolf, her attention was focused wholly on her prey, a spot of light just ahead.

He was flagging, limping now. A smile stretched her little lips. It was only a matter of time.

He tripped and she was upon him.

He flailed a bolt of power at her. It missed, but she peremptorily dodged, and he crawled away.

She laughed, a girlish sound that was wrong in this place.

They'd come to a clearing. He was still crawling away as fast as he could, the only sound now his harsh breathing and the scraping of his body on the hard-packed ground. He didn't look back. Filled with the ecstasy of the chase, she followed him at a lazy walk, kicking her feet, hopping from root to root.

"You've nowhere to go, old man. May as well just give up," she called.

He ignored her.

The clearing widened out into the edge of a gorge. He collapsed in front of it, panting, then slowly wheeled around to face her.

They were similar — both warped hominin echoes, though on different ends of the spectrum. She was a pretty, perfect doll, devoid of emotion, and he was an aged troll — his elongated face drooped, pointed ears flopped, nose bulbous and lined.

He braced the end of his staff in the ground and heaved himself up onto his knees.

"Yes, beg me for your life," she purred.

His lips drew back over his teeth in a beastly version of a smile. An animal, backed into a corner.

"It won't do any good," he rasped.

She laughed again, twirling her skirts. "How do you know until you try? I may let you live."

His eyes never left hers. The intensity of his gaze unnerved her.

"You're right," she said bluntly. "I am going to kill you, regardless. Just like I did to the rest of your stupid little village."

His 'smile' stretched further. He slammed his staff into the ground. The sound echoed oddly in and out of the trees, as though a living creature in itself. She tensed without meaning to.

"Yes, that may be true. You and your wicked kin may wipe me and mine from the eye of Time, but the universe has ways of making people like you suffer."

"Is that it? That's your dying threat? Let me tell you something, old man. The powerful rule this universe. It bends to our will. The Gods bend to naught. Your death will mean nothing, and you will be forgotten, and I will live on."

He laughed. The sound made a shiver crawl up her spine.

"Why are you laughing?"

He didn't stop.

"Shut up!" she screeched, and sent bolts of her power at him. They tore his body. Blood stained the dry ground, which sucked it up with the thirst of the dying. Still, he laughed. She screamed and darted forward. Despite her slight frame, she was very strong; she easily lifted him by the throat. His knees dragged on the ground, legs limp.

He choked, burning gaze still locked on hers, and as his life bled away, the flames in his eyes grew hotter.

"Why won't you die?!" she shrieked and threw him down. He bounced in a shower of dust and came to rest with his legs hanging halfway off the cliff.

Shaking with rage, she approached him. Laboriously, he lifted his head and looked up at her through streaming blood and swollen cuts. His gaze seethed with hatred and power.

"You will suffer," he wheezed. And despite that he kept talking, she couldn't seem to make herself move to shut him up. "For the rest of eternity, you will suffer. And when millennia have gone by, you will beg for the death that you fear above all things, the death that will even then be denied you. This I promise you. With the end of my life, and with every life you end, you will bear our pain a thousandfold."

His whisper called to an answering whisper of winds among the trees.

Screaming in shrill fury, she reared back and kicked him for all she was worth. He sailed out and fell, disappearing into the mists at the bottom of the gorge and into silence. The wind conjured by his staff and words suddenly whipped around her, howling. She dropped to her knees and covered her ears, crying out incoherently.

When the inexplicable windstorm died down, she found that she was shaking. As he'd fallen over the cliff, he'd held her gaze. She was unable to look away. The image of hatred on his contorted face would not be banished, scorched into her. When she closed her eyes, his face floated before the darkness in swirling shades of color.

With her eyes open but unseeing, she crouched on the ground in silence like a child hiding from the bogeyman.

After an eternity of waiting, she hesitantly stood.

The forest around her was silent now, as though reverent to her power. It soothed her.

He was dead ... dead! There was nothing he could do to her. Idle threats. Scare tactics. Well, Goddesses were afraid of nothing, so he'd just wasted his dying breath!

A voice echoed through her mind: "You will suffer for eternity ... even if I have to give up my final resting place."

She spun around, but she was alone.

The voice of the man she'd just killed said again in her mind: "I spare no sympathy for you ... but I pity those who have to share my fate."

With an animal whimper, Ichiryu shot up out of her bed, arms around herself.

She stared at the vanity directly across from the bed, whose mirror remained covered unless she needed to use it. She couldn't abide reflections. Her hand trembled as she wiped away the wetness on her cheeks.

Bending over, she buried her head in her hands.

***

Redd stumbled into her and Ara's shared room late that night: exhausted, drained, but calm. Chani and the young man who had helped her, named Roland, hadn't left her side for an instant as she'd been instructed on the basics of psyker control.

I'm a psyker, she thought with exhilaration and wonder. *Not a freak. Not a monster. Just a totally commonplace human mutation.*

She rolled onto her cot, aware that Ara was already asleep across the room. She felt bad for her friend, but her emotions were dampened for the moment. She wasn't allowing it to get to her. She'd apologize properly tomorrow.

As soon as she closed her eyes, her mind replayed the events of the day. She watched the training again as an impartial observer: the demonstration of the 'firestorm,' an unleashing of power so destructive it ignited the very air, and how Roland had just walked through it and laid hands on the poor soul who had volunteered to undergo it, and stopped it.

She'd seen firsthand what she had almost done, and what Roland had done to prevent it. Even from across the room, his soothing power could be felt. He was a TKer, the Race of Man equivalent to the psyker mutation, but in the exact opposite direction. They used telekinetic wavelengths emitted by the brain to control objects around them, and — nobody knew quite why — TKers could soothe a raging psyker. Chani had called it the Creator's love of duality.

The older psykers, fully trained, reinforced what Chani had said. They'd also expressed amazement that she'd gotten so old and hadn't had a firestorm yet, especially considering what she'd gone through. They praised her for her natural control, and told her stories from when they first started to manifest. The camaraderie was comforting.

Psykers lived on the edge of a knife, their power completely tied to their emotions. Their training regime started early and was intensive, but necessary. Considering what she'd seen — and more than that, how being in the same room as a firestorm almost brought her spiraling back into it herself — she could see why.

But having the older psykers to speak with her, to have someone who knew exactly what she was going through, eased her mind.

She thought, as she fell asleep, that there was hope.

SIX
Decisions

Redd's eyes opened in the middle of the night. She'd fallen asleep on top of the cot, without even pulling the blanket over herself.

Something was wrong.

But she didn't — or maybe couldn't — move. Maybe it was lucky she didn't, maybe she would have been struck down if she had.

A mental whispering came to her.

Mistress, we have arrived. Your will be done. She will die.

Suddenly, she thought of Ara, asleep in the other cot. An assassin sent by Lucifer? Not sure what she could do but damn sure she wasn't going to let them kill Ara, she quickly rolled off the bed.

A dagger speared her pillow. Alarms blared inside the room, and echoed outside. Redd tackled Ara, hefting the angel over her shoulder, who squawked in sleepy fear and surprise. A shadow slashed with something sharp enough to split the air. It whined as it passed close by.

Her power responded to her heightened emotional state — the fear and desperation. It came to the forefront of her mind, calling for her to use it, *use it*. Redd relented. Time slowed.

Unconsciously Redd shaped the power and shot it out from her, blowing a hole in the wall. She dove through the opening, and deposited Ara, who rolled into a sitting position, on the other side.

Redd swept her gaze in an arc, simultaneously seeking her enemy and taking stock of where she was. The busted wall led to one corner of the main square, the open area between all the buildings.

Something pinged her senses.

She whipped around, her heart pounding, and threw another ball of her power at the shadow as it darted out after her.

Too fast! It came at her, avoiding her clumsy attack, and sliced for her throat. She jerked her head back and nearly lost her balance, flinging her arms up to block her face. She cried out as the dagger came again on the back-swipe, cutting deep gashes in the flesh of her forearms.

The pain triggered something. She screamed gutturally and power burst from her like the detonation of a grenade. The shadow rocketed back into the square, incinerated.

Armed soldiers poured into the square from the other side. Another shadow rushed her, knocked her sprawling. It was on her in a moment, its blade streaking toward her throat — which stopped only inches from her flesh.

The shadow visibly struggled, pushing the blade down with both hands. A vision burst in Redd's head of Ara down on her knees, glowing faintly white, her hands clasped before her in prayer. The gentle warmth of Ara's power covered Redd's skin palpably, protecting her somehow.

Taking advantage of the delay, Redd bucked the shadow off of her. Acting on instinct, she viciously kicked it, her speed and force enhanced by her power. It made a sound like screeching metal and writhed, knocking her away. Redd rolled backwards gracelessly and managed to scramble into a crouch.

The injured shadow stood up and turned towards her. Two more came out of the darkness, surrounding her.

She gathered her power to her, keeping it close, as they approached. The center shadow made its move and Redd exploded.

Her show of force shoved them back and stunned them long enough for the soldiers to take solid aim from across the square. Three soldiers fired once each, and the shadows dissipated. Crystals tinkled to the ground in the sudden quiet.

Redd turned on the rifle-bearers like a wild animal. One of the soldiers called out, "Someone get Roland!"

The soldier's voice cut through her haze. She swallowed and closed her eyes, beat down the power running rampant through her, shoved it into a box.

"It's okay," she managed, holding up her hands. "I've got it."

She opened her eyes again and went to Ara, kneeling down beside the little angel. Startled out of her trance, Ara looked up. She grabbed Redd's wrists, turning them to show the deep gashes on Redd's forearms from the shadow's blade.

"You're hurt!" Ara cried.

Redd stared at the wet glimmer of her own blood. The Ranger camp was well-lit at night, but the two girls sat in a pool of deep shadow behind the building they'd blown through, beyond the main lights.

Maybe it was just the shade, then, that made her blood look so strange.

Redd tore her mind away from the spiral it was teetering on the edge of, smiled (and winced) as Ara got to Healing her wounds. Healings weren't comfortable, but she was glad when the pain — which had flooded in after her adrenaline began to fade — lessened.

A disheveled Chani ran up, dressed in a loose tank top and shorts, which showed off impressive musculature previously covered by her coat (*She's jacked,* Redd thought in awe despite herself) and pajama pants. She'd obviously been roused from bed.

"Redd? What happened?" she called, then shook her head. "No, you know what? Come to my cabin. We'll talk about it there."

***

Chani's cabin was pretty spacious compared to other places Redd had seen in the temporary camp; it had its own bathroom, a meeting or living room, an attached bedroom, and another little area with a few machines Redd didn't know what to make of. The 'living room' consisted of a couch, flat-screen monitor, terminal on one side, and in the far corner, a desk flanked by two huge cabinets. Chani had the girls make themselves comfortable on the couch, then she disappeared into the unknown room.

"Coffee, tea, what?" she called.

"Tea for me, please, plain. I am not hungry," Ara responded.

Redd felt drained, and with all the adrenaline gone, very tired.

"Something with sugar … a donut, a muffin, something," she called back. "And maybe some coffee, if it isn't too much trouble … with chocolate, milk, sugar, the works."

Chani came back a minute later with a tray, and delivered the girls their requested items. Redd got a double-chocolate muffin with chocolate chips and a creamy filling. Chani had a large cup of black coffee and something Redd didn't recognize. It was apparently edible, because she was eating it.

Chani flopped down on the couch across from them, blowing out a breath that puffed out her cheeks.

"Alright, we all good and calm? Yes? What happened?"

Redd obliged, starting with her sudden wakeup and the whispers.

Chani put down her coffee and rubbed her hands down her face, then back through her hair, sweeping it back.

"Creator," she sighed. "And they called to a 'Mistress'? You're sure?"

Redd nodded. "I thought they were after Ara, because they said *'she* will die.' But they attacked *me*, even when Ara was alone. I don't know if that's because I fought back and so because of that they saw me as a threat, but that wouldn't make sense if ..." She trailed off, not wanting to finish the sentence.

If they truly were there to kill Ara.

"Who would want to kill me?" Redd went on.

"Could they have been sent by my father?" Ara asked in a strained voice. "If he *was* ... trafficking ... if he saw you as *his* ... what happens to escapees?"

"There'll be an investigation," Chani said decisively. They weren't to work themselves up theorizing. But that didn't make the questions go away, and both girls descended into a sullen, unsettled silence.

Redd looked down at her half-eaten muffin, abandoned. The fight was somewhat of a blur in her memory, just the feeling of heat, pressure, pain ...

She frowned at a specific memory. "Ara?"

The little angel had been staring at her toes. She looked up at Redd's voice.

"What did you do?" Redd asked. "During the fight, you ... protected me, somehow."

"I ... I prayed." She looked down again, clearly uncomfortable with the attention. "I am a Healer. I have studied the higher magical arts to a degree, but I am not a practitioner of magic, per se. My focus is the body, the spirit. However, when I saw you in danger, I ... just prayed for the Creator to shield you."

"I suppose it makes sense," Chani said, amused.

"How?" Redd asked.

"The angels had a special connection with the Creator. Metatron spoke for him, the Zeruphim were his chosen warriors, the Seraphim — "

"So it is true?" Ara cut in, her voice tight with excitement. She covered her mouth and flushed. "I — I mean, there were once more of us?"

Chani grinned. "Do you know how old I was when the Elysian attacked?"

"You were alive?!" Redd exclaimed. "I thought that was like, three hundred years ago!"

Chani regarded Redd for a moment, then went on. "Do you remember Roland? The difference between TKers and psykers?"

"TKers are … Race of Man? And psykers are human."

"Right. I am Race of Man. Humans are just about the only sapient species in the universe who rarely live longer than a couple centuries. They burn. Like suns. Their souls are incredibly powerful, and they have incredible potential, but they are the weakest of the sapients, physically. They are wreathed in chaos, which is why most human-dominated worlds are still uninitiated. Man is different. I'll tell you the whole story later. Suffice to say, if we aren't killed, we live up to a thousand years."

Chani shook her head. "Anyway. Ara, what happened was that the Elysian went after Godholme, the place where the Creator resides." She snorted. "A really poor idea, but it just shows how arrogant they were. We didn't know how numerous they had gotten, nor how dangerous. We didn't know that they had any sort of leadership. They just seemed like yet another Creator-damned scavenger group preying on the outer edges of the universe where we can't protect everyone, because — " Chani cut herself off and her mouth twisted like she'd bitten into something sour.

"It was a lot of 'didn't knows.' Not that it's an excuse, but the Elysian were almost impossible to get any information on. They attacked Godholme and the Creator sent them packing. Needless to say, that pissed them off. They turned their eyes on the angels, since they couldn't get to the Creator directly. The angels had left *this* world, Assisi," she pointed at the floor, "which was their home planet, to protect a small colony world closer to Godholme, expecting retribution to happen there."

Chani looked down, but her eyes were unfocused. "One Seraphim was left here, as well as several small contingents of the other subspecies of angels. For the most part, the planet was … undefended. No one expected what happened. When we heard they had attacked, we rushed here, but it was too late. Scans found no life." Chani looked up, apologetic. "We don't know what happened to the others. They kind of disappeared. We can only assume they ran into a trap set by the Elysian and were wiped out."

"So we truly are the last … " Ara whispered.

"The Rangers and elves are happy to see you, trust me," Chani said emphatically. "We thought you were extinct. It was a sad, sad day when we reported back about that bit of business, I can tell you that much …"

"What happened to the Elysian?" Redd asked.

"They vanished," Chani said, shrugging. "There was a great expenditure of power in one corner of the universe one day, but by the time we got there, whatever had been in the spot had been reduced to cosmic dust. We figure there was some kind of civil war or internal fighting, but the Elysian as a whole haven't been seen since." She picked her coffee back up and muttered over the rim, "Good riddance, too."

Another silence descended.

"Chani?" Redd finally broke said silence.

"Hmm?"

"What's a 'Creator'?"

Chani tilted her head back like she was thinking hard. "Let's see, modern Chaos Earth — yeah, your people didn't really have a concept of a 'progenitor,' huh?" She leaned over to pat Redd's forearm, seeing the blank look, then stood. "We'll talk about it later. For now, we should probably get some rest. Why don't you stay in my room tonight? I'll sleep here." She kicked the couch lightly.

"Wait," Redd said. "Persephone told me my planet was Federated Earth."

"It's both. Federated Earth is its proper name, yes, but Chaos Earth is, ah, a nickname."

"Oh."

"Like I said, we'll talk more about it later. Go get some sleep."

Redd nodded and got to her feet. It hit her just how exhausted she was. She took one side of Chani's big bed, and Ara took the other. Chani made sure they were comfortable, then turned out the light and closed the door.

Redd was awake for a long while after that, though, her mind chasing itself around without ever resolving a thing, hardly completing a thought.

After a couple of hours of fruitlessly trying, she slipped out of bed and went back into the main room with the intention of getting some water from the replicator.

She blinked to find Chani still awake.

"Can't sleep?" the older woman asked gently. Redd shook her head. Chani patted the space next to her on the couch.

The silence stretched between them. Chani was comfortable to be around, Redd realized. She was doing something on a variety of different little electronic pads, things Redd had seen around but hadn't asked about yet. It looked like work. The symbols that flashed across the screen weren't anything Redd could read.

But Redd's mind was still too full.

She drew her legs up to her chest, looped her arms around them, and rested her chin on her knees.

"Chani."

"Hmm?"

"You know about my planet, right?"

"Mm-hm."

"What … what do you guys think of it?"

"What do we *think* of it?"

Redd made a face, trying to find the words. "How is it perceived? Out here."

"Well," Chani said with a sigh, looking up from her work, but not at Redd. "It's uninitiated for a reason. I don't think you're in a mental place to know details. But we don't consider it a nice place."

"It isn't."

"Why don't *you* tell me what it was like?"

Redd hesitated, considering if she should. But the words bubbled up and poured out of her anyway — about her isolated childhood, being raised by a terminal, the things she saw on said terminal as her only information on what life outside the walls of her home was like, the megacities and the miasma and the weird rules, how she was pretty sure everything she'd been told was a lie.

This time, talking about it — despite the knot in her chest — helped. Just a bit.

Chani's silence was warm and understanding. She didn't try to explain or dismiss; she was just there to hear. Redd blinked away tears. She'd never had someone do that for her. With Ara's family bullshit — and how it was clearly affecting the angel even though she'd refused to talk about it, Redd had subsequently refused to talk much about her own issues, aside from what came out past her volition. The last thing she wanted was to add on to her only friend's woes.

But Redd was quickly growing to trust and like Chani.

"Have you heard of the Heroes of the Revolution?" Redd asked suddenly.

"Yes. Winged figures in gold-and-white armor, Federation legend. The heroes that liberated the North from repeated attacks by the other nations and helped create the Federation."

"How did you know that?"

"The Ranger Archives. I'm the Special Projects Commander, so I have to know lots of things about lots of places."

"Were they angels? Did angels liberate my people? But all the angels I've met have horns, and the Heroes of the Revolution didn't." Redd sounded suspicious even to her own ears. "My planet is uninitiated, so nobody's allowed to interfere, right?"

"That is correct."

"You're not going to tell me about the real history, are you?" Redd asked, a touch petulantly.

Chani glanced at her with sympathy. "You almost firestormed not twelve hours ago. I know you're curious and the drive to know the truth can be all-consuming, but you need to give yourself some time to adjust."

Redd buried her face in her knees, burning with frustration and embarrassment. But she knew Chani was right, as much as she loathed to admit it.

"I'd better try to get some sleep," Redd muttered and unfolded from the couch, heading for the bedroom.

"Hey," came from behind her. She paused, only because of the honest concern in Chani's voice. "It'll get better. I promise."

"Yeah," she agreed without much confidence, then went back into the bedroom and climbed back in bed.

***

Redd did doze off, but woke again some time later as Chani opened the door with a mug of coffee in her hand, dressed in what Redd would describe as work-out clothes and looking generally put together.

Redd wrinkled her nose and glared at her blearily. "You have no right to be so awake."

Chani just laughed. "Sure I do. More years of this schedule than I care to admit to. It gets ingrained in you after a while." She jerked her head. "Come on, I've got some stuff for you."

Chani's 'stuff' turned out to be soldiers' uniforms, bereft of the patches, name plates, and other adornments Redd had seen on everybody else. Chani called them 'rec-suits.' Redd studied herself in Chani's mirror after putting it on. Ara came up behind her. Redd couldn't help but laugh.

"Man, I thought *I* looked odd — kinda cool, maybe, but odd — but you ... that stuff doesn't look right on you *at all*."

Ara scrunched her face up, clearly uncomfortable. Chani appeared and patted Ara on the back.

"What's so bad about it? It's a Healer set; see these?" Chani tapped the intricate bracers covering Ara's wrists as part of the armor. "They augment healing powers. You might find that even after your clothes are cleaned, you will want to wear these. And you," she addressed Redd, "why aren't you wearing the circlet?"

"What, this?" Redd reached down to Chani's bedside table and picked up a thin metal circlet with the Rangers' sigil on a circular crest. "I couldn't figure out how to get it to stay on."

"Yeah, I guess it doesn't come with instructions, huh?" Chani murmured and took it from Redd.

She pressed a thumb on the sigil and the circlet disappeared *into* the crest. Chani stuck the sigil to Redd's forehead, and, as soon as she released the crest, the rest of the circlet popped out, fitting snugly around Redd's noggin.

As Chani stepped back, Redd reached up to feel it, wonderingly.

"Cool."

"This will help augment and control your psyker powers."

Redd took a moment to concentrate. "I can feel that." Then, after a moment, she ventured hesitantly, "Ah, Chani?"

"Yes?"

"What's with the, uh … the tube?"

Redd gestured vaguely at her crotch in hopes Chani would understand.

“Ah. That allows you to expel liquid waste without having to stop. The electronics in the suit recycle the lost nutrients and water while disposing of the waste and toxins.” She reached out to lift the edge of Redd’s collar. A tube stuck out on either side, craftily hidden there. “See these? One is for water, one is for a nutrient boost.” She released the collar and detached Redd’s belt buckle. On the back of it was an electronic screen. “This is a biometric monitoring system. Check it often to see what you’re lacking in.”

“I don’t have that,” Ara commented.

“Your suit is a variation made with angelic physiology in mind — thank Fug we had a couple on hand — and since angels don’t expel physical waste, you wouldn’t need it. This is all in Ranger 101, but I guess you two will kind of have to get the lessons on the run. There’s a lot more to the rec-suit that you should know about, but we don’t really have time for full lessons.”

Chani ran her hands back through her hair, taking a deep breath that puffed out her cheeks when she let it out.

“Alright. Today you’re gonna meet the Commandant of this outfit, and we’ll decide what to do with you.”

Redd’s stomach twisted. From the look on Ara’s face, she was experiencing something similar.

“You’re free to chill for a little bit, though, unless you want to come out and do PT with me. I gotta be out to formation here in a few. Ah, actually. This is also a bit ahead of schedule but you’re really going to struggle if you don’t have one specific thing.” Chani pulled out a tube about the same length and width as a finger — maybe slightly larger — and looked at Redd. “In here is a translation implant. It’s ubiquitous in initiated spaces, to the point where everybody speaks their own language because they’re so used to everyone else having one. You’re free to refuse it, but you probably won’t understand literally anyone else from here on out. Ara and I have been speaking Federated Common with you, but a lot of other Rangers won't."

"Oh, so that's why I sometimes couldn't understand when the angels talked to each other," Redd said. "Um, do I need surgery ...?"

"No, not at all," Chani said. "This tube is a hypo; a self-contained system that injects the implant under your skin. I won't get into *how* it works, but you're free to look it up on the terminal if you're interested."

"Inject?" Redd echoed, an edge of fear to her voice. She sought Ara's hand unconsciously, and felt it slip into hers. She gripped.

"It's painless," Chani assured. "The tip has a quick-acting local anesthetic. You won't feel a thing. Though it might take some time to get used to the translator's effects on the brain."

Redd looked at Ara, sure her terror was showing on her face. Ara tightened her hold on Redd's hand and gave her an encouraging look.

Redd took in a deep breath and closed her eyes. "Okay," she said, hoping Chani would do it before her resolve wore off. Her heart was pounding in her ears, so she barely heard Chani step close enough to be within arm's reach.

Chani seemed to respect that she was afraid, because it was over within a second. Redd felt Chani's presence, heard a hiss (which made her flinch), felt a momentary pressure behind her ear.

Then Chani said, "Finished. Well done, kid."

Redd breathed through the panic. She tried to be proud of herself, but the panic chased off any other emotion. With the doubly-soothing presences of Ara and Chani, though, she was able to calm her heart rate and keep her power from responding.

"What about Ara?" she asked, breathless from the effort of distracting herself.

“Angelic biology doesn’t ‘do’ implants. They’re not physical enough for that.” Chani held out a hand to Ara. “Want to show her the knowledge transfer?”

Ara gasped. “Oh, I’ve read about that! I’ve always wanted to try it! Are you certain?”

“I’m offering, aren’t I?”

Ara visibly screwed up her courage, glanced at Redd, who gave an exhausted smile, then took Chani’s hand and closed her eyes. Her lips moved as though she were reciting something — but impossibly fast. It made Redd’s eyes cross, so she looked away.

She heard shuffling and looked back. Ara had a hand to her head and looked dizzy, but recovered soon enough.

Chani spoke.

What Redd’s ears heard was the grinding of boulders tumbling down a rocky hill.

But her brain interpreted it as: “How are you two doing?”

“Oh! I understood that!” Ara exclaimed with the unflappable excitement of a scholar. “That was dwarven, correct?”

“Redd?” Chani looked at her.

“I — I got it. You’re right, though. That’s fucking weird.”

Chani burst out laughing and patted her arm. “You’ll get used to it. Okay, now I really will be late for formation. Who’s coming with?”

***

Redd was curious, so she agreed to come with for ‘formation.’ Ara stayed behind to have some quality time with the terminal.

Redd hung out on one side of the large open area in the middle of all the buildings. The soldiers filed out of their respective buildings in groups, then formed up in the center in a grid pattern, neatly spaced and totally still. They were all wearing similar outfits to Chani — comfortable clothes one would exercise in. Three soldiers came to the head of the crowd, facing them. Chani went to stand by them. 'PT' was initiated by some pomp and circumstance, a head count, and something that sounded like a motto shouted at the top of everyone's lungs in perfect harmony. Chani and the three at the front led the rest of the soldiers in a long series of exercises.

Redd got the sense that Chani didn't need to do this, but she seemed to honestly enjoy interacting with the soldiers, and there was a lot of laughing. The soldiers respected her; that much was very obvious.

When they were done, Chani caught Redd's eye and gestured her over. The two women crossed the compound, passing the cafeteria (delicious smells wafted out, reminding Redd that she hadn't eaten since that sugar bomb at one in the morning), to another large building that pretty much looked damn near exactly the same as all the others.

Inside was an austere-looking office, including a desk, at which sat a man in uniform. He looked up as they entered and set down the pen he was using, folding his hands before him.

"Commander Abyssterilon."

"Good morning, Commandant."

This 'Commandant' looked past Chani to Redd. "Ah, this is the source of all the trouble yesterday, hmm? Has Lord Barandor returned yet?"

"Not yet. Haven't heard a damn thing from him since he left."

"Hmm. I suppose it doesn't matter. We got his intel on the subject, correct?"

"Yep."

Redd was not impressed by the way he dismissed her without even acknowledging her as a person. The fan-shaped door opened and she glanced over her shoulder. Ara, looking frightened, was led in by a blank-faced soldier, who then left. The door closed behind her.

"This is Ara Luschia Invenes, the daughter of Lucifer," Chani said.

"Ah, so this is who I really need to see."

"In a manner of speaking, but, honestly, the intel we've already gained as well as what Pheonix was able to bring us back from Lutius Invenes is probably more accurate than anything we could get from her. She was unaware of her father's activities. And our psyker friend will need to be taken to Terelath as soon as possible. Is contact back up with the elves yet?"

"No, last I heard there's still interference in communications."

The Commandant shook his head. "What the hell is going on with this planet? Did they at least figure out what that breach was all about last night?"

"I'm not sure. I haven't spoken to anyone about it yet this morning. The crystals were sent to the Grey Wizards but it will be a while before we hear anything back. On a separate subject, I was thinking of bringing this psyker, the Invenes girl, and Cadet Rivios to the surface with me."

He looked up in surprise. "This is unusual; why?"

"If anyone should babysit them, it probably should be me." She cracked a grin. "Aside from that, they have some formidable abilities I think I could make good use of on my mission. I *am* one of the best trainers the Rangers have. They won't go wrong with me."

"I'm aware of your credentials," the Commandant replied a little sharply, then spread his hands. "Fine, Abyss, if you want to take it on your shoulders, have at it. With communication with the elves down and Lord Barandor missing, we can't get in touch with Terelath anyway, and I don't have time to deal with a gaggle of kids."

Redd had no idea what any of that meant, aside from the fact that Chani apparently wanted to take her and Ara someplace. The part that concerned her, however, was that Chani was including Cadet Rivios — the horrible bitch who had almost made Redd detonate. She was bursting with questions and protests, but restrained herself for the moment as Chani and the Commandant went on to discuss the particulars of their journey, none of which Redd was able to follow.

Eventually, Chani turned and Redd followed her out. They were two steps out the door when she couldn't hold it in any longer.

"What was all that about? What's your mission? Do I have to come with you, and more importantly, do we *have* to take Imae?"

"Come on," Chani said evasively. "Let's head back to my place; we'll get some breakfast."

Redd pouted, but didn't see the use in arguing.

***

Redd, Chani, and Ara arranged themselves around Chani's little living quarters in much the same fashion as the night prior. Chani had what she called the 'vid-viewer' on with the volume lowered for some background ambiance, and everybody had a meal in their lap, before Chani was willing to talk.

"As you know, I am the Special Projects Commander — that is my technical rank and title. So, my services aren't really needed in this camp specifically, as it was established to deal with … ah, what is happening in Haven. But that doesn't mean I'm here for shits and giggles; I do have a legitimate mission from HQ."

"Okaaay…" Redd extended the word.

"I'm here to scout the surface. The brass wants to know if there's anything, or anybody, down there, especially with the intel that something is interfering with communications; especially now that we know that the angels are still around, even in small numbers. We want to know for *certain* if the survivors from Haven are the *only* survivors."

Chani rolled her eyes. “There’ve been some theories that this planet is barren, but I think that’s a crock of shit. Where they didn’t destroy a planet entirely, the Elysian left a wave of mutations in surviving and new-evolving life, either through radiation or corruption, or by imbalancing the planet’s ecological equilibrium. And there was one Seraphim left here when everybody else went off to the colony planet near Godholme. They aren’t easily taken down, Creator knows, so that Seraphim may still be hanging around, weak or injured, or there may be evidence of her passing somewhere. If she is dead, then, well, we’ll need to make the appropriate arrangements.”

“That makes sense. But, why take us?”

“Well, like I told the Commandant, I think you two could be an asset, and you won’t be happy being quarantined here while they try to figure out a way to ship you off to Terelath.”

“*That’s* true. But why Imae?”

Chani sighed, and was silent for long moments.

“Imae is my responsibility, at least for now.”

Redd took a breath to question it, then let it out. The unspoken ‘don’t ask’ hung in the air, and Redd, begrudgingly, respected it.

She fumed in silent impotence as everybody tucked into their food and the vid-viewer took over as the loudest thing in the room. She felt heat rising in her body in tune with the instability in her emotions, and, sickened, closed her eyes to clamp down on the reaction. Anger gave way to cold despair — was this what the rest of her life was going to be like? Trying not to explode at every little thing? The other psykers told her it got easier, but she wasn’t even sure that she would last that long. Too much stress.

Or was it better that she face difficulty now? Would control come easier with practice, or would it only bring her dangerously close to a firestorm? With Imae traveling with them, the likelihood of the latter happening seemed far too high. There was so much she didn’t know, and no time to sit and learn.

And as if all that wasn't bad enough, there was still the issue of the attack. Chani hadn't said a single word about it since relegating it to an investigation. Redd supposed that made sense, but she didn't have to like it. And she couldn't help her mind from ruminating on it.

The logical thing would be to think that the assassins were sent by Lucifer, but they'd called out to a 'mistress.' She hadn't heard anyone refer to Lucifer thusly, so … a partner-in-crime?

It couldn't possibly be Persephone.

And *had* they been after Redd or Ara? Redd strained to remember why she'd assumed it had been Ara from the outset. She was just trying to protect her friend. But they had only ever attacked her, Redd, even while Ara was unprotected.

The more she thought about it, the more it made sense that they'd been after *her*. If they had been sent by Lucifer, it would make sense. One of those 'if I can't have you, no one can' kind of things. He'd already shown he was capable of violence in retribution.

Redd unconsciously reached up to touch where the needle had pierced her neck, in that dark hallway after the trip to the market.

Why would he kill his own daughter for running away, especially since he'd kept her so carefully oblivious?

No, I was definitely the target, Redd thought with a chill.

But the 'mistress' part was the enduring mystery. Lucifer hardly seemed the type to want to relinquish power to anyone, as arrogant and controlling as he was. So a partner-in-crime seemed unlikely.

Could there possibly be someone else who wanted Redd dead?

Her breath caught.

My parents.

Fuck, it was no wonder Redd had hated and feared Lucifer. He looked at her in the same way she'd caught her father doing when he thought she was distracted — with that same possessive calculation.

The mistress could be my mother, I guess, Redd thought. She was actively shaking and had to close her eyes and clench her fists, breathe through it, before Chani and Ara noticed.

When she'd calmed a bit, she glanced at them to ensure they hadn't been paying attention.

The panic and adrenaline dropped away, plummeting her straight into depression.

What the fuck am I going to do?

The thought of running briefly crossed her mind, again.

Yeah, if she were attacked again and caught out on her own, it would be game over. Still, part of her didn't trust the Rangers. Once this was all over, she'd essentially be what she'd just escaped twice.

Enslaved.

Or fucking close enough.

But she'd just recently been down the tracks of this train of thought. Her situation wasn't any better now than it had been the last time she considered an escape plan.

Hell, if anything, it was worse now that she was a known psyker. The Rangers wouldn't willingly let a walking bomb gallivant about willy-nilly.

She could either go with Chani and deal with whatever Imae could throw at her, or run, abandon Ara, and risk falling into worse hands or being caught and punished, or whatever the Rangers would do to her.

No, she was stuck. Her only hope was that Chani could control Imae.

And that Redd could control herself.

"When do we leave?" Ara asked quietly, interrupting Redd's gloomy thought spiral.

"Tomorrow," said Chani. "Dawn."

SEVEN
Clouded Judgment, Clouded Planet

Dawn came far sooner than Redd would have liked, despite weathering the long hours of another mostly-sleepless night. When Chani opened the door and barked out "Good morning" and "Get the hell up" in the same breath, Redd groaned in protest and rolled over.

She and Ara had been allowed to continue to stay with Chani for their protection, an arrangement that seemed to work out for everybody involved. Redd sat at the edge of the bed, feeling exhaustion drag at every bone in her body, and dreaded the day.

They ate breakfast quickly and quietly, not so much out of a need to do so as much as being caught up in their own private thought processes. Redd resisted the urge to touch the minds of her companions, instead focusing on her eggs. Over-easy this morning, with a thick slice of meat and white rice. A hearty meal for what Chani assured her would be a difficult day.

Redd had seen Ara only eat fruit, but this morning she had a pile of flowers on her plate. Redd almost asked about them, but the look on the little angel's face warned her that conversation was not welcome.

After eating, Redd, Ara, Chani, and Imae gathered in the main square while Chani spoke one last time to the Commandant and several other people who looked to be high-ranking. Redd let her attention wander, but snapped back into reality when Chani turned to the girls.

"Ready?" Chani asked.

Ara smiled, Imae scowled, and Redd shrugged.

"As I'll ever be," Redd grumbled.

They got underway. Each had been outfitted with packs filled with generic supplies, weapons (which Chani had gone through a very brief introduction of, but she amended that they probably wouldn't need to use them, smiling at Ara, who looked like she was going to be sick), changes of clothes, and all those fun little micro-camping stuffs that Pheonix had used, which were, Redd was learning, fairly standard.

This wasn't a new experience for Redd, nor was it a particularly difficult one.

To a certain extent, Redd was used to hiking. Her family had gone on a camping trip to the artificial forests inside Jewel City once a year, a sort of sabbatical away from her father's high-stress, high-tech business life. He liked to pick the most remote place he could find; thus, the hiking. Redd figured it had something to do with those things that parents talked about when they thought their kids weren't listening, the ways that life pulled at them that they hoped not to show, or they hoped their children won't notice. But Redd had noticed, just like all kids do. She'd never been to her father's work, but whatever he did wore him down in a big way sometimes, even when he tried to hide it behind bad jokes and a fake smile.

Just another one of those weird things that parents did.

But being in the deep wilds was the only time Redd's father had ever really seemed to relax, releasing some tension so constant that she didn't even take note of its presence until it was gone. Out there, in the quiet, he would sometimes joke about never going back.

Her parents had insisted — despite the fact that her education came from a terminal — that she do exercises, which had kept her in relatively good shape. She hadn't gone out of her way to be physically active, but she also hadn't hated it. In fact, looking back on it, there was very little she had strong feelings about one way or another, like she'd been moving through a dream.

Though her mind was wandering, and she was allowing it to help the time pass, she recoiled from the rabbit hole that thought would lead down and pulled herself back to the present to take stock of her surroundings.

The terrain wasn't too terrible — limited underbrush, very few thorny plants, almost no hills. Some of the trees were so large they had to be circumvented, or their roots broke the surface of the soil and the four women had to scramble over them or find another way around, but other than that, the only real problem came in the form of distance and boredom. It was a beautiful day, clear blue skies and a slight fresh breeze, which made the going easy and enjoyable.

At least, for Redd, Imae, and Chani.

Ara, however, was struggling, and needed frequent breaks.

Chani had woven the little angel's long hair into a many-stranded braid to keep the voluminous locks from snagging on local flora or getting dirty. The older woman's light-hearted suggestion about cutting it had made Ara turn ashen, and Redd had laughingly teased Chani about her own hip-length hair. Chani had smiled, shrugged, and turned away.

The day wore on with mind-numbing predictability. Walking, stopping to eat or let Ara catch her breath, batting aside the prolific apologies, more walking. Conversation was sparse. The scenery was beautiful, but there was only so many times one could see a tree before they all started to look alike, especially given the other aspects of the circumstance.

Said trees thinned out sometime in the late afternoon, and by early evening, finally became grassy plains. Looking to either side, Redd could almost imagine the edge of the island; there was an undeniable feeling of *narrowing*, as though the island wasn't entirely round, but oblong, and they were traveling longways across it.

"Chani, where exactly are we going?" she said aloud.

Chani stopped and pulled a thin piece of metal with an electronic screen on one face out of a slit in her jacket. She'd been consulting it on and off all day. Redd assumed it was a MLUS (mobile location updating system, a way to track where you were in the megacities) of some sort.

The troop trundled to a stop while Chani turned around and stared off into the distance.

"According to our surface scan pre-deployment, there were strange structures somewhere near the eastern end of this island. I wanted to check them out before rendezvousing with the transport that will take us to the surface. We're close, but I doubt we'll make it before nightfall, so we should probably strike camp here."

She dropped her pack heavily to the ground. Redd watched her without moving, rolling the implications of that last statement around in her head.

"Do you think there's something dangerous there?" Redd glanced between Ara and Chani; Ara had never mentioned any inherent threats on Haven, and City Center seemed peaceful enough … at least from external threats.

Chani straightened and studied Redd. "What makes you think I just don't want to trip over something in the dark?"

Redd snorted. "Come on, you've got those fancy lights. You could make it as bright as daytime if you wanted to." Redd hesitated. "Well, Pheonix did, anyway."

Chani laughed. "I'll have you know that Pheonix's gear is hardly standard, but yes, I do have something 'fancy.'" Chani reflected for a moment. "It's a combination of factors, really, but in my line of work, you learn to be careful." Smiling, she bent to her pack. "I'll tell you about it someday."

Redd floundered, confused, then sighed and shrugged her pack off as well.

***

Nighttime came like a silken sheet in a summer breeze. It was comfortably cool, but near the fire (which Chani had provided), it was also comfortably warm.

Funny thing about that ... when Chani'd first talked about a fire, Redd had expected to be sent out to gather dead wood. But Chani hadn't asked. When Redd questioned it, she was told that Chani had much more efficient and safe fuel for a fire than wood; aside from which, the Rangers strove to be as no-impact on any environment they inhabited as possible. Being a purely spacefaring culture (the Rangers had no home planet, Chani had bluntly said, and Redd was too afraid to ask what that meant), they respected planetside environments probably more than most native cultures.

Redd sat in the entrance of her little pup-tent some ways away from everyone else, courting sleep but letting her mind work while she still had the energy to think.

Ara had already gone to sleep. Poor thing; as soon as she'd eaten she'd just wilted. Chani had had to force her to retire early. Ara'd been insistent on staying up and pushing herself hard to keep up with the other three women, but being a sedentary scholar was hardly good training for even easy traveling, especially over long distances.

But there was no arguing with Chani. Redd was glad for that. She felt a strong kinship and an even stronger protective instinct towards Ara — maybe as some sort of need to repay the little angel for nursing her through withdrawals, or maybe just as a result of the bond they'd formed in adversity. Redd's lazy mind shied away from it — she wasn't in any state to psychoanalyze herself just then.

Realizing she was nodding off, she crawled into her tent and buried herself in her sleeping bag.

It was just as sleep was about to claim her that she heard the voices — Chani and Imae.

"I don't want to talk about it," came the muffled, angry voice of the cadet.

"You don't have a choice."

There was silence, laden with tension. Redd was caught between moving and letting them know she was awake, or inadvertently eavesdropping. Indecision made her decision for her.

“You don’t seem to understand how much trouble you could get in,” Chani prompted; then, when Imae didn’t respond, she continued, “If it weren’t for me and your parents … ”

Redd moved her head quietly and found that she could see their silhouettes through the thin walls of the tent. Might as well eavesdrop efficiently.

Imae wordlessly exploded, arms flung up and out, then at Chani’s hissed command, subsided.

“My parents?” Imae seethed. “What the hell do my parents have anything to do with this?”

Chani must have done something soundless — a look, perhaps — because Imae apologized gruffly.

Chani, standing in front of the fire, spread her arms. “Why do you think I’m here? For my health?” She paused to let that sink in. “HQ didn’t send me; I requested to come. On the behest of your parents, once they found out you’d skipped ship.”

“Yeah, well, it was probably just so I wouldn’t embarrass them.”

Chani shook her head and turned slightly away. “Creator almighty. You’re hell-bent on becoming a statistic, aren’t you? You know your family, you know what happens to them. It’s the first damn thing you learn. You’re brilliant, kid. Yeah, things suck right now, but if you can get through this, you’ll be a hell of an asset to the Engineering Corps. I know you like mechanical systems more than people and half of me doesn't blame you.”

Chani sighed heavily into Imae’s sullen silence. “But this isn't the way. Take it from someone who skipped ship more than once. You’re lucky *we* got to you before some pirate skiff. We’ll find some way to make it easier on you, but you’re going back.”

The Commander turned and disappeared from the circle of firelight, and therefore Redd's vision. Imae sat there so long that Redd fell asleep waiting for her to move.

***

The next morning, the tension was thick. Maybe it was just her imagination after having witnessed last night's argument, but as Redd went through the motions of taking her tent down and packing her stuff up, she surreptitiously watched Imae. The youth seemed ready to break and run at any moment — Redd didn't need her burgeoning telepathy to see that. But what was equally obvious was that she had nowhere to go.

Just like me, Redd thought glumly.

Not that Chani wasn't good company or Redd didn't feel grateful for what the older woman had done for her already. It just wasn't easy to feel like a prisoner, even if the prison was a situation outside anyone's control.

In the nature of their prisons, though, she and Imae seemed to be very different indeed.

Redd hefted her pack onto her back with a groan as Ara approached. She offered Redd a little smile and Redd hesitantly returned it.

"How are you doing?" Redd asked.

"I am well," said Ara, smiling. She *did* look better for having slept. Chani joined them.

Hooking her thumbs into her pack, Chani twisted to look for Imae, who was just coming up to join them — purposely hanging back, though, it seemed.

"Ready?"

The girls nodded, and they set off.

Within two hours, they came to a ring of woods framing a slight bowl carpeted in springy green moss and studded in flat boulders. Chani checked her map thingie and led them right down into the bowl. As the tall, thin trees enveloped them, the almost-transparent foliage transformed the light green.

A shallow grade made for easy going, and the trees spread out even further as the group reached the floor of the bowl. Chani gestured for them to stop at the trees' edge, and the look on her face alerted Redd. She strained to hear or see anything out of place, but the forest seemed as innocuous as before.

Stretched out in front of them were the ruins of buildings, obviously old, for nature had begun to reclaim what was left of them.

Chani wandered forward, appearing completely at ease, which further confused Redd. About fifty feet away from the girls, Chani halted, tilted her head, and called out, "Yo!" She then gestured to the girls to come forward. Redd glanced at Ara, who shrugged.

They finally understood as a huge, winged, armored figure popped up from behind a crumbling wall. Pheonix rotated stiffly to face Chani and called back a greeting.

"What are you doing here? I thought you'd be off-planet by now. Don't you have training to complete?" Chani yelled.

"Curiosity." Pheonix met Ara's eyes; she straightened self-consciously. "Miss Ara?"

"Yes, sir?"

Pheonix held up a hand, an amused look passing over his face. "Calling me sir is *really* not necessary. And you shut your mouth."

That last bit was directed at Chani, who was actually trying really hard not to laugh. She slapped a hand over her mouth and turned away.

"Just Pheonix. Please."

"Very well," Ara said.

"Not much exploration was done up here, I take it."

"No," Ara agreed, puzzled.

He knelt down behind the wall and came back up with an armful of books. Ara gasped.

"I doubt, then, that your people knew that these were here."

"Are those … " Ara began, then lost the breath for the words. She cast a wondering glance at the ruins. "This place … "

"Is from before the time when these islands were raised, yes."

"So these buildings were brought here. What happened? Why did we not settle here, a pre-built location? Why did we not know it existed?" Ara bit her lip and proceeded to answer her own questions. "My father would not let his people travel, we were not allowed to pioneer new villages, although everyone knew we had ample space in Haven. Of course we didn't know it existed."

"I guess we'll stop here," Chani said, "I should probably look around a bit more to have something to bring back to the brass, so I'll let you guys have some time."

Redd sat some ways away, munching on a snack, while she glared at Pheonix.

Ara had taken some kind of weird shine to him, and she didn't like it one bit. While Chani was off exploring the deeper parts of the ruins, looking for who-knows-what, and Imae was sulking somewhere near the bottom of the hill, Ara had gravitated towards Pheonix and the two had gone into one of the buildings (which Redd had overheard was a library).

It wasn't that he was rude or rough with Ara; no, just the opposite … he kept his distance and his voice down as though she were a rabbit likely to be startled at a sudden movement. Almost double her size, he kept his wings curled in and hunched his head down slightly like he was trying to be smaller. He almost seemed aware of his appearance and how he came off as a terrifying figure.

Was it protectiveness over Ara sparking Redd's annoyance? No, because Pheonix didn't feel like a threat. Was it that she felt she'd lose Ara to Pheonix? No … when Ara and Chani had extended conversations (which they did often, Ara was terminally curious about this new world they found themselves in), Redd was content to listen.

Redd blew a breath out through her nose and closed her eyes to try to calm down, aware that her irritation was threatening to activate her power. But the questions kept coming.

Do I hate him? she thought in a kind of despair. She pressed her hands to her temples, as if using physical force would impart some kind of order to her increasingly-disordered thoughts.

Clarity came suddenly, like the parting of clouds.

He makes me feel safe, she thought wonderingly. *So why does that freak me out so much?*

Footsteps interrupted her. She straightened quickly and looked up to meet Chani's eyes.

Chani gave her an odd, questioning look; Redd shook her head. Imae trailed behind Chani, but Ara and Pheonix had to be pulled out of their engaging conversation. As Ara drew near, she separated from Pheonix and approached Redd, the remnants of her excited state still visible on her face.

Chani, like a mother duck with her chicks in tow, turned to face Pheonix, her stance casual.

"So where are you off to from here?"

"The surface."

"Soon?"

Pheonix glanced over his shoulder. "Probably."

"How were you intending on getting down there, just out of curiosity?"

From anyone else, that question may have sounded aggressive, but Chani's tone was neutral.

Pheonix didn't bat an eye, but he did spread his wings slightly. "They do work, you know."

His wings were malformed. The top curve was feathered, but they became increasingly sparse and tattered further down until all that was left was folded, leathery skin. While he was able to spread his wings slightly, the motion seemed strained, and it became obvious that he couldn't open them all the way.

Even that hindered motion, though, produced a span of probably ten feet.

"What are you, an angel?" Redd asked before she could stop herself.

Pheonix's gaze flicked to her and he relaxed his wings against his back again. With a completely blank expression, he said: "My species is currently unknown."

"Well, I've got a transport arranged, why don't you just come with us?" Chani suggested.

Pheonix looked at Chani. If he was considering it, Redd couldn't tell. She wasn't about to peek into his mind.

Something told her that would be a very bad idea.

Finally he shrugged. "Alright."

***

They got moving. Chani informed them that the transport was parked at the long end of the island, probably another hour's walk. When Redd asked her what was waiting for them at the surface, Chani laughed and told her, "That's what we're here to find out."

Chani and Pheonix pulled ahead, Redd and Ara in the middle, and Imae at the back. Still lost in her miserable thoughts, Redd didn't talk much and soon lost track of time.

On the horizon, maybe a mile or so away, a metallic object shone in the sun. Several black, amorphous blobs stood around it — probably their Ranger escort.

At this point, as they walked, Chani gave a short safety briefing, including how to interact with their escort, how to board and disembark from the transport, and how to act within the transport. She also assured them that in an emergency situation, the transport would automatically hover, rather than plummet out of the sky. Redd had never been in anything flying, so that last point was likely because of her probably-palpable terror at the prospect.

One of the soldiers noticed them as they got within clear visual range and called attention. They snapped to what Redd was beginning to recognize as the 'attention' pose, and the one who'd called it saluted.

They exchanged pleasantries and Chani spoke in incomprehensible military-speak with the soldiers, which Redd didn't bother to listen closely to.

Chani gestured the girls ahead of her into the transport. Pheonix held his hand out to Chani to help her in with a smile that was only part mocking. She shook her head and preceded him without taking his hand. Entering the ship, Chani reached to the hook to her right, to the helmet hanging there. She settled it onto her head and moved to allow Pheonix entry.

Tall, wide-shouldered Pheonix, made even wider by his armor and wings, had to scrunch up and bend down quite a bit to get in, but he seemed used to it and did so smoothly. Their escort of soldiers brought up the rear.

The transport vehicle was a simple, one-room affair; though Redd figured there must be a pilot, she couldn't see one. Benches lined the walls. Ara and Redd sat on one, Imae on the other. Chani joined Imae, and Pheonix sat next to her. The soldiers stood against the wall near the door.

Chani glanced around and gave the all-clear into the helmet.

Oh, Redd thought, *the helmet must be to communicate with the pilot.*

The transport lifted so easily that Redd wouldn't have even known it was moving if she couldn't see out the single window that was directly across from her. She watched with some vertigo in the pit of her stomach as Haven dropped away beneath them. The transport turned; then, all she could see was open air, and clouds, gently rolling like waves on the ocean. She was briefly stuck in time, the breath caught in her chest, at the beauty of the scene before her.

The horizon itself was painted in shades of blue from a rich near-violet where the atmosphere thinned out to a pastel where it met the clouds. The clouds, as heavy with moisture as they were, had an iridescent sheen that made them look like they'd been coated in rainbows. The transport hovered for a moment, then plunged forward — and down —

— into the clouds, colors of all hues flashing by, then darkness, lit only by red. It was eerie and called to Redd's paranoia but was over quickly.

The quality of light changed. It was very dark still; but now spots and variations in color and texture dotted the darkness. As the transport circled lower, the source of the light became clearer. Phosphorescent trees, what looked like giant-stalked mushrooms, smaller quicksilver bunches … flora adapted to the heavy cloud-cover. The ground was mostly flat and rocky, and in places there were jagged upheavals and long black scars of canyons that spoke of the planet's violent past. The flora, while gently glowing, was sparse, as though it fought for purchase in the malnourished soil.

"A city," Ara breathed.

Something in Redd tightened. She leaned over to peer past Ara, aware that everyone else in the transport was doing so, as well.

At the distance they were at, it was hard to see details. Some things were immediately clear: the city was backed up against incredibly tall, sheer cliffs, had a cluster of five ivory towers, set closely together, and two walls. Just outside the outer wall was a dark glimmer with liquid reflections. Water?

"Creator almighty," Chani whispered, awed. "A city. A living city."

"But peopled with what?" Pheonix asked.

"Bring us closer," Chani said into the mic attached to her helmet.

The transport pushed forward — and abruptly dipped.

Chani opened her mouth, then it hit them.

A staggering, debilitating *plea for help* — not in any polite language, not even in words. Just an overwhelming need to find the one crying out and rescue them, fight for them, die for them, whatever sacrifice was necessary.

Buried in the wave of need, the pilot lost control.

Redd barely heard Ara's gasp.

"*Seraphiel?*"

It was over as soon as it had begun. There was a moment of dead silence, where the only movement was that of the transport slowly coasting to a stop. Redd looked at Chani, her brain ringing with the after-effects of the cry. Chani was gripping the sides of the bench with white-knuckled fingers and leaning forward. By all appearances, she had been preparing to leap out of the transport, probably to her death, in answer to the call.

"I wasn't the only one that felt that, right?" Chani asked, her voice quiet and harsh.

Voices lifted in agreement around the cabin.

"Anyone else feel pulled toward the city?" Pheonix asked. Redd hated him for sounding so calm. Her heart was about to jump out of her chest.

Chani took a deep breath and let it out in a wavering sigh. Her voice, however, was strong. "I have a mission. You're free to go check it out once we land."

"I will."

Chani directed the pilot to set them down on the stony, barren flats, probably several miles outside the city. Rather than giving in, rushing off to heed the call, Chani had closed up. She was wary, and Redd didn't blame her, once she spent a few minutes thinking about it. They didn't know anything about the provenance of the call nor the occupants of the city.

The transport settled down and its door hissed and opened silently. The crew filed out much the same way as they had gone in. Standing in front of the ship, Redd breathed in and looked up. From this distance and with almost no light, she couldn't even see the clouds — it was like the whole of oblivion hung over their heads. She looked down quickly, uncomfortable. Ara came up beside her.

Chani spent a few minutes talking with the soldiers. They saluted and went back into the transport one by one. They returned carrying boxes and bags; Redd remembered seeing some of those supplies hanging up among the general crap on the walls, and stacked in the back corners.

"Hey," Chani called. "We're making camp here for now."

Redd watched her as she turned to help the soldiers set up. "What?"

"Situation's changed," Chani responded without turning.

"Well, can we help?"

"Nah. Just sit tight. Eat something."

Redd looked at Ara, who just smiled and shrugged. She still looked shaken.

Redd dug through her pack for something to eat. Ara had wandered a little ways away by the time she straightened up again, and was inspecting one of the nearby groups of mushroom-like trees. Redd came up beside her, munching on one of the fairly tasty, nutrient- and calorie-laden bars that the Rangers had provided as travel fodder.

"This is remarkable." Ara said quietly. "A little over three centuries, and the planet has changed so much."

"What was it like before?"

"Like Haven. After all, Haven was raised from here, the surface. It is like a little slice of the past — which is evermore evident seeing the state of the surface as it stands now."

"How do you know?"

"Books."

"Right." Then, after a pause, Redd said, "Honestly, this place reminds me of where I came from. Every night, the miasma would roll in and we'd be quarantined to our homes. Some areas were off-limits entirely because they'd been flooded with it. I've seen what it looks like outside the megacity walls. Uglier'n here. 'Course, I wasn't supposed to know any of this, but I … picked it up."

"How? If you don't mind me asking."

"A channel on the terminal. It didn't take me long after using it as an older kid, around nine or ten, to figure out how to get past my parents' attempts to control what I could see. There were quite a few subversive channels, though it was sometimes a pain in the ass to tune into them because they kept jumping networks. Sometimes they'd disappear entirely for a time. Somebody out there hated the Federation, though I don't know why, specifically. The Federation was corrupt as fuck, maybe that's reason enough. Anyway, the one I watched was aimed at 'Specials,' people who had powers. See, the Federation taught that people with powers were dangerous, and if they weren't brought to heel *by the Federation*, they would destroy everything."

A heavy silence stretched between them.

"Yes, now you know why I don't really trust the Rangers, even though I like Chani as a person," Redd whispered. Then, at a normal volume, she continued, "Anyway. The Federation was always looking for us, for Specials, and by and large the people in the megacities supported the pursuit. As long as a Special was owned by the Federation, they were acceptable. But if they weren't …"

"So there were groups … somewhere … who were trying to help the Specials escape," Ara said.

"Survive, Resist, Escape," Redd said distantly. "Yes. The methods they taught me are the only reason I walked away from what my parents did to me." She gave a short, humorless laugh. "As fucked up as I am. Being alive is better, I guess."

"Being alive means you have a chance to make it better, to take back your life," Ara said forcefully. She reached out to grab Redd's hand tightly. The angel's calming essence flowed through the contact and Redd let out a shaky breath.

She nodded once and Ara released her, looking away as silence fell again.

After a moment, Ara said, “The miasma sounds like corruption. Elysian spread it. Corruption is at least partially responsible for this.” Ara waved an arm to indicate the wasteland around them.

“If anything like the Elysian existed on Chaos Earth, they kept to themselves — which I find hard to believe, just based on what I’ve heard about them. The miasma was some toxic fog, origin unknown. If anyone in the Federation did know what it was, they made sure it was kept tightly under wraps. Supposedly it was being studied, but if that’s true, nothing ever came of it. Don’t know why they bothered.”

“‘Why they bothered?’” Ara echoed.

Redd made a face. “Science wasn’t … utilized. Not like it is out here. Whatever the Federation said, that was what people did. They didn’t question how the Federation knew what it knew. Or if they did, it didn’t get out.”

“Sounds familiar,” Ara said sadly.

Redd glanced at her, then looked down. “... Yeah, I guess it would.”

Redd chose a little outcropping of dusty rock some few feet away, settling down on it. “Ara?”

“Hmm?”

“You said something, when we were … when that … weird thing happened, before we landed.”

Ara became very still. Finally, Redd prompted, “Ara?”

Ara tilted her head, lining Redd up in her peripheral vision. “I heard you.”

“And?”

“I don’t know. I am … still processing.”

Redd let her friend think, and focused on eating.

“Seraphiel,” Ara said finally. “That’s what I received. Seraphiel.” She said it again, tasting the word.

“Do you know anyone by that name?” Redd asked.

Ara shook her head and sat next to Redd. “It sounds angelic, I can say that much. We angels are a … unique people, even among the vastness and variety of the universe. *If* the city has angels still extant within its walls, *if* they watch the skies, it's entirely possible they have a warning system, or a beacon. Or maybe a singular angel managed to reach out."

She looked past Redd and her eyes locked on something, tracking movement. Redd followed her gaze and was immediately irritated.

Pheonix stopped about ten feet away from the two girls.

"May I have a word with you alone?" he said to Ara.

A tension seeded in Redd's stomach and spread through her limbs, ending finally at her face. Her cheek twitched.

"Redd!"

Chani's bellow from across the campsite startled her out of her growing rage. Refusing to look at Pheonix, she got to her feet and stalked past him.

***

Ara felt the heat building in Redd. Anyone could feel her fury.

Why?

That was the question. Why did Pheonix irritate her so much?

Ara returned her attention to the tall warrior as he hesitantly approached her. She stood, not wanting to seem rude.

She watched him. In her eyes, Pheonix was an intelligent, withdrawn young man. She had not had much time to observe him, nor much time to talk with him, but so far he was polite to a fault, and Ara suspected that was part of what was setting Redd off. Bland politeness could, to some people, be taken as disrespect.

Redd's planet was the most propagandized place Ara had ever heard of (from Redd's own stories about her childhood), and Redd herself was not only uninitiated but suffering from acute trauma. She understood where Redd was coming from in her highly fragile state, but that wasn't an *excuse*. Thankfully she hadn't outright done anything cruel, but Ara worried it was only a matter of time.

Ara was torn between the two people: her best friend, and the young man who was quickly finding his way into her affections.

Thinking of that, she flushed. He stopped in front of her, close enough for his scent to hit her; it was subtle — cinnamon and open woodland, with the undercurrent of metal.

"My presence bothers her," he said, and Ara chose not to respond. "Is there anything I can do to make things easier for her?"

"I suspect there isn't," Ara said sadly, "but I can't be sure because we haven't talked about it yet. I wouldn't want to bring it up. But rest assured, you aren't doing anything wrong. She's just in such a delicate place …" she trailed off with a sigh.

"Well, *she* can rest assured that she won't have to deal with me for the foreseeable future," he said with the slightest ghost of a smile. "I'm headed for the city."

He tugged one of his gauntlets off and offered her his hand. "If you find yourself in the city as well, and I am still there, I would like to speak with you again."

After a moment, Ara placed her tiny hand into his and smiled. The hope on his face blossomed into a huge grin as he bent down to kiss her hand. Her heart thumped.

"I will look forward to it," she said, quietly.

"Take care of yourself." He straightened and slipped his gauntlet back on.

"And you."

He turned without looking back, took off at an astonishing speed, and was gone in the gloom in moments.

EIGHT

All That Is Gold Does Not Glitter

No one had seen Imae for a while.

Perhaps, as they all sat around planning routes, goals and schedules, that should have worried them.

Then the transport door shut with a hiss. Chani, whose back was to the vehicle, half-stood and looked over her shoulder, a question on her lips. The engine whirred to life, the transport lifted …

Chani took in the scene at a glance. Ara and Redd were across the camp, but alarmed and looking at the vehicle. Pheonix was hours gone. Chani's small contingent of soldiers were sitting right in front of her. The only one missing?

Chani reached inside her coat for a hidden remote. She activated it; the transport was barely airborne when it stopped and drifted back down to the ground.

Chani smiled grimly, imagining she could hear the cadet's cry as the detention-bracelet flared into life, causing every nerve in her body to scream.

The transport door opened. Imae appeared out of the gloom of its innards, leaning on the doorframe. Her eyes were ablaze.

Chani stood in her way, still openly holding the remote. She made sure the cadet took note of it. "Didn't check your boots, eh?"

“Fug off,” Imae muttered.

The bracelet had done its work; her voice was slurred, and she was having trouble standing. The nerve damage was only temporary, thankfully. Chani regretted having to resort to using it, but the cadet had been exhibiting all the signs of preparing a getaway. Only someone supremely careless would have missed it, and Chani wasn’t about to go tromping all over this planet trying to reclaim her. Better to head it off at the pass.

“Is that any way to talk to your commanding officer?”

Imae growled something, a little drool spilling from the corner of her mouth. Chani sighed and tucked the remote back into her pocket. She signaled to one of the soldiers, and between them, they steadied Imae and set her up in her tent.

“Sleep it off, kid,” Chani murmured as she turned away. She said to her soldiers, “I want her watched,” and winced mentally at the harshness in her own voice. Her stride was a little long, her muscles a little stiff, as she headed back for the middle of the camp.

The anger was there, yes; but it was the bitter disappointment that really got her every time. In her time as a Ranger, she’d worked with, trained, and gone into battle with more young soldiers than she could count. They all went through it, but it was the worst for officers’ kids. And Imae had it hard; she had to give the kid that. But maturity had to come. It *had* to. And she’d given Imae a chance to show that she could be mature, suck it up, shrug and say, “Oh well, I tried.”

And Imae had chosen to throw a tantrum.

Even worse, with the Rivios wild streak and the stigma of Damien still, Ages later, hanging over the clan’s heads, she really couldn’t afford to misbehave like this. It frightened the higher echelons to think that another Damien could be born, so Imae really needed to fly under the radar lest she be branded a risk and shuffled off to some distant post, never to return. The kid just didn’t understand how close she already was to that happening.

Chani thought back to Imae's parents, the current heads of the Rivios clan and both General Specialists. Anastasya Rivios, Imae's mother, was a little fireball with a wicked sense of humor. Her specialty was hand-to-hand combat. Igor Rivios, Imae's father, was an observant, opinionated man. Extremely driven, with a mind like a whip. Of the two of them, Chani had gotten along with Ana better, although Igor was a man that didn't just simply command respect; he siphoned it out of you whether you wanted to give it or not.

As individuals and soldiers, their records were long, decorated, and spotless. Together, they were a force to be reckoned with. Since they'd taken over as the Rivios clan heads in the Fifth Age, that infamous wild streak had been tamped down almost to a non-issue, something the other clans were abjectly grateful for.

As the only child of a pair of General Specialists who were also the heads of a powerful clan, a lot was expected of Imae. As unfair as it might seem to her, the way she was being taught was necessary, and in a way, she had it easier than a trainee. As a cadet, an officer-in-training, she was given far more options. Cadets usually knew what they wanted to do by the time they were Imae's age, and that included not becoming an officer — or not being a Ranger at all. They weren't given special treatment, per se; the Rangers worked hard to ensure that everyone was on the same level, but there were certain leadership courses Imae was required to take. It was meant to give her a primer on what she could expect if she decided to be an officer, sure; but more importantly, it would clue her in on her parents' responsibilities in a way that they oftentimes couldn't express themselves.

That was the bad news. The good news was that once these required courses were over with, that was it; she could move on and do whatever it was her little heart desired. Her parents had explained to Chani that they'd tried over and over to make the strong-willed Imae understand that, but she just wasn't getting it. She kept claiming that she was being forced into a mold that didn't fit her. They had almost pleaded with

Chani to try and make their daughter understand — and that was serious, coming from powerful people like the Rivioses.

Even with how many soldiers Chani had trained to be successful, she was not looking forward to this. If she were honest, her biggest fear was that Imae would be one of her few failures. The girl was just so Creator-damned hard-headed.

Chani ran her hands back through her hair and swept her eyes over the camp. Thinking about it made her head hurt. The memories she was grappling with were not pleasant, and they threatened to drag her down into a dark place.

So she did what she always did: arranged her face into a mask of nonchalance, like the whole debacle hadn't bothered her a bit, and headed off to check on Ara and Redd.

***

Redd had been complaining to Ara about Chani's little 'talk,' and, not surprising Redd in the slightest, the little angel chimed in on Pheonix's defense. Much of what had been explained to Redd was about Pheonix's training and his upbringing, and some of his history with Chani.

Apparently he'd fallen through a tear into Terelath — the main city on the elven home planet of Availeon — right in front of a troop of elves and Chani, who was a guest in that particular patrol during one of her many visits to the elven homeworld. He was covered in blood and had all the life experience and personality of a robot (in that, Redd didn't think he had changed much). Chani hadn't gone into much detail, but she had said there was literally no one else in the universe quite like Pheonix. The influences that shaped Pheonix were the Rangers' highly-ordered militaristic society, and the elves' almost painful political-mindedness.

But, Redd thought angrily, all this effort was being put forth to make her understand Pheonix. Did anyone bother trying to get him to understand her? Hadn't she suffered enough? Why was it always her that needed to change?

She closed her eyes and hunched her head down between her shoulders, propping her upper body weight on her elbows, which were in turn propped on her knees. She could feel Ara's consternation and confusion. She was obviously torn.

That, and only that, was keeping Redd from freaking the fuck out on everybody around her. Part of her realized she was being selfish and immature, but she wasn't listening to it.

Half psyker and half teenager did not make for a logical thought process.

Watching Imae get zapped had lightened her mood a bit, though.

She felt Chani approach and lifted her head.

"Hey, what's up?" Chani asked as she settled beside the two girls.

"Nothing. We got a plan yet?" Redd asked shortly.

Chani ignored her attitude. "Pretty much, but I gotta deal with Imae first to make sure she isn't going to pull another stunt, and for that, she's gotta wake up."

Redd slumped again. "Beautiful."

Chani chuckled ruefully. "She should only be out for a little longer; the nerve inhibitors are pretty mild. Basically what we're looking to do is get the lay of the land from the air on the bug," Chani jerked her head back to indicate the transport, "assess any dangers, locate any surviving angels that the Haveners may not have been aware of, etc."

"We aren't going to the city?" Redd asked.

"Eventually, if Pheonix determines it's safe. If it is, Pheonix is more than qualified to make first contact as a liaison for both the elves and the Rangers. He can handle things there for now, and he'll give us a visible signal depending on what he finds."

"How long do you think it will be?"

Chani shrugged. "That depends. I'm not a surveyor, so I'm not going to survey the whole planet, but I need enough to satisfy the brass." She reached over and clapped a hand on Redd's shoulder in a gruff, friendly fashion.

"What do you think we will find?" Ara put in.

Chani seemed to think about that, then shook her head apologetically. "There's no way to tell. Too many variables. I'm sorry, Ara."

"If you're not a surveyor, why did they even send you here?" Redd asked.

Chani pursed her lips in an unusual show of negativity. Her quick change of expression told Redd that it was an unintentional slip.

"I volunteered." Chani was back to casual confidence, as if nothing had happened, but the slip nagged at Redd. She remembered the overheard conversation between Commander and cadet, and wondered if Imae wasn't the only reason Chani was here.

"Because of my position in the Rangers, I could hardly pass up coming to check out the state of the angelic homeworld after three centuries of isolation. The situation with Haven is well handled, so I offered my services in starting the surface operations. Never know what you may find here. Hell, the planet could have been overrun with goblins for all we knew, so," she shrugged, "I'm capable of handling anything we may run into, within reason."

"Makes sense," Redd said, keeping her suspicions about Imae to herself.

"There's one thing I need to tell you girls about Pheonix, though, before we spend any more time in his presence," Chani said unexpectedly, so serious that it almost startled Redd. "Once all this is over, whenever we rejoin metacosmic society, you'll hear a lot of people calling Pheonix 'Lord Justice.'"

Ara gasped and her hands flew to her mouth. Redd glanced at her, confused.

"Pheonix," Chani said to Redd, "is the Ascended of Justice. Chaos Earth doesn't have anything resembling Ascended, culturally speaking, so I can't draw any real parallels for you, Redd, and I'm sorry about that. The closest I can describe it is that they are stronger even than the Heroes of the Revolution, and they answer only to the Creator. When we are settled in, I suggest you do some research on the terminal to familiarize yourself with them."

There was a muffled series of expletives and the sound of rustling from the opposite end of camp. Imae emerged from the tent, looking like a storm. Chani stood.

"Better go deal with that," she said quietly.

Redd hopped to her feet as Chani retreated, shooting a devious grin at Ara. "I gotta see this. Coming?"

Ara smiled slightly and shook her head.

***

They were scattered across camp when the creatures attacked.

For Redd, it happened in slow motion. She looked up because she caught movement in the corner of her eye. What she saw froze her in place. Like something out of an all-too-recent nightmare, it was a thin, stretched version of a humanoid with a leg shape more reminiscent of the hind legs of a quadruped. A thickly muscled, long tail stuck out from behind it, helping it to balance upright on its backwards-looking legs. The creature was pale and glowed with a slight phosphorescence that made it seem almost transparent. It wore a breastplate of some kind of beaten metal and a loincloth. Lanky hair streamed back from a skull-like visage with a short, upturned nose but a huge jaw and jagged teeth jammed into what was more of a spiky slit in its face than anything else. Its eyes were huge and the black-on-black of a creature fully adapted to a life in almost complete darkness. Several short horns protruded from various places on its skull.

It leaped, covered about twenty feet, and was on the soldier standing outside of the transport, who was closest to it and with his back to it, before the man had any idea what was happening. It tore his throat out with its long claws from behind.

Then they came pouring into the camp.

Chani was quick to react — she'd pulled her guns and was firing like a woman possessed.

It was hard to tell where the creatures were looking, but as the one covered in blood looked up, Redd just *knew* its gaze was trained on her. That was the last thing it did. Redd saw its head explode as if she were watching some gruesome high-speed video. A hole opened up in its left eye socket, and then everything neck up was goo. Its body slumped onto its recent kill, and Redd numbly looked towards Chani.

Redd remembered the firearm that Chani had given them, but it was in her pack — across the camp.

After that, Redd had more pressing problems.

She heard Ara cry out and whipped around, adrenaline sparking and pouring through her body like a bonfire from hell. Gripped in the need to save her friend, Redd surrendered to her power. It blossomed and filled her, and the world became something else. Her eyes fed her what they saw, and her opened mind fed off of the power and mental signatures around her, and merged that information with the visual; so she saw, heard, felt, and understood in one moment. Her brain shifted and adjusted to the new, multi-tiered input instantly, moving into the new awareness like an old hand.

A gesture from Redd, and the creature advancing on Ara slammed into the ground like a ragdoll catapulted from the hands of an angry child. Redd heard something crack, *saw* the carapace breaking, *felt* the life fading — and was almost lost.

The sparking blue-white lightning of electrical currents along synapses, nerves firing and receiving instruction, shut down in an instant, leaving behind a terrifying void. In sensing these signals, Redd had formed a tentative link, and when it dissipated, she was almost drawn with it into death, or oblivion.

That, too, she instantly adjusted to. Like muscle memory, deeply ingrained from years of training, her mind cut off the link and swung around to the threat coming up from behind her. She whipped around. Instead of leaping on her like she was expecting, it stopped, chittering like an enraged monkey, and an odd sort of tension rippled through its body. Redd didn't understand what it was doing until it was too late.

Psionics!

Something hit her like a battering ram. She flew backwards and tumbled to a stop amongst clouds of dust, the world a fireworks display of silver and black pain-sparkles and her breath gone. She came to herself in time to catch the creature as it landed on top of her, at least a hundred and fifty pounds of rock-solid muscle. Her brain on the auto-pilot of *fight to survive*, it did an instantaneous shell-game of shutting down some nerve pathways and activating others, and she found the strength — so abruptly it surprised her — to throw the creature off.

It dug its three-toed back feet into the rocky ground, found purchase, and spun around to face her again. This time it seemed to be hesitating, gauging; Redd was now not prey, but a threat.

Then that tension was building again, and now she knew what it preceded.

Lifting her hands to guide her power, she formed it into a wall. The creature's psionic blast was negated, and she quickly reformed her wall into a spike, which she drove at the creature.

It barely avoided the strike by leaping straight up. Redd moved to just underneath it and drew a fist back. As it fell again, it windmilled its tail in an attempt to change its trajectory. With no time to charge up another psionic blast, it dropped like a stone — right into Redd's power-fueled punch.

The punch didn't kill it, but did send it rolling claws-over-tail, kicking up clouds of choking dust. Redd stepped back, panting, and in a blink, the creature had recovered and jumped up into a crablike crouch once more.

Redd groaned at its resilience. She wasn't sure how much more of this she could handle.

Ara shouted Redd's name in warning. She risked a glance to her side and saw another creature lining her up for a sneak psionic attack — but apparently Redd wasn't the only one to hear Ara's call. A hole opened up in the would-be attacker's chest and it fell, its huge maw wide in a silent scream.

By then it was too late. Redd's original combatant had turned its gaze on Ara.

In blind terror for her friend, Redd focused on the one place she'd always turned to when things had gone too far: the golden light ever waiting at her core.

It pulsed in time with her desperation, her heightened emotions, weaving its threads into her very essence. Energy even her psyker power bowed to.

The golden singing pounded in her ears, both a whisper and a shout, reverberating the world in her vision like waves in a pond.

Afire, she shot forward, feet an inch from the ground but never touching, and tackled the creature before it could reach Ara. The two of them landed heavily with Redd on top.

It thrashed, but the weight of Redd's power kept it pinned. She braced herself with one hand on its chest, and gathered the golden light into the other, clenched into a fist.

The fist raised.

***

"Redd!" Chani heard Ara shout.

She slammed the butt of one of her energy-pistols into the snarling countenance of a creature and jerked to the source of the cry.

She took in the scene within a second and lined up a shot. The creature's midsection burst. Spine-shot. Instant kill. It dropped like a sack of shit, momentum causing it to roll over and come to a stop with an almost disappointing lack of grace.

With no other immediate threats, Chani went to help Redd. She stumbled and blinked furiously. Where the redhead had been, now she was not. In less than the time it took her to blink once, Redd had somehow traveled a good twenty or thirty feet and was now — effortlessly — holding down her opponent with one hand.

One.

Hand.

Chani gaped. She'd grappled with one or two of these things and they were devilishly strong. The creature flailed and raked at the steel-like arm pinning it down. Redd ignored the wounds. Something else about the scene was wrong, but Chani's brain was overloaded enough that it refused to compute.

Then Redd raised her fist.

There was another movement so fast Chani couldn't track it. The creature's head shattered into a spray of black blood, bone chips, and gray matter. Its struggles ceased, legs and arms jerking spasmodically, then falling limp.

The rock below Redd cracked and splintered as the power pouring from her grounded itself into the earth.

Chani had seen a lot. She was a lot older than she was willing to admit to the girls, and she'd lived through thousands of engagements across hundreds of planets. She'd trained soldiers beyond counting, had been through wars with vast armies and tight battles where she was the only one left alive. She'd scraped by by the skin of her teeth, had been captured and tortured, and had enjoyed effortless victories. She'd seen planets and stars and meteors covering the spectrum: hot, cold, beautiful, toxic, wet, dry … she had encountered hundreds of variant species …

This … felt horribly familiar, from some part of her buried so deeply, it was like a visceral reaction.

The shock lasted only a moment.

She shook sweat from her eyes, thrusting the thought from her mind, and cast a practiced eye over what had been their camp — now a battlefield — as the adrenaline bled from her. Her instincts told her it was over, and she had been through enough combat to trust them implicitly.

Bodies. Everywhere.

The sharp stab of fear that accompanied the thought was tempered by logic; Imae was behind her, panting with the effort of assisting in the fight after being KO'd by the detention bracelet. Her soldiers were dead — *Creator damn it* — and the bug was belching smoke from a huge dent in one side. That was not a good thing.

Ara was fine, though clearly shaken. Redd …

Chani swore under her breath and sprinted to the helplessly retching redhead. She dragged Redd a few feet away, propped her against a shoulder and pulled her hair back. Chani murmured platitudes into her ear. Poor kid hadn't even made it off of the corpse before she'd been overwhelmed by the sight.

The mixed fluids were already soaking into the crack-riddled ground to be, thankfully, drawn deep into the earth and beyond sight or smell. Redd shuddered and gagged noisily, like she could exorcize the horror of what she'd just experienced through physical expulsion alone.

When she'd stopped vomiting, Chani helped her to a relatively untouched corner of the camp, where the majority of the bodies were shielded from view by the hulk of the bug. She held Redd while she trembled, silent tears pouring down from wide-open, staring eyes.

Somehow this seemed different from how it took most kids, seeing their first skirmish. Their first kill.

Long ago, Chani had realized she could read people — their emotions and, sometimes, if it was strongly associated with an emotion, a thought or intention. It didn't take an empath long to figure out when someone was reeking of vengeance or anger that something was about to happen.

And when it came to basic emotions, most species were alike.

Redd was terrified. So much that Chani doubted there were any coherent thoughts banging around in her head. The vomiting had been a subconscious response to the revulsion of killing, but this shaking fit had to be related to something else.

Memories came flooding back — memories of battle, but not combat — so similar to this.

Chani held a child, barely old enough to begin learning about the world. This child became distracted and distressed and frightened by anything and everything around them. And the nightmares that most children suffered through were, for this child, a lamp, or a word, or an image, and it happened while they were awake, and all the time ...

How often had Chani held that child just like this, while they screamed and cried, unable to take any respite from the trauma of simply existing?

Chani closed her eyes, shutting it out.

They're okay now, Chani reminded herself.

Ara ran over and fell to her knees in front of Redd, reaching out but hesitant. She looked at Chani for guidance, her big eyes rimmed wetly. Chani shrugged as well as she could with Redd resting against her.

"Redd?" Ara called quietly.

Redd's breathing slowed. She blinked and her eyes focused.

"Ara? Ara — " she whispered, and threw herself at the little angel. Ara held her, talking too softly for Chani to hear. It seemed a familiar thing to both girls. Ara had such a mature, comforting presence, Chani felt even her own apprehension smoothing out, becoming distant. Ara's energy was like a balm for what was, to an empath, an extremely rough world, full of sharp, negative emotions.

Redd pulled away, tears streaking her cheeks, and stared up at Ara. She babbled something, over and over, too broken to understand clearly. The gist of it was, "What am I?" and Chani frowned, not understanding.

Then Redd lifted her arms.

Her flesh was gouged deeply from the struggle. The blood running from the wounds …

It was like liquid gold, glinting in the lights set up for their camp. Ara was frozen, staring.

Chani stood, her mind working furiously.

Great. Another weird kid with weird blood. Why. Why?!

I don't believe in coincidences.

Chani swore mentally, a long litany, an epithet of invectives that made her feel slightly better (but only slightly).

Then, with the discipline borne of long practice, she forcefully redirected her thought process. Weird blood and its implications later; battlefield now.

There was nothing she could do about Redd, and she had to focus on the things she could do something about. Let the kids calm down without her interference.

Imae was hunched over by her tent, unhurt. The soldiers were dead. Chani turned to the transport. The creatures must have thought it was an enemy, or a living thing, because they had torn into it pretty hard. The metal was peeled back in some places and smoke was pouring out. Dents peppered the hull.

Chani stepped inside to check if the comms system was still functional. If she could get enough juice to contact the encampment on Haven, she could still salvage this mess.

The creatures hadn't thought to get inside, apparently, because aside from what had been knocked off the walls from external jostling, most of the supplies were undamaged. The console was flashing a red error message. She tried to access backup power, but it didn't respond. One of the lines must have been broken.

Emerging outside again, she took stock of the bodies of their assailants. At least a dozen — they would have been easily overwhelmed if these creatures hadn't gone after the bug so hard. They obviously were intelligent or advanced enough for pack behavior and basic tactics, but didn't seem much more than that. Or they had had little or no contact with technology, which would make sense considering the state of the planet.

They sure as hell hadn't been here before the Elysian, and that meant no experience fighting Rangers. At least there was that.

A new evolution of creature in three hundred years? How in the great Commander Fug's name was that even possible, and *what* had they evolved from?

No; now wasn't the time for that.

"We've got to move," Chani called. "Gather what supplies we can and get the hell out of here. Head for the city."

The survivors gathered around the bug.

There was a question on Imae's lips, but she glanced past Chani to the bug and it died there.

"Busted," Chani confirmed.

"Is there nothing we can do?" Ara asked, sounding lost.

"I can take a look at it," Imae said before Chani could speak up. Chani lifted a brow at her. Imae scowled defensively. Chani stepped to one side and held her arms out towards the broken vehicle; an invitation … and a challenge.

Imae disappeared into the interior. There was some clanking and crashing, and then quiet. Chani gestured for Redd and Ara to come around the other side of the bug, away from the carnage. Being surrounded by it made Redd look like she was about to faint.

Ara settled Redd down and sat beside her, then worked a Healing. Chani watched with interest; it had been a long time since she'd seen an angel Heal. There were few species that could Heal with magic — elves being the foremost since the angels' disappearance — but even among the angels, true Healers were relatively rare. And here was one, so young, and without any proper training. It boggled the mind.

The gashes in Redd's flesh knitted together in an odd strand-over-strand weaving motion that hurt Chani's brain to watch. Chani held herself firm, forced herself to keep watching until nothing remained but clots of blood and dirt.

"Here's what we've got to do," Chani said. "I doubt the bug can get us anywhere without extensive repairs that we don't have the tools for, even if Imae knows proper procedure. I'm hoping she'll be able to at least get communications back up long enough for me to send out a generalized distress signal."

Redd stared at her, wide-eyed, and shook her head.

"Her? She's … she's barely older than us. What makes you think she can do any of that?"

"The kid has a bad attitude but she's really good with mechanics."

"Oh."

That was a grave understatement and Chani knew it but she didn't have time to explain it properly … not to people unfamiliar with Ranger tech. Although the bug was literally a dump-and-run (it could be detonated if necessary), it was still a complicated piece of machinery. Based on a fluidics system, the holo-controls were comprised of a localized, compressed gas that reacted kinetically when touched. In order for Imae to 'fix' it, she'd have to reroute the remaining fluid to power up the electronics controls and manually control the flow of gas.

Not for the first time, Chani really hoped they could find a way to get Imae into the Engineer Corps.

"Anyhoo," Chani went on, "I'm hoping she also does it fast. A group like that is most likely recon or hunting, depending on their society, and they'll be missed sooner rather than later. I don't want to still be here when backup comes."

"Do you have any idea what they were?" Ara asked.

"I was hoping you could tell me that." Chani pursed her lips again momentarily. "You've never seen anything like that on Haven?" Ara shook her head. "Heard of anything like it?" Again, a head shake. Chani swore under her breath, her quick mind shifting to the next set of objectives.

“While Imae is in there working on the bug, we’ve got to salvage anything we can.” Chani cast a sympathetic look at Redd. “You should rest for now.”

Redd’s brows lowered. “I’m not — ”

Chani lifted a hand, closing her eyes.

“Kid ... ” She sighed, stopped, started again. “Redd. Trust me. Just rest. Let it settle in.”

“Redd, please,” Ara begged.

Redd put up her hands and tried to force a smile. “I guess I’m outvoted.”

“That’s my girl,” Chani said, and pushed herself up to stand. “Ara, check the bodies of these things. See if there’s anything we can use. I need your scholar’s eyes; *we* need to have a better idea of what we’re up against.”

Ara nodded, though her ‘scholar’s eyes’ were wide and scared, and went to kneel next to a nearby body.

Chani approached one of her soldiers, a man named Rich. She knelt down next to him and touched his shoulder in a silent gesture of respect. He could be revived, but a death was never a pleasant thing to endure.

Chani did not envy herself as she stripped the soldier of his undamaged gear and piled it up. She didn’t know how long they would be stuck down here, or even if the nearby city was friendly.

She and the girls had survived the attack. Now came the matter of continued survival in an environment that had proved hostile. Oftentimes that was the harder task.

Once she had scavenged all she could, she got down to an even dirtier job.

Chani’s wrist-comm was special.

There were many like it, but this one was hers.

Aside from that, hers was a Commander’s unit, which gave her some *extra*-special capabilities. The bulk of a wrist-comm itself was a bracer usually extending behind the forearm-side of the wrist bones (or equivalent place in a non-humanoid body) to just below the elbow joint. Some had extensions that went onto the fingers or extra bracing on the palm, depending on what the wearer used it for.

Chani didn't use hers for combat, and, being a gunfighter primarily, she disliked having her hands encumbered in any way. Having those bracing parts on her palms would change how she gripped her weapons, and that was undesirable.

But the heavy lifting of a wrist-comm was done by the rounded bump extending from the top-side; out of it slid a tiny panel containing several sampling tubes and a spiny crystal. Chani took the crystal and another replaced it immediately, manufactured by the unit itself.

She rolled one of the soldiers onto his face, glanced around to make sure the girls weren't paying attention, and ran a hand down the spinal reinforcement of his armor. Her fingers encountered a button: pressing it made a small port at the base of the spine open up. She tucked the crystal into it and waited.

That crystal was the key to Ranger gene-seed technology. While she crouched amongst the debris of combat, a lattice of its construction — manufactured nano-crystals — spread along every nerve in the body, taking a snapshot of the entire nervous-system in its last moments.

But that wasn't its only purpose.

Memory, conditioned responses, psychological makeup, and more — the things that made up the personality in a sapient mind — were both physical and nonphysical. The crystal copied what it could, what was imprinted in the brain and nervous system … and then released a bio-agent catalyst which would break down the connections between individual nucleotides that made up DNA.

Out of the resulting puddle of goo (it also dissolved armor and gear, for the obvious reason that they couldn't leave Ranger tech just sitting around for anyone to take), Chani picked up the crystal and the soldier's Ranger identification chip.

As awful as it was to have to do it, this was procedure for any bodies unrecoverable in a hostile situation. Evil was well-known to find and utilize Ranger corpses for stealing genetics, transferring consciousness, cloning, or necromancy.

This was mercy.

People misunderstood mercy as kindness. It wasn't. Mercy was knowing when to end it.

She moved from body to body, performing the same ritual for each.

On the other side of Chani's wrist-comm from the crystal origination point were a series of round ports. She pressed the crystals, one by one, into the ports, which downloaded their contents to the wrist-comm's harddrive and dissolved the crystal's artificial structure (they'd never been able to get this system to work with natural crystals) in the same moment.

"Hey."

Imae's voice.

"What's the status?" Chani called over her shoulder.

"I got the comms system up and sent out a generalized S.O.S., but it can't handle more than that. I left a message summarizing what happened and that we'd gone towards the city, just in case someone comes looking for us."

"Good work." Chani jerked her head to indicate the bug. "How much do you think we can carry?"

Imae shrugged. "I can probably handle a hundred w-units over a short distance. How far is the city from our location?"

"The early reports we got from the air indicated about thirty killiunits. With Ara's pace," Chani gave a lopsided grin to show she wasn't being derisive, "we'll get there in two, maybe three days."

Imae made a face. "How much of the gear is really necessary?"

Chani bit back a grin. Imae was opening up a little bit; the chance to do something she was good at and contributing had softened her anger and attitude a little. Now Chani was edging her into making decisions and analyzing the situation. If they made it out of this, then let it be a learning experience, at least …

"Probably not as much as we think, but we also don't know what we'll be confronted with on this planet." She glanced up as though the sky itself was plotting against them. "At least we *know* there's hostiles here now." She looked back at Imae. "I'll leave it to your judgment."

She lifted her brows and Imae nodded after a moment's hesitation.

Chani stopped her as she turned to head back into the bug. "Hey. No more escape attempts, right?"

Imae scowled deeply.

"I'm not going to lecture you," Chani said shortly. "The next few hours may decide whether or not we survive. But that also means we can't have you sabotaging us. Truce for now?"

"Yeah, I guess."

Chani clapped her on the back. "Good girl. Let's go."

She took in a deep breath when Imae was out of sight, and let it out heavily. One crisis averted. There was still the matter of Redd — Chani could feel the vortex of emotions emanating from the girl's direction, and the last thing she wanted was for it to become a firestorm.

At least Ara's presence seemed to be keeping her calm. The girls had really formed a very strong bond, and for that, Chani was grateful.

Speaking of the angel …

"What's the word?" Chani asked as she crouched next to Ara.

"Not much, honestly. Obviously nocturnal, but in a land of eternal night that is hardly a revelation." She gestured to a piece of exposed bone. "Their bones are very strange, though. They are like hardened cartilage. Their flesh emits light, which could be a hint towards their diet, but these," She delicately lifted the lip of the corpse, showing sharp teeth and elongated canines, "speak otherwise."

Chani whistled. "In all the time we've been here, even flying overhead, I didn't see any animals, did you?"

Ara met her eyes, and there was a statement in her gaze.

“I have not seen anything living on this planet so far, *aside* from these creatures,” the angel said. “Not an insect, not a small animal, and certainly nothing larger. My lack of visual confirmation does not prove or disprove anything, but it is a conundrum for certain. One cannot sit in the forest of Haven for more than a minute without cataloging at least a dozen species.”

“As is the norm for most stable ecologies.”

Ara nodded assent. The question of what the creatures ate hung in the air between them, but Chani didn’t want to address it and neither, it seemed, did Ara.

“Going back to the original point,” Ara continued, “these canines could simply be a sort of adaptational mutation. Unusually thick, rough, and stiff skin, these horns, their bones, general body shape, oxygen-deficient blood, a lack of body hair …” Ara sighed and sat back, unconsciously wiping her hands free of blood and detritus. “Honestly, they remind me of insects.”

Chani shook her head and stood just as Imae walked towards her, a hefty pack slung over her shoulder. Ara stood up, Chani caught Redd’s eye and gestured her over. The redhead picked a path through the bodies with care, trying not to look down.

“Pack up. We leave now.”

NINE
Chaos

The storm outside the castle raged.

Much like its mistress, within.

None of Ichiryu's other servants had been willing to approach her at a time like this, with her failure so evident. Temperjoke cursed them for cowards as he rapped on her door. She could not hurt him — they both knew that — but his resilience to her anger didn't mean he enjoyed it.

The heavy door swung open without the handle turning and he sneered. Being tied to Chaos had its disadvantages. He wasn't just one personality, but thousands. He didn't have a conscience per se; but Chaos dictated his actions, be they to pick flowers or dismember babies. It had been so for as long as he could remember. And today, he wasn't in much of a flower-picking mood.

Ichiryu was lucky he still needed her. For now.

He stepped over the threshold to be enveloped in Ichiryu's presence. Her power was like the decaying, dry wheeze of an open tomb in the back of his mind. She sat in the shadow at the far right of the oval, in front of a large round orb suspended on three spindly legs. Inside the oval was a gentle golden spark surrounded by swirling blackness accented in purple and crimson.

Temperjoke stifled a sigh. Always the theatrics with this bitch. He couldn't wait to be done with her.

Curled protectively in her left arm was a worn and worried teddy bear, collared with a fraying blue ribbon, and in her bony right hand rested the dark gem she normally embedded in the hollow of her throat. She used it to conjure the creatures that served her, though Temperjoke had no idea where she'd acquired the fel thing nor how exactly it worked. With his inner sense he could make out a matrix of evil energy surrounding it, tied somehow to Ichiryu's own twisted soul. Certainly he could figure it out if he wanted to, but he didn't.

As he watched, she slid the gem back into its place.

"The assassins failed," she said.

"Yes."

Ichiryu watched him expressionlessly. He could feel the fury swimming behind her half-lidded eyes. She wasn't used to being thwarted; the creatures she had sent were a few of her best.

However, they had chosen to attack the target in the middle of a Ranger encampment.

Despite the legends and what those who had actually met him had to say, he wasn't unaware of his surroundings, incapable of understanding, or evil. Far from all of those things, in fact. Chaos was a cruel mistress, but a neutral force and a necessary one.

He had remained with Ichiryu for so long because he knew his part to play in what was to come. But that didn't mean he respected her. Again, far from it. He *knew* he was a mistake. Those — like Ichiryu — who allied with their own false sense of Chaos for petty aspirations to power only gained his ire.

Ichiryu stood, putting the stuffed animal down where she had been sitting, and turned her back on Temperjoke. Her attention shifted to the globe, but she said over her shoulder to him: "I have decided to give this assignment entirely over to you. I won't make the mistake of underestimating her again."

Temperjoke's brows raised, but he said nothing.

"You can deal with her how you see fit. I care not for what happens as long as she dies. She *must* die." Her head turned slightly to display her delicate profile. Her lips quirked into a humorless smile. "I trust you."

The irony of the statement was not lost on him. She trusted no one. Hell, he'd wager she didn't even trust herself, but her tyrant's ego kept her from showing that particular weakness.

But the bigger irony was one he knew her to be unaware of: yes, the girl had to die. But not for any of the reasons Ichiryu named. It took all Temperjoke had to keep from giggling.

Chaos clouded his judgment more often than not, but that golden light was as a lighthouse in the fog: the girl would fulfill his purpose. He'd known it for three hundred years.

As long as he followed the path he could only barely see the edges of, she would finally release him from his torture.

The storm outside eased.

***

The lack of conversation as they traveled, this time, was a precaution against another attack. Neither Redd nor Imae were by any means recovered, but by tacit agreement, everyone pressed on despite individual pains. Ara was pallid even for her and breathing heavily, but they couldn't afford to slow down or stop for very long.

The creatures obviously had psionic abilities, though how far beyond combat they extended was unknown. Could they be used for tracking, teleportation? The group also had no idea how many more of these creatures there were, or if the distress signal would reach anyone.

Survival relied on caution in this case.

And speed.

Frankly, Redd was grateful for the constant activity and burden of exhaustion. It kept her from thinking. More specifically, it kept her from sleeping. Sleep brought nightmares. Lately they'd been bad, and after the skirmish, they were bound to get worse.

So she trudged along, entering a sort of meditation of sleep deprivation and the rhythmic one-two of walking.

When Chani finally called a halt near a small grove of squat mushroom-trees, Redd almost didn't want to sit down. As soon as she stopped moving, her brain started up again. It insisted on going over and over the events of the previous day. She looked up, feeling divorced from herself, and glowered at the clouds. With no sky visible, there was absolutely no way to tell the passing of time. Certainly Chani had some sort of odd contraption that told universal time or some such thing, but Redd couldn't find the words or the desire to ask.

To distract herself, Redd plopped down next to Ara. "How are you holding up?" she asked.

Ara opened her mouth, then closed it again and gave a tight, humorless smile. "My first urge is to downplay my complete and utter exhaustion — the simple fact that I ache from head to toe in places that I knew to theoretically exist due to my studies on humanoid musculature and skeletal structure but were only mere conjecture and now have unequivocally and emphatically been proven to exist through pain alone … but perhaps it would be better to be honest."

Redd chuckled. "At least you still have your sense of humor."

"You seem to be no worse for the wear."

"I'm dead; please leave a message," Redd said flatly.

Ara giggled.

Redd dug through her pack and pulled out a nutrition bar. She didn't even really taste it at this point, and she wasn't hungry, but it would give her something to do and she probably needed the calories.

Shortly after, the march began anew. What felt like hours passed again. Thus existence compressed into the pattern of clomping through the unchanging, bleak, and dark environment, stopping to rest or force down food no one tasted in tense silence, the fear of another attack driving everyone to their feet to start the cycle again.

Redd dipped in and out of her inner space during those long hours of trudging, taking bits of energy from the golden light to keep her on her feet.

To Redd, who didn't know of Chani's empathic abilities, it seemed like the Commander was uncanny in her knowledge of when her companions were literally about to drop — when it would be dangerous to push them any further without serious reason, and thus stopped them for sleep.

Redd awoke aching. She'd fallen into her tent and apparently hadn't moved at all. She sat up, hunched over in the confined space, taking stock of her body. Her hips, legs, knees and feet hurt. She rubbed her neck, trying to gather her thoughts.

She didn't remember a damn thing after they'd stopped. She must have set up the tent, unless she'd just zonked out while still on her feet and Chani had done it for her, then dragged her into it. She hadn't dreamed at all, for which she was glad.

Chani, Imae, and Ara were sitting around in a circle, eating. Chani gave her a bright grin.

"Morning, sleepyhead. We were just about to leave you."

Redd grunted and humped over to plop down next to Ara. "How kind of you. You sure it's morning?"

"Close enough."

Redd took the steaming cup offered by Ara and hoped it wasn't coffee. She took a sip and sighed. Heavily sweetened floral tea. Ara knew her so well. "Did I ever tell you how much I hate how chipper you are, Chani?"

Chani just chuckled in response.

After tea and food, Redd felt better. The horror of yesterday's battle, her first (messy) kill and the disturbing revelation of her blood's color now seemed distant, like it had all happened to someone else. She tried not to think about it anyway, not wanting to deal.

She listened with half an ear to Chani and Imae strategizing and sharing observations about their surroundings, Ranger procedure, when they could expect to see a rescue squad, and how much longer they might expect to be on foot.

"We're heading for *a* city, sure," Imae was saying, "but we don't know what's in it."

"Protocol tells Pheonix to fire one of two flares when he reaches his destination: white for friendlies, red for hostile," Chani said. "Which would be damn hard to miss in this environment. So we keep moving in his general direction while we await the flare."

"But what if we get halfway there and we see a red flare? And what if he was captured before he could fire it?" Imae pressed.

"To your first question: we have enough data to assume with fair certainty it isn't a hostile situation. We've seen no signs of extraworld evil occupation, which leads to the conclusion that the only possible occupants of the city are either angels or those creatures. My assumption is that it's an angelic fortress that somehow slid under the radar. That's not to say we rely one hundred percent on guesses, but we *can* make goals based on them in the absence of knowing the relevant variables, bolstered by contingency plans. We couldn't have stayed where we were; the simple fact is, sometimes you have to act on incomplete data, even if it isn't the ideal. And, c'mon, you know who Pheonix is. Anything that could capture or harm him … we're probably a lot more fugged than we know."

"Think we could get picked up by a patrol?" Imae asked, changing the subject.

Chani thinned her lips. "Hard to say. Did you see that wall around the city? At first it didn't make sense, but after yesterday … if I'm right and it's an angelic fortress, the citizens there must be in constant conflict with those things.

They hardly seemed like the type to share territory. But it really depends. Patrols could be too dangerous."

"What would we do, as Rangers?" Imae asked.

Redd felt Chani's heart quicken. She frowned, becoming aware that she'd unintentionally opened her mind to see the thoughts and emotions behind the words. For now, she left it open, but reminded herself that curiosity killed the cat.

Something in Chani exulted at the question. Her mind said to handle it delicately, to *teach without teaching*. Redd wondered at that, glimpsing a deeper connection between cadet and Commander.

Chani sighed and shifted, affecting the movement to cover her brief pause. Redd laughed inwardly. What a charlatan! But it was so natural, the only way Redd could tell at all was by reading the woman's intentions.

Then Chani looked up, right at Redd.

Redd closed down her mind quickly. She was surprised, and that honest reaction must have confused Chani, because she narrowed her eyes at Redd, then turned her attention back to Imae.

Redd realized her heart was pounding. Apparently, Chani was a hell of a lot more sensitive than she'd suspected.

She listened absently to Chani talking defensive tactics and wondered how in the hell the woman could have sniffed her out. Well, she amended ruefully, she wasn't exactly experienced at this sort of thing yet. Maybe she had given herself away somehow.

Maybe this should be a reminder not to read people without their consent.

After a couple of deep breaths, she'd calmed down enough that the instinctive reaction from her psyker power to buzz beneath her skin at the rise in her emotions had receded.

Abruptly, the talking stopped. Redd looked up as Chani surged to her feet, her face drawn and ashen.

With only a moment's hesitation, Chani sprinted for the gear, grinding out a stream of curses.

Redd half-stood, straining to figure out what had alerted her. She looked at Ara, who was clutching her pack to her chest. She seemed just as perplexed as Redd.

"We need to get out of here. Now," Chani said in hushed, hurried tones.

Redd's gut reaction was to reopen her mind. She felt her friends like bright spots, each with what Redd had begun to call a 'mental signature' — a different frequency to their thoughts, chemical makeup, life-power. She went cold to feel alien signatures quickly closing in on their location.

"It's too late," she whispered, and the creatures came swarming into the grove.

She tried to get to Ara, but was cut off and thrown backwards by a psionic detonation at her feet. She hit her head on something hard and sharp, and the world swam. Panic flooded her and forced out any coherent thought, but the encroaching darkness of unconsciousness was stronger still.

***

When Redd awoke, it was to pain and nausea. She groaned and rolled over onto her side, trying to get vertical without opening her eyes. Something weighed her down and she lashed out at it.

"Hey, chill out," a cool, deep voice cut through the fright. Redd forced her eyes open, gulped back the sickness that threatened to rise.

"Chani?" She sounded horrible even to her own ears.

"Not quite."

Startled, she tried to open her eyes and move. "Lutius?"

Her vision swam. She couldn't focus. The speaker was a large lump in front of her, vaguely human shaped and human colored. It was neither of the two male angels — she could tell that immediately. And it wasn't Pheonix.

Slowly, her eyes cleared.

The man was a giant. Shorter than Pheonix by (Redd would guess) a few scant inches, he was easily twice Pheonix's width. His generous shoulders and arms bulged with muscle, thick neck supporting a broad, square face with a prominent jaw and chin. Redd took in a thick brow, deep-set eyes ringed with dark circles, thin lips, slight stubble on skin that was just darker than her own, but reddish, turned almost mauve in the sparse light. Short black hair was slicked back, a few strands falling down over his forehead. He had silver eyes, metallic like her own. They reflected the light in glinting flashes as his gaze moved.

He wore a simple, tight, black t-shirt, black pants, black boots, and a silver necklace.

Her instincts told her to run, but her body would not obey.

"Who are you?" she blurted.

He smiled and offered her a hand the size of a dinner plate with thick fingers and rough calluses. She didn't take it, which made something flash across his face, so quickly she couldn't quite be sure she hadn't imagined it.

Something flickered behind and through him in that moment. Something familiar. Like something from the nightmare …

She closed her eyes and then opened them hastily, torn between shutting out the world and having to deal with the — the — *thing* — in front of her.

She backed away from him on hands and knees, beginning to panic.

"Get away from me," she rasped.

He sighed theatrically and tilted his head to one side. It was such an odd movement from such an intimidating man that it made her pause.

"This is what I get for trying to help?"

"Help? Where am I?"

"Your friends aren't far. I'll bring you to them in a moment. I just figured we should be properly introduced." He smiled again, that creepy wolf's grin. "I feel like I know you so well, Redd."

"What do you mean? Stop playing freaky games."

"My name is Temperjoke."

"Okay. You obviously already know my name. So now we've been introduced. Can I go now?" She clung to sarcasm like a rock in rapids.

He was silent, staring at her like he'd been flash-frozen, his face stuck in that rictus of a smile. "You know something? I know who you are."

He laughed; it was a high-pitched, unsettling sound that made bumps cascade across Redd's arms. If she were a dog, her hackles would be raised; a cat, her tail puffed up. As it was, her whole body was ready to flee at a moment's notice. Oddly though, her psyker power was not reacting to her heightened emotional state. That rang an army's worth of alarm bells in her head.

"But she doesn't," the giant man continued. "She discounts you as a minor threat, but a threat nonetheless ... one that must be eliminated. She doesn't know why you affect her like you do, why she's drawn to you." He clicked his tongue and shook his head. "She'll find out soon enough if she keeps pressing you. In fact, I might just help." He leaned forward, close; too close for comfort. Her nostrils flared. He had no scent.

Anger shocked her out of her stupor. "What the *hell* are you talking about? Enough of your fucking bullshit! *Where are my friends*?"

He chuckled, the rocky rumble of an earthquake deep within a mountain, and put his hands up in defeat. "Alright, alright. They're just that way, in a grove. I'm sure you'll be seen before you see them, though, so no worries. Do you mind staying a moment, just to hear me out?"

Redd hesitated, though she wouldn't have been able to say why, even if asked. "I guess."

He smiled warmly. The expression rang false. "Just let the Rangers know that I'm not an enemy. It's time I moved on." He held up a hand to forestall the protests hovering around her lips. "Don't worry if it doesn't make sense now. It will. Go on, your friends are worried."

Slowly Redd stood, unsteady on her feet and dizzy. The movement inspired waves of pain and sent her stomach into her throat. She forced herself to walk in the direction he'd indicated, stiffly and stubbornly, not taking her eyes off him.

Suddenly he was in front of her; one moment he wasn't there and the next he was. She gasped and drew back, but he caught her wrist.

She went to jerk her arm away, but he raised her hand to his lips and kissed her fingers. The touch burned with familiarity. "We will meet again."

Then he was gone.

Redd doubled over, clutching her stomach and shaking.

She ran, heedless of the nausea that welled up, the pain that spiked in her head with each step — until a black figure drew up in front of her. She grunted in fright and skidded to a stop.

The noise drew more shapes. She fell back, ready for the end as they converged upon her …

Then one called her name.

"*Chani?*" she gasped. The black mass parted and Chani ran up. She dropped to her knees and hugged Redd.

"Thank the Creator. We thought we'd lost you, too."

Before she could ask about the 'too,' Chani was helping her up and into the midst of the black forms. Redd briefly resisted, but relaxed upon noticing that they had faces. One even smiled at her. Then it clicked — they weren't literal shadows, but people in black outfits.

She was having trouble focusing, trouble thinking. Her brain was sluggish, and prone to equating anything she saw just then as a nightmarish hallucination. It was all she could do to cling to Chani and reality.

Chani led her into a grove, a thicker arrangement of trees than she'd seen yet on this planet. Redd sat down and felt worse again. As the adrenaline drained away, the nasty bump to the head came to the forefront. Silently, the black-robed people surrounded them. Redd eyed them warily.

"It's alright, they're here to help us," Chani said. Redd's vision greyed and she saw two of everything, so she clamped her eyes shut to wait for it to fade.

"Hang on," Chani said. Redd felt her lean forward, then hands messing with her belt. She almost lashed out, but Chani shushed her. "Okay, you've got a concussion."

She felt another body approach, saw a flash of light behind her eyes, and suddenly felt better. A Healing. In surprise, her eyes opened.

A man of medium height crouched in front of her, swathed in black robes held tight to his body. A cowl of black covered his head, but a silver-grey beard cropped short to a wide jaw hinted at the color of his hair. He had bright, crystal-blue eyes and a friendly smile.

"Feeling better?" he asked. At Redd's nod, he said: "I'm Cira."

"Redd. What happened?" she asked.

Cira settled himself in front of her cross-legged, resting his hands on his upper thighs, elbows out. In that odd position, Redd was shocked to see that the shadows behind him moved — wings! Black wings.

"Are you angels?" Redd asked, surveying the group. They were all dressed like him; all with dark wings.

"Indeed we are, friend."

Redd turned wide eyes on Chani.

Chani grinned, tired but elated. "They're from Everdark. The city. A patrol."

Cira offered a lopsided smile. "Not a patrol, but we were patrolling."

"What happened?" Redd repeated, urgently.

Between the two of them, Redd got the story. Redd had been taken down quickly. The creatures, whom the angels of the distant city called *erukahl,* which in their native tongue meant 'born of darkness', converged on Chani. She'd held her own, but there had just been too many. Dark shapes had flowed out of nowhere, and Chani had found herself surrounded again, but this time with a dagger at her throat from behind.

Chani laughed and shook her head at that. "Been a damn long while since someone has been able to sneak up on me, but I was also exhausted and outnumbered."

"Excuses," Cira chuckled.

Listening to their bizarre exchange, Redd decided she'd never understand soldiers.

"We got to talking," Chani continued. "These angels are the only ones of their kind left — that they've been able to tell, that is; but regardless, they've been pinned in by the *erukahl* for two centuries and fighting constant raids. Cira here has been around since before the Elysian conflict, so we're lucky he was the one heading this group. I told him I was a Ranger and he offered to escort us to the city."

Redd shook her head. Chani was talking fast, excitedly — it was hard to follow what she was saying.

"What are we waiting for?" Redd asked.

"We are out on a mission and cannot return until we complete it," Cira said apologetically. "The *erukahl* work off of a hive system, following the orders of their Queen. Under her are matriarchs who head smaller family groups. A matriarch of a nearby family group has been acting erratically, sending her drones out ranging far and wide, and thus has butted heads with us rather often. We were sent to find out why."

"But it's a simple recon mission, so we should be there in no more than another day outside of our original estimation," Chani added.

Redd looked down, then around at the dark shapes surrounding them. The sense of wrongness that had pervaded the entire conversation was now coming into sharp focus. Suddenly she felt sick again, sick at heart, and before she'd even asked the question, some part of her knew the answer.

"Where's Ara?"

Chani met her eyes evenly.

Redd struggled to stand, the sickness growing. "*Where is Ara?*"

"They took her," Chani said quietly. Redd felt the breath leave her like she'd been punched in the stomach and reeled back to rest a hand on the tree behind her. The 'bark' was smooth and slightly springy to the touch; it felt warm.

"Is she —" Redd gasped.

"She was still alive when I saw her, but I couldn't get to her in time. I don't know what they plan on doing with her."

Redd looked pleadingly at Cira.

He shook his head slowly, his expression conveying his sympathy. "They have stolen ours before, but for varying reasons. I cannot give you any insight as to what they mean to do with her."

Redd sank back down, burying her face in her hands. Some oddly calm part of her mused on how it was amazing how close she was to the edge of fully falling apart at hearing that Ara was in danger. She had to fight it. After torture, nightmares, and all the close calls and weird shit she'd been put through in the last several years, to break down now was almost laughable. She had to beat back the fear and despair.

She took a deep, shaky breath. "She may still be alive?"

Cira nodded slightly. "We have recovered some of those who were taken. We must get to her quickly, though."

"Let's go, then," Redd said.

They stood, and that seemed to be the signal for the other angels. They were creepy, Redd thought, moving almost soundlessly. Like wraiths, living shadows.

Cira indicated a direction and Redd and Chani followed the general flow of bodies. As they moved, Imae came out of the shadows and joined them. Redd glared at her.

Why couldn't it have been you? she thought acidly.

Time ran together as they walked in a way that was familiar, almost comforting given the circumstances. She could sink down into forgetting once more, into a haze of nonbeing where she could lie to herself that Ara was fine, was just behind her or beside her.

Tapping into SRE's teachings once more, she dipped into her mind to taste the golden light when her mind needed a break.

Chani tapped her on the shoulder. Redd jerked, unaware that the Ranger had even approached. Chani touched a pocket on Redd's rec-suit.

"You look like hell," Chani said for her ears only as Redd dug around in the pocket, coming up with a little pill. Unthinking, Redd threw it back and sipped some water from her throat-tube to let it slide down.

"What did I just take?" Redd croaked.

"Stim pill. Quick dissolving. You should feel the effects here in just a minute."

Chani was as good as her word; soon enough, some of the exhaustion sloughed away as she walked. It didn't help the anger or the sense of hopelessness, but with every step she convinced herself that she was coming closer to Ara. If they didn't stop, they'd catch up. It repeated as a mantra that kept her on her aching feet.

The angels and Chani were like machines. They didn't eat, didn't sleep, didn't talk. Hours later, Redd pounded along, breathing heavily, the pill's effects long gone, afraid to ask Chani if she could take another, despairing now that she'd be walking forever, in the dark, alone in a crowd …

With no sun or clock to tell her the time, Redd had no way to track how long they marched. The angels stopped once and Redd was allowed to eat and drink. She barely tasted it.

She listened with half an ear to the quiet words exchanged between the angels. Chani and Imae joined her, but they didn't involve her in their own conversation. She didn't care.

After a few minutes, Cira appeared and crouched before Chani.

"We will be drawing near our objective soon. The matriarch is agitated and aggressive, so the drones are as well. If need be, we will take her down. I don't intend on starting a full-scale war before we're ready, but a family group this far from the main complex shouldn't draw too much attention."

"What strange creatures," Chani said after he'd left. "There aren't too many humanoids that work off of a hive system."

"The less I see of them and the sooner I get out of here, the better. This planet is starting to look less and less appealing," Imae grumbled.

Chani snorted. "See why we don't skip ship?"

Imae looked away and Chani dropped the subject.

The angels stood as one to some silent stimulus, and the group was back on the move.

Redd retreated into her mind as she plodded forward.

Suddenly the line of angels in front of her stopped. A few broke off and trotted ahead, disappearing into the shadows as though they never were. Momentarily distracted, Redd peered into the clearing they were approaching.

Cira (or, she thought it was Cira; they all looked the same) came around and gestured for the three non-angels to get low. Redd took the opportunity to creep closer. Chani and Imae were right behind her, although she only peripherally noticed them.

Before her was a large clearing that dipped down into a little gully; one side was a cliff and the other flattened out into a roundish, bowl-shaped valley that eventually became forested again well off to her right. At a forty-five-degree or so angle to Redd's hiding spot was a large cavern entrance going into the cliff face. *Erukahl* wandered in and out at a slow pace.

The only light in the whole place emanated from a gigantic crystal, about twenty feet tall and half again as wide, across the clearing from where Redd and the angels lay in wait. It was an iridescent blue-green-purple-pink, somewhat translucent, and shone with its own gentle inner incandescence.

Immediately Redd hated the thing, despite its aesthetic appeal. It grated on her in a way she couldn't place. She ground her teeth and, perhaps foolishly given the situation and her current mental state, focused on the crystal to see if she could suss out the feeling. Immediately she was awash with psychic energy of such magnitude that it made her skin crawl, which tripped some warning signal in her head. But rather than imparting clarity, it only added to Redd's growing frustration.

One of the *erukahl* approached the crystal, which made its light flare. A dim shape in the center of the crystal moved, like a spasm. Redd blinked at it and stared hard. Was she hallucinating again?

It moved again. As she focused on the shape, weakness spread through her limbs, too late to be fought. She was being drawn in, captured by the light. It surrounded her in a pulsating prison of power. Someone hissed her name, but she couldn't respond.

And there it was. The heart of the crystal: its evil purpose.

She felt it and was repulsed even as she couldn't help but be captured, just like the poor creature there already.

Redd knew it for what it was by the connection formed: a limited sentience that allowed it to sense those of power, call them, encase them, grow over them, become one with them, and slowly drain their life to feed the *erukahl* psionic webs.

The consciousness within was familiar. It cried out for help, but it was as incapable as someone tied up and shoved into a box.

The golden light within her seethed suddenly, throwing off the yoke of the crystal's call, and Redd's mind snapped back.

Angels rushed around her, meeting the *erukahl* threat as they leapt forward with beaten metal weapons and clubs.

Under the hypnosis of the crystal, Redd had left the safety of the forest and walked out into the open. Under the hypnosis of the crystal, she'd briefly merged with it and had seen who was inside.

Ara.

Her vision hazed over with crimson at the edges. Redd kept herself in check, barely, with the frantic thought that she daren't hurt Ara. The power boiled over and around her, filling her with elation and adrenaline. The golden light pulsed within, like a second heart. Its singing rose to envelop her: both a comfort and a call to battle. The *erukahl* streamed around her to engage the angels; she didn't question it.

She moved through them, vaguely aware of the sounds of fighting around her. She approached the crystal and it lashed out at her with psychic power. She could feel from it a primitive sort of fear based only out of survival instinct.

She brushed off its attack and came within arm's reach. The crystal's glow intensified and centered around the small, frail body in its core. A threat. It would choke the life inside if she didn't retreat.

Rage battered Redd like a storm, calling to the golden star within her. Its pulses were painful now, the heat building under her skin, searing away her control bit by bit. She wanted to explode and kill *everything*.

As delicate as a balloon in the vortex of a tornado, Ara's consciousness reached out to Redd — and the drive to destroy shattered. Redd took in a deep gasp that was half-sob.

But Ara's connection to Redd wasn't a cry for help — it was a warning. Without telling them to, Redd's feet shuffled her away from the crystal. Though she was retreating, she couldn't look away from it.

The crystal's sheen subtly changed, becoming more opaque, but in a sick way that made Redd feel ill to behold. Cracks appeared on its surface like a spider-web.

As open as she was, Redd felt it all: the crystal's panic, its structure rapidly changing in ways Redd couldn't identify, the pressure emanating from Ara like the little angel had somehow become a gravity well. For Redd, on the edge of that influence, it made her light-headed and feel as though she might burst.

Which is exactly what the crystal did.

The fissures within its surface deepened suddenly with loud cracks, then the whole shape shattered, spraying crystal chunks and slivers and glittering dust everywhere.

And in the middle of it sat Ara, apparently unharmed and blinking too much.

With the pressure receding, Redd darted forward out of pure instinct and scooped up her friend.

That was how Cira, two of his angels, Chani, and Imae found them after the battle was over. Redd was cradling Ara as though she'd never let her go, with Ara whispering platitudes. Ara's pale hand weakly fluttered at Redd's upper arm.

Chani burst out laughing at the scene, dashing tears of relief from her eyes. As Redd noticed the Commander and her companions, she stood and helped Ara up as well. The angel seemed extremely drained; the color was leached from her flesh in a way that made her look almost like porcelain or marble.

A pair of black-winged angels ran up and spoke in quiet voices to Cira. He gave them an order and turned back to the girls, shaking his head.

"So it happened again. When we first became aware of the *erukahl*, it was because several of our young had gone missing. We traced the kidnappings to hive offshoots like these, and crystals where the children were being used as power sources." He looked sickened, his voice was hard. "We put a stop to it immediately."

Another angel approached him, this one carrying a small cage made out of crystal. Cira took it and raised it to eye level. A squeak issued from the creature trapped inside.

"Don't eat me! I'm a summoner! I can … I can call a dragon to eat you!"

Cira watched with amusement glittering in his eyes. "I will not eat you, little sister, although I do doubt your claim."

The tiny thing slumped against her bars and heaved a sigh. A moment later she was at them again, her three pairs of semi-translucent, feathery wings fluttering in a miniature iridescent storm.

"So you'll let me go free?" She stopped and seemed to realize what he had said. "Hey! I'm serious, I can squash you like a bug!"

Cira rumbled a chuckle. Chani reached in to poke at the winged person.

"What *is* it?" she asked.

The creature's wings fluttered in, what Redd assumed, was indignation. "It? It! I'm not an it! I'm a fae!" she cried.

"I would not talk so big were I as small as you," Chani taunted her merrily.

"Small! Small?!"

"I think we shall keep you in there a bit longer, little sister." Cira said seriously, barely containing his laughter. "We wouldn't want you squishing my angels like bugs."

Again the fae's face fell and she beat at the bars of her cage futilely, squeaking threats and pleading alternately. At a hand motion from Cira, the angel carried her away.

"Come, we must leave before they notice what was done here. We will have time to talk further once we reach Everdark," Cira said.

By the time Redd, assisting Ara and with Chani hovering nearby, reached the treeline, the angels of Cira's group had set up a sledge, onto which they helped Ara. Ara offered to Heal their wounded, but she could hardly stand by herself, so her offer was gently turned down. They started moving again, pulling Ara along on her sledge and refusing to let her walk, with Redd sticking to her like a burr. Redd did her best to ignore the buzzing in her ears, the exhaustion that was rapidly creeping up on her.

She was lucky, though, and they stopped within the hour, after getting far enough away that if any reinforcements showed up at the scene of the battle, there would be no evidence of the angels. Ara had fallen asleep along the way, and after checking on her, Redd found a semi-comfortable place and followed suit.

***

Redd woke up, muddy-headed, to Chani nudging her with the toe of her boot. Chani pushed some food into her hands; Redd bolted it down without even recognizing it and rolled to her feet, taking a few sips from a canteen the Ranger Commander offered next. Not even fully awake and with no idea how long she'd been out, she found herself stumbling along with a crowd of soundless black forms, like an escort of ghosts.

Time passed.

The angels stopped, as always, to some unknowable signal. Redd plopped down gracelessly, letting her breathing and heart rate settle. Chani came next to her but didn't speak; she was watching the lead figure, barely visible in the darkness only as a shadow in more shadows. Redd assumed it was Cira.

Her assumption was confirmed as the figure broke away and headed back to Chani and Redd. He pulled his hood aside to reveal his face. His eyes darted, betraying an uncharacteristic nervousness. Chani seemed to instantly pick up on that.

"What's wrong?" she asked, quiet but direct.

"I'm not sure. It's a … feeling, an impression."

"Of ... what?" Redd asked after no one else seemed inclined to.

Cira looked like he'd just been startled from a dream as he met Redd's eyes. "... panic. Or, warning."

"An attack?" one of the angels whispered.

"I can't say." Cira responded, hushed. "But I can't seem to move."

"I feel it too," Chani said apprehensively. Redd glanced at her, and realized that, for some reason, she was frozen as well. The anxiety at the thought of staying put and perhaps getting overtaken by *erukahl* was far outweighed by this new fear of moving forward even a foot.

"A trick?" someone asked.

Cira shook his head mutely, indicating that he didn't know.

Redd looked up just before it happened.

The clouds parted. Light flooded in and she threw an arm over her face in a knee-jerk reaction to days in darkness. Cries of pain and confusion all around her were quickly drowned out by a mysterious rumbling, then an ear-shattering crash. Shockwaves raced along the ground. Redd lost her footing and slammed into something hard. She clung to it as the ground shook for long minutes.

Then ... silence.

She realized she could hear herself breathing heavily, feel her own heartbeat. Pain quickly made itself known, but a mental systems-check found everything in working order — just bruised. She heaved herself up and got to her feet shakily, slowly climbing up the boulder that had sprouted out of nowhere in front of her. The top gave her a vantage point to see the destruction wreaked ... and its cause.

A mountain now stood where before were flat plains and a forest of thick mushroom-trees. Redd gaped at it.

It couldn't have come from the sky ... could it?

A chill ran through her, fear so strong it locked her muscles.

There was only one thing a massive mountain from the sky could be.

"Redd!"

Redd jerked towards the sound of her name. Chani crawled out from underneath an overhang that led into a deep crack. She was supporting a limping Imae.

"Chani, where's Ara?" Redd called in panic, climbing down from the boulder as quickly as she could without tumbling down it entirely.

"Not with me. The angels?" Chani asked, her speech clipped.

"I don't know."

Chani picked her way around the boulder and up a slightly less steep part of the hill. Imae was right behind her, barely able to help support her own weight. Redd followed.

The angels were regrouping. Cira stood in a knot of them, his face dead white. The other angels shifted nervously, whispered.

Redd scanned the group anxiously. She wasn't sure if she could handle the thought of losing Ara twice in such a short period of time. Hysteria hovered at the edges of her mind.

Then, behind the angels, a glow: Ara! She was sitting propped up against a rock, Healing an angel kneeling in front of her. Redd bit her lip. As she watched, the injured angel's arm, twisted at an odd angle, rotated and set right. The angel bowed to her and stood up. Ara lifted her head and caught Redd's eye.

Ignoring her own pain, Redd dashed across the intervening space, fell to her knees, and wrapped her arms around the little angel. Ara returned the hug to the best of her ability, the grip from both girls desperate with fear and relief. Redd released Ara after a moment, wiped her eyes, and sat back on her heels.

"You okay?" she asked quietly.

"I was not seriously hurt," Ara managed. "And you?" Her brows were creased with genuine worry as her gaze quickly flicked across Redd's body, seeking any obvious injuries. Redd was too exhausted to even be sarcastic.

"I'm — I'm okay, physically. Just some scrapes. Nothing worth Healing. I'll be honest, though, I'm not sure how much more of this I can take."

As one they turned to look as a shadowy angelic shape took a few tentative steps toward the mountain.

It was Cira, and he looked lost. Then he seemed to get a hold on himself and he shook his head minutely, faced his patrol.

"Are we missing any?" he asked.

"Four."

Brief pain flickered across his face. "We can't waste time. We need to get home, to Everdark. I feel … pulled."

TEN
On Survival

It took them two exhausting days to get around the mountain and back onto the plains. The city they could see as they came around the bend was a reassuring sight, and the pace, which had slowed from days and days of walking with no surcease, picked up slightly. Ara had been recovering in her little sledge and it was there, despite several attempts and assurances that she could walk, she remained. At the point where the city was coming into view, Cira hazarded aloud that they were only a few hours from its sanctuary.

That was the good news.

The bad news was that they had experienced several more earthquakes and had witnessed at a slightly less ground-zero vantage point exactly what was causing them. And it was bad news, indeed.

The islands of Haven were falling.

The angels, when Redd asked, had no idea why that would be occurring. They were short-tempered, the ever-present pulling and the feeling of panic pervading the group frayed everyone's nerves. Ara went completely silent after seeing the second island drop and hadn't said a word for almost a day. When they finally stopped to rest, Redd ignored her pressing need to sleep and sidled up to her friend.

"If I am right," Ara said without prompting, "this city that we are approaching, Everdark — in antiquity, it was Pirroun, a fortress originally built to monitor the northern mountains of Silencefall, in the depths of which are housed some of the most dangerous things on this planet. Haven lost contact with its inhabitants during the Elysian attack and assumed everyone had perished. Apparently, it remained a fortress, this time against *erukahl*. I grew up with the thought in mind that we, on Haven, were the last of our kind, and when my father proved himself a villain, I lost all hope that the angels would survive ... but now ... "

She dropped her head into her hands.

"But how do I face them? After what my father has done? Will they even accept me, or will I be branded traitor with him? What of my mother and uncle? With the islands falling, are they even alive?"

Her voice was harsh and hushed, and Redd touched her shoulder gently — a question. Ara leaned in and Redd folded her arms around the slight shoulders. Ara didn't cry, but curled in Redd's embrace, breathed deeply and raggedly through the emotion. Redd rested her cheek on Ara's head and closed her eyes, trying to provide a calm presence through her own turmoil.

And too soon, it was time to get walking again.

The approach to Everdark was a long stretch of dusty rock, broken only by odd wave formations, like the frozen surf of an ocean, which was itself studded with the occasional ravine or crack. Behind them was the forest from which they had emerged, and to either side, more dense forest funneled them in towards the city, eventually meeting the edges of the cliffs. The ground was vaguely sloped upward, which made this, too, not an easy trek.

Everdark was built into the side of a mountain, in the most literal sense — almost as if someone had scooped a triangle-shaped indentation out of the side of a wall of several-hundred-foot sheer cliff. The only viable approach, then, was the front. Smart, for a fortress, she supposed.

She looked back. The lovely new mountain that Everdark citizens could look forward to viewing from now on was about halfway between the edge of the forest and where the trees really got thick at the far end of her view.

The soldiers manning the perimeter of the water defense lowered a bridge from the inside and raised a ponderously heavy door. Redd's group crossed over … and another hour's walk stretched out in front of them. She groaned.

The trudge uphill was brutal. They moved through what she assumed had probably once been farmlands, though they certainly weren't any longer. Now they were crowded with people and things of all types.

There were legions of elves in golden armor with winged helmets, and buildings that looked unnatural to this place. Further uphill were short, bearded people and more buildings. Beyond that, lizard-like people were standing on two backwards-looking legs, like the *erukahl*.

There was more to see, but she was just on this side of delirium and couldn't pay attention to it all.

They reached the inner wall. The massive door cranked up, and into the heart of Everdark they went.

The cliffs had been narrowing steadily the deeper into the fortress they got, funneling them in, and the feeling of being closed in made her edgy. Past the inner wall, Redd's group made their way down a main thoroughfare, which seemed to be a straight shot all the way to the huge, foreboding building made of black stone directly up against the rock, alongside the point of the triangle. Next to that building was the tower cluster she'd noticed from the air.

Those were just about the only standing structures in the place, aside from a few buildings here and there seen over the sea of ruin. But even here was a swarm of activity: an army of hominin-shaped machines, each operated by a figure at their center, removed rubble, tore down structures still half-standing, carried and bullied large boxes into place.

Redd watched a building start to grow out of a box. Her mouth hanging open, she stared until they were too far past for her to see it.

The whole thing was surreal. The machines, growing buildings, creatures that weren't human, large open spaces contrasted by towering cliffs so high up she almost couldn't see their top edges … with how dead exhausted she was, she almost felt it could all be a hallucination.

Then they were turning off the main thoroughfare and into a complex that seemed to mostly have survived whatever had reduced everything else to debris. It did show signs of having been recently repaired, though.

Redd was dying of curiosity. Ara had said this place was a fortress against dangerous things, and it had only been three hundred years since the Elysian attack — by all accounts, a very short time for a species like the angels. How had things gotten so bad in that time? Was all of this destruction *from* the Elysian? If the battle had happened in the city, how had anyone survived at all? Or was this the *erukahl's* doing?

Her wandering thoughts were brought around as they were directed into what she found to be a medical center. She was checked over by an elf in a yellow robe, then settled into a cot and told to sleep. Which she did most gratefully. The questions could wait.

She came to partial consciousness once in the next several hours only to catch Pheonix leaving. With an annoyed grunt, she rolled over and went back to sleep.

At some point, a random Ranger roused her fully. She and Ara were the only ones left in the medical center of the group who had come in. The soldier brought Ara and Redd, still bleary, across the main thoroughfare to another series of original buildings, and into one — which seemed to be a bunch of bedrooms all in one big building, similar to the barracks at the Haven Ranger camp.

She didn't listen to much of what the Ranger said at that point, only to note that Ara's room was next to hers. Once she was alone, she fell into the bed and was out in seconds.

***

A red sky.

Clouds boiled over the horizon, lightning flicking through and across the bellies of the great heavenly formations, attracted by the immense amount of power channeled and concentrated below. The earth was naught but bare rock; it had long ago been scorched free of whatever vegetation it may have supported in a previous life.

And bodies.

So many, piled atop one another. Pieces and bits and parts and blood, as if someone had upended an anatomy book and spread the images on the ground. A forensic team's nightmare.

In the midst of it all, a girl.

All familiar ... the repeated nightmare that had plagued her for years.

But ... this time, something was different.

This time she looked through another's eyes. She saw herself the way he — how had she known it was a boy? — had, so long ago.

Her conscious mind rebelled, tried to pull away. But something about it gripped her, wanted her to see, needed her to understand some facet of the dream that still tortured her.

The girl was merely a waif of a child, dressed only in a long, undecorated tunic. Red hair fell to her ankles in a matted mess of gore and tangles. Blood ran in rivulets from her head to her feet, spreading in all directions as though fleeing. Pushed by the waves of power radiating from her.

While Redd herself could feel nothing of the mind she currently inhabited, she recoiled. But she was trapped — chained — into this body that wasn't her own.

The girl turned her head, met the eyes of the boy, and, through him, Redd.

Golden eyes glowed like twin suns in the cherubic, dispassionate face. Within her gaze was a straight-shot glimpse to the soul of something as old as time, second only to the Creator.

The air began to waver, distort, as the girl tilted her chin upward. This time her gaze followed, pierced into the clouds. The thunderheads in the sky parted, and attackers poured down in a wave of writhing bodies, kissed by lightning and trailing wisps of incandescent crimson. They screamed for her head, her power. She was their greatest threat. She was the first of them. And she would be the last.

Like a red sun rising over the desert, the little monster smiled.

Redd awoke with a jolt, a scream caught in her throat. Her eyes darted wildly.

Cream-colored room, sparse but homey. A small, comfortable bed, fresh flowers by the window, slightly phosphorescent …

Dark.

She settled back, her breathing and the whisper of her body on the sheets the only sounds.

Everdark.

That's right.

They'd been in Everdark for several days. Though she'd been able to talk with Chani briefly, she'd mostly been alone. In the few minutes she'd gotten to talk to Ara over the last few days, she'd found out that the little angel had been unofficially inducted into (and was being trained by) the ranks of Healers. Chani was, obviously, at the center of everything.

Which left Redd to her own devices.

She had been given leave to wander around the inner city, sometimes watching the rapid construction taking place, sometimes climbing up onto the inner wall to get a view on the happenings in what had probably been farmland in another life. Now they were camps for armies of multiple species.

Which, now that she was more lucid, was suspicious as all fuck. What was all this about? Clearly Pheonix had done his job as a liaison just as Chani had said he would. Yes, Everdark was fairly razed: supplies made sense. The angels that had managed to survive living here were all holed up in the 'Keep' at the rounded apex of the triangle-shaped slice out of the cliffs. The Keep was a series of tunnels and rooms carved *into* said cliffs: from the outside, It was just a stone wall with a massive door and multiple tiny windows dotting the stone. So the people she saw rebuilding or fortifying the walls and buildings made sense. But the profusion of heavily-armored bodies, grim faces, and large weaponry did not. Were they there to protect from the *erukahl*, or preparing an offensive?

Frankly, to Redd's civilian eye, it looked like they were gearing for war.

She rolled to sit on the edge of the mattress with her feet dangling. Hunched over, she looked at the ground from the strip of reality seen past the tangled red curtain of her hair.

She closed her eyes to drop into the meditative state she was so familiar with, leaving behind her physical shell but for an ephemeral tether. The golden light blossomed in front of her inner eye. It had been erratic of late, battered by her constantly-shifting emotions and stress she couldn't escape. It seemed calm now, and she basked in its steady glow and its multisensory music to recenter herself, before surfacing once more.

She slipped off the bed and wandered over towards a mirror hung on the far wall. Pulling off her sleeping robe, she tossed it on the bed, intending to get dressed for the 'day.' As she pulled on her rec-suit, she studied herself in the mirror.

She'd lost too much weight but had gained some muscle. She wasn't okay with the former (when she started seeing bones against flesh, it reminded her too much of when she'd been really sick and brought her mind back to a bad place) and was secretly pleased with the latter. She was envious of Chani's muscles — with strength like that, no one would ever hurt her again.

Perhaps, in a mind with no future but 'survive,' a goal like 'get stronger' could be acceptable.

She sat to consider her itinerary. Hunger loomed, but after the nightmare she didn't really want to be alone. She pulled out the communication crystal Chani had given her during one of their too-brief meetings, and concentrated on the Commander's face.

After a moment, she got a reluctant answer. She blinked — it was weird the way these things worked. The crystal was a little sliver, barely an inch or two long, with a small brass-colored dial that encircled it. But when she looked into it, she could see Chani's face clearly.

"Yes?" Chani said, a little abruptly.

"Did I wake you?" Redd asked, trying to quell her annoyance at Chani's attitude.

Chani rubbed a hand across one eye and then grinned ruefully. "Yeah. I got to bed late. What's up?"

"Oh, um … "

Redd felt a little silly. Why was she bothering someone so important with something so petty?

"What is it?" Chani asked again, this time more gently.

"I just … I mean, I'm hungry, and … " She trailed off, not able to say that she was lonely.

Chani laughed. There was the sense of her moving, like she was sitting up while holding the crystal. Redd caught the impression of another body behind her, the flash of bare flesh and folds of sheets.

Come to think of it, she knew next to nothing of Chani's personal life. The thought of Chani having a sexual partner was embarrassing. Redd remembered the conversation between her and Ara in the Ranger camp.

"Well, I'm up, I should eat," Chani said, distracting her. "Be there in a bit."

The crystal darkened.

Redd left her room and went one door over, figuring she'd see if Ara was around. Her light knock was answered with such speed that she came to the conclusion that Ara'd been up and waiting for someone.

"Redd?"

"No, the Creator," Redd answered a little testily. Ara gave her an odd, slightly hurt look, and Redd sighed. "Sorry."

Ara smiled, accepting her apology, and opened the door a little further. Her room was a copy of Redd's. "Come in."

Redd paused by the door and looked everywhere but at her friend. It annoyed her that she felt so awkward, so she decided to just get it out. "Waiting for someone?"

She didn't look at Ara until the angel's silence demanded that she do so. Ara was looking down. And suddenly, she felt like an ass.

"Hey," Redd said gently, and waited for Ara to look up. Redd put a hand up in question, Ara nodded. She stepped forward and gathered Ara in her arms. After a moment, the angel hugged back.

"I'm sorry," Redd said, and meant it. "It's Pheonix, isn't it?"

"Yes. He's going to take me to see the Master Healer here. He says she wants to speak with me."

"Well," she said, feigning cheerfulness as she pulled away to put Ara at arm's length. "That's alright. I'm off to get something to eat with Chani. You'll tell me how it went, right?"

Ara's eyes expressed that she didn't believe Redd's sudden change of heart and Redd just smiled crookedly. There was nothing she could do about her dislike of Pheonix. She stubbornly recoiled from thinking about the realization she'd had, that he made her feel comfortable, but it was accompanied by the sinking sensation that she'd have to address it sooner or later.

With him here in Everdark — which definitely meant he would be spending time with Ara — it was likely to be sooner than later.

Finally, Ara sighed. "I will."

Redd turned to leave.

When she opened the door, she found Pheonix and Chani on the other side. Chani looked a little tired, but she was grinning. Pheonix looked as impassive as ever, but he did incline his head to Redd slightly as a greeting.

"I was coming down the hall, and look who I ran into!" Chani said. "What a co-*inky*-dink." She drawled out that last part, her eyes shifting to Ara.

That made Redd laugh, and she jabbed Chani in the boob. "Don't tease her. I saw what you had in your bedroom."

Chani glanced at Redd with surprise on her face, then laughed and slung an arm around Redd's shoulder. "Okay, okay, you got me. Once this is all over, kid, and you join the Rangers, you'll understand. But for now, come on, we'll get some vittles."

Redd gave a silent wave good-bye to Ara as Chani led her down the hallway and out onto the main road through Everdark. Once outside, Chani dropped her arm.

"Do I really *have* to join the Rangers?" Redd asked.

"It's not so bad, Redd. Trust me. Psykers have to have special accommodations to live normal lives. That's all it is. You'll get a steady paycheck and have access to just about anything you want at HQ."

"But I'm stuck there, right? I don't have a choice and I can't leave?"

Chani thinned her lips. "You *need* training. You'll be required to go to Ranger HQ for that, yes. But that's to *help* you. After your training concludes, you'll be given the decision of whether to stay or go. If you stay, it's a job, like anything else. Not all psykers are soldiers, although a lot of them do choose to become fighters because it's a great release for the natural stress of what they are. We take very, very good care of our soldiers, Redd. Even the lowest joe is more important than, say, me. Anyway, don't worry about it too much right now. Once this is all over, you'll have plenty of time to figure it out."

Though Redd wasn't at all pacified, she allowed Chani to shift the conversation. They eventually chatted idly as Chani led the way into the Keep, which was just as dark and closed-in as it appeared from the outside. This wasn't the first time Redd had been there, though, as a lot of essential operations (like the dining facilities) were being hosted inside its thick walls. She was learning she didn't particularly like small spaces, even ones lit jauntily with both technological and phosphorescent lighting.

As they made their way through the halls of the Keep, Redd was assailed with smells that made her stomach cramp and growl. She hurried over to a replicator to order pizza and a drink. She knew she shouldn't be surprised the replicator could give her something from her planet — she'd eaten from them before — but she wasn't used to it yet. Chani actually got something Redd could recognize: a pile of rice, vegetables, and some weird gnarled clumps of meat.

"It's weird how so many things exist in so many places. Like grains," Redd said as they sat, gesturing at Chani's rice.

"Well, some of that is by design. At least regarding the species you'll likely see a lot of: hominins, elves, angels. All made directly by the Creator's hand, and their home planets with them. Since a lot of us share elements of physiology, we needed similar planets, and that created similar flora and fauna. But it's been a long time since then and epigenetics is a hell of a force. There *are* differences, sometimes major ones, which is why replicator technology reads biometrics, to ensure no incidents. Trust me, there are plenty of foods available from those replicators that would instantly kill you and me, planets that would do the same, and people that don't look or function anything like us. You just haven't seen any of that yet."

"So what is that, then?" Redd asked, gesturing at Chani's plate.

"Marinated and grilled avian feet and rectums."

Redd stared at her. "With so many other options, why pick that part of the body to eat?"

"Protein is protein. It's just a preference. Frankly, I like the squeakiness and the texture."

Redd dropped it. After a few minutes of eating, she said: "Can we talk about what the 'Creator' is, now?"

"I s'pose. Well, most species have a genesis legend. Basically, how that species came to exist. Usually this involves some form of higher beings. Like the Ascended I mentioned. Did you ever have a chance to look them up?"

Redd shook her head. "No, I wasn't able to do any research, but I do think Chaos Earth had some similar story. There was an old, old legend about how we were 'raised' by some powerful something. But I don't know a whole lot about it. Not the kind of thing the Federation really wanted circulating."

Chani gave her a look that made it plain that she was questioning how Redd had found out about it, but rather than asking, she said, "The Creator is sort of like that. But it's not a legend, it's real. The Creator is a being incomprehensible to us, possessing unimaginable power. It created — well, everything you see."

"That's ridiculous," Redd snorted. "And impossible."

"Really? How do you explain yourself? Your power, your blood? Is that impossible?"

Redd looked down at her food, her eyes unfocused.

"There are things in this universe that no one understands," Chani went on more gently, "not you, nor I, nor the longest-lived beings we know of. Just because you don't understand it or it doesn't fit with your preconceived notions, doesn't mean it isn't possible or doesn't exist. You're here to learn, and you *have* to learn, to survive."

"I know all about survival," Redd said flatly.

"The only thing you do know, huh? Is that what you're thinking?" Chani asked.

Redd stared at her plate without seeing it. "Seems like it."

"I know more about survival than you'd think," Chani said, and something in her voice made Redd look up. "Maybe

I'll tell you about it someday. Try to give yourself some grace. You've had it exceptionally hard and this is not how we generally handle uninitiated people."

Redd fell silent, struggling against her emotions. Chani, unflappable as ever, waited calmly and ate.

"So, the Creator?" Redd asked finally, her inner tension audible.

"We really know next to nothing about it. How it came to be, if there are any others like it, how it functions — all we know is that it exists, and that it has more power than anything else. The Ascended exist, and they answer to — you guessed it — the Creator."

Redd grunted but didn't pursue the line of inquiry further.

"So, what's a hominid?" she asked instead. "And hominin? I've heard both those words."

"A hominid is a general term for species from the hominin-genome plus the primate-genome. They all tend to look about the same — one head, a torso, two arms, two legs. That sort of thing. You'll most likely hear 'hominid' being used in the context of 'hominid-shaped,' since there are so many species that fit that profile — even elves and angels. Homi*nins* are specifically those in the human genome. Both you and I are hominin, since you're a human and I'm Race of Man."

"So, wait. There are humans everywhere, but not all of them come from Chaos Earth, clearly. Why are there so many of us?"

"An ancient species, the Arkitekts, was given the task by the Creator to seed the 'verses. I can only imagine they got bored, or lazy. Or maybe they just took their jobs too seriously. Whatever the case, they did a whole lot of seedin'. Some things we have evidence to attribute to them, some things to the Creator." She hesitated for a split second, enough for Redd to take notice of it as a hesitation. "It is also said that the Creator created evil to balance the universe. The elves believe that balance is the Creator's ultimate goal, and so they protect the balance above all things."

"Oh yeah, the 'balance.' You mentioned that before." She said uncomfortably, feeling as if someone were standing behind her and shouting: *That's not right!*

It wasn't just that it wasn't 'fair,' but that it wasn't *right*. She was certain, on a level she couldn't begin to rationalize or explain to Chani, that the Creator most certainly did not want any sort of balance, but an eradication of all evil. The realization shook her to her core, so she stayed silent.

She'd only just recently heard of this 'Creator' thing and now she was sure of its intentions?

She ate mechanically for a few minutes, and Chani let her process.

"So, who was this … seed-bearing species? Are they still around?" Redd asked finally.

"Not that we're aware of. We actually don't have much information on them, aside from a few cryptic artifacts that we can't make heads or tails of. They left nothing behind — no homes, cities, planets, ruins. They, apparently, just disappeared."

"Seems to be a common thread," Redd said sarcastically.

Chani laughed, then said, "Ah, hold on."

Redd looked up from a bite of pizza to see Chani digging around in her pockets. She pulled out a communicator crystal and looked into its facets.

"Yes?" Pause. "Roger. Out."

"What's up?" Redd asked, a little knot twisting in her stomach.

Chani sighed and put her elbows on the table, clasping her hands together in front of her. She met Redd's eyes levelly.

"I'll be honest; I didn't just agree to come today because you asked."

The knot twisted tighter.

"Then, what?" Redd asked, trying to keep the tremor out of her voice.

"The plan currently is to get you through to Terelath as soon as possible, then transfer you to Ranger HQ when the time is right. In order to do that, I'd have to be with you every step of the way, since I know your specific situation better than anyone else. I was going to take you there right after we ate, but we have to delay for a bit since the King and Queen of the elves are coming through shortly and I'll need to be there for that and the war councils after. You're free to wander around or hang out in your room until — "

"*War* council?"

Chani made a face and said, "Yes," but didn't elaborate. Redd stared her down, and finally Chani sighed heavily.

"We are preparing for a siege. Almost as soon as Pheonix got here, he received word that there were not only ships approaching in space but also an army on foot. We don't have a lot of time, so — "

"So you're going to shuffle me off as quickly as you can?" Redd asked with an edge.

Chani lowered her brows and for a moment Redd feared she may have gone too far. "This is for your *safety*."

"You said on Haven that you could use my abilities."

"I said what I had to, to get you out of that camp. I wasn't *actually* expecting to find hostiles here."

"But you acknowledge that it was a possibility you'd considered, and you agreed to let me come anyway. You've seen me handle myself."

"*War*," Chani stressed the word, "is no place for the untrained. Scraping through a few skirmishes doesn't mean you're a combat expert, kid."

"Put me in a place where I can't possibly hurt anyone. You said it yourself: psykers can find release in battle. I haven't firestormed yet."

"Just because you haven't, doesn't mean you won't. We don't know all your triggers. I don't get why you're arguing. You *want* to stay?"

"I *want* to help," Redd said quietly but stubbornly. "This is Ara's home. Ara's people. I wouldn't be able to live with myself knowing I walked away, when I have the power to do something, anything. You know Ara won't consent to leave. I'm not abandoning her." She felt her lips tremble on the last words.

After a heartbeat, Chani gave a little disbelieving laugh. "Creator, you really are alike."

"What?"

"Don't worry about it." She stood. "Listen. When I said we don't have time, I meant it. I'll bring it up at the war council. This isn't a decision I can just make arbitrarily. There's protocol. For now, we really do need to get down to the square. The King and Queen should be coming through very soon."

ELEVEN
Hearts and Minds

As Chani and Redd approached the square, they found it packed. There were people everywhere, almost too many to move through — angels, dwarves (the short people with beards), lizard-guys, elves, some species Redd simply didn't recognize at all, and a few hominins here and there.

Chani skirted the crowd, head on a swivel, until she found a particular group set aside from everyone else. Following Chani on instinct, Redd glanced over the heads of and in between gaps in the congregation. At the far end was a large open space surrounding what Redd assumed was the portal to Terelath.

The portal wasn't what she would have expected. It didn't glow or sparkle. It was just a slight distortion of air around what appeared to be nothing more than a large, round door without a frame. Redd squinted but she could only make out subtly-shifting blocks of color. Mostly green and white.

She supposed that the elves who surrounded the portal were these Ladies she'd heard of. Dressed in simple robes, they each hovered several inches off the ground. Curious, Redd opened her mind. Instantly she clamped her eyes shut, reeling back into someone standing behind her. The person recoiled, and began to berate her.

She barely heard them though, her senses blown out completely by the power that emanated from the elven women. It was like looking into a supernova — from two feet away. When Redd opened her eyes, she found she was being stared at by the three Ladies that floated around the portal. Redd ran to catch up to Chani and hide behind her, but she felt watched even so.

Chani didn't seem to notice.

"Oh, is this one of our young charges?" asked an elf standing across from Chani, his brows raised. When Redd met his gaze, he grinned. His dark skin was mottled with green, as though he were perpetually standing in the shade of a tree. His hair was twisted into green ropes that cascaded thickly down his back, several of which were wrapped in gold rings, jeweled pendants and metal spirals. He seemed more muscular than most of the willowy male elves she'd seen so far, with wide shoulders, a defined chest, developed abdominals, and thick legs. Strapped to his back was a bow almost as long as he was tall, green-colored and shot through with metallic golden that glittered and shone as it caught light.

He was bare-chested, which again seemed strange for an elf (Redd couldn't help noticing the lack of body hair — but not just that, no nipples or navel, either). Around his waist was a thick, stiff belt from which draped a half-skirt of green chainmail, and below that, brown leggings.

It wasn't lost on her that Chani was giving him a quelling look, either, which it appeared he was completely ignoring.

"Redd, this is Ruemilanthrasia, Prophet of Spiraea Lady of the Woods, the Ascended of Nature. He's here with the elite troops from Terelath."

Chani then gestured to the dwarf standing beside Ruemilanthrasia; he was larger and more well-kept than most she'd seen so far, who seemed to like to adorn themselves with rotting humanoid parts and keep snacks in their beards. His own beard (which, along with his hair, was jet-black) was braided in thick chunks, which were clasped closed at the bottom with golden casts of the heads of ugly little vaguely humanoid monsters. He wore plate armor, a circlet across his forehead, and carried a hammer that, when the bottom of the handle rested on the ground, was taller than he was. It was made of metal from head to tip and covered with runes. The head of the hammer, bigger than the head of its wielder, was rounded on the front and arched back into the likeness of an eagle. His skin — what little was visible through all the armor and hair — was an ashen brown and looked like he was literally made of rock.

"This is General Stonebreaker, acting Regent of the dwarves and the commander on the field of the dwarves from Doom's Furnace," Chani said.

"Called so because every weapon forged there is the doom of *something*," a high-pitched voice from the person standing next to Stonebreaker put in. "Most often goblins."

Redd focused on the speaker and tried not to look too far down. He stood less than half her height, and she had a hard time finding his physical being through all the tools. Every pocket was stuffed with bits of twisted metal that she supposed were useful but couldn't imagine what for. The belt he wore was afflicted with this clutter tenfold — strips of cloth had been sewn on top of other strips of cloth in order to create more places for things to reside.

He was pale, with large, watery blue eyes and a simply enormous schnoz that was slightly reddened at its blunt tip. He twitched and blinked several times every few seconds, seemingly incapable of staying still. This ticking affected his hands worst of all; with disconcerting hyperflexion, he was constantly rolling a large silver coin back and forth over his knuckles.

Most oddly, he was sitting in a white chair that seemed perfectly contoured to his body … and floating.

"Tinkerfist, the Master Tinkerer of the Third Level and Diplomatic General Extraordinaire. He's here with the gnomes, who should be arriving sometime soon," Chani said as an aside to Redd.

Stonebreaker burst out into raucous laughter. He slammed the butt of the hammer down into the ground, Redd guessed to emphasize how comical he thought the joke to be, although it only served to startle her.

"Aye, an' that they do well! For there are none better than we dwarves at crushin' a goblin skull or three, eh?" Stonebreaker belted, and began laughing again. Tinkerfist watched him, seeming sad or confused because of his slightly wilted features, although to be honest, Redd couldn't tell what he was feeling, at least not from his expression. She wasn't about to open her mind again. Fuck *that*.

"And the Shellmaster of the drakkan forces is here with us for this battle." Chani nodded formally to the lizard-person — a drakkan, Redd guessed — on the far side, nearer to Redd than herself. Redd turned towards him and was rewarded with a slight nod as she met his slanted green eyes. He was quite a bit taller than Redd, covered in interlocking, iridescent blue-and-green scales, similar to what Redd figured a reptilian peacock would look like. In fact, this drakkan looked evermore like a peacock than any of the others she'd seen around — for the massive, beautiful, feathered ruff jutting from his neckplates.

His face was slightly elongated and his jaw oddly shaped. His thin lips bulged — teeth, most likely. He had pointed ears (in fact, as she looked at him, she noticed a lot of elven features and wondered at it), a lithe, narrow body, and a stout tail, which he'd curled around one leg.

The only clothing the drakkan wore was a scale-like metal belt with a loincloth to cover his crotch, which she supposed was proper because he grew his own armor. Everyone else was decked out to the nines in full suits of armor — but the fact that this creature was so 'naked' in comparison told Redd the scales that covered him head to toe must be hard indeed. His black hair was tied back in a simple ponytail.

In his claws was a long spear with a wickedly curved tip.

"Yes, this is Redd, the uninitiated psyker we found on Haven," Chani said, sounding as though she'd repeated it a thousand times.

Heads nodded around the circle.

Stonebreaker looked Redd up and down (he only came up to her chest, which Redd would have thought comical in another situation).

"So, lass. Have yeh been trained in any other types o' weapons?" he asked in a voice slightly too loud.

"Er," She glanced at Chani again, pleadingly. "I haven't had a chance to — "

"*Ha!*" the dwarf roared. He slammed the haft of his hammer into the ground again. "See, there's the problem! A perfectly bonnie lass, were she only teh grow a beard and learn teh use an axe! Yeh cannae rely entirely oan the gifts the Creator gave yeh! When will yeh learn?" He was addressing Chani. Redd couldn't tell if he was actually serious or not, but judging by the barely-held laughter of Ruemilanthrasia, he probably was. No one answered for a moment. Stonebreaker seemed to be eagerly awaiting a response.

Out of nowhere, Imae snorted. Redd had forgotten she was present. "You're one to criticize, with that smooth beard," Imae said with a lopsided grin.

Stonebreaker puffed up visibly and sparks shot from somewhere under his beard or armor. "WHAT?" he bellowed. "I — I — MA BEARD NEEDS TEH BE WELL KEPT. All yeh — *prissy dandy* species requiiiiiire a dwarf be *brushed* an' an' *clean* — cannae be WALKIN' ABOOT COVERED IN DETRITUS — "

"Yeah yeah," Chani interrupted, waving a hand. "That sounds like a 'you' problem."

Steam belched from under Stonebreaker's armor but the rest of the circle laughing uproariously (excepting Redd, who had no fucking clue what was happening) cut short the impending explosion.

Chani wiped tears from her eyes with her pinkies and an exaggerated expression — mouth agape, eyes lolled upward — and said, "Whew. Okay. Enough shenanigans. Stop poking the dragon. The King and Queen will be through shortly. Right?"

She knelt and slung an arm around Stonebreaker's neck, which broke the last of his stormy mood. He chuckled gravelly and shoved her off, muttering something Redd didn't catch.

Chani just gave him a cheesy grin in response, then excused herself and Redd. They moved off down an alleyway lined with guards of all species. Imae came to stand next to Chani, who put her head in her hands as soon as the group turned a corner.

"Oh, Creator," Chani laughed, "it's been too long since I've been around dwarves; I'd forgotten what it's like." She rounded on Imae. "And you! Why do you encourage him?"

Imae just offered a cheeky grin.

"Commander Abyssterilon," a voice called.

A couple of angels headed towards them, escorted by an elf and … and ...

Redd's eyes lingered on the elf. He was taller than her by a few inches, and easily the most gorgeous creature she'd ever seen.

He oozed easy confidence. He had bright cerulean eyes, short hair — nearly shaved in the back, with bangs that fell to just above his eyes. The strands an inch on either side of his center part were the same color as his eyes. Whether or not that was natural, Redd was unsure, but she also didn't care.

He had skin a shade or so darker than her own light brown and (from what she could tell) the trim physique that spoke of someone who was not a stranger to hard work. He wore a set of armor that looked like tight-fitting chainmail, and across his chest was a plain brown harness. Attached to the harness was a brown sheath that was undecorated except for a single sunset-colored flower with silver leaves.

The body of the sword seemed to be one piece (insofar as Redd could tell from its place inside a sheath), and was a glimmering, multifaceted cerulean-and-neon purple that shifted colors when the light hit it. Glass or — crystal, perhaps? Its hilt was simple and silver.

He was also adorned in several pieces of silver jewelry. He wore a thin chain around his neck and a circlet made of silver filigree, which was inset with opals and feathered with silver leaves, around his forehead. Many earrings decorated his long, pointed ears asymmetrically, the largest of which was a silver sword.

A sensation flooded Redd — a not unpleasant one, but strange. It made her want to shiver.

Ara's words came back: *Your body wants to be touched, or to touch someone else.*

She did have the inexplicable urge to run her fingers down the back of his exposed neck.

Oh, she thought, *this must be what attraction is. Ara's right. This is a bother.*

She let a brief grin flicker across her face, since he wasn't looking at her anyway.

But I like it.

"Hey, Little Shit, what's up?" the Commander called as she met up with him. They clasped hands enthusiastically. The angels hung back. There were several more that Redd hadn't noticed at first.

"It's 'Lord Little Shit' to you," the elf retorted, feigning indignation. His voice was medium-toned, rich, full of humor. Chani laughed.

"I guess I don't have to ask why you're here," she said.

"Had to come, especially with new reports about what we'll be facing, but we can cover the boring details later."

The elf's eyes flicked past Chani and lit upon Imae, then Redd. A shot of heat ricocheted, lightning-quick, up her spine. She offered him a half-smile, but he'd already looked away.

"Oh, right," Chani said. "This is Redd, a psyker we picked up on Haven, and cadet Imae; she's accompanying me on my mission. Girls, this is Lord Tyyrulriathula, a Bladesinger and Commander of the Phoenix Legions."

"Nice to meet you," Tyyrulriathula said, offering a small but elegant bow to Imae, and then Redd. Imae saluted stiffly and Redd nodded, trying not to drool.

Tyyrulriathula then moved to one side, allowing the angels to come up to the forefront. Chani introduced her to Veric, the cobalt-winged, stern-faced military adviser, and Freija, the sticklike, bald, serious high priestess. The others represented trade and commerce, food statistics, crafts, democratics, and utilities, but Redd didn't pay much attention to them. Her eyes kept meandering back to Tyyrulriathula, as though drawn there magnetically. More than once, she caught him also looking at her.

After a few minutes of sterile conversation, something signaled Chani, Tyyrulriathula, Veric, and Freija to look in the same direction, towards the portal. Redd looked, too — then realized the crowd had gone silent and people were moving away, shuffling to the outer edges of the courtyard.

"Come on, we gotta head over there now," Chani said, at the same time Tyyrulriathula offered, "Shall we?"

Redd cast one last glance at him and then jogged to catch up with Chani.

As they broke free of the crowds that surrounded an outer ring of guards, Redd finally saw the whole picture. Tyyrulriathula, Imae, Chani, and the angelic council went to stand about thirty feet in front of the portal. Pheonix and Ara emerged from the crowd to join them. Redd hung back with the assembled onlookers. She saw no reason she should be up there. Ara gave Redd a slight smile as she took her place in line. The little angel wore a white robe and Pheonix was dressed in a decorated set of red-and-black armor. Redd squinted, trying to make sense of the colors as they seemed to shift before her eyes. She thought he looked uncomfortable and, strangely, the thought tickled her.

They waited only a few moments before the Ladies beside the portal lifted their arms simultaneously, and the shimmering colors sharpened. Redd briefly caught a glimpse of a paradise world: huge trees with emerald green leaves, cloudless crystal blue sky, and buildings seemingly made out of living foliage. Then the first pair walked through: a male elf wearing an outfit very similar to Tyyrulriathula's, holding the arm of a Lady. In fact, as the procession continued, Tyyrulriathula himself edged up from one side and smoothly took the arm of a Lady that came through by herself, as though they'd rehearsed it. He caught Redd's eye, gave her a devilish smile and a lift of the brow. The Lady whose arm he held didn't notice. She barely touched him, her arching brows held high as she gazed off into the distance with an altogether unpleasant look on her face. As they stopped in the line of other elves, she released him and floated there impassively.

Each male elf was dressed in the same manner as Tyyrulriathula, and while some of them wore their scabbards at their sides instead of across their chests. Each one also had his Lady.

As the last pair took their place, they turned towards the portal in one motion, and there was a pause.

Redd was beginning to get restless. The sheer force of power in this courtyard had her sweating and dizzy. Her barrier wasn't good enough yet to block it all.

She heard rustling behind her and turned to see the audience kneeling. Veric knelt as well, though the rest of the council remained on their feet. Redd hastened to follow the crowd so she wouldn't stand out.

The portal rippled and two elves that Redd could only assume were the King and Queen came through, arm in arm.

Redd was instantly struck by an almost overwhelming sense of sadness. Belying calm smiles, something in the eyes of the two elves suggested a deep sense of loss. The King was on the short side, a dark-skinned elf with a neatly-trimmed mustache/goatee combo (very odd, since every other male elf Redd had seen was bare in face and body — at least insofar as she could tell) and jet-black hair swept away from his face. Both he and the Queen wore delicate, understated crowns of the purest white leaves. He wore a beautifully ornate green and black suit of armor.

The Queen beside him was unlike any creature Redd had seen thus far. Wavy red hair fell to her waist, bright against a robe of green and black. Slanted red eyes were ringed with long, thick lashes, and her lips were perfect and full. Her porcelain skin was ethereal, as though she were carved from flawless marble and stood in a perpetual beam of sunlight. She was achingly beautiful, beyond anything Redd had ever seen or even dreamed.

One of them must have gestured, or something, because everyone kneeling stood, with the exception of Veric, who kept his head down and said:

"Welcome, my Lord and Lady Firstborn. It has been long since we have seen elves here, long before this place came to be known as Everdark. I am Veric, master of military operations. I personally do not remember the days of the elves, but when I was young, my parents told me stories of the honored place we once held as partners in the light of the Creator's grace. For the sake of my people, I extend the highest gratitude towards you for your assistance. I hope we can return to the peace and fellowship we once knew."

"We shall make every effort to see that happen," the King responded, a genuine smile on his handsome face.

One by one, the council members introduced themselves.

One of the Ladies came forward and held out an ornate wooden box to the King and Queen. They took it, each with one hand supporting it in perfect balance.

"Secondborn," they said as one to the angelic councilors, "we present to you your rightful place in the Book of Races, and with it, a gift."

Freija, the high priestess, came forward, bowed deeply, and took the box. As her hands touched it, her eyes widened slightly. Almost distractedly, she returned to her spot.

"If you will, Councilors," the Queen called, her voice like the rain, "merely wait a moment; we may adjourn to more serious discussions. We have several individuals we wish to speak with first. Lord Justice."

Pheonix rose slowly and approached them.

The Queen smiled at him. “We thought the angels were lost to us. To find that the boy who rang the bells is fulfilling his destiny so early … ” She inclined her head. “Thank you.”

Pheonix bowed without saying anything, and returned to his spot.

Chani approached without being called, sporting a cocky grin. She gave a flourish and a salute, at which the elven royalty chuckled. Redd was beginning to get the sense that all of them had had some kind of contact with Chani, or knew about her, which made the respect Redd felt for the veteran Ranger grow even further.

“My lieges,” Chani said.

“Can’t you show a little reverence, just once?” The King asked, playing at being exasperated.

“Nope, your Highness. Incapable of it, your Highness,” Chani quipped, eliciting laughter.

“We wanted to thank you as well for your cooperation. Your experience has been invaluable,” the King went on. “We hope to be able to speak with you further once time permits, but for now … ”

Chani saluted again, beaming, and went back to her place in line.

The Queen’s eyes shifted to Ara, who tensed. The Queen’s smile broadened just a bit in apparent amusement and possibly a bit of pity, and she beckoned the little angel forward. Ara froze. Chani pushed her gently, just enough to get her moving. She stiffly approached and settled onto her knees before the tall elf. She looked close to tears. Redd’s heart went out to her.

“Ara Luschia Invenes. We have heard much about you, and the potential you have shown for the Healing arts. We would like to extend you an invitation to come school with us in the spellcrafting Teaching.”

Ara stared at the Queen, her lips parted as though she were going to say something but it had died on her tongue.

“Say yes!” Chani whisper-shouted. Scattered chuckles could be heard from the audience. That seemed to break Ara from her trance.

She nodded and stood. “I would be honored and delighted.”

Her voice was soft and dignified, but Redd could hear the tremble that lay beneath. She performed a surprisingly refined bow for one with little contact with the outside world, and shuffled quickly back to her place.

There were commendations, people were introduced, and the meeting began to break up.

Chani approached Redd and said, “Alrighty, we’re off to council.”

“Oh. Um. What will I do?”

“My suggestion? If you truly do want to fight, to protect this place, get some serious training in.”

***

Redd hesitated until well after most of the crowd was gone, then wandered off in the direction of the training grounds.

She choked back the overwhelming sense of having been abandoned, reminded herself that the others had jobs to do.

But, now, so did Redd:

Train. Become worthy of Chani’s trust and respect. Help defend the last of the angels. This, she’d decided for herself.

Redd turned a corner, trailing her fingertips against the rough stone of the building beside her, and the training area opened up before her: a large dirt area, loosely fenced in, lit alternately by magic lamps and phosphorescent plants to combat the constant darkness from the cloudcover. At the far end were weapon racks. She stopped by the fence, kicked off her boots. She wanted to be able to *feel*.

She entered through a gap in the fence, her bare feet kissing the soft dirt, and let her mind scatter in preparation for the meditation of physical movement.

She'd found this place while wandering around, bored out of her mind, shortly after they'd arrived in Everdark and everyone had separated like a startled school of fish. Chani had shown her a few basic moves to practice in the time they'd been traveling, and this had been a fine place to work on those since being in the fortress.

What Chani had taught her was mostly used as an exercise routine for now until she could get more formal training, but she imagined she could make use of it in a fight if she needed to. Up until now her few skirmishes had mostly been brute-force berserker meltdowns and that had to change. Without control, she was more dangerous on a battlefield to her allies than to the enemy. Part of that meant training her body and learning how to physically defend herself.

Redd had also found that she liked physical movement — the visceral kinetic dance of punch, duck, weave, twist, kick.

Fighting the constant rage simmering just underneath her control was made easier when she moved. Imagining invisible opponents to focus her innate ire on, she could slip beneath it, letting the preternatural serenity of the golden light fill her mind … and body.

Tapping into the golden light in this way made it brighter even when she wasn't using it. She still spoke to it often, but didn't have to completely shut off her external senses to do so. Its music was a continual background to her thoughts.

Though intellectually she figured she should probably be concerned about this … evolution … of a thing she'd never heard of anyone else possessing, she couldn't muster the emotion in actuality. It kept her calm. Wasn't that what they all wanted? Maybe that's why she hadn't talked to Chani or Ara about it. She didn't want to face their concern.

She reached the center of the ring, spread her arms to either side, closed her eyes, and took in a deep breath.

The golden light within awoke from its half-doze, spiraling out to fill her veins with warmth and strength. She smiled.

But today wouldn't be about the physical, as much as she knew her internal tension could use the release. No, today she had to work on control.

By opening her mind completely, surrendering her consciousness, her *self*, her surroundings opened themselves to her.

She'd found that she was able to detect things on various levels of existence she hadn't even known existed prior to seeing them with this internal eye.

Elements, life, spirits, matter, energy, souls, thoughts, power — all showed up as something different, and with no control, she saw them all at the same time, intertwined and overlaid. It was extremely confusing and would probably take her a long time to sort out.

However, she was making progress. The more time spent sitting in that space and watching things go by, the more she learned. She found she could move around in it without releasing the tether to her body — like stretching an arm out while in a sitting position. And by moving, she came to the realization that the things she saw *reacted to her*. By experimenting with moving her awareness, or whatever part of her existed in this space, she'd eventually realized she could also affect the things she saw.

It was this muscle she was working in today's training session.

***

Several hours had probably passed by the time Redd came back to her body. She took a deep breath and opened her eyes to view her handiwork.

In front of her in the dirt was a portrait of Tyyrulriathula. Not a bad rendition, if she did say so herself. She was no artist, but a little simplistic drawing made with one's mind instead of hands was probably no feat to sneeze at.

Laughing, she stood up and stretched her stiff muscles.

She turned her back on the portrait and arched her hands over her head, groaning with the simple pleasure of it. She finished loosening up, then thrust a strong punch out in front of her. Ducking to one side as though dodging a blow, she jammed an elbow, then a fist, into an imaginary enemy and twirled around, exulting in the power and fluidity of the motions.

After running through a few sets of the routine, she straightened, bouncing on the balls of her feet. She tossed herself into the air and extended her awareness, catching her own body and changing its position in the universe, tossing herself about like a ball. She flipped and landed nimbly on a post of the fence, lost her balance, snatched herself up, and moved herself to somewhere else. By now she was feeling the strain, so she set herself down in the center of the ring.

Suddenly the absurdity of it all hit her — how much things had changed, but also how much *she* had changed — and she doubled over laughing. Her eyes caught on her little magic-mind-power dirt portrait of Tyyrulriathula again.

The memory of him filled her mind's eye, from the glint in his eye to the glint of his jewelry. She sighed. The image of his sword again floated to the forefront.

She approached the weapons rack, sliding the practice sword out of its spot. She hefted it, feeling silly, and tried a couple of clumsy strikes.

Laughing, she dropped the sword to her side.

"Oh, what am I doing?" she lamented to the universe.

"You just need a little practice, that's all," a familiar musical voice said.

***

Chani was getting nervous. Pheonix hadn't shown up to the meeting yet, and to be tardy or absent wasn't like him at all. Several of the elves seemed to share her concern.

Just when she was about to excuse herself and go look for him, Pheonix passed under the decorated arch of the council room, striding towards Chani purposefully.

She might have been fooled, but for the slight smile and the remnants of a flush on his face. Perhaps no one else noticed — she knew him better than most — but she instantly recognized the difference. She laughed quietly as he came up beside her, and leaned over to him once everybody's attention had shifted back to what a council member was saying.

"Been with Ara, have you?" she joked.

"How can you tell?" he murmured back.

"She's the only person I've ever known to make you blush."

Pheonix gave her a lift of the brows over slitted eyes and a little cocky grin, then rearranged his face to the bland mask he normally wore. It was all Chani could do to keep from laughing out loud.

She was glad those two had hit it off — Pheonix was sometimes just too antisocial for his own good. A partner would help loosen him up, and help him grow up to be a good person. And Ara in a relationship could be a disaster waiting to happen. But Pheonix, having been trained by the elves and the Rangers, would undoubtedly hold his partner in the highest regard. All in all, they seemed good for each other.

"You know I'll beat the snot out of you if you hurt her," Chani whispered to him, half-joking.

"I don't intend to, and I'd like to see you try."

Chani just shook her head and turned her attention back to what was going on … and it was then that she noticed the not-all-that-surprising lack of one other key player.

She rolled her eyes. This place was becoming hookup central.

***

The room stood with its door and large window open, not that the only occupant seemed to care about her privacy. Not large enough to feel cavernous but not small enough to be cramped, the room was furnished with maple furniture and red coverings. It was a lavish, but strangely sterile space, like an unoccupied showroom.

It overlooked a small garden, ringed in manicured bushes, beyond which was bare earth melting into grain fields in the distance. Under a red sky, the waving stalks were almost white.

She watched the children that played at the edge of the field, each daring the next to go a single step closer than the last … closer to the castle of the tyrannical Goddess that ruled them.

They were simple people, who had to make do with what was given to them. Ichiryu didn't allow much. The clothes that covered the childrens' dirty bodies were homespun sacks, probably made from the tough fibers of the very plants they played near. Two of the children were hominin, but one had light fur covering her body, a snub pink nose, and little pointed and tufted ears higher on her head than the others.

The watcher's own tufted ears twitched. She closed her eyes, snatches of memory, like echoes in a tunnel, trying to come forward. It gave her a headache.

The children's shrieks floated on the air as they scared each other and ran full-tilt back towards the village she couldn't see.

She downed the shot of burgundy liquid she held in one hand, slammed the glass down, and turned. She gasped and stopped short on finding that someone had been standing behind her.

The man was about her height, and he watched her with serious, hazelnut-brown eyes. They were deep-set in his face above a short, round nose which was tipped slightly up and dusted with light brown freckles that extended across his cheeks and forehead. The bangs of his brown hair flopped into his eyes; the rest was shoulder-length but pulled back into a ponytail at the base of his neck.

She went to push past him and he caught her arm. “Tisaki. Hey, I’m here on business today.”

Tisaki yanked her arm from his grip and went to a cabinet on the other side of the room. She opened the double doors and dug out a bottle, pulling the cork and taking a swig. She turned to find him frowning at her.

“You’re drinking again?”

The bottle popped as she pulled it from her mouth. She swallowed, making a face. “So? What’s your business, then? To berate me about my personal habits?”

He watched her for a moment with confusion in his eyes, then sighed and approached. She let him take the bottle and put it back in the cabinet. “No, I bring news from the Lady.”

“The Tyrant, you mean,” she retorted.

He pursed his lips at her in disapproval. “If she hears you speaking like that … ”

She pushed past him again and went to the window, laughing without humor. “What will she do, Hop, hm? What could she possibly do that could be worse than what I live every day?” She spoke quietly, almost without any inflection, despite the words.

“Death is a lot worse.”

“Says you.” She turned with a flourish, waving her arms. “Oh, but I’m so sorry, go ahead and give me the news from your precious ‘Lady’.”

He stared at her in pained tolerance.

“Well?” she goaded.

“Temperjoke has defected.”

Tisaki blinked. “Defected? The Chaos Ascended?” She gathered herself and snorted, crossing her arms over her chest. “He’s been with her for centuries, hasn’t he? Who would have guessed.”

"We've been put on his assignment. This is the second time the Lady has failed with this particular case and she's raging about it, so we'd better not screw up," he said over his shoulder, then left.

Tisaki stayed by the window for a few minutes longer, feeling frozen. The wind whistled in the garden below her, sounding desolate.

Decisively, she strode across the room once more, yanked open the cabinet, and snatched up the bottle Hop had taken from her previously.

She took a deep draught from it and went to the window again, the dirge of the wind outside calling an answering despair from the woman whose broken heart couldn't remember why it had cracked.

TWELVE
Bladesinging In The Rain

Redd jerked her head up, frozen in what was assumedly an incredibly awkward position, as the Lord Tyyrulriathula sauntered across the ring.

He was even more beautiful in motion.

He'd apparently changed his attire at some point, because now he wore an embroidered long-sleeved tunic that opened to reveal the cleft of hairless pectorals. His pants were green, boots brown. The plainness of his clothes was a stark contrast to the armor he'd worn previously, and framed his intricate sword even more fully. He was also wearing his scabbard across his back: she could see the silver handle poking over his right shoulder.

He stopped an appropriate distance away and cut her an elegant bow, which he held. Slowly he lifted his head, looked up at her through his bangs, his full lips quirked into a half-smile.

"Redd, right?" he asked.

She almost melted into a puddle then and there, but somehow managed a nod in response. She had absolutely no idea how the hell *to* respond. A bow, like she'd seen others doing? But which kind? The conundrum sparked the gears in her mind to begin turning again through the honey his presence threw on them.

"Y — yes. And you're … I'm sorry, do you mind helping me with your name?"

"Tee-rool-ree-ah-thew-la," he said easily.

She plonked the tip of the sword in the dirt and looked down, saying the unfamiliar word several times under her breath. She repeated it back finally, raising her gaze to meet his hesitantly. He'd straightened again while she was otherwise occupied, and tilted his head with a smile. His earrings tinkled softly.

"Well done," he said.

A beat of silence stretched between them and Redd felt herself go hot in a flush. "Well, I'd better — " she started, turning toward the weapon rack.

"Would you like some pointers?" he asked at almost the same moment, then grinned ruefully. He held out a long-fingered, calloused hand.

"Sure," she said. She didn't really care about the sword, but if it meant keeping the conversation going, she'd do what she needed to do.

As he approached, she mused on what kind of books Ara had been reading that had described *this* feeling.

"It is most efficient if I guide you through the motions," he said, his hand hovering near the one of hers that still held grip on the sword, but not quite touching. He circled her, both too close and too far away. "Can I touch you?"

The phrasing was *technically* formal and correct, but it could also be interpreted (she thought) completely differently.

"Sure," she repeated, unable to manage anything else.

At her confirmation, his hand dropped onto her wrist, sending a jolt through her. His other hand came to rest on her opposite shoulder to gently guide her body into what she supposed was the proper form for that particular sword. She wasn't paying attention to anything beyond his warmth and scent and the quiet wash of musical words from his silver tongue that she was sure had meaning, but which she couldn't be bothered to chase. Willing putty, she followed his direction. It was all she could do to remain standing.

Keeping firm hold on her wrist, he guided her through a few strikes and blocks, then stepped away. She missed a step, almost stumbled, but recovered and turned to face him. She was lightheaded and breathing fast, even though it hadn't been a particularly demanding set.

"Does it make more sense now?" he asked. Again: completely polite, detached words. But behind them …

"No," she said bluntly, and he laughed. She grinned crookedly, not caring if the expression made her look silly. "Honestly, my attention was somewhere else."

Humor flitted over his face. This close, with him holding her gaze, Redd could see that his pupils were star-shaped. Eight points, she counted quickly.

Man, everybody's weird around here, she thought, remembering Pheonix's sharp teeth, Ara's horns, Chani's oculus pupils and the thin purple lines that ran down her sides, the metallic dots under her jaw.

And Redd's own metal-golden eyes and blood-crimson hair.

"You're supposed to be with them, aren't you?" Redd asked, jerking her thumb to indicate the square.

"Technically," he said. "But they don't need me. I'm just here to lend muscle, not to participate in politics. And that's all that's going on in there right now. Honestly, I'd rather be out here."

"Won't they get mad if they see you hanging out with some random uninitiated rescue?"

"Perhaps. But I'm used to their disapproval."

"A misfit, huh?"

He grinned. "Rare as it is among elves, yes. One misfit to another, try not to take their opinions of you too seriously."

"What makes you think I'm a misfit?" Redd asked, a little snappier than she intended.

He remained unflappable. "A guess, based on how you described yourself. 'Rescue' is a strong word."

Redd sighed. "I don't think I've presented exactly the best impression to anyone initiated that I've met so far, that's for sure."

"*I* think you're doing fine. Though I'm sure you've heard this many times already, you can't help what happened to you. Folks like Chani and Pheonix, they can't *not* help people. It's kind of a sickness. They'll be forgiving of whatever you think you've screwed up."

"You know Pheonix?"

"Since he fell out of that tear in Terelath, yeah. I was supposed to be one of his trainers, but he quickly outpaced me. I had to settle for friend."

"Is he really … that thing they say he is?"

"Ascended? Indeed. I've seen it with my own eyes. He's terrifying, and I'm glad he's on our side." He studied her face. "You don't like him?"

Her lips twisted. "He annoys me. I can't say why."

Tyyrulriathula let out a full-throated laugh. "You're in good company. I can't think of a single person he *doesn't* annoy. But we love him anyway. He's single-minded in his pursuit of Justice and claims he barely feels emotions, both of which can make him impulsive, self-sacrificing, and oddly short-sighted. It's a task to wrangle him. I can see how he'd be pretty abrasive for someone who's been through the kinds of things you have."

"How do you know what I've been through?"

"I don't. All I know is that you're an uninitiated psyker pulled from a sapient-trafficking situation. Even if that's the end of the story, that's enough. I can imagine it isn't the end, though. But I'm not here to dig into your past; it's none of my business, unless you choose it to be."

"Why *are* you here?"

"You can answer that."

She met his steady gaze and the heat twisted in her lower belly again. Her breath hitched. To cover her reaction and recover, she turned to shuffle across the ring to return the practice sword to its spot.

Turning back, she said, "So, *Lord* Tee — Tee-roo … shit. I'm sorry."

When she met his gaze apologetically, he was grinning again. “Elven is hard for a lot of non-native speakers. Don’t stress it. Do you have a suggestion for an alternative you can call me?”

“You’re asking me?” Redd asked, incredulous. When his expression didn’t change, she thought about it … though thinking about anything with him looking at her was doubly difficult.

“What are the first few letters of your name?” she asked. “That’s normally how I’d shorten something.”

“T, Y, Y, R, U.”

She frowned, concentrating. “Well, T and Y would be ‘tie.’ So … Ty?”

“Ty … ” he repeated as though tasting the word. “I like it.”

“Yeah? Lord Ty sounds kinda weird, though, huh?”

“You can call me Ty. Being a Lord is a formality at best. I am Bladesinger first. The deference for having been chosen is asinine. I’d much rather be judged by my accomplishments.”

“You lost me. Bladesinger?”

He chuckled and patted the sheath on his chest. “This sword is a Lawblade. It denotes me as a chosen of the Ascended of Law, which is known as a Bladesinger. Additionally to the Lawblade, all Bladesingers are given a spot on the secondary elven Council, which comes with some political responsibility — supposedly — and the title of Lord. I love my blade, but I’d just as soon part ways with all the political shit. Ah — sorry, that’s a lot of information to just dump on you.”

“I did ask, and it’s very interesting. You know I’m uninitiated. All this stuff is new to me.”

“But we don’t want to overwhelm you. We need to start slow.” He took a step forward, the gentle phosphorescent light glimmering on his jewelry and sparking a mischievous look in his eye. Again with the double talk. She wasn’t sure if it was intriguing or aggravating or some mixture of both.

"Yes, we should," she murmured in agreement, "... take things slow."

One moment, his gaze was boring into hers, and the next, he'd glanced up over her head, tracking motion. Laughing, he stepped away with his hands up. It was a very 'oops, got caught' kind of posture.

Surprised, Redd turned.

Chani stood by the entrance to the dirt ring, arms crossed over chest, face saying she was torn between irritation and amusement. Pheonix hovered behind her.

"Okay, okay, you got me," Ty called to Chani as she and Pheonix crossed the ring. Chani shook her head, a smile tugging at her lips.

Redd looked between the two of them. "What's going on?" she asked.

"Lord Tyyrulriathula here snuck out of council." Pheonix offered. Was that … *humor* she heard in his voice? Perhaps a trace of a smile?

"Yeah, whatever, Pheonix. I've seen you with that little blonde thing around the city," Ty retorted.

Pheonix shrugged a shoulder. His armor shifted audibly with the motion.

Redd snorted. "Ex*cuse* me, but 'that little blonde thing' happens to be my best friend."

"Alright, enough," Chani said firmly but not without amusement. "Come on, kids, we need to get going. Boring it might be, but it's important. And yes, Lord Little Shit, I know what you're thinking, but you *are* required to be there."

Ty shrugged exaggeratedly, turning that mischievous grin on Redd as he passed her to leave the ring. She watched him go, and her heart skipped when he paused to look back.

"Oh, and Commander, I want Redd at the council meetings with me."

Chani lifted her brows and hesitated. Then she flourished one hand and held out her palm in a gesture of benign acquiescence. Ty met Redd's eyes briefly, then he and Pheonix disappeared.

Redd stumbled back a few steps and rested against the fence, wondering how her legs had held her for so long. She was shaking.

Chani, bless her, was quiet while Redd gathered herself. The aftermath of Ty's effect on her was one of deep loss, longing, and … fear. At how strong their connection had been, and how much she wanted it back.

"What is wrong with me?" she whispered.

"I didn't think it would be so relevant, so soon," Chani sighed, "but we just didn't have enough time to tell you everything about psykers. Sexual attraction for you is almost as dangerous as anger. Part of the reason that psykers need to be confined to the HQ during training is that they have to have easy access to null-shielded rooms. *Any* lapse of control or high emotion — including those involved in a sexual encounter — has the chance to trigger a firestorm. Psykers aren't called 'planet-crackers' lightly."

Redd stared down at the ground, feeling empty, drained. She wanted to cry, but the tears wouldn't come. Chani made a noise in question; Redd nodded, and the older woman slid an arm around her shoulder and squeezed once before dropping her arm.

Stepping away from the fence, Chani laughed. "I gotta say, you got some taste."

Redd looked down, embarrassed. "Shouldn't you ... uh, we? Get back to the meeting?" She asked tentatively.

"We have a few minutes."

Redd looked at the ground, grateful for the time.

"I've done my studies on Chaos Earth," Chani said, without prompting. "For most sapients, sex and physical attraction feels good. It's a normal feeling, and it's normal to want to indulge that feeling — safely, in an appropriate place, with any and all parties' enthusiastic consent. One of Chaos Earth's many problems as a society is that it associates sex exclusively with creating a child. Almost no initiated sapient species look at it that way."

"So that's what 'attraction' is … wanting to have sex?"

"It can be. There's lots of different ways to engage with someone. Sex is one of them. I don't have time to go over the particulars with you now, though, and I'm sorry. Like I said, I didn't figure this would come up until we were at least in Terelath. It's your body and your choice, though, either way."

She leaned forward, holding Redd's gaze intensely. "*If* something happens, try to remember to be safe, and I'm always here if you have questions or need help. I'd suggest, if you're worried about your self-control, or if you're just curious, doing some terminal research on some of the basics of biology that may have been lacking in your education. Being informed is the very first step to safety."

Redd nodded, appropriately impressed by the gravity of the situation.

"You said … most sapients. How do elves do this sort of thing?" she asked.

Chani made a face. "Elves are stuffy. The average elf does what they want, as do most citizens of the Accord. If we're talking relationships, the propriety for political players — even unwilling ones like Tyyrulriathula — is strictly regimented. There are, of course, exceptions. Tyyrulriathula purposely flouts the accepted norm of his people. He thinks elves are too stuck in the past, stagnated, and that in order to grow, they need to accept their emotions again."

Chani laughed once. "He's pushing some buttons, but they can't do anything about him per their own rules. But, to address the question you aren't asking: humans are discouraged as lovers or mates. The mere two hundred or so years a human would live is just a moment in the lifespan of an elf, and that's true of most longer-lived species, who all usually avoid humans."

Before Redd got too upset, Chani went on: "*But,* he did seem interested. I've known the little shit for most of his life. Did you think it was a coincidence that he snuck out and happened across you out here all by yourself? You're both young. Nothing wrong with having fun and not really worrying about the 'forevers,' yeah? C'mon, let's get going to the council."

"Nobody will say anything?"

"Not with the mighty Bladesinger and Commander of the Phoenix Legions Lord Tyyrulriathula sponsoring your right to be there."

"Man, how do you say his name so fast?" Redd lamented as she pushed off the fence.

Chani laughed and slung an arm around her shoulder.

They made their way to the Citadel, the tower cluster next to the Keep, a place Redd had heretofore not been to. It was five, massive, parallel, ivory towers, contrasting sharply — possibly intentionally — with the obsidian stone cliffs and dark stone buildings surrounding it. The largest of the five was the central pillar, with the four others being smaller and set off at equidistant angles from the main column.

Now that she was closer, Redd noticed that the entire base of the Citadel sat at the center of a circular building connecting all five towers.

The main entrance into the base of the Citadel led to a round room with a huge table at its center. Redd glanced up at the ceiling, wondering about the rest of the tower.

Chani took her into one of the four satellite rooms: probably the 'war room' Redd had heard mentioned, where they were holding the war council and strategy meetings. What the other three rooms were, she had no idea.

The war room was circular internally as well, with columns set around the perimeter evenly. The walls were smooth white stone with grey-blue swirls. The floor seemed to be the same material, but a deep blue flecked with yellow, green, and black. An even mixture of all the species she'd seen outside crowded inside, here, as well.

On the far end of the circle from the entrance was a raised dais, just a few steps, with a line of heavy unoccupied wooden chairs arranged across it. The room was dominated by a giant table with so many documents scattered across it that Redd couldn't be sure how anyone made any sense of it. Smaller tables were scattered similarly around the edges of the room. At one such table sat Ara, a few other angels, some elves in yellow robes, and someone who must have been the Master Healer, Arrista Legaia. The Master Healer was a short, round, aqua-haired angel with multi-colored wings that, coupled with her bouncy demeanor and ready smile, made her resemble a parrot. Redd had heard of her from Ara and her appearance was too distinct to mistake her for anyone else.

The other tables were out of Redd's view in the press of bodies.

A few people glanced her way as she and Chani entered, but when Ty appeared at her side and offered her a hand, that was the end of it. Luckily, with so many people around, Redd was too nervous to be overwhelmed by the sexuality he exuded, though he hadn't tuned it down at all.

He took her to one relatively out-of-the-way corner and leaned against the wall, crossing his arms over his chest.

"Why am I here?" Redd asked.

"If you're going to be involved," he said, "you have a right to know what's happening. You don't have a chain of command like most everyone else, and we can't assign you one. So, I'm volunteering to be your liaison. Misfits stick together." He flashed her one of those dazzling smiles, but she was too tense for it to take effect.

People around the table started talking, but Redd's translator seemed to be ignoring it. She glanced around. Nobody else seemed to be having a problem with it. She leaned towards Ty to say under her breath, "I can't understand a single word." She worried she wouldn't be able to understand him when he responded.

"You wouldn't," Ty said quietly, to her relief. "It's Ranger Battle-speak. See them?" He gestured subtly at an elf each standing near every group of angels in the room.

"They're translating. Why *did* you think I took you over here?"

She gave him a scandalized look, to which he responded with a low chuckle.

"Anyway," he went on, "they're going over current intel. The *erukahl* have somehow teamed up with a mix of space pirates, goblins, dark elves, and orcs. The extraworlders are who is approaching us. The *erukahl* are likely going to meet them along the way. Apparently, at the same time we were rediscovering the angels, those on the side of evil also were."

'"Side of evil'?" Redd asked dubiously.

"Has anyone explained the balance to you?" At Redd's nod, he said: "Without going too deeply into the particulars of metacosmic society, evil has proudly taken on the mantle. They hide behind the balance. *We* aren't the ones who claim them to be evil, *they* are."

"That's … a thing."

Ty snorted in derisive agreement, leaned closer and dropped his voice further. "I'll tell you this much: it's all too clean. We show up to help the angels and the very next day a mixed army of factions that would normally never work together comes bearing down on our heads? And through a tear? Stinks of outside interference. As far as anyone knows, the *erukahl* are incapable of manipulating tears, and if the *erukahl* had had prior contact with these other species, they would have struck Everdark down long before now. Someone's gotta be acting as a go-between."

"What's a tear? Why is that important?"

"A forced portal between two places, usually magic-based. Messy, unstable, and temporary."

"The *erukahl* are psionic, they couldn't have managed it using those powers?"

Ty shook his head. "Unlikely. Granted, we don't know a *whole* lot about their physiology or capabilities, but the timing remains the biggest indicator that it wasn't them. The angels here in Pirroun were nearly routed long before now. Why wait to do it when reinforcements arrive?"

Redd, who didn't know anything about strategy or war, just nodded. She supposed, with the logic she'd been given, that it didn't make sense.

Unable to understand what was being said by those around the table, her mind started wandering, and the reality of *war* started to settle on her. The Federation had gone through its share of historical wars, though its narrative was vague at best. The destruction wrought had spoken for itself; one of the theories floated for the miasma's existence was some great calamity that had happened during the fight for freedom. Either way, there had at one point been many megacities, with only eight surviving to the day Redd had learned of them.

"They're going over orbiting vessel composition and what we can expect on the ground," Ty murmured, interrupting her thoughts. "It's dry, so I won't recount every little detail. We're looking at about one-hundred-million strong, give or take a few squads."

Redd had to physically put her hands over her mouth to stop from crying out in shock. She turned to Ty, eyes ablaze.

"How the hell are we supposed to defend against that many?!" She hissed.

Ty glanced at her coolly. "You know why evil hasn't been completely eradicated, balance or no?"

Blinking and thrown off from her shock, Redd mutely shook her head.

"Quantity over quality. Early reports indicate the goblins are the main aggressors. They have no regard for life, even that of their own, and would sacrifice anything to see one elf or dwarf die. The majority of the forces we'll be facing will be a single clan of goblins, their soulless undead shock troops, those they have enslaved, and their machines. One clan averages at one-hundred million, thus the estimate. On our side, one well-trained elven Legionnaire can eviscerate a thousand goblins alone. With ranged or magical backup, that number goes up. With an entire squad, the number goes up exponentially. This is not even close to the first time we've had to deal with goblins in this almost exact manner. We're used to this. We have an Ascended on the field, multiple highly decorated war heroes and their dedicated troops, and the Seraphim."

"Ohh-h," Redd said sarcastically. "You mean the mysterious ruler of Everdark that nobody has seen or heard from in over two centuries?"

Ty gave her an admonishing, tolerantly amused look.

Redd shrugged, lifting her brows and widening her eyes.

Ty looked towards the sky. "She's here. She's always been here. Weakened, yes; the whole angelic species is right now, from being removed from the Book of Races. Now that they have been reinstated as the Secondborn, they will be given that power back. We've already spoken to her. She regains her strength as we speak."

"What happened?" she asked. "To the angels, to Haven ... all of it? Ara didn't know."

"From what we've been told, Haven was raised by angelic sorcerer-priests as a sort of pleasure-gardens, a place for the citizens of Pirroun to escape to. As you can see, Pirroun was meant to be an installation where they would be able to hunker down and defend in the case of an attack from Silencefall. It was a functional place."

"So Haven was like a vacation spot," Redd supplied.

"Sort of. And a last-resort escape in the event of a disaster. Volunteers were to go up, build and maintain the infrastructure."

"Lucifer …?"

"Invenes was a minor trading house. He took his wife and brother to Haven, he and several hundred other families. Each was to be given a parcel of land up there on the condition that they create or maintain something. A business, a garden, a building, a craft — it didn't matter so long as they contributed meaningfully. Then the Elysian attacked, and cut Haven off from Pirroun. The Seraphim crouched over her city, protecting the last of her people as was her role, while the storms raged and the Elysian destroyed everything around her ears. And when it was all over, she sent people to Haven to see if anyone had survived. The messengers never returned, and eventually no one could try because the *erukahl* had taken to knocking the angels out of the sky … then they were trapped."

"That's not enough time to evolve a whole species, though, right?"

"Yeah. We said the same thing. The angels of Everdark studied the *erukahl* when circumstances allowed — through skirmishes, finding the dead. They said the erukahl aren't natural. They feel … manufactured. The evidence they did manage to gather about *erukahl* biology led them to assume that the *erukahl* evolved out of one of the many animal species on Assisi before the Elysian attacked, though not which one. As to *why* they are the way they are, the problem was likely twofold; the Elysian left the planet in such a state of imbalance that any flora not inside the Seraphim's shield — the shield that steadily drained her power and left her with almost nothing — mutated.

But the true folly came with the inclusion of an ever-flowing spring, magically fed, into the largest of the islands. The excess ran off the edges, into the atmosphere. In a stable ecology that wouldn't have made much of a difference, but with the planet already out of balance, it created the cloud-cover that drove the direction of the mutations to creatures that thrived in darkness, and cut the angels off from the sun and sky and stars."

"Man, that's shitty."

Ty laughed softly. "It is."

Redd narrowed her eyes at him. "Are you making fun of me?"

Ty regarded her for a moment, then leaned close. His lips hovered close enough to her ear for her to feel his breath.

"You interest me," he murmured. "Honestly. The Rangers and elves, while doing much good for the universe, are both regimented and too formal. I'm surrounded by people too willing to issue forth whatever it is they think they *should* be saying, even if it's opposite what they really think. You are sincere, which is refreshing."

Her eyes closed halfway as he spoke, letting the throaty music of his words wash over her. "I wish you wouldn't do that," she mumbled, half-protesting. "At least, not in public."

"Do what?" The chuckle was in his words.

Pulling the dregs of her self-control together, the same that he'd so effortlessly brushed aside, she opened her eyes and turned her head to flash him an indignant look. "You know very well what I mean."

He lifted his hands in a posture of surrender, but his ever-present grin would not be banished. "Okay, okay … where were we, then?"

"The Seraphim. Haven."

"Mm, yes. For some reason, the *erukahl* hate the angels. Or, more specifically, I should say the *erukahl* Queen hates the angels. Maybe it's a predator-prey thing — as you can imagine, there hasn't been much philosophical thought on the subject.

"So the Seraphim had to constantly fend off attacks from the *erukahl* as well as watch over Silencefall. With both her and her people weakening, it was a constant struggle for her. We understand now that the reason the islands began to fall was because she just didn't have the power left to suspend them."

"Wait. Has Haven — "

"As soon as we spoke with the Seraphim and were apprised of the situation, we began to evacuate the remaining angels."

Redd sighed in relief, internally surprised at how strong the emotion was. Persephone and Lutius had risked everything to not only take her in, but then help her escape.

Even if they hadn't been Ara's family, she would have been worried about them, given the current situation.

But the relief was compounded now that she knew that the fear that her soul-sister had silently carried around would be alleviated.

Turning her mind back to their conversation, Redd asked, "But, if she's that weak, how is she an asset?"

"Seraphim is a title. They are the Creator's chosen, in the literal sense of the word. There are only twelve allowed to exist in the universe at any one time, the ultimate ascension for an angel. This Seraphim will be back to her full power soon, and, with the elves and Rangers supporting her, will be a juggernaut. She is indispensable, not to mention what she means to the angelic people as a symbol alone. Without her, they would have no will to fight or go on."

"I see."

Something shifted subtly. Redd glanced over the room; Ty did so as well.

"It looks like things are breaking up," he commented.

Redd felt her stomach tighten suddenly. In a room full of people, she could be polite and hide her attraction, but she was terrified to be alone with him — even if a part of her desperately wanted to be.

She was relieved to see Chani work through the crowd and angle towards them, Pheonix trailing behind.

"Hey," Ty called. "What's the word?"

Chani sighed and ran a palm over her face. "It's difficult. We're not sure how we can separate the main bulk of the *erukahl* army since they're all underground, and orbital scans show that the cave systems go for miles and miles. Bombing isn't an option, and magic wouldn't be effective because of that damned psionic net. We're toying around with bombing anyway; maybe we can take out the majority of them by collapsing the tunnels, but … if we don't kill them with the initial collapse, they'll just dig their way out in a matter of hours and we'll have wasted the ammo." She fell silent and shrugged. "At the moment we're at a standstill, so we're taking a break."

"Where are you off to?" Ty asked.

Chani spread her hands in a gesture of 'I don't know,' then laughed ruefully. "Away? I just need to get out of here."

"And you?" Ty asked Pheonix, who cracked a little grin.

"Accompanying the Commander. Away."

Ty jerked his head toward the door and pushed off the wall. "Well, let's take a walk, then."

And so Redd found herself following the other three through the halls of the Citadel and down into Everdark itself. The city was less empty by the minute, as more and more troops poured in from the portals set up in the main square, people from all over the universe coming to help the angels.

Perhaps by accident, they ended up at the training grounds.

Ty broke off from the other three and strode into the dirt ring, his bardic laughter ringing out.

"When I caught her, our dear Redd was playing with a sword." He turned around, spread his hands slightly, grinning. "It was cute."

"Hey, it's not my fault I haven't been taught how to use weapons yet," Redd said irritably, her cheeks and ears burning.

"Well. Let us continue our instruction," Ty said.

"What?" Redd asked.

The elven Bladesinger pulled his blade from across his chest as his answer.

The blade, as it cleared its sheath — and something wondrous happened.

Its plain silver hilt 'blossomed' into a flower of silver filigree studded with the same opals as his circlet. The thought flashed across Redd's mind; *How does he wield it like that?* Only for the question to be answered immediately.

He didn't.

The blade left his hand to float nearby, and six additional blades appeared in the space around him at staggered intervals. One burned, one dripped ice crystals, one was a vortex, one was made of shifting earth, and two were mere distortions of space, visible only as they passed in front of something solid.

And as the swords came to be suspended around him, he began to sing.

His song cascaded over her, drawing goosebumps from her flesh — its melody existed beyond mere sound, somehow encompassed all senses.

He held her gaze. The swords swirled around him slowly, like the dance of cosmic bodies.

She felt Chani shift next to her, felt the mute disapproval, but couldn't fathom why. She wanted to ask any number of questions, but couldn't look away.

And then his eyes, wild with some emotion she couldn't place, shifted to Pheonix. He stopped singing, though the fingers on both hands gracefully twisted with the melody she could almost still hear if she strained. He spread his arms wide and lifted his chin.

"Come, boy who rang the bells. It has been a while since we last sparred."

"I suppose it has," Pheonix replied blandly.

Pheonix passed through the gap in the fence. As he walked purposefully, two swords materialized out of nowhere into each of his hands. They were rather plain, but elegantly curved. One had a saw edge and the other crackled with power. Pheonix took one in each hand.

Instantly the two men were a blur of motion Redd almost couldn't follow. The song shifted, became something darker and harsher, but with a current of lively energy that was almost at odds with itself. Her brain didn't know how to process it. Ty danced in the center of the zephyr of flying weaponry, bending like a reed while his blades flashed and struck, parried and feinted.

Pheonix was no less fluid, but he was an economy of motion. Whereas watching Ty was like watching a performance, Pheonix was a machine: cool, easy, confidence incarnate. The difference between the two was remarkable.

Pheonix struck with both blades, Ty rebuffed, and almost before the elf could respond, Pheonix reversed and his weapons were scant inches from Ty's legs before an ethereal sword parried them. It became clear very quickly that Pheonix was faster by far, as it took longer and longer for Ty to counter his attacks.

The song changed again, to an unearthly wail that was physically repulsive to listen to. Redd clapped her hands over her ears, fighting nausea.

Chani tensed, took a step forward. She called out to Ty; the elf didn't respond. The blades whirred, their movements frantic and jerky. A wind picked up, emanating from the elven Bladesinger.

Pheonix and Chani seemed to know what was happening, and their reactions fed a growing concern in Redd, who did not. Pheonix's stance altered dramatically. Ty's burning sword came at him — Pheonix performed a calculated sweep, timed and angled to knock it down, where it buried itself to the hilt in the dirt, flames extinguished.

Ty's swords dropped one by one, planting in the loose dark soil like some empyrean graveyard. Pheonix darted, avoiding the blades still in the air, and with a final thwack, rendered Ty defenseless.

The winds buffeted Pheonix as he pressed forward, his sword streaking for Ty's head — Redd gasped and reflexively closed her eyes.

She heard Ty hit the dirt.

When the winds died down, she opened her eyes to Ty laying in a furrow. She hesitated for just a moment, then ran up as Pheonix straightened — past him, to Ty's side. She was expecting to see blood … but found none. Ty pushed himself up on his hands and knees, shaking his head, raining granules.

He looked up at Pheonix — silent, pissed off — and got to his feet.

A huge bruise was already spreading over his cheek where the flat of Pheonix's blade had connected.

He stalked out of the training ring and disappeared into the gloom of the Everdark without saying a word or looking back.

Redd, still crouched, glanced wildly between Chani and Pheonix. Pheonix showed essentially no reaction to what had just happened, but his dark brows were lowered, giving his strong features a stormy cast. Chani was thin-lipped with calculating introspection and concern.

Redd stood up and ran after Ty.

***

She found him some few blocks away, leaning against the outside of one of the ubiquitous buildings that filled Everdark and made the city into a honeycomb. She approached, trying to be quiet, but he whipped around and fixed her with feral, bright eyes that rooted her to the spot. He relaxed when he realized who it was, and tried to smile.

"Guess that was pretty careless," he whispered.

"That … being what?" she asked softly, reverent to his heightened emotions.

Ty's smile faded. "A loss of control." He laughed shortly, humorlessly. "The vaunted control of the elves. Perhaps I take my own instruction too literally … or … "

A hesitation, then a hand raised, long fingers stretched to gently caress her cheek. She closed her eyes, welcoming the darkness behind her lids, and leaned into his hand.

"No," he rasped, voice filled with a dry humor.

His body was drawing close; she could feel the heat of him.

"Why?" she murmured huskily, amused.

Her world still wreathed in black, she felt rather than saw his approach; the breath on her lips, the touch of his hair as it grazed her cheeks, his chest and leading thigh brushing hers tentatively, then pulling away as though he were wavering on his feet. The sensations, without sight, intensified, sent heat and prickles along her body.

"Because one of us has to have some self-control … " The words were barely spoken, but she could sense the shape of his thoughts. He was completely open. She felt his reasons for sparring with Pheonix, and she almost laughed. A pure, base need to impress her, to show off his battle prowess. He had been about to say; *perhaps I take my own instruction too literally, or perhaps it was because of you.*

"Why?" she asked again, the question twofold.

And it was then, as predictably as clockwork, that they heard Chani call out.

Ty hesitated. He was torn; Chani called again, and he leaned away.

Redd opened her eyes in the manner of one long asleep, vision taking a moment to focus. And focus it did, on the slightly-embarrassed, rueful, and mischievous smile on Ty's handsome face.

Chani came around the corner and stopped. Redd turned.

"Aw, mom, you ruin everything," she lamented loudly, so Chani could hear across the intervening space.

Chani stared, her brows drawing down, mouth open. Redd had never seen Chani so … out of sorts. The Commander, recovering, shook her head. She didn't smile. The look she gave Ty was a guarded one — Redd didn't have time to wonder at it.

"Look, you two, snog later; it's time for work. Just got word that the last of the angelic refugees from Haven are coming through … with Ara's father."

THIRTEEN
Family Trials

"We've had another outbreak among the village refugees." Master Healer Arrista looked tired as she consulted the list on the top of her datapad.

Ara nodded, feeling a pang of sympathy for the aqua-haired angel. Ara was feeling the strain of the last few days herself, but with Pheonix supporting her and with all the activity, she'd been managing to keep up.

"It's those thrice-damned *erukahl!*" The third member of their group, an elf named Riayulinathan, cursed and slammed her hand into the table.

Arrista sighed and asked wearily: "Do we have anyone left in the lower ranks who hasn't had a chance to fight this thing face to face?"

"Not that I am aware of," Ara responded. "How have the elven Healers been faring?"

Riayulinathan made a face. "Same as yours, although we have power to spare. We can keep it from spreading and, if we get to the affected in time, delay death, but without a cure …"

She trailed off poignantly, but then continued, "We can take over fully for you for a little while ... let everyone recuperate?"

Arrista nodded. To Ara, it seemed as if she was trying not to look too abjectly relieved.

"We — I mean I," Arrista corrected herself, smiling ruefully, "would appreciate that."

Ara looked out over the council room, emptier than it had been in days now that the Lords, most of the Ladies, and the King and Queen were gone, back to Terelath.

She sighed, thinking about what had brought the three Healers here today.

This sickness in question was little more than a trap laid for the angels' Healers by the *erukahl* — though for what purpose remained unknown — and it was not new. It had been around for decades, traced back to an *erukahl* drone that had somehow managed to get past the outer wall. When the drone was killed, its body exploded, releasing some kind of toxin into the air, which spread from there.

The biological part of the weapon caused sickness, but as soon as the Healers reached out to the sufferer, the toxin somehow drained them of power. So far they had just been dealing with a shortage of Healers to stave off the symptoms of the afflicted, but it was getting to the point now, with the angels in close quarters and immune systems compromised by stress, where there were more patients than there were angels with any power left.

And as Riayulinathan had stated: without a cure, they were only delaying the inevitable.

Ara frowned. The worst part was that there could be no cure without investigation. And no Healer could use Sight without the spore attacking, same as if that Healer were to try and Heal. Other than the fact that it targeted Healers, they weren't even sure what its composition was or how it worked.

Ara's hands clenched into fists. All she'd read, all her studies, all her experiments, all her knowledge — it meant nothing if she couldn't *use* it, if she couldn't save the lives of her people!

A commotion in the hallway outside brought Ara from her thoughts.

A Blackwing, so distinctive with their black wings and black robes, who Ara didn't recognize, appeared in the doorway and offered a bow.

"Miss Invenes?" the Blackwing said.

Ara half-raised out of her chair and the other two looked over their shoulders.

"Um, yes? Can I assist you?" Ara said.

"If you would please follow me. The last refugees from Haven are coming through now."

Ara's heart thudded and she suddenly felt dizzy.

She met Arrista's eyes; the aqua-haired angel nodded. Head in a fog and anxiety twisting her gut, Ara followed the Blackwing down a few halls and into a large room.

Inside was a small portal. The entire angelic council stood before it, as well as a few angels unknown to Ara, and several elves. Cira and a few of his troop were there as well; Ara's Blackwing escort left her at the entrance and joined them.

The portal shimmered and a few frightened humans, then a few angels, came through. When Ara saw Lutius, she froze with abject relief to see her uncle alive. He looked haggard and tired, his normally jovial expression hardened.

She dared to hope that she'd finally find relief from her biggest fear. She searched the faces of the angels and humans that poured through the portal, looking for her mother.

Some of the newcomers were led off in groups, passing Ara as she hovered by the open door; others were directed to stay. Her uncle was one of the ones who remained. Ara balled up her hands at her sides, her eyes trained on the portal. Waiting.

She was just beginning to lose hope when the portal shimmered and a woman stepped through. A wave of emotion rocked Ara; relief, happiness, piercing grief, shock at how bad Persephone looked. That was it, then.

Lutius had been successful in rescuing her mother. Ara closed her eyes and breathed out, shakily, trying to quiet her pulse.

When she opened her eyes, it was to her father. As soon as he was through, Cira and two of his angels came up and placed slender metal half-disks around his wrists —

something blue and glowing finished the circle, binding him. Persephone stared at him, dry-eyed and hard-faced. Lucifer held his head high, his face frozen in a mask of impassive haughtiness.

"Lucifer Invenes, you are charged with high treason against the angelic species," Freija began, her tone even and cold. She listed his crimes, while he stood motionless in the arms of his captors.

Ara's father had never been much of a father to her. He was a criminal, greedy and cruel. But that didn't keep the pangs of regret from nearly choking her.

She regretted that she couldn't have changed the past and prevented it from happening, somehow. But there was no helping those who didn't wish to be helped. And her mother had already done all she could to save those her father had harmed. It had almost meant her death.

She took in a sharp breath and realized she was crying; hot tears dripped down her cheeks.

Something must have alerted him to her presence. Perhaps he heard the intake of breath, though she didn't imagine how he could have from across the room. His eyes flicked to her, but his expression remained unchanged. No recognition, no love.

No sorrow — nothing to show he knew his actions were wrong.

That broke her in two. She put a hand on the doorframe as he looked away, the world spinning and blurring with tears and emotion. Something seized inside of her, taking the hurt and the anger and the betrayal and crumpling it up into a knot. She locked it in a box and threw it, and the man who was not her father, out of her heart.

"Do you have anything to say in your defense?" Freija concluded.

Lucifer remained silent.

"Sad though it is, your crimes are not limited to your own species, and now that we have contact with our brethren again, contact *you* deemed fit to deny us, you must be judged by a higher court made of all those you have wronged," Freija finished icily. "I doubt you will find any advocates here, but you are entitled to choose counsel. Your counsel will have twenty-four hours to put together your case, and at that time, you will be tried."

Veric nodded to Cira and the other two angels. They took Lucifer away. Persephone, Lutius and several others were drawn aside. Ara didn't wait to see what they had to say.

***

A knock came at Ara's door. At first she was tempted to ignore it, but as it sounded again, she reluctantly rolled off her bed and opened the door a crack.

Seeing Redd, she frowned slightly and opened the door wider. Redd stepped aside and Ara caught a glimpse of the worried, drawn faces of Persephone and Lutius.

"Thank you for showing us her room," Persephone murmured. Redd nodded, glanced in briefly at Ara with concern on her face, then returned to her own room next door. Ara stared at her mother for a moment, almost afraid to touch her — that if she did, she would wake and find that her mother's presence was just a dream.

Persephone reached out to touch her daughter's face, which broke the spell. They clung to each other. The tears came again, and for a while, Ara gave in to them.

Her mother's scent was soothing. How ironic, she thought, that she had sometimes wished for an adventure, for something more than her sequestered life. Now she realized the books had it all wrong. There was no glamor or glory in this. She wasn't cut out to be a heroine. She was exhausted, heartsore, overwhelmed, and wanted it to be over.

"I was so afraid," Ara hiccuped. "I was so afraid you were …"

Persephone shushed her.

Lutius offered her a cloth when the crying subsided. She dabbed at her eyes, blew her nose, and pulled back from her mother, still hunched over.

"When we first made our partnership official," Persephone said after a few moments, "we lived here, in Pirroun, but … things were so different. We accepted the opportunity to go to Haven, to prepare it for the others. Lucifer said it would be a wonderful start to our family."

"He was always so ambitious, hated being a minor trader," Lutius added in a low monotone. "Hated our father for being 'satisfied' with just the life of a 'peon.' He just hated everything."

Ara looked at her uncle. Lutius rested against the far side wall, arms across his chest, gaze down, shoulders tight with anger.

"I was prepared to support him. He seemed so damned *sure*," Persephone said. "But the Elysian attack changed everything. Dumping their power into the atmosphere, they altered the way our planet functioned. The clouds gathered, and there were storms for weeks. We thought it was the end. Many of those that came with us died. Those who were left went into hiding until we were sure the Elysian … " Her voice thickened. She cleared her throat, and went on, stronger: "... were gone. We didn't have enough to rebuild. Lucifer brought up the idea of modifying the portal we'd used to get us from the surface to Haven. At first, there was pushback. But eventually more and more relented to his side, as the time went on and we simply didn't have enough people to do the work needed for survival.

So we did it. Modified the portal. Brought in humans to help us. We — the rest of us — thought there was no one left on the surface." She took a deep, shaky breath. "Lucifer never told me about the messengers."

Ara had been watching her uncle while her mother spoke, but looked back at Persephone. Her mother's lashes were wet, but she shed no tears. Dark circles shadowed her eyes and lines marred her porcelain skin; her hair was matted, clothes rumpled and creased.

"What about the slaves?" Ara asked in a whisper. She could barely get it out.

Persephone closed her eyes.

"After a while, he — Lucifer, he met someone through the portal. I don't know the man; I only saw him a few times. Lucifer changed dramatically, almost overnight, after that meeting. He became a monster. The humans originally brought in were told they were full citizens, and afforded the selfsame rights. But then Lucifer started demanding more work, more control. Armed men started showing up … they … " Her voice failed. " … They killed anyone who resisted. I don't even know where he got any of them — the troops or the humans. The man he met through the portal, maybe. The others stayed in fear, and Lucifer somehow opened more portals, started trafficking … I st — I tried… I begged him to stop, to just … that we would make it on our own … he … " She sighed shakily. "... Threatened me.

"When your friend, the psyker, showed up, I could see how … how interested he was in her. She would have made him a fortune, if that was even his goal. I don't … I don't know what he wanted. I knew I couldn't sit by any longer, even if it … ended me."

The last words were so hollow and without inflection that Ara felt like she had to throw up. She was cold with horror.

"Why, mother?" Ara asked.

"I don't know. I don't know. We didn't have anything. No resources. With how few of us were left … I think it started out as denial, pure and simple … he wanted Haven to be his paradise, after struggling for so long … after so many deaths. And not just for him, but for the rest of us, as well. And he obviously didn't want help from the surface … maybe he didn't want to admit his failure. He was always so proud, so proud … " Persephone's eyes were tortured. "I just wanted to protect you … keep you from his evil. But in doing so, I … I was complicit. I should have stopped him sooner … so many lives … ”

Ara had moved beyond horror and was in some numb state on the other side. She gathered her mother in her arms. Persephone didn't cry, she just sat there, stiff, breathing heavily, unevenly.

"There was nothing you could have done," Ara heard herself say. "The only reason you made it out was because of the Rangers. Had you tried earlier, before they began the investigation, you would certainly have died. Then what would have become of me and Redd?"

Persephone was silent. Then, unexpectedly, she laughed — the sound was not joyful; rather, ironic and dry. She sat up, wiped her eyes.

"Ara … my beautiful, pragmatic girl … only you could manage to comfort me with those words."

Her mother turned and hugged her so tightly Ara felt like she was going to break, cutting off any reply she might attempt to make. The pressure eased after a few moments.

Persephone dug out a small cloth to more efficiently wipe her eyes. "I cannot say that things will be better now, but at least we don't have to live in fear any longer."

Ara looked down at her hands, mulling over the question she knew she had to ask, but wasn't sure if she wanted the answer to.

"What will happen to father?" she asked.

Persephone was quiet for long moments.

"I don't know. The council has never faced a situation like this. No one has ever betrayed us so. But even with the heinous level of his crimes, they cannot kill him. It goes against everything we stand for."

Someone knocked on the door.

Ara hesitated, then said: "Come in."

Lutius moved out of the way, and the door slowly swung inward.

Ara took in a sharp breath. Pheonix ducked under the doorway, angling so he could get his wings clear. He stopped, his eyes flicking between Persephone, Lutius, and Ara. His brows raised slightly in question.

Ara stood stiffly and gave him a little bow. "Pheonix. This is a surprise."

No sooner had the words come out of her mouth than a body rushed past her. Persephone threw her arms around Pheonix, who froze in place until she released him. Ara met his eyes; she tried to convey in hers her apologies for Persephone.

"Hello again to you as well, Lady Persephone," he said.

Persephone wiped her eyes with her cloth. "I never got a chance to properly thank you for helping Lutius rescue me."

Ara looked at Pheonix with wide eyes. He'd gone *back*? This was the first she'd heard of it. Why hadn't he told her?

"No need. I was only doing my duty," Pheonix said.

Persephone slapped his breastplate with the cloth. "Nonsense. I will find some way to repay you. It's only right."

Pheonix smiled and wisely didn't argue further.

"I'm sorry we could not meet under more favorable circumstances," he said instead, "but I am glad to see you here, safe. I didn't mean to interrupt, but it's serendipitous to find you all here."

"Is that so?" Lutius asked.

Pheonix looked at him and gave a slight dip of his chin. "You have all been requested to attend the trial of Lucifer Invenes, to be held tomorrow at TT 1400. Also, Lucifer has chosen Lutius Invenes for his counsel."

Lutius swore.

"Uncle?" Ara asked in surprise.

Lutius looked at her sharply. "He knows I won't lie." The words came out with the force of a whip, in answer to the unspoken question. "I'm sure he did it to torture me; he's always hated me, but he knows me. If there is a grain of truth in what he has done and what he claims, I will uphold it, even though I despise him. That Creator-damned goblin-fucker."

Ara bit her lip. Pheonix looked amused; Ara narrowed her eyes at him inquiringly, but he didn't explain the expression.

She began to say something, but Pheonix was already crossing the room. He held out a hand. Cradled in his palm was a clear blue crystal Ara guessed to be about three inches long. She took it carefully.

"I will contact you when it is time, using this. If you need to speak to me beforehand, just concentrate on an image of me," he said.

Ara nodded. He turned to open the door, but paused and gave another little bow to Lutius and Persephone.

"Perhaps we will be able to converse informally in the future, once time and circumstance permit. Have a pleasant evening."

The door shut softly. A few moments of silence passed while Ara stared down at the crystal. She knew she was blushing.

"Well," her mother said, and Ara almost flinched. "He's cute."

"*Mo-ther!*" Ara gave her laughing mother a withering glare.

"I'm sorry, dearest, really; I'm happy," Persephone chuckled, wiping tears away. "He seems like a sweet young man." She sobered and pinned Ara with a sharp look. "You aren't having sex, are you?"

Ara could have died. She put her head in her hands. "No, mother," she said from behind her palms.

"So I suppose I don't need to give you that talk?"

"For all that is holy, *no.*"

Persephone gave Ara a kiss on the forehead. "I think it's time we go find our quarters. Some rest for all of us is in order."

Persephone moved out of the way and Lutius came to give Ara a hug.

"Remember, you always have us," he said in her ear with gruff affection. Ara nodded and squeezed him.

"I love you both," Ara called as they left.

The door closed on Persephone's smile. Ara let out a gusty breath, then fell backwards onto her bed. She dug out the crystal and looked at it, admiring its color — that of a pure stream in summer. Closing her eyes, she concentrated on an image of Pheonix and felt the crystal flicker in her hands. When she opened her eyes, his face peered up at her.

She smiled shyly. "Hi."

He gave her a mischievous grin. "Hello."

"I apologize for my mother, she — "

Pheonix's smile deepened. Slightly incensed and embarrassed, Ara stopped.

" — tries," she finished.

"Don't worry so much," Pheonix said.

"I wonder something."

"Hmm?"

"I wonder why you were smiling when you told my uncle about my father's decision."

"I hate slavers," Pheonix said after a moment, "more than I hate anything else in this universe. I was raised by slavers from infancy. Were I anyone else, I would have died. They tortured me, beat me daily, and finally put me in the arena, where I stayed for over ten years."

Ara had no idea what to say.

"Your species has been isolated for so long," Pheonix continued, "there are certain technological advancements developed of which you are as yet unaware. Let's just say I take pleasure in the inevitable outcome of tomorrow's trial, regardless of who he chooses as his counsel. I am sorry that it is your father on trial, but that is the truth of my feelings, and I will not lie."

"He is no father of mine," Ara said quietly, hoping to convey the depth of her conviction through the crystal. "He has never been a father to me, as far as I can remember. So I have washed my hands of him and his reprehensible actions."

"I am glad to hear that." He did, indeed, sound relieved.

"Pheonix," Ara started, feeling like she should say something.

"You don't need to feel sorry for me."

"I don't feel sorry for you," Ara hastened to say. "I just don't see how anyone could mistreat someone as special as you."

Pheonix opened his mouth, and then closed it. "I don't know what to say."

"'Thank you' is usually appropriate in such situations," she said.

"Then … thank you." A slow smile crept onto his face. "And, regarding how I was treated as a child … I could say the same thing about you, and your father's actions."

Embarrassment kept Ara from responding.

"You know, 'thank you' is usually appropriate in such situations," Pheonix said.

Ara's mouth opened in shock, then she laughed. "Thank you."

***

The trial opened with a statement of the alleged crimes and the statement from the defense. Officiating were Chani, representative of the Rangers; Pheonix, who was impartial as an Executioner and Ascended of Justice; Zasfioretaeula, Prime War-Bladesinger, therefore representative of the elves; and the angelic council. Lutius was grim-faced but did his best to put forth his brother's wishes; Lucifer had pleaded not guilty. Ara and her mother sat in the crowd, awaiting their turns on the stand.

According to Ara's father, he was working to set up an inter-world trade. The angels were stagnating, that much no one could deny, and without resources or commerce, they would eventually die. He claimed that the man he'd been doing business with turned out to be evil, and forced him into using his mansion as a center for trafficking. As to the messengers sent to Haven from Everdark, Lucifer said there had been none.

First up to the witness stand was Ara. She placed her hands out before her, centered over the electronic pads set into the stand as she had been instructed, and the screen behind her lit up.

Her memories played — forbidden tomes, guards, humans coming in, staying as 'servants,' and then gone, Persephone's haunted face, a myriad of images of Redd and Ara's time spent nursing her back to health. Lucifer blanched and the haughty expression he'd been wearing since being led into the makeshift courtroom transformed into something sickened and afraid. Ara's eyes were downcast, and tears silently coursed down her cheeks. When the flood-tide of memories ceased, she lifted her hands. Pheonix was right there; he assisted her down from the stand, remaining close by until she returned to her seat. Her mother folded her arms around her briefly, but then it was her turn.

Persephone was evermore like a queen as she rose to the stand. She stood tall and proud and placed her hands, straight-armed, on the pads, her chin high. Her eyes met her husband's in defiance; the disgust and anger she had never been allowed to show before was now flaring from her gaze.

Lucifer's jaw clenched.

Persephone's memories were more detailed; she had seen the portal, and knew how it had been modified, but not where it led. She'd seen the dungeons, the opulent underground meeting rooms, the 'breaking-in' of slaves for bed and arena, many of whom she had secretly given treatment and comfort to, and in some cases, the release of death, breaking every taboo in angelic society. She'd seen the man who'd orchestrated it all at her husband's side, and the wealth — oh, the wealth, and the weapons, and the black market items … all hidden underneath the mansion.

She was trembling by the time she left the stand, but remained strong and dry-eyed. She sat next to her daughter and the two gripped hands.

Lucifer was called up next. He stood and slammed his hands down on the table.

"This is preposterous! It's all lies! How can I be sure all of," he paused and waved dismissively at the screen, "*that* is genuine? It's easy enough to prevaricate a person's image using today's available technology! I *demand* that you grandfather this case to the time of the alleged crimes against the angelic species, which is what, need I *remind* you, this trial is *supposed* to be addressing, and produce real, hard evidence against me, *if you can!*" He banged a fist on the table, punctuating those last few words.

Lutius hid his eyes behind a hand.

Several things happened at once. Chani surged forward as Pheonix came at Lucifer, Pheonix's swords already streaking towards the angel's head — then stopped.

Chani had somehow reached Lucifer and put herself in between him and Pheonix before the young warrior could strike. His swords hovered millimeters from her back. Stone-faced, Chani stared down at the horrified angelic traitor.

"Let me remind you of something, Lucifer Invenes," Chani said, cold and direct. "This trial is both a formality and a courtesy. Not to you, but to the angelic species. You are technically a war criminal — of not one, but two wars. It is both Ranger and elven policy, as the appointed lawkeepers of the universe, to allow a culture, species, or people to prosecute their own who commit crimes against their own, in their own fashion. These are unusual circumstances, in which said species cannot take care of themselves; and that brings me to my second point. Behind me stands a man who abhors slavers, and this is important because he is not just an Executioner but the *Ascended of Justice.*

"Just in case you don't happen to remember what that means, his authority, granted directly by the Creator, supersedes any other in this universe barring the Creator himself, *particularly* in unusual circumstances. In this courtroom, today, you almost died, and I am breaking our own law by restraining this Executioner from *his* appointed duty. This is all inevitably trivial. We found more than enough evidence in your base of operations to convict you a thousand times over. And memories cannot be tampered with. Therefore, you are guilty and will be punished, but not by me or the very, very angry man behind me, as much as he would feel satisfaction in doing so."

She lifted her head and glanced back to the angelic council, many of whom were in various poses of getting out of their seats and had frozen at the scene unfolding in front of them.

"It is the judgment of the Rangers through the authority granted to me, Special Projects Commander Chanilinaicanau M'tyoiderit Abyssterilon, that this man's punishment be left to those he has wronged the most: his own species."

She looked next at Zasfioretaeula. "What say the elves?"

Zasfioretaeula gestured to Pheonix, who also had the authority to speak on behalf of the elves, giving Pheonix the chance to make a final choice: complete what was technically his duty and end this evil — or leave the decision in the hands of those he had wronged.

Pheonix was a statue. Then, his swords disappeared and he straightened. "Seconded," he grated.

"What say the angels?" Chani asked.

Freija, Veric, and the angelic council looked at each other. Finally Freija straightened, ashen-faced.

"We — we cannot make a decision of this magnitude. The true ruler of our city is, and has always been, the Seraphim. Without her guidance — "

"Such a thing …" a voice said from nowhere and everywhere. Lucifer, who was looking worse by the moment, gripped the edge of the table.

"... has never occurred in our illustrious history. Even the schism," the voice continued as a woman coalesced in the room, "is recorded as an unfortunate event spurred on by a minor disagreement and an unwillingness to change by both parties."

She looked exactly like Arrista. Small, round and beautiful, with piercing eyes. Her aqua-colored hair, unlike Arrista — who wore hers in a series of small braids and loops held close to her head with gold wire — was styled in loose ringlets that just brushed her shoulders. A halo pulsed behind her head, and her six wings were the purest white. Her eyes fixed on Lucifer, who was petrified and agonized.

"It saddens me beyond any ability I have to articulate that one of my own children has done something so reprehensible, but the angels do not believe in execution, no matter the transgression."

Tears spilled from Lucifer's eyes and his mouth opened and closed spasmodically.

The Seraphim drew herself up. She was not physically tall, but even so, she filled the room.

"Therefore, the decision of the angels is to exile the traitor to Silencefall." She lowered her head and closed her eyes. It seemed as though the next words pained her greatly. "Perhaps something there will dispatch him in the way that his crimes deserve … in the way that we cannot."

The Seraphim looked up once more. "To be carried out immediately," she whispered.

"Witnessed," Pheonix echoed, anger still evident in his voice.

"Witnessed," Chani said with the finality of a falling guillotine blade.

Angelic guards took Lucifer away. He said nothing, did not fight. He only stared at the Seraphim, tears pouring down his narrow face, his eyes begging.

She did not look at him.

Outside the room, Lucifer began to scream, the howling of a crazed animal. Shaking, Ara threw herself against her mother's shoulder to hide her face. Pheonix glared at Chani, then crossed the room to stand beside Ara. Chani looked up and sighed, her shoulders slumping.

"You could have waited to break his mind," she commented to the Seraphim, half-sarcastic and half-lamenting. "We needed to know who his contacts were."

The Seraphim looked at Chani, a little sad smile curling her lips. "You make it sound as though I did it intentionally. Worry not, my brave Commander. I have the information you require."

Chani watched her solemnly for a moment, calculating. Then she bowed with elegant reserve. "Of course, my Lady."

The Seraphim turned away. "My aides will deliver it to you. If you will excuse me, Commander, I believe my people would take solace knowing that their Seraphim can be with them for the first time in three centuries … even if it will be on the eve of battle."

FOURTEEN
A Nail In The Coffin

Pheonix found Chani hunched over a mug of dwarven ale in the temporary Ranger mess inside the Keep.

"What, you gonna chew my ass, too, kid?" she asked, voice flat.

"I should have killed you in there," he replied, without inflection. She met and held his eyes, didn't move. The truly remarkable thing was that she was not frightened of him; at her very core, Chani didn't fear a damn thing. Then, after a pause to make sure his words sank in, he continued, "But in retrospect, I'm glad I didn't."

Chani scoffed and took another mouthful of beer. "You, glad for anything? Must have to do with Ara."

Pheonix ignored the Commander's unusual show of spite. She'd probably gotten her ass reamed by HQ covering for Pheonix, yet again. It was no wonder she was drinking.

"Yes, it does," he said, and smiled slightly. "She's suffered enough without having to watch her father beheaded in front of her."

Chani grunted, face in the mug. "Hindsight sees all. But it's nice to hear you say it. Have you visited her yet?"

"No, I was about to, after I talked to you." He grinned. "See, I'm on top of it."

Chani laughed. Pheonix felt a flicker of relief. Chani was one of the very few people that meant something to him, and she'd put her career and her life on the line to prevent an action of his that, while 'right,' was also wrong. To see her suffering over it was unjust. He'd had to correct it.

"You alright?" he asked.

Chani sighed, and, for a moment, didn't respond.

"Yeeeeah," she drew the word out in a sigh, "I'll be fine. Go on, get out of here; let me get some quality time with my booze."

Pheonix saluted. Chani made a face at him. Still grinning, he turned on his heel and left the Commander to her business.

***

Persephone had stayed with Ara long enough to help her daughter calm down and begin to process the trial and some of the new horrors she'd learned about, then said her goodbyes. Ostensibly, she'd left for Terelath already, but she'd told Lutius to go ahead and she'd meet him there. Such a good pup, he'd obeyed without voicing the questions in his eyes.

Now she stood in front of an intricately-carved stone door deep inside the Citadel.

A place most people didn't know existed.

"Hullo, ma'am," said a rough, deep voice from behind her.

Persephone stifled a sigh. "How did you even get in here, Paul?"

Paul, a hominin Ranger soldier so bland in appearance one might never look at him twice, shrugged and only offered an infuriating grin in response.

The silence stretched between them. Persephone's eyes traced the contours of the door as though she were committing every curve to her core.

"When are you plannin' on tellin' her?" Paul asked.

Persephone frowned. *Of course* Paul knew. Of course he'd poke at that sore spot.

"Soon," she said, then shot him a scathing glance. "When are *you* going to stop hiding?"

Paul's smile disappeared. "Why, I suppose it'll have to be soon as well. Somehow I doubt *Lord Justice* will let this state of affairs go on for much longer."

***

"Why have you come back?" Ichiryu said into the darkness.

Temperjoke pouted and dug a toe into the ground. "What, not happy to see me? And after all we've been through?"

She surged from the decorated chair that was her throne, her eyes blazing red in the near pitch-black.

"*I COULD KILL YOU FOR WHAT YOU DID TO ME!! I COULD RIP YOUR BODY LIMB FROM LIMB, BATHE IN YOUR BLOOD AND USE YOUR SKIN TO MAKE MY ROBES!*" She screamed, unhinged, but she did not attack; and after a moment, she subsided, panting.

Temperjoke hardly seemed worried.

"No, you couldn't, because you are one of the few who knows what being tied to Chaos really means." He smiled grimly, tight-lipped. Ichiryu sneered at him, her clawlike hands gripping the arms of the chair.

Temperjoke held his arms behind his back and paced stiff-legged back and forth in front of her 'throne.' She sank down and followed him with eyes consumed by hatred.

"But you found my replacement already, I see," he chuckled. "I just think this whole thing is a mistake."

Ichiryu snorted, recovering her composure.

"I took your counsel before as a matter of respect for what you did for me. No longer. I know that your feelings are now involved, and that makes you weak."

Irritation flashed across Temperjoke's face, and Ichiryu smiled like a cat with a mouse. After a moment, his bland expression returned and he shrugged a powerful shoulder, resuming his pacing. "Think what you will. You are flawed, and you will fail. This is not prediction or false hope; this is history."

She leaped at him. Her sharp nails and the force of the blow ripped a hole in his upper chest, underneath his collarbone; her hand punched straight through with a sick squelch. She came to rest with her shoulder up to her mid-forearm buried in his body, her elbow down to her hand sticking out the back. They were nose to nose. For a moment the only movement was his black blood running over both of them.

He smiled into her gaunt face, spattered in black. "Well," he said in a childish lilt. "I was going to leave it up to Fate, but now, I think I'll intervene. That bitch gets to have all the fun anyway."

He picked her up by the throat, removed her arm from his body with a vicious yank, and tossed her into her own chair. She moved to get up; he was there leaning over her, both meaty hands supporting his body weight. The blood from the gaping wound in his upper chest dripped down in rivulets.

"You already made one fatal mistake," he whispered, his voice thick with malice. "You trusted me."

He pushed himself upright and skipped down the steps of the dais, his capricious manner changing its face again.

"Trusted … *me!*" Temperjoke giggled.

He disappeared, leaving the babbling giggle to rebound off the walls and echo into nothing. Ichiryu remained where she lay for a moment, her harsh panting becoming the only sound in the empty, stone room.

She slid bonelessly off the chair, rolled down the steps, and curled up into a fetal position. Her hands scrabbled at the cold, bare floor, gouging marks and drawing blood from her fingertips. She writhed and arched and screamed as the impotent rage took hold.

She scrambled to her feet, to her throne; it was no small weight, but she picked it up and hurled it, where it broke into two pieces against a pillar. The pillar cracked and a portion of it came loose and fell with a ground-shaking thud.

The castle whispered, *Temperjoke is gone.*

***

Redd wandered into the war room. It was late and most everyone was resting, but she was craving Ty's companionship and thought, perhaps, he would be there. The elves didn't ever sleep, it seemed.

But it was empty.

Thwarted, she wandered the room. This was the first time she'd been in it while it was empty, so the first real good look she'd managed to get of it in its entirety. The two leftmost doors were the gilded golden elevators that she'd been told led to the Seraphim's room at the top of the middle tower. She climbed the dias stretching across the right side of the room, intending on inspecting the door behind it.

Said door sported a visible glowing sigil on its face and emanated a very 'don't touch' energy. She turned her back on it, and focused on the only other door in the room, just off the dias and to the right of the main entrance — which was slightly open. As she approached, she found a light was on within.

Her heart fluttering, she pushed the door open — and Pheonix looked up.

Feeling like she couldn't back away now that he'd seen her, she entered. She couldn't remember what this one was for, but by the abundance of documents everywhere, she guessed it was some kind of a strategy room.

Pheonix watched her for a moment more, then returned his attention to the papers, which, as Redd came close enough to see, turned out to be maps.

"Hello," he said.

She peered over his shoulder, careful not to get too close, and let her eyes range over what he was looking at.

"Hey. Whatcha working on?"

"Same thing I've been working on."

Redd tried not to take his factual statement as rudeness. She succeeded, but only partially. He sat up and ran a hand through his hair, pulling the long black strands away from his face.

"What I mean is, we're still trying to figure out how to separate the *erukahl* army from the goblins."

Redd pulled up a chair, interested, and leaned over the maps. Obligingly, Pheonix moved to allow room.

There, was that so bad, to answer my question directly since it's not like I know what the hell it is you specifically have been working on? she thought, with only mild acidity.

The largest map dominated her view. There was a long squiggly line cutting off the upper-right part of it, onto which a small, coin-sized mark was stamped. A few inches left of that (west, she supposed, glancing at the directional key to verify), spread a network of lines from another coin-sized mark. The mark looked like a bloated spider with hundreds of broken legs, and was over ten times the size of the eastern mark. There were symbols all over that were self-explanatory — mountains, trees, terrain markers, rivers, lakes — but others, still, that she couldn't begin to fathom.

"What's that?" she asked, pointing to the eastern, coin-sized mark, pressed against what now appeared to be a mountain range.

"Everdark."

She frowned and moved her finger to the spider-like shape. "Then what's that?"

"This main area right here," Pheonix gestured to the circular mark, "is the central *erukahl* cave, as far as our various intelligence sources can report." His fingers moved to indicate the lines that looked like legs. "And this is the proposed spread of the *erukahl* tunnel system, with smaller, branch family caves indicated."

It took a moment for that to sink in. "But … that … there's so many of them."

Pheonix remained silent while she tried to swallow that bit of information.

"How … why haven't they just overrun Everdark?" She finally managed.

"The first reason is the Seraphim. She has a shield over the city that repels the *erukahl* from just jumping over the walls. It also extends underground so they cannot tunnel in. The second is this," he tapped a small, blue-lined swoop encircling the outer rim of Everdark, "which no doubt you've seen; the water defense. The *erukahl* cannot swim, and large bodies of water seem to interrupt their psionics, so they can't jump over it, either, and that prevents them from just swarming over the walls."

Redd digested this, and time passed while she stared silently at the maps. Pheonix did so as well, occasionally shuffling the papers around to look at something lower in the pile.

She realized abruptly that her attention had drifted off and she'd been picking out shapes in the representations of the *erukahl* tunnels out of boredom. She went to stand up, but something caught her eye. Barely visible was a small, winding blue line that crossed close to one of the northernmost tunnel entrances, one that had been crossed out with a red 'X.' She frowned and leaned closer, peripherally aware that Pheonix had moved away to give her room.

If she hadn't been so engrossed in the patterns, she never would have seen it.

"What is this?" she asked, placing a fingertip on the blue line. She had an inkling, but she needed to know for sure. She felt somehow that there was something important there, something just out of reach.

"A river," Pheonix said slowly, and it seemed to Redd that he immediately grasped the significance.

"And the X?"

"A abandoned tunnel exit." Pheonix stood, his hands on the table. "The angels' reports show that they were scouting the area and found it by accident."

Redd traced from a bend in the river to the tunnel mouth — it was less space than the curve of her nail took up. To scale, it would probably be several hundred feet.

She straightened, feeling rather accomplished. Pheonix looked at her — *really* looked at her, in the way that made her feel that he'd been looking through her up until that moment.

"Very good eye. I must go and begin preparations. We have little time."

***

Within minutes, both the war room and its satellite room were packed. What had been before an atmosphere of frustration was now buzzing with optimistic energy. All the major players had shown up, and Redd was hanging out against one of the walls, watching, arms crossed over her chest. Ty approached, smiling. He bowed respectfully, then took up a spot next to her.

"So I heard this whole rigamarole was your brilliant plan?" he asked.

"It was more of an accident. Whatever you guys are gonna do, it's on Pheonix, not me."

"Well, Pheonix is attributing it to you and everybody's wondering how they didn't see it."

"I've got an answer to that," Chani put in, coming into view. She stopped next to Ty and Redd, looking tired and a little disheveled but sporting an ear-to-ear grin.

"Good job, kid," Chani said, then turned to gesture expansively at the people filling the room. "What we have here is a selection of some of the most respected and talented war tactics geniuses this universe has to offer, and what that means is that the simplest answer, which is often the most effective, is also often overlooked."

"So what's the deal now?" Redd asked.

"Well, we've sent a messenger to the Seraphim with the question of genocide."

Any lingering embarrassed satisfaction in Redd chilled instantly.

"W — what?"

"We need to know if we need to kill all of the *erukahl*. It's a big decision, wiping out a species, and the Seraphim has seen them from their beginning. If anyone would know if they were worth saving, it would be her. They're accidental mutants, but that doesn't mean they don't have value as a species and deserve the right to exist."

The room shifted by some silent cue and everyone turned towards the dais, onto which Freija, Veric, and the others of the angelic council filed. Freija stepped forward, her sharp chin held high. A priestess, face hidden under the cowl of a white lace hood draped over her head and shoulders, moved up with her. In her arms was a bundle of white cloth.

"The Seraphim has spoken," Freija said, her voice carrying.

A penny dropping would have seemed like the booming of a cannon.

"Her decision towards the *erukahl* … is to cleanse them all," Freija continued, casting her bright eyes over the room. "She informs me that there has been a queen egg laid by one of the lesser matriarchs. In fact, it was this same matriarch that kidnapped the child of our lost Invenes family."

Redd stiffened.

"She has tasked us with this: to retrieve the egg before the flood is released, that we might raise the new queen and teach her the true way," Freija said. "To atone for the deaths of millions by recreating the *erukahl* species and teaching them to respect the balance."

Cheering and clapping started on one end of the room and swept in a wave over those assembled. The priestess just behind Freija's exultant form bounced the bundle in her arms, her head lowered.

Little, pudgy white arms emerged from the cloth.

"Furthermore — "

Freija turned as the priestess with the bundle joined her at the front of the dais. The priestess handed her the bundle carefully; Freija smiled warmly down at it. She gently pulled back several layers of cloth, like peeling flower petals, and raised it for all to see.

The child within blinked and looked out over the audience with startling clarity. Even from her spot near the door, entirely across the room, Redd could see that the infant's eyes were a bright yellow-green, and the pupils slitted vertically against the light. From what Redd could see, the rest of the child was, what she would consider, hominin.

"My Lord King and Lady Queen of the Firstborn have graced us with our right as a species; our angelic dragon!" Freija cried out.

Redd had no idea what she meant, but it must have been important, because the cheering began again. The child didn't seem to like the noise — its face scrunched up like it was about to start squalling — and Freija held it only a moment longer before allowing the white-cowled priestess to carry it swiftly from the room.

"What the hell was she yammering about?" Redd murmured to Ty, leaning towards him so he could hear over the noise. He chuckled.

"Each species is gifted with a special dragon. Consider it a melding of the dragons' powers and the powers unique to each species."

"Dragons exist, too?"

Ty turned to look at her appraisingly, his brows lifted.

Redd glared at him. "Stop making fun of me for being uninitiated," she grumbled, incensed. "Hell, I'm still getting used to the idea of talking to an elf."

Ty chuckled again. "Put it this way," he said. "There's a reason your planet, and your backwards, underdeveloped species, 'imagined' us; elves and dragons and fae and angels. Think about it."

Veric moved up to stand beside Freija before Redd had time to consider Ty's words.

"We have a slight snag in the rerouting of the river already. I'm sure some of you expected this," Veric said. "Preliminary intelligence suggests that the Queen of the *erukahl* has a barrier around her tunnel-complex much the same as the Seraphim has around Everdark."

"Our scouts tripped some kind of alarm and barely made it back," a Blackwing Redd didn't recognize put in, "but when we sent in a solo operative, he made it fairly deep into the complex and back out again without being noticed. The area that the barrier has to cover is much larger than that around Everdark, so that could account for the focus on quantity rather than quality. We think that a skilled assassin could get inside and kill the *erukahl* Queen."

"This would be a pincer move," Veric continued, "timed so that just as the assassin was returning to safety, the rerouting of the river would be complete. Without the Queen, the *erukahl* would be fragmented and confused, so even if for some reason one or the other failed, we'd at least have a greater chance of success in implementing both." He sighed and became very serious. "But this will be an extremely dangerous task and I will not assign anyone to it, so I ask for volunteers."

There was only a momentary pause, and then someone spoke up.

"I'll go."

Pheonix's voice.

Veric looked around until he caught sight of the young warrior. Veric's eyes widened, and he inclined his head as a gesture of respect.

"We are honored. If anyone could accomplish this thing, it would be you, Lord Justice." He hesitated. "The other issue is who will go to retrieve the Queen egg. Granted, this will be much less dangerous, but at the moment, even going outside of Everdark's walls is risky enough."

"We volunteer."

Redd realized two things simultaneously; one was that the voice was Ty's. The second was much more immediate, and much more disturbing: Ty was holding her arm up.

The sea of people shifted. She could feel Ty grinning.

Veric, from across the room, looked between the two of them, confused. "Lord Tyyrulriathula?"

Ty put Redd's hand down, but continued to hold it. Redd stood unmoving, blinking too much.

Veric glanced at her, then back at Ty. "Ah, very well then, my Lord Bladesinger. I will not refute your right to take on this task … nor your right to bring whomever you wish. You obviously think her qualified. Just know that it must be done as soon as possible to minimize risk." He turned back to the assembly.

Redd was irritated, embarrassed, and hurt over how Veric had dismissed her — felt the heat rising in her in response to the emotions. As Veric went on to other concerns, Ty squeezed her hand. She looked at him; the smile he gave her was so gentle, so knowing, that it quelled the angry heat immediately.

"Admit it, you're just bringing me along to get me alone," she murmured.

"What, sex in an active combat zone with a psyker and no null shield?" He laughed softly. "I'm not *that* much of a thrill-seeker."

***

Ty let out a big breath as he plopped down, cradling his elven wine in a pitcher-flower: a flower that grew to the size of the average elf's forearm, in which the elves had taken to storing their wine. Chani raised her mug to him in greeting (dwarven beer, always), and Pheonix, next to her, nodded. He had nothing in hand; Pheonix didn't generally drink.

They'd agreed to meet in the mess hall after the meeting. It was crowded, noisy, redolent with the smell of food — just the kind of place a soldier needed to unwind.

"So," Chani said sharply, immediately. "Taking Redd along."

"Oh great, here we go," said Ty.

"No, no, you listen to this." Chani pointed a finger at him. "She's an *uninitiated, untrained psyker.*"

Ty looked a little genuinely offended. "I know that."

"I can't believe I have to tell you this, but we need to be *protecting* her, not sending her out on a fuggin' mission in an active combat zone."

"She feels like Pheonix," Ty said. Chani's brow lowered.

"How so?" Pheonix asked.

"A shared destiny, perhaps," Ty said after a moment of considering it. "It's hard to explain. The power is there, undoubtedly, but it goes beyond even psyker. And I'm not just saying this because she fascinates me."

"Okay, yes," Chani said by way of reluctant agreement. "She's exploding through all the training we've been giving her so far. She eats it up like she already knows it. She's getting *bored*, making up her own shit, and that turns out to be more effective than what we're teaching her! It's like she understands what she is on a level even other psykers don't. For Fug's sake, she shouldn't be learning jumping for another ten years, *at least*, and I caught her doing it! And, yeah, that just does sound awfully familiar, doesn't it?"

Pheonix chuckled, low in his throat.

Ty laughed loudly.

Chani snorted, not entirely unamused. "And that worries me, because … well."

"Could be coincidence," Pheonix said.

"You *know* I don't believe in coincidences, Pheonix," Chani said, then took a pull from her mug. "Anyway, I'm not going to waste resources on that line of inquiry at the moment. Back to the *point* … I need to know that if she firestorms, you can handle the situation."

"She hasn't so much as *threatened* a firestorm," Ty insisted. "I'm calling it right now: whatever she is, it isn't a psyker."

Something serious flickered across Chani's face.

Responding to it, Ty lifted his hands in a defensive posture. "Alright, yes, I'm sure I can handle both her and the enemy. I'll prove to you that you can trust us."

Chani pinched the bridge of her nose between thumb and forefinger. "Fine. But *get out* if it gets bad, and know that I have backup plans."

"When don't you?" Pheonix said.

The other two ignored him, knowing the comment for what it was; mischief, Pheonix style.

Ty grinned, wide and cocky, leaned back in his chair, and spread his arms. "Come on, what are you really worrying for? It'll be simple. And she's with Lord Tyyrulriathula of the Phoenix Legions, the most talented young Bladesinger to be seen since Andural! What could go wrong?"

"Oh, yes, because asking *that* fuggin' question before a mission always goes well, hmm?" Chani drawled sarcastically.

Ty raised his pitcher as a salute. "A toast to you, Commander, for being so supportive and positive — "

"Drink your wine, boy," Chani said over the lip of her mug, "before I pour it down your throat."

FIFTEEN
Look To The Day Star

Redd awoke to knocking. Still mostly asleep, she rolled out of bed and rocked unsteadily on feet that felt divorced from her body.

Blinking to clear her eyes, she crossed the room. Before answering the knock, she ran her fingers through her hair, a rat's nest from hours of fitful rest. And of course, given the likely state of her appearance, it had to be Ty waiting at the portal to her room, wearing his armor again. She stood there, frozen, while a smile slowly worked its magic on Ty's handsome features.

"What's up?" she asked, self-consciously crossing her arms over her chest.

"Come on, get dressed. Time to go."

A chill ran through her; fear or excitement?

"Already?"

Ty shrugged a shoulder. "Military. They always want it done yesterday."

Redd scrunched her face up as her tired brain struggled to decode that statement. Ty laughed, not unkindly, and reached out to close the door.

"I'll see you in a minute."

She suited up in her Ranger rec-suit fitted with some basic armor Chani had breezed in one day to drop off. She fit the circlet around her head, feeling the sensors reacting and tuning to her power. Sleepiness completely gone, she now buzzed with internal energy, like she was high on too much caffeine. The feeling had nothing to do with the circlet, which tended to have a similar effect, but everything to do with what she was about to do.

What Ty had volunteered her for.

As she fitted her bracers and gloves, pulling them tight to her fingers, she wondered idly what the hell it was the Bladesinger saw in her. It wasn't his sexual interest she questioned, but why he was involving her in all these things. She was barely in control, not trained at all … and yet, despite the slightly-worried looks she felt she received from some of the more decorated folks around Everdark, Ty had taken her under his wing and there apparently wasn't anything they could say about it.

Maybe it's because he can kill you easily if you get out of control, some dark voice said in the back of her mind. She shook her head. Even if that were true … if they went around willy-nilly killing psykers because they threatened to spark a firestorm, why have TKers to neutralize them? Why even have them around at all? Why not just murder every psyker born? According to Chani, the Rangers had the technology to monitor psyker births, so they could certainly do it.

None of it made sense.

She checked herself in the mirror and decided, pulling her hair back into a ponytail, that her lack of understanding was more than likely the problem.

Ty was still waiting there when she opened the door.

"Are you hungry?" he asked. "We can grab something on the way out."

The suggestion of eating unsettled her already-nervous stomach. She shook her head vehemently.

Once they had walked a few blocks down into the maze of Everdark's ever-growing inner city, she asked, "How are you so calm about this?" She couldn't hide her exasperation.

He laughed. "Don't get me wrong, this is no pleasure walk, but I've had years of training and have seen combat before." He patted the sheath across his chest reverently. "My Lawblade is not just a symbol. It is a real, bloodied blade."

Descending past the inner wall of Everdark was like descending into a busy coral reef. Redd wanted to look at everything all at once. There were large pieces of machinery being set up all around, but she couldn't make out what they were supposed to be.

It was chaos, utter chaos.

Yet Ty moved through it with direction and purpose, a bubble of calm in the frenzied preparations. The crowds of people parted for him and his gentle smile. And Redd was a remora, clinging to his belly — or maybe just flotsam dragged in his wake, she couldn't decide. There were brief greetings and assurances of good luck (*Man, word traveled fast*, she thought), but she could barely hear them.

Surreal.

It wasn't until the bridge was being lowered over the water defense that the sur- dropped away and events became real. Ty led her through the thick, sturdy arches of the main gate.

On the other side, she flinched at the bass *thunk* of the gate closing behind them. No turning back now.

What the hell am I doing here? Redd thought.

"So, where are we off to?" Ty asked.

Redd blinked at him. "What do you mean? You don't know where we're going?"

"Why do you think I brought you?" His tone was light; the words weren't meant as an insult. "You've been to this place before. You're my guide." He grinned. "As much as I like spending time with you, I needed a real reason to drag you out into certain danger. I'm just the muscle."

Redd put her head in her hands.

"Okay," she said, "well, it took us days to get back. I take it you don't want to walk."

"Probably not the smartest thing to do, no."

"So," Redd prompted.

Ty's grin remained infuriatingly unblemished. "So, what are our options?"

Redd clamped down on the irrational anger, but couldn't help the sharpness of her voice and the grit of her teeth. "Well, I *could* do my teleportation thing, but I've never tried to do it over long distances or with another body … do you have any, I don't know, elf-y tricks?"

"Good suggestions, but for two things."

"What's that?" Redd asked, exasperated.

"One: it's not teleportation. The technique you're referring to is called 'jumping'."

Redd lifted her hands and let them fall again, akimbo. "Semantics!"

"No, it isn't," Ty remanded. "These terms are regulated for use in high-stress battle situations — say the wrong thing, you'll confuse someone and that could cost lives."

There was no arguing with that. "Fine, whatever. What's the second thing, then?"

Ty raised a brow at her. "Elf-y?"

Redd pursed her lips and glared at him meaningfully. "First of all, remember when you called my species backwards and underdeveloped? Besides, I don't know what elves are capable of, and I know squat about Bladesingers. For all I know, you have super speed or something. Can't the Ladies teleport?"

"Point. Yes, but I'm not a Lady. The best I can do is run pretty fast, but even then it would take us hours."

"So I'll ' …jump' us, then." Redd lifted her brows at him. "Anything to add?"

"Nope, we're good."

"Well, aren't you helpful," she muttered.

"I try," he chirped.

Sighing, Redd centered her thoughts around what she had to do and away from the relentlessly flippant Bladesinger. He waited patiently — and quietly, which was a blessing — while she unfolded from her physical shell and scattered her awareness into the matter of the universe around her.

She retraced the route back to the now-abandoned caves, using a complicated mixture of sensing the past, psychic remnants of the heightened emotions of the travelers at the time, and other things, unidentifiable, that she could only follow blindly.

Barely feeling her body but sure in its existence, she took Ty's hand and *jumped.*

When she was back in the safe confines of her own mind, she opened her eyes hesitantly. She'd deposited them in the cover of some of the shadow-trees just outside the main, open area around the mouth of the caves — mainly in order to stay out of sight of the troop of *erukahl* hanging out in said open area, sensed from miles away. Both relief and elation that she'd managed to do it flooded her.

Heavily armed *erukahl* wandered back and forth in small clusters. The main group, led by a large female holding a wicked-looking spear, stood off to the side, chittering amongst themselves.

Ty laid an arm on her shoulder and pulled her ear close to his lips. His breath gave her goosebumps, but she suppressed the reaction.

"I'll distract them. You get the egg."

Redd nodded. Ty stood and stepped out of the tree line. Redd sunk down lower so as to avoid being seen, marveling at the poise and lack of fear in Ty's actions, even as he nabbed the attention of every *erukahl* in the area.

Ty drew his sword. He let it go at the apex of withdrawing it from the sheath across his chest, and the other six swords appeared to float in a ragged circle around his body. At the same moment, he began to sing.

The *erukahl* rushed him.

Redd didn't bother to watch. She snuck around the side of the tree line, using it for cover until it ended, then dashed across the open space to the mouth of the cave.

She only had to pause for a moment as her eyes instantly adjusted to the completely lightless interior. That was new.

But that wasn't the only thing that was new. All morning, there had been the strangest sense of anticipation about her. That too-much-caffeine high persisted. It made her twitchy.

Something was going to happen.

She hesitated, then entered the main cavern. There was nothing to do for it but continue on.

This place appeared to be nothing more than a simple cave with a branch-off on either side; its walls and ceiling were rough, and the rocky and uneven floor made it hard to keep her footing. She guessed with their large feet and splayed toes, the *erukahl* had no such issues. This area seemed to be the meeting or communal space; leaves and unidentifiable detritus piled up on the ground in various spots. She gave it a quick glance but didn't see the egg. One of the branch-off caves was where they kept items she could only imagine were stolen from the angels. The egg wasn't there, either.

The other branch-off was another living area, this one opulent compared to the rest. Cloth was actually piled up on the leaves, and a couple of dilapidated pillows lay in disarray around various baubles and shiny things.

Probably the Matriarch's, she thought. How she'd acquired these items was beyond Redd, but it was here she found the egg.

She dug around a bit to get it, buried amongst pillows. Upon picking it up, she was surprised at how big, heavy, and warm it was. It was oblong, the skin a mottled grey and white, textured like sandpaper.

Relieved and ready to get the hell out of the spooky cave, she ran for the entrance. About halfway across the main cavern, she slowed.

A figure moved in the dim luminescence from outside, seen through the mouth of the cave, only just lighter than the full-dark of the cave.

It wasn't Ty.

The figure approached and Redd backed up. "Oh," she said, sounding sick, "it's you. Why are *you* here?"

"Upset it's not your new lover-boy?" Temperjoke said, his voice a tense lilt.

Redd set the egg down and straightened, hands open and ready though her heart was pounding so hard she could barely hear. He seemed to be waiting for her to say something. She didn't indulge him. Finally he sighed and tilted his head.

"To be honest, I can't be sure myself exactly why I'm here," he said. "I did just quit my job."

"What is it you do?" Redd asked, despite herself.

"Oh, this and that." He took a step forward and his hands flowed with the words, the movements oddly sanguine for such a large man. "Today, I'm here to kill you."

Redd shot past horror and ended up at some kind of numb acceptance on the other side.

"Why?" she whispered.

He clucked his tongue impatiently. "Maybe it's because I still feel like I owe her something, or maybe it's because I feel like I should help you."

"Her? Who? What the fuck kind of logic is that, killing me to help me?" Redd could hear the hysteria in her own voice, badly hidden behind sarcasm.

Temperjoke smiled gently. The presence she had sensed within him on their last meeting rose again. Her jumpiness finally made sense, but by then it was too late.

"I'm just drawn to you, I guess."

Redd went to back up, but the electrical impulses carrying the command from brain to feet were hijacked somewhere mid-spine. Temperjoke suddenly stood in front of her, against her.

And then, pain.

Pain so intense it choked her like deep water filling her lungs. She was drowning in it.

He twisted the dagger she hadn't seen, wringing an involuntary grunt from her, then wound his arms around her body. He smoothly lowered her to the ground, making the soft shushing noises one would make to quiet an infant. She convulsed and clawed at the dagger; he took her hands and held them. Her legs flailed, scraping against the ground without finding purchase.

"This may be the last time I can help any of you," he murmured. "Remember this name: Ichiryu."

Fireworks went off in front of her vision.

Confusion — fear —

PAIN.

Worse than dying, the sensation of something not-physical violently ripping away.

She tried to scream, but through the roaring in her ears, all she could hear was the choking of her blood-filled lungs as she struggled — and failed — to breathe.

The pain was in her soul, in her mind — the agony of transformation far outweighing mere physical injury. It was almost a relief when her oxygen-starved brain shut down and dropped her into something beyond darkness, beyond sensation.

***

As the last *erukahl* fell, Ty suddenly became aware of a huge force of power nearby. Without hesitating, he dashed towards the cavern.

He reached its entrance and took in the scene at a glance — the smug, sick grin on Temperjoke's face, Redd's unmoving, prone body splashed in something that glimmered — and sent his blades streaking at the Ascended. Temperjoke disappeared before the ethereal weapons could reach him. Ty swore and sheathed his Lawblade.

"*COWARD!*" he yelled into the empty air.

After a moment, the echoes died away. The Chaos Ascended didn't reappear, to Ty's frustration. But maybe that was for the better: Ty had more pressing matters.

He knelt next to Redd. She wasn't dead — he could still feel her life-spark — but she wasn't breathing. Confused, he checked her pulse. Nonexistent.

Well. Whatever was keeping her soul around, he wasn't about to press his luck with it and waste time.

Mindful of her state, he picked her up, shuffled over to grab the egg, and turned. The best thing to do now would be to get her the hell back to Everdark. He was no Healer, and only they would know what to do with her.

"I don't know what to do with her!" Arrista cried. She stood over Redd, who lay with disquieting stillness in the bed in her quarters. Ty had run at his limit for hours, checking Redd's life-spark as often as he could. He'd been barely on his feet when he finally crossed into Everdark, but had still streaked to the inner city as fast as his legs and the heavy doors would allow. A representative of the Seraphim had intercepted him and taken the egg.

He figured he should bring Redd to her room rather than the medical facilities. Better not to cause drama. Having to run through the city was bad enough; he only hoped he was fast enough that few people had noticed the glimmering golden liquid covering both of them.

THAT had been a shock.

Maybe I'm not so far off with my comparisons of her and Pheonix. As glib as he had been the night before with Pheonix and Chani, the thought sent a chill through him.

But they'd made it, and so far he hadn't heard of any commotion about his arrival. Surely Spiraea was watching over them for Redd's soul to still somehow be clinging to her body.

C'mon, Redd, he thought, something in his chest twisting. *You're too stubborn to die.*

He sat next to the window, exhausted, fingers curled around his necklace for comfort.

"The angels have been cut off for so long, much of our ancestral knowledge was lost," Arrista continued, solemnly. "We're only now able to crack into the Angelic Record again, and I can't find anything in there about this!"

Ty sighed. "But you agree the life-spark is still there?"

Arrista paused and frowned at Redd. "Yes," she said slowly, "it is. I cannot explain it, though."

The door burst open and Ara, crying, ran into the room, clutching a large tome to her chest. Behind her was Pheonix. Ty nodded slightly to him, and Pheonix returned a bow.

"Lord Tyyrulriathula."

"Come, no time to be formal," Ty said. Pheonix nodded in acknowledgment and went to stand just behind Ara, who was fumbling with the book.

"Ara, what do you have there?" Arrista asked.

Ara didn't respond, only muttered to herself, sniffing back tears. She flipped pages, then slammed her fist down on the bed. "I can't read it!"

Ty recognized some of the symbols as they flashed by under the angel's tiny, quaking fingers. His brows went up and he pinned Pheonix with an accusing stare. Pheonix met his eyes evenly and shrugged. Ty made a mental note to ask about the book later. Trust Pheonix to be the one to find the damn thing.

Ara yanked the sheets back and stretched her hands over the form of her friend. Arrista had already Healed the wound from the dagger, but it had made no difference in the redhead's state.

For long minutes Ara poured power into Redd's prone form. Until her hands, haloed in white, were trembling, and she was sweating with effort. Still no change. Arrista laid a hand on her shoulder.

"I can't … I can't … " Ara hiccuped.

Arrista hugged an arm around Ara's shoulders. Ara turned into her, laid her head on Arrista's chest, and surrendered to tears.

That became the only sound in the small room.

Ty jerked his head to look at Redd — dimly aware the others were doing the same — given only a moment's notice before a golden radiance filled her veins, lifting her off the bed. It poured outward in a kinetic wave that blew back his hair and displaced some furniture around the room.

She dropped back onto the mattress bonelessly.

A sharp intake of breath pierced the silence. Redd shot to a sitting position, violently coughing up blood. She curled her knees and fists to her chest while the paroxysms wracked her.

Ty stared.

Though her outward glow had dissipated, he was almost blinded by her life-spark.

It was *changing.*

The life-spark was the marker of the soul. A person was born with it, and it didn't change.

But the bright white burn of a human life-spark sloughed away in Redd, to be replaced by ephemeral golden light …

So much for avoiding drama, he thought sardonically.

He met Arrista's eyes. By the look on her face, she saw it, too.

"Redd?" Ara quavered as Redd's coughing fit subsided.

***

Redd was nowhere.

A consciousness, retaining the distinct sense of self, but with no sensation.

Perhaps the lack should have sparked some emotion, but there was just ghostly tranquility.

Maybe this is what dying is like, she thought, detached. *I guess it's not so bad. I did my best.*

I hope Ty got out with the egg.

Expectation grew of — something. But only nothing remained. What was after dying? She hadn't ceased to exist, but she also wasn't anywhere. Was this it, then? A mind trapped in nothing? That sounded like hell.

Restless, she tried to feel something. Tried to move.

The attempt managed to uncover a source of warmth nearby. She focused on it.

Elation flared: the golden light!

Maybe I'm not dead?

Gratefully she fell into it, only realizing as she did that it had changed. It had always simmered, a transient motion — seen as through glass.

A barrier which was now gone.

The light filled her vision, and she tried to reverse direction, but it was too late.

"So, you've come at last."

The voice reverberated inside of her, a strange mix of child and woman, light and dark, soft and loud. A hint of the halcyon music rose and fell with the cadence of the words.

"It's you," Redd said … or, tried to.

The light enveloping her dissolved into a naked hominin form, floating in the dead space, long hair streaming up from its scalp. A golden, genderless being.

With a hole in its chest.

"What's happening? Where am I?"

"Time," the being said, "is something you will have, but you don't share it. If beheld, the night reveals all."

"Great. Riddles. Isn't that just my luck."

Despite her annoyance, something about this was right … and more than right. Familiar.

"You know more than you know," the being insisted, floating closer. Its arms spread. Redd wasn't sure she had a physical form, but nonetheless she got the sense of a hug.

"What are you doing?"

Redd became aware of a slowly-growing feeling of tugging. Like an invisible hand had taken hold of her chest, pulling — not to direct her, but to siphon her essence.

The being pulsed, and the feeling lessened.

"You're — protecting me? From what?"

"Your vessel is damaged. Without interference, you return to the source." Though it didn't have a face, Redd got the distinct impression of being looked at. "You must fight it, or all will have been for naught."

"Fi — fight what? *Am* I dying? That's what you're saying, isn't it. Tell me, how do I fight it?!"

She grunted, the siphoning returning with a vengeance. The being pulsed again, but it wasn't strong enough to dispel the pull entirely. Panic surged.

"No," the being said weakly. "If you lose yourself, you will lose all."

"I don't — what am I supposed to do? How do you *fight death?!*"

"Do as you have done before."

A ripple echoed through Redd and the space around them, emanating from the consciousness that was Redd. The words echoed with unexpected truth.

The ripples formed images. The scenes from her nightmares. The girl's golden eyes staring out of her cherubic, bloodstained face.

Realization.

Redd reached out to the being. Inside its incandescent depths, she thought she saw a smile.

And as she drew it into her, the music crescendoed, shaking the foundations of Redd and the space around her.

A last whisper wove into the dying throes of the song:

Look to the day star…

***

Somewhere, deep in space, a long way off, a warm golden halo washed over a sphere of hardened light.

A crack appeared.

***

Redd groaned, wiping her mouth. "That fucking sucked … "

Her head was pounding and her chest still hurt — but it was the strange, phantom hurt that she'd experienced previously after being Healed. She had a vague sense that something had happened, but her recent memory was all pain and halcyon light.

"What, the dying, or the coughing?"

Redd fixed Ty with a weak glare, which he grinned at. He looked beautiful even while tousled, covered in dirt and dust, and the dual glittering and black stains of what she belatedly realized must be her own and *erukahl* blood. She wondered how much time had passed that he hadn't even changed out of his armor.

"I'd probably have to say both," she muttered and levered herself up. Her voice sounded raw to her own ears. She looked down at herself covered in golden blood and made a face.

"Anyone got a towel?" she asked with tired sarcasm.

Arrista and Ara cleaned her up and changed her bedding and robe. Redd collapsed, breathing hard and wiped from attempting to help. She was incredibly weak.

"What happened? Who did this to you?" Arrista asked.

When she could speak, Redd recounted the encounter with Temperjoke, up to the last thing she remembered.

"I must have come in just at that point." Ty put in as she finished. "I saw the bastard, but he disappeared before I could catch him." Ty shook his head. "Damned coward."

"Who was he?" Redd asked.

Ty gave her an unusually somber look. "Temperjoke, the Ascended of Chaos."

Redd stared at him for a moment, unsure of how to respond, then snorted. "That's not a very funny joke."

There was no response from the serious faces surrounding her bed.

Redd looked down. "Okay, awkward."

The door opened and Chani's gaze swept the room.

"I don't understand it, either," Ty said quietly, to the Commander's unspoken statement.

"She was human when she came here," Arrista hastened to add.

"I know, everybody felt it." Chani said. "But it's not impossible; we've been fooled before."

"Historically, it's happened with angels, but only when shifting between species," Arrista said. "But she's not an angel … "

"What the fuck are you talking about?" Redd's sharp interjection got their attention. She was trembling.

Chani's eyes fixed on her.

"Your soul has shifted. You … released a burst of energy when the shift happened. Some people are saying it felt like the Creator, some say it felt Elysian — "

Redd's heart lurched.

"I'm not any fucking Elysian," she started, but the panic was taking over.

Ty and Chani spoke over one another, but Redd didn't hear them.

What else could this power be? a calm voice asked inside her mind. *That light you didn't want to talk about? Your ability to fight with no training? You really didn't think you were that special, did you?*

Her mind was unhinging. Pulse racing. It was all happening again, her parents all over. They were going to ostracize her too, or worse. She knew the history, they'd almost destroyed the angels! The Secondborn! They wouldn't let her get out of here; not alive.

Outside noise came in as static — were they saying her name? — paranoia, fear, anger rushed up to overwhelm. Her vision went grey at the edges. She jerked the blanket over her head, unable to fight the panic as it overtook her.

The last thing that registered was Chani's voice: "See, this is what happens when you ask 'what could possibly go wrong?' before a mission, you pointy-eared freak."

SIXTEEN
Ain't Mental Illness Grand?

Redd slept.

The nightmares came again. Eventually, they too receded, and she slipped into deeper slumber.

She surfaced from her recuperation several times over the next few days; Ty or Chani or Ara were always there, forcing her to eat or drink, trying to engage in conversation. Once she awoke to Ara's voice, the little angel recounting the latest details from around the city. Disinterested, she'd fallen back to sleep.

Part of her knew she was hiding, deliberately sleeping to avoid the necessity of confronting her new identity. But, she rationalized, she did need the extra rest. It had been a very rough few days.

She'd technically died.

In all her dreams, the golden figure did not return.

On the third day, she couldn't physically sleep any longer. She laid on her side, silently, unmoving, her head pounding and tummy growling and bladder full … but Ty was in the room, reading a book, and she didn't want to let him know she was awake. She couldn't handle the interaction.

The door opened, and she closed her eyes.

Chani and Ty talked, and Redd let her mind wander.

Elysian. I'm Elysian.

Something inside of her despaired.

She felt dirty, spoiled. If she could throw up and expel the Elysian out of her, she would — over and over, as many times as necessary — but it was there, irrevocably, crouching within her, a fistful of nerves in one hand and a grasp on her soul with the other.

Elysian.

One of the most despised species to ever exist. Responsible for almost wiping out the angels, the Creator's chosen.

Ara's people.

How many had they killed? How much knowledge was lost?

How many other species hadn't been as lucky as the angels, of whom nothing but dust remained?

Elysian.

She shuddered uncontrollably, closing her eyes to let it wash over her.

She was a monster.

Elysian!

The urge to run, to abandon everyone before the situation could devolve into a repeat of her parents, flooded her system. There was no way they'd let her —

"Hey," Chani said, close by. "I know you're awake. Talk to us."

Redd pulled the covers over her head. Chani sighed and sat on the side of the bed. Redd felt the weight of a hand on her lower back. She twitched from the contact and curled up.

"Redd," Chani pressed. The hand, the sudden attention of the two minds in the room, her thoughts still in such a dark place, all combined to send her panic spiraling out of control. She threw off the covers, kicking at Chani's hand (she missed; Chani was far faster) and sat up.

"*What!*" She shrieked. "*What do you want me to say?! I'm sorry?!* ***I*** *didn't even know what I was!* How was I su— what — I — "

The words tumbled into incoherency and Redd gave in to the desperate sobbing of someone pushed way too far.

Chani watched with brows knitted and Redd wanted to scream again for the pity she thought she saw on her face, but the tears wouldn't stop long enough. Chani captured her flailing hands and held them, and Redd collapsed against her chest.

Hazily, through the outpouring of grief, she felt the mattress shift, then a warm presence behind her. Ty's arms curled around her shoulders, his head on her back.

She hated them for staying and seeing her like this — but hated herself more:

For falling apart, for wishing they'd go, for wishing they'd stay, for not being able to make up her damn mind, for not being able to think straight, for the tears that came so hard she could barely breathe.

For not knowing who and what the fuck she was.

For being so weak.

For asking why, if she had all this power, she had let her parents do those things to her.

That was what she hated the most.

Chani let her cry herself out, then helped her clean up, despite Redd's feeble protests that she'd be of more use somewhere else.

"Are you ready to talk now?" the Commander asked gently. Numb, Redd nodded. "You *are not* Elysian. And even if you were, it wouldn't matter, because we're not xeno-antagonist. Actions matter more."

"Then why —"

"I said *some* people. You're more fragile than you want to admit, so I don't blame you for your response. But you have to fight it."

Redd physically startled. That sounded so familiar. Hadn't she heard that recently …?

"Then … then what am I?" she asked.

Chani shook her head slowly. "We don't know."

"You're telling me," Redd said shakily, "that none of you — Pheonix the Ascended, the Seraphim, the Master Healer — none of you — know … *what I am?*"

"At this moment, that's correct."

Redd stared at the blanket, eyes unfocused. "Great." Then, after a moment: "Where do we go from here? What's going to happen to me?"

"Nothing changes. I've made arrangements for you to participate in the action here if your opinion on doing so hasn't changed. You'll still be taken to Terelath and, eventually, HQ, after this is over. Hopefully at HQ we'll be able to scan you and find out more about your biology." Chani put a hand on Redd's shoulder. "Remember what we talked about before. There are lots of things we don't understand in this universe, Redd. I'm sorry you ended up being one of them," Chani quirked a sardonic half-smile and Redd felt her own mouth respond. "I empathize with how disorienting this must be. But you're not alone. We won't abandon you, and we *will* help you find a way through this."

Redd sniffed back more tears, silently rested her forehead on Chani's shoulder. The older woman hugged her tightly and Redd squeezed in return, feeling her strength return.

When they parted, Chani caught her gaze and smiled encouragingly, patted her, and got up to leave.

***

Redd's explosive outburst seemed to help ease the inner tension she'd built up over days of isolating herself, and over the next few days she was able to get up and do a few small things, though she was wobbly — mentally, emotionally, and physically.

Chani explained life-sparks and how there was no way to hide or alter one, not without leaving telltale markers. While Pheonix and the Seraphim couldn't tell her what she was, they *were* loud on the subject that she wasn't Elysian. No one was quite sure how the rumor was started, but Chani informed her they were actively investigating it.

When they could.

There was that invading army, and all.

Even though Redd was awake and moving about, she still wasn't recovered enough to join the others in the preparations, so confined to her room she remained. The others wouldn't leave her alone for long, though, and continued rotating in shifts to spend time with her. Ty was in the most, followed by Ara. Chani, still deeply embroiled in war stuff, popped in and out when she could. Arrista accompanied Ara once to check Redd's vitals and mental state. Even Pheonix came to visit once, with Ara, though that had been awkward.

She'd been gifted a terminal and a basic replicator for her convalescence, which had made things much easier. As much as her friends had gone above and beyond to visit, no one had the time to wait on her hand and foot — and though her physical strength came back quickly, her emotional state remained delicate. It would be bad if she left to go to the d-fac (meaning 'dining facility') and someone flagged her for being 'Elysian.' Better for all involved if she rested as much as she could.

So she'd started some of the terminal learning Chani had suggested, and it was just as illuminating and overwhelming as she'd anticipated.

On the fourth day of confinement, Ty came to visit while she was on the terminal. She plopped on her bed and he took the only chair in the room.

"How are things looking out there?" she asked.

He let out a little breath, ran a hand back through his hair. "Progressing. But slowly. You're still insisting on joining the action?" Redd nodded. "Chani wanted me to confirm one last time. She's got a spot for you in a patrol."

"A patrol? *Outside*?" Redd exclaimed.

"Of course not. Inside the city limits."

"Oh. Why?"

"Our enemy has superior numbers and they're devious — we're not taking the chance that they don't have some way past the barrier. If they get inside the city, we've lost." Ty reached out, stilled her restlessly fidgeting hands with one of his own. "But don't worry. It's a chance, but a very small one. You'll be fine. The patrols are just a precaution."

Redd nodded, uncomfortably aware of him. His hand on hers was warm. She looked up to meet his eyes —

— to find him making a ridiculous face.

She burst out into helpless surprised laughter and he sat back with a self-satisfied, smug grin. So she lobbed her pillow at him, which he didn't bother to deflect. It *poof*ed against his face and fell into his lap.

"Go get me something from the mess hall!" she cried, pretending to be outraged while trying to hold in the giggles, and pointed at the door.

Laughing, he left.

***

Tisaki watched steel-colored clouds slide listlessly over a maroon sky. Sheaves of silver-white grains shifted around her, with her body, with the wind, as she moved through them.

What this planet was called before Ichiryu's arrival, what it looked like, what the people had been like … nobody knew or remembered. By design or by tampering, the people were not long-lived. They had little education, almost no religion, and no form of written communication. Ichiryu made sure to keep them cut off and without hope.

Tisaki didn't know what Ichiryu needed the people for, why she didn't just wipe the planet clean, but she also didn't care.

Standing in the field, immersing her full senses into the planet, she could almost remember …

She frowned.

Remember what? What could I possibly be forgetting? Ichiryu birthed me, from that same foul magic she creates all her servants.

Can that really be true? Something asked. *You hate her with every fiber of your being. You disobey her at every opportunity. Are you really hers?*

Tisaki ignored the voice and took a decisive step forward. She'd wandered far from the castle, either boldly or subconsciously. The village was almost in sight.

The sound of children laughing came to her with a shift in the breeze. She tensed; they came into view. Two of the ratty, dirty brats that inhabited this place, doomed to live a pauper's life under the thumb of a tyrannical Elysian who fancied herself Ascended. The two children laughed, chased each other around, and drew closer …

Tisaki froze like a deer scenting the wolf. All but one movement ceased; her right hand lifted of its own accord, placed her open palm gently on her lower belly.

Something about this motion brought such mental pain it was almost physical. She blinked away sudden tears. The children noticed her then, and her moment was shattered as they cried in terror and bolted back into the inner ring of huts that constituted this village.

Bitter and angry without even knowing why, Tisaki retreated to Ichiryu's obsidian fortress.

She opened the door to her room, and stopped.

Ichiryu stood by her window, looking out of it.

The window that had the view of the grain fields, and the village.

Tisaki swallowed against a tight and dry throat.

How long had she been there? Had she seen … ?

Tisaki bowed slightly as Ichiryu turned just enough to show her profile.

"My Lady," Tisaki said, choosing to err on the side of deference in case the mistress was in one of her many mercurial bad moods.

"The time to strike is now," Ichiryu rasped. "You know I don't tolerate failure."

Tisaki blanched, the heat and life culled from her body. Stiffly, she bowed.

"It will be done, Mistress," she whispered.

***

Redd sat curled up in her bed, reading. It was a good change from the terminal. The Everdark library, large to begin with, had swollen anew with literature from Haven. Ara had donated her personal books, the illegitimate gifts from her father, and it was one of these Redd was reading. The journal of an angel written prior to the Elysian conflict, a female General in charge of watching over Silencefall.

This was how Ara found her.

At the timid knock, Redd called, "Come in!" and immediately set the book down in concern.

Ara had a freaking giant wing on her back (just one, which was odd) — white fading into pink towards the ends of the largest feathers, shimmery when light hit it, almost appearing glitter-dusted. But because of Ara's state, Redd couldn't very well ask about it.

Ara's pale cheeks were streaked with tears. She stuttered incomprehensibly. Redd quickly crossed the room and took the little angel in her arms, hoping to calm her enough to make some sense out of her.

"Pheonix," Ara finally sniffled. "It's Pheonix, he's been gone too long … I can't … he's … *I just know*, Redd!" Her voice dropped to a horrified whisper. "He's in danger. I can feel it."

It was chilling to hear. Redd didn't bother asking how Ara knew, she trusted Ara's intuition. Especially when it came to Pheonix. The connection between those two was so strong she could almost *see* it.

"Have you told anyone else?"

Ara hung her head, the long, white-blonde strands of her hair falling to partially obscure her face. “Chani.”

“So, what’s the plan?”

Ara shook her head, her shoulders curling in preparation for another round of crying.

“Chani said that all they can do is wait … if he doesn’t return … there’s nothing they can do … he, he’s one of the best … if the *erukahl* … if they can … ”

She couldn’t finish, but she didn’t need to. If the *erukahl* could take out the revered and feared Pheonix, that meant, first of all, that the plan had failed. The whole *erukahl* army was probably lying in wait, or at least as many as would be needed to counter whatever the defenders of Everdark could muster up — which wasn’t much.

Even though she didn’t get along with him as a person, that didn’t matter. Pheonix was in trouble.

Redd let the little angel exhaust herself crying, then helped her into bed. Redd pulled the covers over the small form that just then seemed all the more frail. Ara looked up. Her eyes were black with tears and emotion; like the night sky, they trembled with stars.

“I almost lost you. I can’t lose him, too ... ”

The words were so ghostlike, so full of sorrow. Redd’s tentative determination cemented in an instant. She nodded and leaned down to give her friend a hug.

“Sleep, my love. It’ll be alright,” Redd murmured. “I promise.”

***

Pheonix knew as soon as he approached the dam site that something had gone wrong.

The workers were understandably going to be quiet, but this was a silence that stank of death. He called Malol and Bedaestael to him, feeling them wake, and strode forward. He needn't soften his step; he naturally made no noise. Useful in a hostile area.

The work site was in the middle of a forest — the river cut through it — in a small clearing that housed the caved-in old tunnel entrance being excavated for this plan. Emerging from the trees, Pheonix assessed the situation.

No workers, but there were signs of a struggle: a splash of blood here, a fallen tool there, fresh scrabbling in the dirt. Without hesitation, he descended into the depths of the recently-opened tunnel, his eyes shifting to function in the almost complete lack of light.

He followed the winding corridors downward, ignoring the branch-offs that felt like dead ends in favor of the main passageway.

No *erukahl*, no captives, no sound. Not even any corpses. The walls of the tunnel were rough near the entrance, but smooth deeper in. Veins of glowing crystal appeared sporadically in the strata the further down he went. In places, crystal clusters jutted out to form a sort of natural light fixture. Not that he needed it.

He made it to the main thoroughfare near the hollow blister that was the Queen's chamber without glimpsing another soul, which told him his mission had failed. It was too late to turn back now — they would be surrounding him from behind. He had to find a defensible position, and keep moving so they wouldn't become suspicious and launch the assault before he was ready. Malol and Bedaestael were electric in his hands.

The main cavern opened up before him and he was out of time.

A brief glimpse past the outline of the end of the tunnel confirmed his suspicion; empty. He whipped around. He felt them before he saw them, but the two senses were so closely linked that it took a mind like Pheonix's to notice any delay. They came in a river of sleek, phosphorescent white bodies. The first one that tried its psionics on him got a nasty surprise, and lost its head.

Psionics didn't work on him. He was immune to much magic and much mental trickery. Just another peculiarity of the enigma known as Pheonix.

He was in no mood for theatrics as they converged upon him, clawing each other, trampling, shoving. He aimed to kill in one strike, to conserve his energy. They had numbers, but no skill. At least not enough to spar with him one on one.

And yet they still poured into the tunnels, and that forced him back against the walls. No matter how many he killed, more launched over the fallen and came at him, and he knew that they would take him down by sheer bulk. Eventually, they would swarm him so he couldn't fight back.

He greeted this knowledge with the same stoicism he used to deal with all things, but for one small regret.

I'm sorry, Ara.

His body was a machine, cleaving a milky torso in half here, taking a head off there, gutting another, cutting a leg off at the thigh here. He would take down as many of them as possible.

He could do that much to assist the war effort; let his death mean something.

***

With Ara asleep, Redd stole out into the ever-teeming streets of Everdark's inner city. No one took notice, thankfully. She'd equipped herself with her Ranger gear, her stomach full of butterflies on methamphetamines. The last time she went outside the barrier, she'd died.

But this was for Ara.

The thought gave her strength.

At the inner wall, she looked up — and was momentarily taken aback that she could *see* the barrier now. In some strange way it was there and wasn't — a shimmering veil over the city that consisted of pure love and prayers, tied to the Seraphim's power. It was amazing.

And she had to get through it.

Hopefully the Seraphim would be distracted. Hopefully no one would notice her. Hopefully the barrier just kept things out, not in.

There were a lot of ways this could go wrong.

Fucking tick tock.

She opened her mind and …

The universe revealed itself to her comprehension in a way that it hadn't before. It was absolute chaos, and for a moment, she almost blanked out. Then her mind went about sorting and shutting things off — *tuning* — like an experienced technician with a complex rig.

Just as she'd done with the ambush at the landing site.

When it settled, she was left a little shell-shocked. She could sense everything around her, but in a muted form. Were she to focus on any one thing, she could bring it to the forefront and examine it from any number of angles, but she wasn't ready to figure it out just yet. She shifted her focus upward and outward.

Pheonix's trail was easy to spot; the man's psychic residue was like fucking fire. She followed it at a speed that was incomprehensible, even to her, and 'jumped' to the mouth of the tunnel leading down into the bowels of the Queen *erukahl*'s lair.

Opening her eyes and coalescing into her body at once was a relief and a regret. To say that she was only confined to her five human senses (one of which was useless in this scenario — she wasn't about to lick the ground) and her psyker senses would be a falsehood; she was beginning to realize that the way her brain worked had changed on a fundamental level. Whatever had happened when she'd given off that light (she still didn't remember) had left everything different, but not in a way she could readily, intellectually grasp.

A heady sense of power and confidence flooded her.

She strode into the darkness, not surprised that her enhanced vision could pick minutiae out of the gloom with no troubles.

Down, down, down, until the sounds of battle reached her. Her heart jumped. She sensed him — cold flame, a contradiction of controlled chaos.

Pheonix was still alive!

She used her modified jumping ability to float forward, speeding along in a way that would probably look like she was phasing in and out of existence. It was quiet and fast.

It wasn't long until she ran into the outskirts of the group of *erukahl* trying to get a piece of Pheonix. They'd piled up so far back along the tunnel that she couldn't even see the stone-faced warrior.

She hung back and released herself to stand on her own two feet, back to the rough earth. She peered around a corner, hoping to stay undetected until she had a better sense of what the hell she was doing here and how she was supposed to help one of the universe's most prized and powerful warriors.

He'd even beaten Ty.

The thought paralyzed her with indecision and absurdity just as long as it took for a small *erukahl,* struggling to get past its mates and being constantly turned back, to notice her. It peeled back its thin lips, showed a mouth full of needles, and hissed. Then it leapt.

Despite the surprise, instinct took over. Charging her fist with power, she slammed it into the creature's dome. It dropped, twitched once, and lay still, its head caved in like a watermelon smashed with a hammer.

Her power filled her veins as more *erukahl* turned to face her, all too ready for a fight. The first few were easy to take down, but as the numbers grew and she eventually was surrounded, doubt infested her like maggots in dead flesh. Enhanced punches and blasts of psyker power carved through them, but she was fighting a losing battle on a much less even field than Pheonix, who was both better trained and better equipped.

Desperation fueled her to rapidly drain her power reserves to fight the oncoming flood and keep them from getting their claws on her, but it just wasn't enough.

Her mind a vortex of fear, she reached inside for something more, some second wind, anything to stave off death — and something responded.

The golden light.

The sense she got from it had changed. It had always felt like it was listening — which made sense, in retrospect. During her recovery, she'd remembered most of what had happened in that in-between space after taking Temperjoke's dagger. She'd probably merged with whatever fragment of personality the golden light had contained, not that she was ready to think about that just then. Now it was just power.

Power she could pull from — and pull she did.

It raced through her veins, both burning and warm, bringing with it elation.

She was a firework, ablaze with energy barely held back by the thinnest of membranes, and she would burst if she didn't release it …

The singing filled her head, that indescribable cacophony — at once meaningless noise and the most exquisite symphony.

The *erukahl* almost seemed to have stopped moving, several in mid-air. She lifted a hand, saw through hazy eyes that it was glowing golden from the inside out — and laughed.

She pushed the *erukahl* in mid-air, fascinated at how it inched towards the ground … then punched it. It launched into a rock wall and burst, but the liquid remnants of its body froze. She laughed again, giddy, and wove through the crowd of them, watching with delight as they scattered into bits at her slightest touch. She drew the power within her to her fingertips and let it arc out, lances of golden light that disintegrated anything they touched. She giggled with joy and spun into the air, floating effortlessly.

Hundreds of *erukahl* fell before her, and she lost sight of her goal to kill them in curious and inventive ways.

She was light, she was ecstasy, she was power and destruction and retribution …

She was unstoppable.

Then, a gap opened in front of her, and through it, she saw Pheonix jerk his head to look up at her. Unlike the *erukahl,* the warrior moved at her own speed. His eyes widened (the most expressive she'd ever seen him, but at that moment it seemed so … unimportant), and Redd dispatched the few *erukahl* still surrounding him.

She waved at him jauntily, tittered, and curled in on herself. Her power crackled around her, encouraged and nourished by her desire for destruction, and shot out in all directions. Pheonix tensed, but he needn't have worried — *she* controlled *it*, not the other way around. The remaining *erukahl* burst into ashes.

She straightened out and approached him, the light she threw off illuminating him and the piles of bodies uncountable at his feet. She opened her mouth to speak and found herself unable to. The world slanted sideways, and the power abruptly drained from her.

Despairing, she grasped at it — but she was wrong in one thing: the golden light controlled the power, not her. It faded, folding back into itself, into a locked place inside her mind, and took with it its boon.

Redd cried out in anguish, and fell to blackness.

SEVENTEEN
It's A Bother, But I Like It

Sensation returned faster than cognitive thought or memory.

A groan — her own?

Shifting, somewhere nearby, and a voice that refused to resolve.

Her mind was too busy going about parsing and checking and collating — physically she was fine, aside from some serious aches and pains …

She was laying down on something soft, covered in something else soft …

She took in a deep breath. That seemed to trigger her brain to work properly, because she found she could open her eyes.

Ty had perched at the edge of the bed when she'd first begun to move — the shifting — so it was him she saw first. He smiled, and she returned one, shakily. Ara came into her view and launched herself at Redd, who caught her with a chuckle. Ara pulled back in horror, and Redd shook her head.

"I'm actually feeling okay," Redd assured her. Ara dove back in for a tight hug and Redd squeezed her back. Ara cried, and clung to Redd, and thanked her, and admonished her, and Redd cuddled her and smiled and waited for the little angel to let it all out.

"You better?" Redd asked.

Ara nodded, but sniffled convulsively a few more times.

"How's Pheonix?" Redd asked.

"He is well." Ara smiled, a little weakly. "You know him. Water off a duck's back, as they say."

Redd closed her eyes and sighed deeply in relief. So her recklessness hadn't been for naught.

"Speaking of duck's backs," she said finally, "did you want to explain *that* to me at some point?" Redd asked, gesturing at Ara's wing, which Ara self-consciously tucked closer to herself in response.

"Ah, well. Where do I start?" Ara said.

"I've always wondered why you didn't have wings in the first place. I just didn't want to ask. I figured you'd be sensitive about it."

"I am … I was," Ara mumbled after a long silence. She reached up to gently touch one of the three opalescent horns arcing back from her skull. "There are many subspecies of angels. Too many to name. I am an archangel."

"How come I only see regular angels around here?" Redd asked, then thought about it. "Um, do I?"

"You don't. Angels and archangels are all that's left in Everdark — though the archangels you see here are all from Haven. The angelic species has had two schisms in our history; the first separated the fallen from the rest. The second happened during the Elysian conflict."

"You know the story?" Ty interjected, asking Redd. "About those that left to defend the colony near Godholme?"

"Yeah," Redd said, "Chani told me about it. That's why there are no more of the others?"

"Partially. Most left, many were killed. The rest disappeared." Ty said.

"So what's the difference? Between angel and archangel. I can't tell."

"Angels," Ara said, "are born with their wings. They are the basest 'form,' I suppose. Archangels, of which I am, are often born without wings. We must earn our wings, and our haloes. Angels do not have haloes. And most archangels earn their wings within months, years. I did not."

"Oh, Ara," Redd murmured.

Ara shook her head, smiling slightly. "I don't want pity. Or sympathy. It merely is. Like I said in Haven, angels as a whole are not like other species — in a lot of ways. Another is that we can move back and forth between subspecies. One can be born an angel or an archangel and become a nephilim, or a zeruphim, and from there, move on again."

"Wow. Why were there only angels stationed here, then?"

"Because of that ability to shift, if any subspecies of angel becomes gravely injured or put in a situation where they are, say, cut off from the Creator, they can shift downward to angel. You've questioned how I can eat flowers and fruit and get enough nutrition. Remember what Chani said about angelic biology? We're only physical enough to be able to interact on this plane. If you cut me, I bleed Creator energy. Angels are the most physical of the angelic subspecies and require the least Creator energy to survive."

"That's wild. I have so many questions, but I probably shouldn't ask them now. Well, I'll ask one." Redd pointed at Ara's wing. "How *did* you earn that, then?"

"You remember the plague?" Ty interjected.

Redd thought about it, then snapped her fingers. "Yeah, I heard about it. Some sort of spore, right? What happened with it? Everybody was all abuzz about it, and then, nothing, but I kept forgetting to ask."

Ty held his hands out towards Ara in a very sort of 'ta-da' gesture. Ara straightened, sticking her head up and her shoulders down, which made her resemble a turtle.

Redd laughed, glowing with pride for her friend. "I knew you had it in you."

"I — I'm not even sure *how,*" Ara stammered. "I just did. But, thank you."

"I guess you're held to a higher standard than the rest of us, then."

"Maybe you're right," Ara said, and sighed heavily. "I wish I could stay, but you still need your rest and I have a lot to do."

Ara gave her one more encouraging hug, then Redd waved silently as the little angel left.

"So what happened at the river site?" Redd asked Ty when Ara was gone. "I don't remember anything."

"Ah, yes, that." Ty spun to face her, folding his long legs. "Firstly, let me also tell you what an incredibly poor idea it was for you to leave *by yourself* to try to assist an *Ascended*."

Redd hung her head. "I'm sorry."

"I won't compose a Song about it — but by Spiraea's petals, you had us worried. I'm glad you survived."

Redd nodded silently, shrinking further into herself. Ty reached out to tap under her chin to encourage her to raise her head. When she met his gaze, he was smiling slightly. He leaned back.

"So — that out of the way. When you got to Pheonix, you were some kind of glowing energy being. And you decimated the *erukahl* ambush force. By yourself."

Redd was silent a moment to let that sink in. "Uh. A … 'glowing energy being'? I guess I'm past asking if you're serious. How did I get here?"

"You passed out after your light show, and Pheonix had to carry your unconscious ass back."

Redd hid her face in her hands briefly.

"Oh. So now someone has had to carry me back twice. Great. I'm doing a *great* job at being an asset … to the enemy."

Ty laughed softly, rolled one broad shoulder. "Hey, Pheonix got out alive. Even he admitted he wasn't certain he would until you showed up. I'm sure he was more than happy to do it. And you're a lightweight compared to some of the blanks *I've* had to haul around."

Redd tilted her head questioningly.

In response to her look, Ty explained, “Metal blanks. I’m an apprentice smith. Some of my tools aren’t anything to sneeze at, weight-wise, either.”

“Oh, that’s cool,” Redd said, genuinely. “I’ve never met anyone who could make things. I can’t even draw a straight line.”

“Mm, everybody has their skills. I can’t become an energy being and take out a whole army by myself.”

“Sure, keep bringing it up. Are we sure I’m not Elysian? That sounds awfully Elysian.”

“We’re sure. But as to the capabilities of Elysian … beats me. There’s almost no information on them. They were reclusive at best and murderous at worst, so it wasn’t like they’d answer a friendly questionnaire. They disappeared before we had a chance to learn anything from other methods. Before my time, anyway.”

“Before your time? I thought all elves were like … ” she trailed off, not wanting to insult him like last time.

“I’m seventy-five, which,” he said, grinning, “is young.”

“Um … wow,” Redd said, then after a moment: “So, how heinous is our age difference?”

He laughed loudly.

“It’s *really* hard to draw linear parallels between immortal and mortal growth. Remember that for an immortal, even a human at the end of their life would be a spark in the bud at best.”

‘“A spark in the bud?”’

“Elven procreation doesn’t create a zygote as in hominins; it creates a sort of — spark. To create a child with at least one elven parent, the genetic material is extracted by an ent and put into the bud of our renewal tree. The bud is tended by ents until the elf inside is ready to emerge.”

“You don’t know your parents?” Redd asked.

Ty shook his head.

“That’s really different. So you guys are never kids? Do you remember what it’s like being in the ‘bud’?”

"Being in the bud isn't like being in the womb, but we do remember it. We're … softened … when we first emerge. We all look sort of alike. But we're fully grown. Over the time period known as First Life, which is from emergence to one-hundred True Years, we learn and become who we will be for the rest of that life."

" … What do you mean 'that life'? Like, until death?"

"That's one way," he said, then hesitated. "Supposedly, we can remove our garlands," he tapped the silver-and-opal circlet around his forehead, "and … become … someone else. I've never met anyone who has done it, though."

"So, there's First Life, then … "

"Second Life, and adulthood. First Life is when you learn things like who you are, emotional regulation, how society works. Second Life is where you fit in society, what you want to focus on. Adulthood is, obviously, where you implement what you learned."

"And adulthood starts … when?"

"After two hundred."

Redd did some quick calculation.

"Adulthood was twenty-seven in the Federation. I'm probably seventeen now, which is over halfway there … you're not even close. Am I robbing the cradle?"

Ty, after he picked himself up from laughing so hard he couldn't stay upright, said, "See why we don't really compare?"

Redd furrowed her brow at him. "No, really, is this weird? Will people be concerned? You're not, like, a legitimate child, are you?"

"I'm not *that* young," he said petulantly, which didn't help his case. "Elves are typically expected to have relationships starting around my age. Since procreation is an intentional act between multiple parties, there's no real taboo about young elves … exploring."

His gaze met hers with such intensity that the now-familiar heat blossomed again in her lower belly.

"What about the Federation?" he asked, distracting her. She looked down at her hands.

"I don't know," she said shortly. "You had to have some kind of license to breed, but it was never explained how breeding even worked. I can only assume any kind of sexual contact outside the legally licensed kind, regardless of age, would be illegal."

He made a thoughtful noise. "Sounds like population control to me."

"I don't really want to talk about it."

"That's understandable."

She watched her hands play with the blanket, though her eyes were unfocused. Her mind was spinning around a wild thought, one that made her pulse race.

"Teach me."

She blinked and it took a moment before she realized the words had actually come out of her mouth. She jerked her head up. He hadn't moved from his position at the foot of the bed, though his brows were raised.

"Teach you … ?"

"You — you know more about this than I do, right?"

"I suppose, yes, I've had a traditional education on the subject," he said coolly.

She felt heat rise on her face. *Maybe this was a mistake.*

"But you can learn all that from the terminal," he continued. "What exactly is it you need *my* instruction for?"

Oh — he's being cheeky.

"Now I get why Chani calls you 'Little Shit,'" she grumped.

He chuckled and reached out to brush his fingers under her chin. "Lesson one," his voice dropped, a low murmur that sent a shiver up her spine. "Consent is paramount. For there to be consent, there *has* to be clear communication. Neither party can assume or be vague. I'm sorry that it will be difficult for you, but I need to know exactly what you are okay with. And you need to not be afraid to tell me when to stop or go, when you like something or when you don't. If you think that might be too hard for you right now, it's better off that we wait."

Redd closed her eyes and bit her bottom lip in contemplation, his words echoing in her head. His hand still lingered by her chin; she nuzzled into it until he opened his fingers to cup her cheek.

She turned her head to graze his palm with her lips. In her hyper-tuned-in state, she heard his slight intake of breath.

Nervous of what she would see on his face but keenly wanting it, she opened her eyes. The bright cerulean of his irises fairly glowed despite his lids being halfway closed; his full lips were parted.

"I want you to teach me," she said, deliberately, holding his gaze.

His thumb caressed her lips and her eyes fluttered closed again as his palm slid down the side of her throat. The mattress shifted; she felt the space between them diminish. He cradled the back of her neck — and she was grateful, because right then she felt boneless.

"Can I kiss you?" he asked, hovering close enough that she could feel the words.

"Yes," she said breathlessly, and closed the distance herself.

Her first kiss was electric, mind-numbing, both a release and a ton of napalm dumped into a bonfire. Coherent thought fled yelping into the night. He eased her backwards onto the bed, flipping the sheets away from her body, and she reached up to coil her arms around his neck. His lips moved against hers, parting teasingly and pulling back, but not enough to break contact completely, in a rhythm that she quickly picked up and matched with hunger.

Her body went into an autopilot she didn't know she had.

She arched, fitting against his slim form like they'd been made for one another. Her hands flitted across his skin, devouring the feel of him — hair, neck, arms, greedily ducking under the hem of his loose shirt to range across the smooth tight muscles of his back — places she'd glimpsed or imagined and yearned to explore now fulfilled, but it only made her want more. He groaned softly under her fingers' questing, which elicited a purely mental thrill. Maybe he'd wanted her touch as much as she'd wanted to give it.

Her hips found his and she sighed in pleasure with the contact, but he put a bit of distance between them. Disappointment cut through the haze in her head and her eyes focused — on his unearthly beautiful face. He was breathing hard, the desire in his eyes almost too much.

"What? What's wrong?" she asked.

"What about a null shield?"

A null shield? She struggled to remember what that meant. Oh — that thing Chani had said psykers needed in order to have sex. She groaned unhappily.

Wait.

Puzzle pieces clicked into place, one after another. Her psyker power hadn't responded to her heightened emotions in recent times — not with Temperjoke, not during the battle with the *erukahl*, not after her freak-out about Elysian.

"We'll be fine," she said, giggling with giddy relief.

"Are you sure?" he asked skeptically.

"I know my power. I'm sure," she said, and pulled him to her.

His intake of breath in surprise and desire was honey; his powerful body tensing against her was wine; his long, dextrous fingers teasing her robe open to trail across skin that raised goosebumps in their wake — that was better than anything …

***

Chani visited some time later.

When Redd answered the door to let her in, Chani looked past her to Ty (who, to Redd's ultimate humiliation, merely sat up in bed, naked). Chani lifted a brow, then returned her attention to Redd.

I'm going to burst into flames. I'm going to roast in my own confounded embarrassment and die.

"Ah, not a good time?" Chani asked.

"Um. No, it's fine."

"Just came to check up on you and let you know that your patrol is leaving soon. They expect you at the main square at 2100."

"Oh, okay — "

"What's the latest?" Ty called from over her shoulder.

I'm going to kill him, Redd thought, a fireball of irritation, *for being so fucking casual about this.*

"Well, the assassination attempt on the *erukahl* Queen obviously failed spectacularly," Chani called past Redd to Ty, "so right now we're trying to just set up this place to be impenetrable when the opposition gets here. Pheonix did manage to trip the dam on the way out, so the caves are flooded, but there's no way of telling how many *erukahl* were left behind, since they somehow knew about the strike. I'll let you know when I hear something more specific."

"Gotcha. Hey, Chani, just out of curiosity, why didn't you just call my crystal? Or hers?" Ty said.

Chani gave an amused grin. "I tried. Both of yours. I wonder why you didn't answer."

Redd hung her head.

Chani laughed and slapped her on the back with the force usually accompanied by being hit by a small truck. "Hope you had fun," Chani whispered.

Then, with another miniature earthquake inflicted on Redd's back by a hand as hard as rock, Chani twisted on her heel and strode off, hands in pockets, whistling.

Redd slowly wheeled around, closing the door with the same motion, and pinned the helplessly laughing Ty with a homicidal stare.

"It's *not funny!*" she exclaimed and threw a hastily-snatched pillow at his head. He let it knock him down and moved it to one side as she climbed back on the bed and crossed her arms over her chest to pout.

He wormed his way over and laid his head on her lap. "Sure it is. It is, in fact, very funny."

She looked down at him, intent on keeping up her irritation, then sighed and dropped her arms to her sides. "Okay, maybe it was. Kinda."

He chuckled softly, that intimate way she was just beginning to notice and realize with a sort of innocent pleasure that he reserved for her. He reached up to gently touch her lips and she smiled.

"It didn't hurt, did it?" he asked quietly.

"Just a bit. But when you … uh, well, let's just say I was a bit distracted."

Ty righted himself and pulled her in for a tender kiss. "I'm glad," he murmured. "How are you feeling now?"

"A little sore but I'll be fine. It's nothing compared to battle, that's for damn sure."

"I should hope not."

He looked at one of his fingers. "It's almost time. She must have been trying to get a hold of us for a while before she decided to come down in person. You should probably get ready."

Redd sighed and slipped off the bed, bending to gather the scattered pieces of her Ranger uniform from where they lay in the messy room.

"I'd rather not," she grumped. "I'd rather stay in bed."

"You and every other soldier in existence," Ty laughed.

***

Redd was set up with a group of elves and dwarves, and told that she'd be following the orders of the elven Scout

Commander — someone wearing dark leather-like clothing and wearing two sheathed blades at his hips.

She'd been introduced as a psyker-in-training, and an elven scout (whose name she hadn't caught) had been assigned to watch her back. They didn't seem to take any issue with her being a psyker or in training, or even treat her presence as anything unusual, so she wondered if it was common to have people pop in and out of patrols this way.

They traveled a predetermined route winding through the increasingly-complex inner city of Everdark that took them into the housing areas and down past the left side of the inner gate.

Though the rest of her patrol group was professional enough to make her nervous, they themselves didn't seem to be particularly nervous. For them, this seemed routine, and that helped keep her calm.

A different scout approached to speak to the Scout Commander in low tones that Redd couldn't hear, so she leaned against a wall, surreptitiously letting out a huge breath. She was mostly recovered from, well, everything, but she still tired easily, and things still looked and felt weird. She was a little proud of herself that she'd managed to keep up without complaining or letting it show how tired she was, but a break was a break.

The scout moved on and Redd pushed off the wall, sighing softly to herself.

The elf gestured and they got moving again.

Redd wasn't sure how much time it took her and the patrol to loop around twice, but it was thankfully uneventful. Halfway through their third loop, just as they were passing a little open area mostly full of debris that hadn't been taken care of yet, unfamiliar energy pinged nearby. Instantly suspicious, her heart already beginning to race, Redd waved to the scout assigned to her and they crept off together through the deserted streets. As she rounded a corner, voices reached her ears.

A small group of elves emerged from a portal. But these weren't like any elves she'd ever seen. Their skin ranged from dark brown to black to dark purple; they were wiry and short, although their features were obscured by garishly spiked helms or wrapped black cloth. They wore ebony chain and carried strange and wicked-looking weapons. The moment each individual stepped foot through the portal, they disappeared from sight.

Redd's eyes widened.

She opened her mind slightly, just enough to see with her inner eyes. They were cloaked somehow, but only from physical vision.

Behind them came a short but muscular brown-skinned cat-woman with a ridiculously huge scimitar strapped to her back. The portal closed behind her and she looked around with her snub, pink nose scrunched up in distaste.

Redd gestured to the elf with her and they backtracked a ways to be safe, at which point the elf said something into his wrist in a muttered language she didn't understand. She glanced back at him, and he gestured her forward, indicating that he'd follow her. Behind him, past a few buildings, she could see what was approximately half the patrol, though she didn't know what had happened to the other half.

With a little thrill, Redd realized they were telling her to track the enemy and they'd follow her lead. Redd's heart was pounding but her mind was sharp on the 'scent'. A chance to be useful had sparked her determination and she wasn't about to let the enemy surprise anyone or get away.

She followed the faint mental signatures, giving them just enough distance that they hopefully wouldn't sense or hear her and her partner.

While she did, her thoughts roiled.

How? How likely was it that there would be a back door? How'd they even get in? A weak spot in the Seraphim's shield? Some kind of teleportation? Or was it a tear? And who were these people? Some kind of hit squad? Why didn't the Seraphim know about this? Did she?

She just hoped there weren't other such entryways opening up in other parts of the city. Her gut tightened into a knot of fear.

Focus!

She brought her attention back to the mental scent. Oddly, it doubled around a building and came back towards the path Redd and the others had taken.

Creeping forward, she opened her mind a fraction more and pinpointed the other elves down the alley in front of her. The cat-lady was not with them. She sensed confusion as they milled about. With a start she realized what she was picking up.

They were tracking *her*. Or maybe her patrol.

At another moment, she might have found humor in the situation: her tracking them tracking her. Right now, her heart thudded rapidly as it dawned on her that they, for the moment, didn't know where she was. She sent out a tendril of psyker power and formed it into a ball in their midst. Just before she triggered it to detonate, one elf whirled around towards her position.

She ducked back around the corner, giggling as she heard the explosion and cries of dismay and anger. Something about her detonation had de-cloaked them, and the half of the patrol group following her, including her shadow, rushed forward to engage. She was vaguely aware that the other half of the patrol had come from another angle, boxing the other elves in. But she only barely noticed it through a sudden dizzy spell.

She rested against the wall to let the feeling pass. She still wasn't entirely recovered — maybe the psychic bomb had been a bit flashy, but hey, it had worked. The sounds of battle came to her ears. She knew she needed to be with them, but had to wait for the world to stop spinning.

Before she could fully recover, a footstep at the mouth of the alley alerted her. Only by ducking at the last second did Redd avoid the strike that would have stuck her to the wall.

Redd rolled to the side on instinct and came up in a crouched position. Distantly some part of her mind was glad she'd done all those drills.

The cat-lady stood at the other side of the alleyway, illuminated on one side by phosphorescent light. She snapped her arm back and the scimitar thudded into her palm. It was connected by a chain to a bracer around her forearm.

"Hey," cat-lady called, smiling maliciously.

Redd didn't respond, just held her position and watched warily.

Why didn't I sense you? Redd thought incredulously.

Swinging the scimitar on its chain, the cat-lady took a few nonchalant steps toward Redd. Redd tensed again, her eyes flicking between the shadowed face and the weapon.

"Just wanted to say hello to the bitch who has been ruining my life the last few months," cat-lady said with false cheer.

Oh no, what now? Redd thought. *I don't have the strength for this...*

"Who are you?" Redd blurted. Maybe if she kept talking, the patrol would finish with the other elves and come to her rescue. At the moment, scimitar-wielding murder-eyes had the advantage. Redd was backed into a corner and depleted.

The cat-lady smiled slightly, keeping silent. Her shoulder twitched, and Redd rolled to one side, avoiding the second strike. When the cat-lady caught the scimitar, she'd advanced almost halfway down the length of the alleyway.

She launched the scimitar again. This time Redd blocked it with a burst of psychic power. It ricocheted off a wall, spraying sparks, and Redd's assailant had to leap aside in order to avoid having her ankles chopped off.

Seeing her chance, Redd busted past the woman's mental defenses and snatched thoughts and memories from her mind, none-too-gently.

She dimly heard a gasp, and as she pulled back, she shook her head.

"Your name is Tisaki … you work for … "

As the stolen knowledge settled into her mind, Redd went cold.

"Ichiryu … "

Temperjoke leaning over her, blood filling her lungs, that name echoing in her ears …

But it hadn't been important at the time because of all the dying she'd been doing.

During Redd's moment of lapsed concentration, Tisaki swung the scimitar. It hit Redd full-on in the chest, and she sailed backwards. Under normal circumstances, it would have cut her in half and probably splattered her remains into teeny tiny bits all over the alleyway, but Redd's armor saved her somehow. The blow only knocked all the air out of her lungs and slammed her into the wall. Not that that wasn't enough — stars burst before her eyes and she convulsively gasped for breath.

She threw up her arms and with it, a psychic barrier that deflected the next strike and drained her of a little more of her power. Sure, she couldn't be chopped in half, but that didn't mean she couldn't be bludgeoned to death!

A desperate plan formed. She quickly calculated the timing of Tisaki's strikes, then strategically let the barrier drop. She dodged the next strike, barely, and nabbed the scimitar by the handle out of mid-air.

She met Tisaki's startled gaze. Latching onto the chain with the other hand, Redd wound it around her hand. "Where do you come from?" she shouted, anger bubbling up.

Tisaki hissed, beastlike, and tugged on the chain. She was very strong, but Redd, even in her weakened condition, discovered she was stronger.

Damn it, I'm not going to let this glorified housecat get the better of me!

Redd wound another loop of the chain around her hand and dragged Tisaki another few feet across the cobbled ground.

"Were those others sent from Ichiryu, too?"

Another loop, another foot across the ground towards the furious Redd. Tisaki thrashed, drawing blood from her own arm.

"Who the fuck is Ichiryu?" Redd demanded. Tisaki was only a few feet away. "*And why the hell do you fuckers want to kill me?!*"

Tisaki was inches away. She lunged at Redd, claws bared, but Redd was ready. Pouring the last of her power into her fist, she drilled the cat-woman right in the teeth. Tisaki dropped like a stone. Panting heavily, Redd fell to her knees to make sure she hadn't killed her — there was still a pulse, though her face was pretty torn up.

"And stay down," Redd gasped.

With shaking hands, she wrapped the woman in her own chain, tying the scimitar into the loop so she hopefully couldn't work her way free if she woke up before help arrived. She tried to stand, but collapsed against the wall, exhausted with the adrenaline draining away.

That was how the dwarf found her. He gestured wildly to someone outside the alleyway, and two elves followed him as he ran towards her. They hauled up the insensate Tisaki and dragged her away. The dwarf called to someone else, and another elf, this one in the yellow robes of a Healer, knelt before Redd.

He smiled shyly and lifted a long, thin metal implement. Redd stared at him, uncomprehending, and he tapped her on the forehead with it. Instantly she was out, and remembered no more.

EIGHTEEN
Homicidal Stalker from Space

Chani wove through Everdark's inner city, transformed into a maze by being perpetually built/rebuilt.

She'd heard about the portals opening, but it didn't concern her too much. Assassin teams, most likely. It had been handled; the dark elves from all the teams had been killed and Tisaki — the only outlier — taken into custody. Normally the Rangers and elves (who were, let's face it, running this war), had a strict policy of no quarter, but the Seraphim and Redd had intervened in this case, so Tisaki was being held until they had time to deal with her.

That's why they had patrols.

Any hit squad was doomed from the start, coming into the city itself. Most of the nonessential civilians had already been evacuated through the portals to Terelath, which had then been closed as the enemy neared. If the hit squads had had a specific target, they'd be hard-pressed to complete their mission without running into dozens of hardened warriors who could see through the kind of cheap tricks that dark elves usually employed. And if the enemy had been simply bent on causing mayhem, well, that had failed too.

Funny that Redd (and Pheonix, who had tangled with a nasty from one of the other assassin teams) had to be the ones to run across them; but, like most leaders who'd had boots on the ground, Chani didn't believe in coincidences.

She could hear the goblin war-drums already. The flat plains leading up to a sheer, several-hundred foot cliff face acted as a soundboard, even though the enemy was still fairly far off. They were advancing *quickly*, though, a little more so than she would have hoped. The defenders still had some shit to take care of, but what Chani was en route to do just then was one of the last preparations and she'd feel all the better having it off her plate.

Damn goblins, why did they insist on making so much noise? As a scare tactic it was laughable. It just made her angry — but worse, it was starting to give her a headache. Tinkerfist and his gnomes were working on a specialized shield generator to bolster the Seraphim's. She just hoped it'd be ready soon.

She shook her head and turned a corner. Stretched before her was the demolished skeleton of a park. A few trees stood like silent sentinels, but the space was open enough for what she intended.

A sleek blue-and-silver drop ship noiselessly flew so close to the tops of the buildings that had there been any weathercocks, they would have been turned to *coq au vin*. With pirate ships around, one couldn't be too careful, so she didn't think anyone would complain if a few shingles became roadkill.

This was an important drop-ship.

It hovered in the largest open area between the trees, perhaps eight feet off the ground, and a hatch opened from its pregnant belly.

Chani made her way towards it. As she got closer, she could hear a soft, low-pitched humming. She waited twenty feet from the craft as sixteen people dropped out of the hatch, one by one.

First came five humans and five Men dressed in Ranger light tactical combat gear. The only difference in these two groups were the symbols on the breasts of their armor. An outsider would have considered them to be all the same.

Because Chani couldn't sense life-sparks, she only knew the difference from experience.

The next five were heavily ensconced in pseudo-armor, made from a mixture of dwarven metals and cybernetics. It was matte, dark grey stuff, meant to let them fade into shadows, and near skintight to offer the most range and sensitivity. They wore helmets with lighted visors, with a range of gear and ammo strapped to various parts of their bodies according to each individual's personal preference. One thing was shared among them: each carried a sniper rifle almost as tall as the individual that carried it, with tripods neatly folded and placed into shoulder-holsters. These Ranger-made weapons fired caseless, kinetically-propelled energy rounds, and each had a seventy-five centiunits long, snake-thin barrel with a slightly flared end. A mixture of Ranger and gnomish engineering and dwarven metals made them the perfect long-range, single-target weapons, though a good shot could take out several targets with clever aiming if necessary … or to show off.

The last person birthed from the ship was Imae, who gestured to someone still within. Boxes dropped from above, and, with hand motions from several of the Men, stopped midair. The fifteen moved towards Chani, segregated slightly into groups. The boxes followed the five Men like obedient dogs.

Imae held back, patted the ship on the side as was custom, waited for the hatch to close, and jogged to catch up.

The fifteen fanned out around Chani and gave a smattering of salutes. She nodded in greeting and waited for Imae to join before speaking.

"You've been briefed?" Chani asked, bluntly.

Heads nodded.

"Good. The suborbital bombardment and artillery will commence shortly. Let's get you to your positions."

She jerked her head and turned, hearing the quiet footsteps of the group as they followed.

"Rivios, up front," she called back.

Imae came up to her side, keeping pace. "Yes, Commander?"

Chani smiled briefly at the use of her title; for once, there was no reluctance or sarcasm in the words.

"I need you to run this force," she said, loudly enough for the rest of the crew to hear. She waited until the words sank in. Imae didn't argue, but Chani could sense her apprehension. "I have to be elsewhere but I'll be in touch if you have any questions." Chani tapped her throat-mic.

"Yes, Commander."

The kid didn't have any experience leading soldiers, and they both knew it. But if not now, then when? She couldn't stay a cadet forever. And hopefully having the responsibility of command (if not the reality) would make her a little less apt to rushing headlong and more likely to think things through.

Besides, a 'commander' for this particular group was pretty much redundant. They were damn near self-sufficient. Chani hoped Imae didn't realize that. She needed to take this seriously.

Imae dropped back and gave specific instructions as to how she wanted her people to approach the battle based on current intel. They seemed to be listening to her without complaint, but that could just be based on who her parents were.

Or, perhaps it was just because *Chani* had told them to.

She grinned.

It didn't matter, really. Imae was not the type to put others in danger needlessly, even if she didn't hold herself to the same standard. As fugged up a strategy as that was, it was pretty typical of (good) officers. The kid had potential, if she'd stop being so immature.

The sad truth was, becoming one was usually the only option for any kids of high-profile, high-ranking officers. Those kids simply didn't thrive anywhere else after growing up in such a specific household.

Everdark opened up and the group passed through the inner wall and out onto the former farmlands, where there wasn't enough room to spit without hitting some squad or machinery. Between the Rangers, the elves and their artillery, the angels themselves (although many of their warrior-class had either died or disappeared, many angelic civilians and the few soldiers that were left had gallantly offered to help defend their homes), the dwarves, the drakkan, and the gnomes and their weapons, they'd stuffed this place as full as a sensimite in the recruit barracks.

They reached the outer wall and Chani led her group up the stairs. At the top, Imae and the whole line of them passed her, and Chani broke away to approach the battlements. She leaned on the rough stone. The enemy was clearly visible now, although the intervening distance made it hard to make out their rate of travel.

They stretched from edge to edge, as though someone had planted some particularly malicious moving grass. Luckily, Everdark — well, Pirroun — had been built in the perfect spot to withstand a siege. The cliffs funneled the enemy in — no back entrances, no sealed tunnels into the cliffs; at the time this place had been built, the angels were still in constant contact with the rest of the universe. When a portal could be opened up at any time, why risk a physical 'back-door' that could be a possible entryway for your enemy?

Historically, that never went well.

Chani looked up; the clouds parted and a ship descended. A sub-orbital bomber. It was a sort of double-humped design with smooth lines and thin wings. The upper pod, set forward, was the cockpit. One pilot, one crewman. The bottom pod, set towards the rear, was a tightly-packed cargo bay full of fusion bombs.

Objects streaked towards the ground, into the 'malicious grass.'

If she listened and looked closely, she could hear the bass thuds of the rounds exploding, see goblins cartwheeling in the air. From this distance, it didn't even look like the bombardment made a dent. And it wouldn't.

But, as she'd said: any small advantage could mean saving this place … or losing it forever.

The goblins had already overtaken and squatted in far more places than they should have. Chani'd be *damned* to let it happen here too.

The bomber pulled up, looping around for another pass. There was a heartbeat's delay, then she heard a 'shot out' call over comms.

Chani stood with her arms crossed, legs spread, as a wall of objects almost too dense to see through arced over her head. The first wave of artillery gained speed and height, and eventually slammed into the masses approaching — but by that point, they too were too far away.

Up against the inner wall where Chani could barely see them were the majority of the long-range artillery. Elven heavy and light ballista, gnomish cannons in two calibers, and four different types of dwarven artillery (among all the species, the dwarves had the most experience with sieges). Ranger kinetic railguns were mounted on the inner wall itself. Though she couldn't see them, she knew the drakkan artillery had been deposited up on the cliffsides, because they were magic-based and couldn't be used within the Seraphim's range for fear of interfering with her own magic.

On the outer wall itself, the main attraction were the four dwarven 'one-ninety-five-calibers' — chain guns in the most literal sense — giant grappling hooks attached to a massive chain on a huge swivel. Typical dwarven engineering. Interspersed along the wall were ranks of elven archers (called Rangers, but in fact they predated Chani's organization) releasing arrows in perfect harmony, Ranger mortars and rocket launchers firing with deadly accuracy, and the snipers of all species taking targets of opportunity.

The suborbital bomber came around for another pass and the artillery quieted — except for the dwarven guns, which whipped their chains and clunked back into place. Nothing dwarven was quiet.

If the goblins hadn't known that they were dealing with dwarves yet, they did now, and Chani could imagine the havoc that was going on across the plains. The one-ninety-five-caliber was a fearmonger among goblins. The ranks that saw it would panic, try to run, and most likely be trampled by those behind them who remained unaware. A goblin army on the move was like the march of time; it didn't turn aside when you fell and it didn't notice you when you died.

All part of the plan.

The artillery resumed, the dance continuing.

Then dark shapes dropped out of the cloud cover. Pirate interceptors — ships cobbled together out of whatever tech the pirates could salvage and scrounge from wrecks and the poor souls who ran afoul of them — swarmed the bombers, firing ballistics and photons. The bombers aborted one by one and pulled up before they could be seriously damaged. Suborbital bombers were shielded and could withstand a few minutes of sustained fire, but protocol was to flee. The bombers had no forward weaponry and couldn't fight back against the more agile fighters. That meant that soon, she'd be seeing —

More shapes zipped overhead to meet the ones approaching. She knew these without needing to see them clearly. Ranger fighters: streamlined, stylized, navy blue vessels shaped somewhat like a falcon, wings arcing around towards the front-end cockpit in a graceful curve.

The pirate interceptors ascended abruptly, bursting through the cloud cover with the Ranger fighters hot on their heels.

But having pirate interceptors in the air made it unsafe for the bombing to continue, because pirate interceptors were specifically designed to take out Ranger bombers, but didn't stand a chance engaging directly with the more agile, better-equipped Ranger fighters. The pirates would focus on their target, the bombers, despite being harried by Ranger fighters, so it was too much risk to keep the bombers in the line of fire. For the Rangers, one lost life was one too many.

With the bombers pulling back, artillery picked up the slack to slow the enemy's progress.

Chani turned away from the battlements and headed back down the stairs. This part of the siege would go on for a while. Best see if Redd was awake yet.

Redd had, in fact, awoken some time earlier. She and Ty were talking when Chani knocked lightly on the open door and stepped in.

Redd put down the snack Ty had brought her and smiled. "Hey, what's up?"

"Gotta get your report of what happened with the patrol, if you're up to it?"

Redd nodded and recounted what she remembered, with Chani asking clarifying questions throughout.

When Redd was done, Chani sighed. "I get that your life was on the line, but for the future, don't go busting into people's minds without more training." Redd shrunk into herself slightly. "That mandatory warning out of the way: what did you find?"

"Not much. Uh, the only important thing was that she works for someone named Ichiryu. It's a name I've heard before, but — Chani, what?"

Chani had put her head into her hands.

Ty leaned back and whistled.

"Creator, I never thought I'd have to hear that name again," Chani said quietly.

"Who is it?" Redd asked.

Chani waved a hand. "Before that, you said you'd heard that name before. Where?"

Redd averted her eyes. "Um. Temperjoke. Right before he … killed me."

"Why in Fug's name didn't you mention this earlier, Redd?" Chani asked flatly.

"I forgot," Redd said sheepishly. "The name didn't imprint at the time because, you know, *dying*, and I wasn't reminded of it until I found it in Tisaki's mind."

"So Ichiryu is connected with Temperjoke," Ty murmured.

"Seems that way," Chani agreed.

"Who is Ichiryu and why is it bad that she's hanging out with Temperjoke?" Redd demanded.

"Ichiryu," Chani said, "was some Elysian we'd taken into custody some hundred or so years ago, but — "

"Woah, woah, hold on." Redd interrupted, incredulous. "I thought they were all wiped out. *Extinct.*"

Chani lifted her shoulders and simultaneously tilted her head to one side, making a face. "Mm, well, the official history books say that *Legion* — their only known social or political structure — was destroyed, but even then, the — the — fuggin' *catastrophe* or *war* or whatever the *Fug* it was that effectively took Legion out of the picture only killed the ones in the area of the energy burst. Granted that was a vast majority of them, but some did escape. Aside from that, we're uncomfortably aware that the mechanism for their creation is still in place, so new ones are still being birthed."

"So which one is this Ichiryu? And how are they … created? I mean — *created*, not born?" Redd asked.

"Slow down," Chani said. "Ichiryu is a survivor, though we don't know if she was ever a part of Legion or precisely how old she is. I know nothing about the Elysian reproductive systems, sorry."

Redd nodded and subsided, but she was unsettled.

"We caught her one day," Chani continued, "trying to break into the artifacts vaults on one of the elven colony worlds. She was brought into a holding cell, where she paced around and muttered to herself and yelled at nothing. Tried to escape a couple times, but the null fields we use in our detention facilities are not nice.

She was carrying this journal with her at the time. We confiscated it. A lot of it was just ramblings about nothing and abstract drawings, but there was a series of lucid entries where she was, for some reason, chronicling her own species. And it was there we finally learned a few key things about the Elysian, including how they are created, but it isn't common knowledge. It was discreetly agreed that we don't want people trying to artificially spawn Elysian, thankyouverymuch. Without breaking security protocol, yes, they are created."

"So … what happened to her? Why is she out and about now?"

"We had to let her go."

"You ' …had to'?"

"The balance."

"What about it?" Redd pressed.

"At the time, her species was known to be almost extinct. The Chosen decided that she should be released because to destroy her would cause an imbalance."

Redd pressed her hands to her head in frustration. "*Damn it*, that fucking *balance* again. I hate that shit. You're just coddling evil, don't you know that?"

In the silence that followed, Redd looked up, expecting anger or disapproval. Instead, she caught Chani and Ty exchanging wry glances.

"What?" Redd asked. "What's with the look?"

"You just sound like someone we know," Ty said, grinning.

Chani sighed and crossed her arms over her chest. "It concerns me, though, that Temperjoke is involved with an Elysian who seems to want to kill Redd."

"You're telling me," Redd grumped. "I'd never even heard of this bitch before now. It's freaky, knowing that someone is out there watching me. She's like a … homicidal stalker."

"Temperjoke has been increasingly erratic lately, though," Ty added. "Even just here on Everdark, he's actively interfered far more than is necessary or healthy for an Ascended."

"He said something else," Redd said slowly, fishing in the depths of her memory. "The first time I met him."

"The *first* time?" Chani asked sharply.

Redd sighed and recounted when Temperjoke found her after the *erukahl* launched their second assault.

"So that's why we couldn't find you," Chani said to herself, then looked back at Redd. "When I met up with Cira and his patrol, we tracked back to where we'd been attacked and you were gone. We assumed you'd been taken, too."

A hazy memory floated up in Redd's mind's eye: Chani rushing to embrace her. *Thank the Creator. We thought we'd lost you, too.*

"So what did he say?" Chani went on.

"He asked me to tell you guys that he's not an enemy."

Chani snorted, hard. "Yeah, excuse me if I don't believe that. He's been poking around where he shouldn't be far too often for me to not quantify him as an enemy."

"I think I agree with that," Redd said flatly. "Stabbing someone doesn't generally foster good will. But he specifically said he wasn't an enemy to *you*, the Rangers."

"Hey, it's like you said: stabbing someone — especially an innocent someone who happens to be one of my charges — doesn't foster good will. I'm inclined to agree," Chani said. "Words don't mean shit unless backed up by congruent action, kid. The earlier you learn that, the easier it gets to sort the bullshit from the genuine. Anyway, try to keep focus on the upcoming battle. Neither Ichiryu nor Temperjoke can get you while you're here. From here you go to Terelath, and *nothing* gets into Terelath. Once you're feeling up to it, join us on the outer wall. You can be up there with the other psykers and magic-users when the enemy starts to get close."

Redd nodded, her mind whirling with too many things to settle on just one. As if Chani knew, she patted the top of

Redd's head gently — Redd offered a wan smile — before she left.

"We've got some time," Ty said once Chani was gone, that mischievous glint in his eye again. "How do you want to distract yourself?"

NINETEEN
Enter, Evil, Stage Front

The dogfights above Everdark lasted for hours, while artillery sailed over the walls and the enemy marched ever closer, undaunted by their losses.

Eventually the goblins' own artillery came into range and started firing, which careened off the Seraphim's barrier. Yet still they kept firing, hoping to wear her down.

The goblins were scavengers like the pirates, but in a much more devious fashion. Because of their massive numbers, they assaulted and squatted on many planets, planets which often contained precious metals and ore deposits. If the planet had inhabitants, they'd be either assaulted to extinction or squeezed out. The dwarves were their sworn enemies, and had been so for as long as anyone could remember. The goblins took great pleasure in taking dwarven colony planets: dwarves knew where the best ore was. But instead of studying what they found to unlock its secrets the way the dwarves had, they melted it all down and fast-tracked their weaponry to fuel their many wars.

Even as the army approached the outer wall, firing boulders and hunks of metal and sometimes, in their fervor, their own kind, the ranks stretched back into infinity. Streaming from behind trees, piling up around Everdark like grains of sand at the bottom of an hourglass, the goblins marched on.

The front ranks consisted of Amalgamations: undead mishmashes of bones, rotting flesh, and metal to hold up the parts that wouldn't work otherwise, into a vaguely humanoid shape.

The goblins themselves were little hominid-shaped people with pointy ears. They came in a wide array of colors and had huge noses, beady eyes, and lined, squat little faces. Among their armor and weaponry, there was no streamlining, no group consciousness, no regulation.

Though one would be hard-pressed to define 'gender' among creatures so cloned that they couldn't breed naturally, it was well known among Accord species that the vast majority of goblins were genetically and biologically designated male. Goblins with uteruses were rare and prized only *for* said uteruses. So when one was born, they were immobilized in specialized tanks, injected with a serum meant to speed maturity, and technologically modified to perpetually crank out babies from a soup of the strongest goblin genetics. Thus *why* the average clan was around one-hundred-million in number. Goblins, on all fronts, were quantity over quality.

Another example of how goblins did everything half-assedly: they could pump out bodies for their armies with the frequency only rivaled by hive species, but they didn't bother to figure out how to birth more goblins with uteruses.

Goblins from the birthing vats deemed 'unworthy' were subjected to experimentation. Those that survived often became Brutes — mindless, hulking beasts.

Occasionally, goblins with uteruses would detonate at birth, often killing their birthers and destroying much of the birthing room. These were shamans, and they were allowed to live because the goblins prized power above all — that they used it on other goblins was immaterial, and sometimes desirable. Some of these shamans could be spotted dancing and gesticulating wildly with bits of wood, dressed in dirty robes looped in talismans and covered in symbols.

Smaller groups of non-goblins were interspersed among them in the marching army. There were clusters of indeterminate-species individuals wearing black robes with cowls (black school wizards), and dark elves — the 'other elves' Redd had encountered on her patrol.

And orcs.

Orcs were humanoid, though only by the loosest of definitions. They had grey to grey-purple skin, though their actual skin color might as well be unknown for the amount of purple-liquid-filled blisters — some as big as their heads — covering them. The purple liquid pooled under their skin in places, ran through their veins, leaked out of every orifice. Many individuals had no skin around their mouth and jaw, leaving naked white bone showing, with a permanent grin of blackened, sharpened, teeth. They were entirely hairless.

Orcs were bizarre, even among evil species, for being worshipers of the God of Pestilence. They drank 'pustulence,' a liquid produced by their God and Elders, which burned the skin off their lower face, rotted the blood as it still pumped through their bodies, and pooled under their skin. No one quite knew how they survived the process nor how they continued living. They were one of the most aggressive species and battled constantly, even amongst themselves, with the express purpose of opening the blisters 'in worship of Pestilence,' which spread the pustulence. Crystalized pustulence on their skin formed a kind of armor. The more of this chitin armor an individual sported, the more attractive, virile, and zealous they were considered to be.

The only difference between 'male' and 'female' orcs were that males had four arms and females, only two.

And lastly, slightly set apart from the rest, were the *erukahl*. Combined intel had revealed that the majority of the weaker workers had been left to die in the tunnels; that was who Redd and Pheonix had fought, albeit a small reserve local to that part of the system. The force present on the battlefield currently consisted of roughly ten thousand drones — the bigger, more brutal soldiers — and several thousand of huge, strong fighters that were the Queen's personal guard.

Then there was the Queen, herself. She stood twelve feet tall on two trunk-like legs, beautiful like a black widow spider. Her alabaster skin was armored in living crystal, some of which had grown into actual stalactites jutting from her body. These crystals glowed softly with phosphorescence. Six horns curled back from her head, the purest of ebony, parting long black hair. Both hair and horns reflected iridescent light. She moved slowly, with grace and purpose.

Her face was the frightening visage of a skull: hollowed black eyes — pits of darkness — thin lips drawn back over crowded rows of sharp teeth, like inch-long daggers. The skin of her face was stretched and lined. Arced out behind her were six mutated shapes, spiked through with crystal shards, black and curled in on themselves. Her silhouette was that of the gnarled, dead husk of a burned-out tree.

As well as the goblin artillery weapons, there were siege weapons and other violent-looking mechanical devices, like the Bashers — five vaguely rectangular machines, like cannons without the smooth lines, wheeling forward without any visible source of propulsion. They used, ran on, and fired a specific type of dark energy and were immune to all types of magic.

Towering above everything on the battlefield were the siege animals, several hundred feet of tortured flesh grafted with metal armor buckled straight onto skin and pierced into muscle. They were controlled by a mixture of magic and pain, had forms ranging the gamut, and were kept well out of the range of the defenders' artillery.

***

"How are we doing?" Chani asked, looking out the window of the Citadel.

"About how we expected," Veric replied.

"It's not slowing them down much," the Seraphim remarked, her soft voice unreadable.

"That's about what we expected," said Chani sardonically.

"We have Ladies standing by for full evacuation," Pheonix said.

Chani turned away from the window. "Hopefully we won't need that. We let the goblins take this city, they'll have the whole damn planet inside of a week."

"Retreat is preferable to death," Pheonix said without emotion.

Chani nodded, then grimaced, covering her ears briefly. "I hate those drums. They always give me a splitting migraine. Makes it hard to think."

"Probably the point," Ty said, grinning.

"Naw, they just like hearin' themselves make noise," Stonebreaker countered mirthfully.

"I guess you would know all about that," quavered Tinkerfist.

Stonebreaker rolled his eyes. "Dealin' with their like day in an' day oot, yeh get to be ah wee tiard of it, Ah'll give yeh that." His wide face split into an easy grin. "But! Makes it all the easier teh kill them if they're pissin' yeh off, eh?"

Tinkerfist made a noncommittal noise, watching his coin rolling across his fingers. "Either way, the shield generator should be operational shortly."

"Thank the Creator," Chani professed.

"How are you doing, Lady?" Veric asked the Seraphim.

She smiled, her eyes unfocused. "I am well, thank you, Veric," she replied. "My shield is holding."

"And our guest?" Chani asked.

"She rests," the Seraphim said. "Her mind took quite a shock; I cannot question her until she recovers." She paused, then said, "They are coming within range."

"Well, that's our cue. Time to get a move on. You comin', Ty? Better get Redd on the wall with the others and check on things." She sighed melodramatically. "A Commander's work is never done."

Ty nodded and followed Chani out of the tower.

***

Redd was nervous as Chani and Ty led her down the crowded hill, towards the wall that stood in the distance. Ty had indeed successfully kept her from stewing on any of the complicated shit she'd been involuntarily involved in … by showing her how to play an elven game utilizing little colorful beads and magic.

But now it was time.

The din had been terrible inside; out here it was unbearable. Between the lines of artillery firing and the goblins riling themselves up, she could barely hear herself think.

"Are we gonna have to deal with this the whole time?" Redd shouted, her voice cracking with frustration and volume.

"Hell no," Chani yelled back, laughing. "Should be in three … two … one … "

And the noise stopped. Redd gasped with the sudden silence, fearing obliquely for a moment that she'd lost her hearing — then the artillery fired again. She turned to Chani wonderingly, refusing to be incited by the woman's broad, knowing grin.

Ty looped an arm around her shoulders and squeezed. "You remember null fields?" he asked.

Redd thought for a moment, then nodded.

"They can be tuned to reduce light, *noise*, radiation, magical frequencies, pollens and spores — all sorts of things — as well as nullifying all of the above *within* the shield. Really quite ingenious."

"Thank the *Creator*," Chani said with some passion. They reached the steps and she gestured the two younger people ahead of her.

Redd felt horribly exposed at the top of the outer wall, but at least they weren't alone. She just had to trust in the Seraphim's shield. Her eyes roamed across the wall. A line of elves, mostly dark-skinned, wearing what looked like molded wooden armor but most certainly was more than that, fired bows in measured intervals. The weapons were all slightly different, apparently unique to the elf holding it. No one seemed to have arrows. Magic, probably, then.

And they sang. It was a different song from Ty's Bladesong, though — a narrative, perhaps? And while the words were definitely not in any tongue she recognized, if she listened hard enough she could almost understand the story. It was earthly and melodic, without the ethereal, emotional quality of Ty's song.

Hearing it, she took in a deep breath and felt energy flow through her, like she'd just taken a stim pill.

There were others, too: Ladies, other elves, lots and lots of Rangers with different weapons, all still recognizable by that black armor, and other people in a different type of black armor Redd didn't recognize.

Then, she got her first glimpse of the army — what and who it consisted of — and froze. Chani went to talk to someone behind her, but her conversation was lost on Redd. Ty stood quietly next to her.

"This … this is what we need to fight — to win against?" she whispered.

Ty must have heard her, because he laughed softly. "Remember — quantity over quality."

Redd stared outward. The front edge of the enemy forces were almost on top of the wall, maybe two miles away, already past the Haven-island-turned-mountain she'd had to circumvent, and advancing quickly. It wouldn't be long. Her stomach twisted in fear. She was vaguely aware of Ty doing something next to her, but couldn't tear her eyes away from the insurmountable task literally at her feet.

She looked at Ty to say something, but the words died.

He was so angry that he was radiating it. Behind him, several others turned to look at him with surprise, too, apparently noticing it as well.

She touched his shoulder and he took in a hissed breath, turning wild eyes on her. It took a moment for recognition to dawn, but when it did, he blinked and closed himself off. Bit by bit, he calmed.

"What's wrong?" she asked quietly.

Wordlessly he gave her a handheld telescope.

"Behind the troops … on a hill, straight ahead," he choked, still fighting himself.

Mystified, Redd raised the telescope to her eye. It took a moment for her to figure out how to use the many-times-zoomed scope, but she finally focused on the hill and found a line of figures. She'd been briefed on a terminal regarding some of the things she'd see during battle before Chani would let her come up to the wall: what to look for, what to avoid, how to manage certain enemies. So she mostly recognized what she was looking at.

The first two from the left were goblins; the very leftmost was a goblin the size of a Brute wielding two ugly weapons. One appeared to have been made from the spine of some unfortunate creature, and the other was some bastard chainsaw. His armor was of high quality and etched with designs, but seemed ill-fitting. His greasy hair was pulled into a bun on the top of his head.

He dwarfed the normal-sized goblin next to him. Puzzlingly, this smaller goblin's armor was split in half; the left side of his body was metal, and the right very similar to what the shamans wore. This goblin took body mods to scary new heights. Shafts of metal and bolts looked to be shoved *through* his round pate. Redd couldn't be sure if it was an affectation or if he was an animate dead, but she was sure that either way she didn't want to know. He carried no weapons.

Next in line was an orc. Redd only knew she was female because she had two arms: she was covered entirely by thick striations of purple chitin. The only part of her that was visible was her face, which was that same haunted ghoulish nightmare she'd seen on other orcs. The chitin built up around her head, neck, and shoulders, forming a jagged collar of stalactites that stuck out at serrated angles. That same purple liquid that oozed out of her eyes, nose, mouth, and ears also oozed out from between the slats of the chitin. She bore no visible weapons.

Beside the orc was a dark elf. She was so out of place that Redd almost did a double take. As exquisitely beautiful as any elf Redd had seen up to that point, she stood with poise and grace, surveying the armies with a smirk. Her skin was a deep brown that was almost red, and her black hair was done in a waist-length series of braids. She wore a tailored black suit with a white collared shirt underneath; a silver metal plate inset with decorations rested over her sternum. At her feet was a male dark elf, wearing a skintight bodysuit. Around his neck was a massive jeweled collar, attached by chain leash to the female dark elf's waist. For weapons, he only wore a single sheath, probably for a dagger, judging by its size.

The final one in the line was another orc, not that different from the first, though perhaps broader around the shoulders. The major difference between them was that this one had four arms. In each hand he carried a weapon: one burned, one steamed coldly as though he'd just taken it from the freezer, one looked like some form of multi-whip tipped in spiked balls. The final weapon was a giant mace shaped out of metal in the likeness of an elven head, pointy ears and all. The tortured look on the head's face was enough to send a shiver down Redd's spine.

Very disturbed, Redd lowered the telescope and handed it to Ty. "Who are they?" she asked.

While she'd been checking out the competition, Ty had calmed. "From left to right, the Clan-Head of this goblin clan, a Warboss clone — the goblins send a clone of their high leader, the Warboss, to each large-scale battle they're involved in — Vathath, a Bound Witch Lady, whose orcish magic-user troops will stay well back from the front … " He hesitated, his lips thinning. His rage threatened to rise again. Redd thought wonderingly, *What would cause this much of a reaction in him?*

"Ty?" Redd ventured.

He gave her a tight-lipped smile. "The dark elf is a Grand Mistress; she probably hired the pirates and slavers. And the one on the end is … Kser." The name came out like a curse. "Kser is a Bound Sword-God. The Berserkers are his. The mace he carries is a Deimmortalizer. The head on that mace was that of a living elf — he still lives, preserved by their magics, and tormented with the knowledge of what he has become. Worse, I recognize him. He is the one whose sword I inherited. When a Bladesinger dies, his sword returns to the Altar of Law in Terelath. One of the reasons our swords are so powerful is because they have been through so many previous lives." His eyes unfocused but fixed in the distance. "Edranthussinlas cries out to me. I must avenge his unclean death and bring his skull back to the Altar of Law, where it will finally be properly displayed with the rest of our honored dead."

Redd didn't respond. The idea of displaying skulls anywhere was a little weird to her, but who was she to judge another culture's practices? She wasn't even sure how she felt about death and belief anymore.

"Just be careful," she said quietly, with feeling. He met her eyes with a small, strained smile.

Chani joined them.

"Alright, Redd, we'll need you here at this position," Chani said. "It'll be fine," she laughed as though sensing Redd's panic. "Just watch your fellows' backs and they'll watch yours."

Redd looked out over the plains. Goblin artillery fired, slammed into the shield, fell, or exploded. The army marched, ever closer, and the drums beat, silently …

It was unnerving.

"What am I supposed to do?" she asked pathetically.

"What you do best," Chani answered, quick and sharp and confident. "Focus on the siege weaponry and keep them from getting to the shield. The less stress the Seraphim is under, the better off we all are." She turned to Ty. "Come on, we've got to check in with the other crews."

Ty took Redd's hand and drew her in for a heart-stopping kiss.

"You'll do fine, love," he said and squeezed her hands with his. "See you soon."

Redd watched them disappear down the stairs, then faced the oncoming army again. Nervousness churned in her stomach. She stood, unable to move, watching as artillery sailed over her head, the earth opened and rose to crush the oncoming mob or swallow them whole, hearing and sensing and seeing the people along the wall next to her firing off spells and arrows and bullets … and the Amalgamations in the front merely marched on, over their broken compadres. Some fell for no apparent reason, to things she couldn't see.

How was she supposed to help? How could she possibly stem this tide? How could *anyone*? She could burn through all her power and die at their feet, and still have accomplished nothing.

Some of the enemy carried long metal planks. As they came close, several things happened: those with the planks split off (apparently protected by something, because as the focus shifted on them, much of the smaller projectiles reflected before making contact) to approach the wall, the goblin long-range fire stopped, and Redd noticed something she hadn't before.

Just outside the outer wall, on the goblin side of the water defense, were Ranger machines. Some were fairly sizable — wheeled, tracked, floating slightly — but all had at least one large gun. She couldn't make heads nor tails of them, but if the smokescreen surrounding each was any indication, they'd been firing for some time.

Redd realized they were guarding the water defense, because the Amalgamations were attempting to utilize those planks as bridges. As groups carrying the planks vaporized, there were dozens to take their place. And in a heart-stopping moment, the two clashed. Amalgamations swarmed over the machines by the hundreds, clogging the barrels, tearing at the metal. Chunks of machinery disappeared, pulled away by the unnatural strength of these undead monstrosities.

One vehicle shuddered and smoked, electricity crackling across its frame. Horrified, Redd watched an Amalgamation reach through the hole it had created to disable the thing, and pull a struggling body from within. A Ranger, by their black armor.

The Amalgamations descended on the Ranger —

— and were blown away, smashed to literal pieces.

Her power screaming through her nervous system like a runaway train, Redd lifted the Ranger up in a sphere of light while she bludgeoned Amalgamations, using her power like a hammer.

The vehicle she'd pulled the Ranger from detonated with an explosion that rocked the wall and scattered Amalgamation parts in a wide radius. She set the Ranger down on the wall. They flashed her a salute, then her attention was elsewhere.

It hadn't occurred to her that there were *people* in those machines. Now that she knew, what she'd been witnessing took on a sudden, sharp urgency. She opened. She felt and saw the shapes of the powers beside her: the Seraphim hovering over everything (a soft glow that shifted like silk in the wind), the psykers (spikes of power, each tuned with a color and texture unique to their owner), the TKers (tendrils of energy with the TKer themselves at the center, like a giant anemone), the Ladies and War-Ladies (bright, white aftershocks that seemed to hold all colors, similar to the image burned into the retina after looking at a bright light). These and more flitted like fireworks, overlaying and sometimes combining.

Redd added her own halcyon to the show, sweeping Amalgamations back. The psykers across the wall joined her, raking the undead bodies like leaves away from the line of machines. Some resumed firing; some were too damaged. Those occupying the disabled vehicles were rescued in the brief respite, and more explosions occurred.

It went on this way, with the mind- and magic-users on the wall controlling the ebb and flow of the incoming enemies.

But there were simply too many, and it seemed like they were fighting a losing battle.

Redd turned her attention to a machine just in time to see one Ranger fighting for their life, but another Ranger was ripped out of the hull of theirs — had anyone else seen? — how could she be in two places at once? — she couldn't communicate — she turned inward reluctantly, terrified, to call to the golden light —

— then every single Amalgamation crumbled to dust at once.

Wrenched back to the scene before her, Redd realized that something she'd been seeing around every undead body — a sort of haze of magic — was now gone. She followed its last traces to the dark stillness that was Pheonix and the burning-and-crackling of his weapons.

He had been down there with the machines, doing the same thing she was, and had done something to incapacitate the Amalgamations.

Someone tapped Redd on the shoulder.

She gasped and came out of her mental tunnel vision with a start. A psyker stood behind her, a concerned look on their face.

"Hey, you need to go get some rest. You've been up here for too long."

A wave of dizziness stilled the protest on her tongue. She nodded and let the other psyker take her place.

***

A quick meal and a nap later, Redd headed back to the wall — and ran across Pheonix going in the opposite direction. She stopped, feeling awkward. He gave her a quick bow and passed her.

“I don’t know why I dislike you,” she said after he was beyond her, not turning to face him. Her hands clenched into fists. “I know you’re a good person.”

Pheonix had stopped walking. But he didn’t say anything.

“Chani told me you’re the Ascended of Justice, whatever that means,” she continued. Pheonix remained silent, which ignited her simmering irritation to a full boil. “What do I know of justice? My whole miserable existence has been one big fucking injustice. Where were you when they were — “ She took a sharp, painful breath in. “And you have the audacity to insert yourself into my life like you belong. You have the audacity to — “

You have the audacity to make me feel comfortable, like everything will be okay.

“Well, everything’s not fucking okay,” she finished in response to the thought, ashamed at her outburst.

“I spent much of my early life as a slave in an arena run by pirates and slavers.” Pheonix’s voice floated from behind her. Despite being said with no inflection, Redd flinched as if he’d yelled at her. “Unarmed, enslaved people were — and still are, because the Bast-damned thing still exists somewhere out there in space — tossed into the ring against vicious beasts and each other. My slaver-masters couldn’t hurt or kill me, though they sure as hell tried. But you know what they did manage?”

Redd was frozen, unable to react, as Pheonix continued in that same calm tone.

“I watched them hurt, torture, and kill people around me. Day in, and day out. All that was unsuccessful on me was successful on people like you.”

She turned slowly. He was still facing away from her, shadowed by the overhang of a nearby building, though she could see his profile. His eyes were cobalt embers: the coldest fire imaginable. It quelled the heat in her.

“People who had the emotional capacity I lack. All the pain that rolled off of me … took root in everyone around me. Had I the capacity for guilt, I imagine it would eat me alive.

But I don't, and how I feel or don't feel doesn't matter, because I have a job to do. I have not been given instruction on how to be Ascended, and it seems none is forthcoming. I don't even seem to *be* fully Ascended. I won't apologize for something I didn't do, and I can't ease your pain, but I swear to you: whatever boon I find in my Ascendency, I will use it to bring evil to justice. Including the people who hurt you."

Tears burned her eyes, but she held them back by sheer will. She refused to break down in front of him, of all people.

Damn him … she believed him. The hope hurt more than anything. She could hardly breathe.

"You'd better," she said at last, though the threat was both watery and toothless. What could someone like her do to someone like him? Before she made a bigger fool of herself, she spun on her heel to stomp off, yelling back over her shoulder: "I don't know why Ara chose you, but she did, so don't fuck it up!"

She didn't know why she'd confronted him, and she cursed herself an impulsive fool the whole way back to the wall, letting the tears fall as she walked.

Maybe because that was the first time we've been alone, and it was in the back of my mind, weighing on me. She realized she did feel lighter, once the humiliation had receded a bit.

She ruminated on his words.

I had no idea he'd gone through something like that, she thought. And he had no emotions? Or … a reduced emotional capacity? She vaguely remembered Ty saying something about that. Some of the things Pheonix did made more sense now, and she understood a bit more as to why they'd been so awkward around each other. Redd operated almost entirely on emotion, so of course someone who was her exact opposite would be unrelatable and maybe even strange.

So much of what he'd said hadn't made sense. He was Ascended — some super powerful creature — but he didn't have all their powers? Weren't the Ascended picked by the

Creator, an even more super-powerful creature? Why would the Creator not guide those it had chosen?

Trying to puzzle it out was giving her a headache, so as she approached the stairs up to the wall, she rested against them and closed her eyes, breathing in and out slowly and focusing on the golden singing to re-center herself.

Then she climbed.

She picked a TKer who was flagging, relieved her, and took her place.

The goblins hadn't advanced in that time, although from the looks of it, they were still making just as much racket.

Suddenly the ten siege animals who had been hanging back, rushed forward. The sky opened for several groups contiguously: two on the enemy side, one on the defenders' side.

The first group were pirate slave-creatures, the second were the vaguely faceted metal pods the pirates used. Out of them poured … pirates. People in hard-point armor and carrying firearms.

And the final group …

Fucking mechs, Redd thought. *It's fucking mechs.*

And fucking mechs they were. Almost the height of the siege animals, these were humanoid-shaped only in virtue of having two things that looked like arms and two columns of metal that supported them in the way of legs. Blocky and sturdy and tough, it was almost as though their weapons were their structure.

Redd determined that they were Ranger in origin, because they dropped facing the enemy, and splashed across the back of each mech were black wings — the symbol she'd seen on every Ranger's uniform.

On Chaos Earth, there was a popular vid program (though Redd had always hated it, her parents had watched it often) where two mechs would tear at each other to get to the pilot inside; the first to kill the opposite pilot got ten million creds. So she was familiar with the idea of giant mechanical creatures, though not to defend people.

Now that she thought about it, using them to defend people made a lot more sense.

She was starting to understand more and more viscerally why everyone called her planet backwards.

There was another type of mech, about half the height of the two-legged one but ten times as wide, with eight long, piston-like legs, shaped like a spider. Two massive guns mounted on its 'head' immediately started firing, as did multiple others stuck out from various places along its body.

The hordes of goblins parted and the collared creatures came to the forefront. Right behind them were the goblin siege engines, and some ways behind them, the mech-sized siege animals.

The mechs shot forward, propelled by something mounted at the heels of the 'feet,' and the titans — the mechs and the siege animals — clashed in a chaotic melee Redd couldn't keep track of.

A mech grappled with a siege animal its size while its support columns (legs?) were flamed by something that looked like a small dragon — the crawler mech created huge holes in the amassed goblins while two collared creatures climbed its legs and goblin artillery rained on it. Another mech knocked over a siege tower as it approached from the far side, preparing to line up with the wall. One of the siege animals, this one with thick, dark fur, six legs, and multiple red eyes, was held in stasis by the combined efforts of the TKers and the psykers, while friendly artillery focused on taking it down. It thrashed in mid-air, carving canyons in the dirt with its lashing tail.

Her heart pounding, Redd scanned the battlefield for whoever needed her help the most. She decided to turn her power against the beast in mid-air.

The thing was torn to pieces, log-sized arrows buried in its hide, holes gushing black blood from gnomish cannons, chunks of its protective plating torn away by the dwarven hook-thrower, and yet still it fought on. As open as she was to everything, Redd could feel the TKers and psykers weakening, but there was nothing she could do to support them in that manner.

She panicked for a moment — it would take too much power to use any of her current techniques to kill it. It was simply too big.

Despite Chani's warnings, she touched its mind but was repelled by the sheer unfamiliarity of it. Nothing doing there.

… But what about its body?

Gathering her courage, she delved within it — and was briefly stunned to find that it worked. Her ability to mentally disseminate extended to physical forms as well, apparently.

She pushed deeper, opened it up from the inside, trespassing within its altered body with the intent of finding what made it tick to turn that switch the fuck off.

She ripped through it, sending bursts of power through its nervous system to overload its synapses, to shut down its muscles and organ function (which had all been bolstered by the goblins' sick technology). Everywhere she went, she left a fatal flaw — changed a blood clotting mechanism here, reversed a vital organ flow there, stoppered a toxin-filter, tied up a group of nerves.

She wasn't sure how she knew all these things (the creature's biology was completely foreign to her), but right then wasn't the time to question it.

She felt its body shuddering, heard the roars of pain, and withdrew so as to not feel its death.

Perhaps sensing its impending expiration, the psykers and TKers heaved the creature, in tandem, to the middle of the goblins standing back to watch the fight. The goblins attempted to scatter, but not quickly enough — the behemoth made goblin pâté on impact with the ground, and probably killed more than a few as it rolled and twitched.

Redd came back to herself and took in a deep breath, leaning on the battlements to make the world stop spinning.

Okay, she thought. *Maybe that was a bit much.*

But there was no time to stop or rest just yet.

She steeled herself and focused on the collared monsters. Something stopped her as she went to do the same to one of them, an enormous tiger-like creature with scars crisscrossing fur dappled in such a manner that it was difficult to fix her sight on it for long. She studied it instead.

It turned toward her as though it were aware of her inspection. She felt that they'd locked gazes, despite the distance and haze and gloom.

And she realized it was intelligent.

It's only fighting us because of that damned collar! she thought in surprise.

She invaded the collar instead, barreling through circuitry and wires in the same manner as she had the more fleshly mechanisms a moment earlier. Exhaustion nagged at her; she ignored it, fueled by emotion.

The collar smoked and sparked, and she released the catch. It thunked to the ground and the tiger stopped, lifted its head, and looked in her direction.

Thank you, came a voice in her head.

The collar? She sent back tentatively.

It stifles my ability to think and to speak, forces me to obey, the rough mental voice said, accompanied by a wave of revulsion. *But it does not make me forget. I remember all.*

Give me a moment, Redd thought at it fiercely, *and I will release your brethren. You will have your freedom, if you will fight with us.*

The creature sent her a blast of agreement/wordless thanks/feral anticipation. Redd turned her mind to the other collars and four more thunked to the ground. The formerly-enslaved gathered in a knot and went off together.

They exploded into the middle of the pirates from the pods. The tiger-creature snatched one man up in his jaws, neatly severing the victim in his mouth with almost gleeful abandonment. That he could do it despite the man's armor spoke of his strength. He roared with triumph and pounced on another, ignoring the bullets that peppered his body, streaked his beautiful hide with red. She could hear the panicked screams through his mind, feel the luxuriation of blood running through his fangs — the hot, coppery taste at once a balm and a frenzy.

She turned her mind to free the rest, all too aware that they were still outnumbered and surrounded by enemies.

By the time the last collared creature joined the bloody melee, it was too late for the one she'd spoken to. She found him lying on his side, his lifeblood pumping out of so many wounds he looked no better than a pile of processed meat. Her mind hovered over him, despairing. She couldn't Heal — that was not her domain. She didn't even know where to start, and she had no time.

I'm so sorry, she sent, her guilt and sadness pouring through their mental link.

Tears of desperation and hot grief stung her cheeks. The creature, whose name was Tygjak, struggled to lift his head.

Thank you, was the whispered response in her mind, full of calm and understanding, *for a glorious death. You have kept your promise. I am free.*

The great head fell and Redd screamed.

TWENTY
Seraphim Secrets and Halcyon Rage

Pheonix looked out over the battlefield from his vantage point on the gate tower of the outer wall.

It was not going well.

Redd's release of the pirate slave creatures had done some good, but it was a drop in the bucket. The goblins themselves, sensing an advantage, were advancing, and with the protective wall of armored vehicles outside the water defense almost all crushed, the mechs and the crawler were pretty much holding this battle. They'd been rotating psykers and TKers out (the Ladies were tireless; the War-Ladies obsessed), but with the main skirmish zone being so close to friendly forces, artillery couldn't do much. They were still firing, but over the mechs' heads, into the heart of the goblins. Any little bit helped.

But the fact was, the goblins were pushing forward steadily, some by simply going under and around the feet of the mechs. Though they'd suffered unimaginable casualties, the goblins' disdain for life was so complete that it bothered them not at all to melt their own dead and tromp through the resulting mudpit of blood and gore.

And now the black school wizards were in maximum effective spell range to put pressure on the Seraphim's shield. With the split attention of the defenders on the wall, the Bashers weren't being taken out as quickly as they should have been, and had fired several times. He could imagine how much of a toll that took, to withstand such a blow.

Infantry would have to take over soon to drive the enemy back, or they'd be in the city in short order.

He cast a calculating eye over the battlefield and barked orders to the two elven scouts waiting near him. They disappeared silently to carry his directions to those who could make them happen — to stall for a little longer until the mechs were freed, to shore up areas that were weakening. In his ear was constant chatter from the defenders as those stationed all around reported the status of their zone, called for help, or offered assistance and suggestions. He wasn't, by far, the only individual of a tactical mind with an eye on the battlefield, and they all worked in tandem with the singular thought tying them together: defense of the city.

A siege animal went down, stapled to the ground by the two-hundred-foot-long extendable deutronium spear that was that psyker/TKer pair's chosen finisher weapon.

Eight down, two to go.

Something pinged his awareness and he instinctively turned, although he couldn't see her from there.

It was that same burning power, like staring into a sun; Redd was activating that strange ability she'd used to save his ass in the *erukahl* caves.

Another scout approached. Pheonix dispatched them immediately to get a medic and a TKer on the wall near Redd.

He wasn't sure if this was some mutant form of firestorm, but if it was, he'd want someone there to calm her. Better safe than nuked.

He mused briefly on Redd. He felt an odd … kinship was the best word for it, although they were hardly as intimate as that term implied. 'Shared destiny' — wasn't that what Tyyrulriathula had said? It was appropriate.

Pheonix didn't trust others easily, and while he wouldn't name her friend, Redd was clearly an ally of Justice, and that was all he cared about. That their personalities clashed was of no consequence to him, though, if he was being entirely honest, he'd prefer not to be a walking trigger to someone already so fragile.

But there was nothing he could do about that, and he was an expert in letting go of things he had no power to change.

Tyyrulriathula had *also* told him, in confidence over a beer, that Redd thought the same way about the balance that Pheonix did: that it only functioned to protect evil.

It had given him serious pause, in a way not many things could. And though only Chani knew, he had made a decision about Redd.

The battlefield shifted. He focused his attention on it. The goblins were panicking.

Now why would the goblins be afraid of Redd's odd power?

Some folks had said she'd felt like both the Creator and an Elysian, so perhaps the goblins thought she was associated with one of those? But then, why would the goblins be afraid of Elysian?

Maybe the Elysian reign of terror extended further than anyone knew. They *had* spent most of their time in Dark Sector.

Crossing his arms over his chest in thought, he leaned against the wall beside him. As he did, something pressed into his side and sparked power.

Immediately he knew what it was, and knew how badly he'd messed up.

Straightening, he pulled a bundle from his belt; the carefully-wrapped item he'd rescued from the ruins of the city on Haven. He tugged the cloth from around it and let it drop, revealing an intricate crown of silver and pure clear crystals and amethysts, with twelve points to represent the twelve Seraphim.

The crown of Ashera, first and rightful Queen of the angelic species. An artifact of ultimate power, handed down to each Queen as she is chosen by her people.

"Shit," he whispered ruefully, and turned.

***

A righteous rage welled up within Redd, and she called to the golden light with open arms. It filled her in a way that felt natural, like coming home.

HOW DARE YOU HURT ONE OF MINE, a wholly unfamiliar voice, golden but also blood-red, rippled from her very essence.

She cleared the battlefield around the rest of the formerly-enslaved creatures, which let them retreat to the outer wall, where they were rescued by psykers. Some of them were almost mortally wounded, and several others died along with Tygjak. The medics and Healers would save them. Redd's assurance on that was unshakeable. No more deaths.

She turned her attention to the siege machines, laid bare and crawling with the speed of a snail to her bullet mind. A touch from her power and the resulting explosion was a beautiful cascade of innate forces: chemical and mechanical reactions, energy and heat transfer, gravity and sound.

The squat machines with the bizarre heads, like battering rams on wheels, were the next thing to grab her attention. She could feel and see the shield weakening each time the fucking things fired, and they were pissing her off for causing the Seraphim pain.

She gleefully destroyed them.

"Gods protect us, it's the Daystar!" A voice bubbled up through the miasma of input to take her full attention. The word was familiar in a way she couldn't place, and that stirred her ire.

She traced the speaker to the line of generals hiding on the hillock behind their armies.

The Warboss clone and the Clan-Head were both shaking violently. The Grand Mistress, her dark eyes large with terror, was frantically tapping on and speaking into a dark crystal. Redd shattered it in the dark elf's face, just to see her squeal. Redd laughed uproariously — the sound must have been akin to a death knell, for each figure flinched.

Suddenly petulant, Redd demanded of them: "*Why do you fear me so? Why am* ***I*** *your nightmare incarnate, when you can raise your weapons to men like Pheonix and Ty without batting an eyelash?*"

"You … you are the light that burns to nothing and leaves not even ash!" The Grand Mistress hissed in fright. "We would fight a thousand false Justices and a million Bladesingers before we would ever face you! We remember Primus-1."

None of that made any sense to Redd, so her rage took center stage again.

"Know this! You forfeited your lives coming here!" she screamed at them, and was rewarded with more cringing. "*I am here. I am the first,*" she found herself saying, without knowing where the words came from, "*and I will be the last. I* ***am*** *the Daystar. Pray to your false gods. See if they will come face a true Ascended.*"

Her control wavered, and with it her vision. She was on her tiptoes on the edge of a cliff — now was the time to back away, before the abyss drew her in.

She let the light ebb away, spiraling into the part of herself that kept it compressed and stored for when she needed it. She was finally in her own mind again — her battered, tired mind.

Her eyes opened reluctantly. She was aware there were people waiting for her attention. A medic, and … someone else. The symbol on the collar looked familiar. She remembered Roland after a moment of searching. This wasn't him, but …

"TKer?" she mumbled.

He smiled at her and took her arm gently. "Come on," he urged, and the medic caught up her other arm. This was a good thing, as she found she couldn't walk without their support. "Time to rest," the TKer said.

Redd stared at them, her thoughts oozing. "Okay."

***

Pheonix made it to the Citadel in such record time, one would swear that he had teleported. The heavily-armed guards at the Seraphim's door looked at him in alarm, but didn't move a muscle to stop his hurried entry into her sanctum. The Seraphim herself sat in the middle of the floor, cross-legged, by all outward appearances resting. Pheonix knew it to be much more than that; while part of her attention remained with her physical body, the vast majority of her was well outside the room she occupied, scattered in a thousand directions to provide support to her people.

"Yes?" she asked in her quiet manner. The strain she was under was evident in her voice, in the set of her shoulders.

Pheonix dropped to one knee and presented the crown on his upturned palms. The Seraphim's eyes opened, fixed on it with a frightening intensity.

"Bring that to me."

Pheonix obeyed.

"Set the crown on my head," the Seraphim ordered.

As the crown touched her brow, a great burst of light blinded him.

For a moment, he shared her vision as the influx of power from the crown — and its connection to the Creator — gave her strength.

Infantry organizing — all suddenly aware of what needed to be done, crowding in ranks before the outer gate to prepare for the final confrontation — making way for the centipod and millipod, the living battering rams that would carve a path through the enemy for the hominin and humanoid fighters — the city would have been lost, even with Redd throwing her entire weight into the fight; the sheer force of the enemy pressing into the shield had moved it back almost past the water defense, and the Seraphim wouldn't have been able to hold out much longer — the ground rumbling as the Seraphim's shield tightened around it —

And praying — the most feverish devotion he'd ever sensed — would have brought tears to his eyes had he the capacity. A channel opened between the Seraphim and the Creator —

The shield congealed, became a solid thing, light playing along its surface like oil on water. The rumbling became an earthquake, then stopped abruptly. The sensation of rising. Pheonix stiffened his legs, expecting a jerk of some sort, but the ascension was smooth, controlled.

A heartbeat.

The shield faded, becoming translucent once more, and dissipated. Light streamed in through the window of the Citadel's main tower.

Pheonix moved to it.

Clouds rolled below and blue stretched from horizon to horizon.

The Seraphim had torn the Citadel tower cluster, her sanctum, from the earth, and lifted it above the clouds.

"Bast," Pheonix muttered and gripped the edges of the window. He hefted one boot onto the sill, and squeezed his seven-foot-frame through. Balancing precariously on the outside of the window like a very large pigeon, he gauged his distances for a moment, then launched with all his considerable strength.

Sailing outward, he spread his arms and legs, then snapped his wings out. The underdeveloped muscles protested at this use, but he put the discomfort out of his mind with an iron will. A pocket of air bubbled up underneath his wings and, subconsciously making slight adjustments to keep himself on course, he rode it into the dizzying heights of the upper atmosphere. He couldn't flap to gain height, but he could glide and descend, and if the infantry was putting boots on the ground, he'd need to get down there.

That Grand Mistress had Pheonix's name written in blood on her forehead. She just didn't know it yet.

The cloud cover burst off to his left and he watched, with mild interest, the *erukahl* Queen, surrounded by her drones and soldiers, rocket skyward. They ignored him, so focused was their Queen on the Citadel and what lay within.

Now with the crown and the Creator supporting her, the Seraphim was damn near indestructible. With the *erukahl* Queen out of the fight below, the chances of survival tipped more towards the side of the defenders.

Hey, that worked for him.

The only thing he didn't understand was *why*. Why lift the Citadel? It seemed on superficial examination to be sort of counterproductive. She'd made herself a target. But Pheonix was not so naïve as to think the Seraphim didn't have her reasons. Perhaps there was more to Pirroun than being a mere outpost to guard the northern mountains.

Regardless, she'd just changed the entire dynamic of the battle.

***

The Seraphim was filled with the power of the Creator. His love for her was his love for his partner Ashera, was his love for all of his children with her, was his love for all of his creations. It was a devotion so strong it was obsession; it was his power and his strength and his source, and so, hers. His children were threatened, and so his love turned to hate, to vengeance, to destruction, to grief. All possible emotions becoming one the way that all colors combined to create white, and light.

But the beginning was always love.

There was no easy way to take a life, even in defense of one's children, but the love made it possible; it was the basis for all things. Under normal circumstances, having to battle one of her own, even so corrupted, would destroy her. But sharing the Creator's unfathomable mind — partaking in the source of all that was and all that would be — sloughed away enough of her personality to see what needed to be done, and execute.

And yet, at her core, she remained — a spark, a droplet — and she called out in anguish:

Zadkiel! Why? Why has this happened? Why have you tormented us, me, your sister, your soul? Why didn't you tell me you remained, and fought? Why didn't you come to me? I love you! I would have protected you, fought with you, died with you!

The response was almost unintelligible. Zadkiel had been gone for so long, in the company only of her mindless children, she had forgotten how to communicate. A tangle of images, impressions, and sensations followed:

The skies turned blood-red with their power, their evil — lightning and aurora-storms raged in the heavens, their very existence an affront to herself and her Creator and all she stood for — but they were so strong, beyond anything she'd ever seen, these Elysian, and nothing could hurt them — still she fought, while her children died around her, and her people were slaughtered — the murderers laughing — the Creator silent in the face of her pleas for help — desperation, numb disbelief, as they struck her down — but they left her alive, unknowingly, and weakened to the sickness they spread into her planet with their presence — it seeped into her body, and turned her, infected her mind — the transformation was painful, so much agony for countless days, stretching moments into eternity, robbing her of what little faculties she still possessed — and eventually, the memories faded ...

And on the other side of the transformation, Zadkiel was gone, and only the erukahl Queen remained.

She slowly became aware, but she was alone. The aloneness hurt, and to combat it, she created children. Her children wandered far sometimes, and they crossed paths with those who were perfect.

The perfection was a damnation, it angered her, and she wanted it destroyed. But there was another, one whose power was connected to her somehow, one who protected the perfect ones. She couldn't leave it behind, but she couldn't approach it. She was magnetized, caught in between two poles and unable to move. The incapability of action ignited her fury, and her fixation, and became the focus of her every thought, although she didn't know why. Even that was fuel for the flames.

The perfect ones must die, and their protector with them. That had been what had sustained her, and now the protector had the crown — she didn't remember its significance, but its power was so great that were she to possess it, her children would never suffer again.

The protector must die, and the crown must be hers.

Zadkiel, corrupted Seraphim and *erukahl* Queen, paused in a rare moment of repose. She floated motionless in the cheery blue sky, a mockery of her lightless existence. It contrasted jarringly with her twisted, pale body and demonic facade. Her strongest children ranged around her in a loose formation, puppets awaiting commands. She gathered and fired synapses long atrophied, attempting to speak.

Her voice was distorted with disuse.

Sera — phiel. I was — abandoned. You left me — to die. But — I did not. You — made me this — way. It is — your justice — that now — you perish — by my hand!

Zadkiel, you were ordered to flee! Seraphiel pleaded. *Why did you not? I had to stay, I was the guardian of Pirroun and its secrets! But you ... you could have saved yourself!*

The broken voice came again, harder and stronger than before.

I was — ***abandoned****. The — Creator — did not — answer my cries. We — were — his — chosen! And now — I will destroy — that which — he loves. It is — retribution!*

Seraphiel, the protector of Everdark, sent Zadkiel a wordless flood of love and support and grief, but it was rebuffed. The corruption was too deeply rooted — there was no rehabilitation for a mind so far gone. There was no negotiation.

There was no choice.

Overcome by sadness, Seraphiel drowned in the music of the Creator's love.

The *erukahl* drones and soldiers shot forward, riding lines of psychic power in the manner of a spider traversing its silken threads. Seraphiel tightened her shield and they surrounded it, taking up posts at all angles to barrage her with psionic attacks. They sought a weak point, to tire her out and distract her.

Perhaps that would have worked in time, but they weren't given the chance. Sleek shapes bulleted through the air in tight synchronicity, and the first set of drones dropped. Puppets with their strings cut.

Ranger fighters shot off into the distance while Zadkiel screamed her fury, but she didn't dare chase them and leave herself open to an attack. When they looped back around, she erected a massive psychic wall. One fighter, too close, rammed into it and exploded. Seraphiel felt the life-spark burst like a mini-supernova, then dim to nothing.

Zadkiel shrieked laughter.

Foreign, white-hot anger surged through Seraphiel. She gathered her power and punched it through Zadkiel's wall, shattering it to allow the fighters through.

More drones and warriors careened into the clouds. Seraphiel felt the pressure on her shield ease.

From above, a giant conglomeration of wood and metal scraps cobbled together into a bloated, oblong ship descended from behind Zadkiel, then another, and another. The Ranger fighters spun acrobatically in the air and dispersed, avoiding the barrage of fire from the pirate frigates. With the fighters out of the picture, the frigates skimmed the cloud-cover, sending up frothy wisps of white, to fan out around the Citadel. With the stress of their weapons added to the *erukahl* probing for cracks, Seraphiel had to pour power into the shield to keep it solid.

There was no way to run dry; the Creator was a bottomless well. But channeling him was dangerous, and she could feel the burden of it already, fraying at the edges of her soul. Too long, too much, and it would destroy her utterly.

Doubt crept into her mind, coloring her prayer. She trusted the Creator with everything that she was, but was unsure of her own ability to withstand the assault and still manage to make an offensive push. It was too much on one body, on one mind.

And there was still Zadkiel to deal with.

The corrupted Seraphim hung motionless between two pirate frigates, radiating glee and triumph. In her mind, she'd already won.

Seraphiel struggled to hold on, fight against the bits of her being swept away in the stream of the Creator's substance. Losing this city was not an option. The secret she protected was far more important than herself, or any of the lives below, and if absolutely and utterly necessary, she would destroy them all to safeguard it.

That was her mission, as it had always been.

Suddenly the pirate frigates took fire. Seraphiel sensed ships descending from the rear: Ranger corvettes. Relief and joy blossomed within her. Ranger corvettes were shaped like giant firearms — blocky, more weapon than ship.

They shot past her in a calculated arrangement. She felt the plasma building in one of the cannons — a planet-disruptor — as the Ranger corvette lined itself up with a pirate frigate. The pirates broke away from Zadkiel and each other, panicking in the face of the Rangers' new onslaught. Their fire was drawn to the corvettes. The planet-disruptor shot a beam of plasma that lanced into the nearest pirate vessel, cutting it neatly in half. A series of explosions from the destroyed ship sprayed debris.

With the pirates and Zadkiel focused on the Ranger corvettes, the Ranger fighters again dropped out of the upper atmosphere and went about taking out the *erukahl* still clinging to Seraphiel's shield like parasites.

The dogfight circled her, rounds and energy and plasma bursts creating a cacophony of action. Her attention freed from them, she turned it to Zadkiel.

Zadkiel's confidence was shaken as she suddenly found herself alone. Seraphiel stretched out her awareness, enveloping Zadkiel in the Creator. The corrupted Seraphim fought, thrashed against the invisible and intangible, and threw her psionics outward like the detonation of massive grenades.

The Creator quelled the psionic power, wrapped her in impenetrable bands, quieted her writhing. Seraphiel watched, a silent witness, as the Creator reached through her and into Zadkiel, and said:

YOU, MY CHOSEN, BORN OF MY TEARS.

Zadkiel screamed to hear the words. She boiled with hate and distrust — and, deeper, grief and betrayal — but couldn't move a muscle or close her ears and mind. The love that cascaded through the link burned her, reminded her of that untainted essence that remained at her core. The disparity tore her apart.

And within her, the images rose again, and she was incapable of halting the tide.

Beyond written history, in the infancy of the universe, the Creator had the Firsts. The First angels were the literal children born of the union with Ashera.

Between the angels and the Creator was a love unparalleled by anything else that had ever been or would be.

The first few angels created sang praises to the Creator as a tribute to that love, that bond; but their voices were too sparse and it grieved them to have an incomplete song.

The Creator couldn't stand to see his children so upset, and wept.

The tears that fell became the twelve Seraphim, and in adding their voices, the angels became a choir. This made Ashera cry with joy, and from her tears were created the remaining angelic subspecies. The choir swelled as new voices took up the Song, and all was good.

Never again was the Creator made to weep by the angels.

Zadkiel was silent, tears streaming down her hollowed, lined cheeks. She ceased to struggle outwardly, but the internal battle yet raged. Corruption versus love, obligation versus the choice that she had made to disobey.

YOU WERE TOLD TO LEAVE.

I — had — to — fight! Zadkiel protested, anguished.

YOU CANNOT BLAME YOUR SISTER NOR ME FOR YOUR FAILURE.

Zadkiel's sorrow was wordless.

WHY DIDN'T YOU TRUST ME? AM I NOT YOUR FATHER AND MOTHER, YOUR HEART, YOUR VERY SOUL? DO I NOT KNOW THE UNIVERSE, ITS BEGINNINGS AND ENDS? AM I NOT THE UNIVERSE ITSELF? PAST AND PRESENT AND DISTANCE ARE MEANINGLESS TO ME. HOW COULD YOU THINK I WOULD MISLEAD YOU?

Shivers coursed along Zadkiel's body, the truth of the words piercing her as bullets and spears never could.

I always — trusted you — Zadkiel begged.

LIAR! IT IS **YOU** WHO HAS BETRAYED **ME**. MY CHILDREN WERE ALMOST SHATTERED HERE, AND THERE WAS NOTHING I COULD DO. INSTEAD OF AIDING THEM DURING THIS TIME, YOU ALLOWED YOURSELF TO BE CORRUPTED, YOU GAVE IN AND GAVE UP. YOU ARE ONE OF MY SERAPHIM, THE ONLY OF MY CHILDREN GIVEN THE PRIVILEGE TO SPEAK TO ME DIRECTLY, ACCESS POWER ENOUGH TO DO AS YOU PLEASE IN MY CREATION — BUT THIS COMES WITH A GRAVE RESPONSIBILITY: TO BE MY HANDS AND FINGERS AND FISTS. YOU KNOW THE RULES; I CANNOT

INTERFERE. YOU SHRUGGED OFF YOUR DUTY WHEN I DIDN'T SAVE YOU FROM YOURSELF, AND YOU DARE TO PROFESS THAT WHAT HAS BEFALLEN YOU IS **MY** DOING?

No — Zadkiel gasped.

THE ELYSIAN REMAINED BECAUSE OF YOU. SERAPHIEL AND THE OTHER WERE PROTECTED, HIDDEN. YOUR ENERGY ATTRACTED THEM. IF YOU HAD NOT RESISTED — IF YOU HAD DONE AS I INSTRUCTED — THE ELYSIAN WOULD HAVE MOVED ON. IT IS BECAUSE OF YOU THAT ASSISI IS DYING, THAT YOUR PEOPLE ARE FRACTURED. IT IS YOUR FAULT YOU HAVE BECOME WHAT YOU ARE, AND I WILL NOT SAVE YOU.

No — please forgive me — Zadkiel whispered.

There was silence.

That was worse than all else combined — even through the shackles wrapping her, Zadkiel convulsed, her face spasming with emotion.

NO — COME BACK — I'M SORRY — SO SORRY — DON'T LEAVE ME — I DIDN'T MEAN — TO DISOBEY — I ONLY WANTED — TO DEFEND — MY HOME!

Her pleading was that of a child, the broken voice innocent in its absolute confusion and sadness. The corruption clouding her mind shattered, and for a moment, her light shone through.

I know what I have done, she whispered, the mental message like the sighing of the winds through trees, *but I can never take it back. I can never set things to right. I will always be this way; it is too deep in me. Seraphiel, my sister, I love you. Whatever strife I caused you, I will amend in the only way I can. Perhaps in the next life, Zadkiel can redeem herself.*

You already have, love, Seraphiel murmured.

Zadkiel smiled, and in that instant Seraphiel saw again the angel she had been: Zadkiel's pale, ash-blonde hair was a halo of unruly curls about her thin face. She was tall, with a slender form that she had a tendency to wrap in loose sundresses and elven robes. With her six yellow wings, she felt like summer. Seraphiel hurt anew for how far Zadkiel had fallen.

The Creator loosed his bonds on Zadkiel, and she lifted her arms, palms out. Her energy streamed from her, leaving the perverted shell, as she gave herself up to the universe.

Seraphiel's heart ached to watch it, but within the sorrow was the seed of hope. Zadkiel's soul would remain untarnished, her penance and sacrifice wiping its slate clean for a new birth. And so she would be reborn. The Creator was nothing if not forgiving. The Seraphim all shared the same life, so until she was ready to return, her energy would be stored in a new Seraphim-to-be.

This was why, when she saw Zadkiel's energy slow down, and then funnel downward to the surface below, Seraphiel was so surprised.

Then she remembered the young archangel who had taken care of the plague, and nodded to herself.

Yes, it would go to the nearest Seraphim-in-potential.

She wondered, *Does the girl have any idea?*

Zadkiel's former shell, emptied of its contents, went limp but didn't fall. Its texture changed subtly. Bits separated, pulled by the light breeze with nothing more substantial than a thought to hold them together, and became dust. It dissipated into the blue sky.

By then, the pirates were thoroughly trounced. The Rangers gave no quarter; the corpses of the frigates undoubtedly spotted the battlefield below.

A kind of peace settled over Seraphiel. Her part was done. The rest was up to the combatants on the plains.

TWENTY-ONE
The Finale

Ara and Redd were on their way back to the outer wall.

Chani, Ty, Pheonix, and the various generals and leaders of the other species loitered below, preparing for their ultimate and individual confrontations with their opposites. Though Redd wasn't sure why they had to go have private duels, she'd been assured this was 'protocol' and had decided to leave it at that. Although Ara and Redd were still not at their peak performance, they weren't about to let others, who had fought just as long with just as little rest, continue while they sat around on their asses.

It was time to see where the battle stood — where they could be of the most help.

Redd was anxious, both to have the shield gone and to have Ara at her side, although the latter was a mixed bag of anxiety, relief, and the need to protect the little angel. She was glad to have her friend with her, and glad to be able to keep eyes on her, but worried about Ara's proximity to the front lines and her own ability to keep the girl safe, which she felt was her obligation.

She tried to convince herself Ara would be fine. Instead of the light robes she'd favored while inside the city, Ara was outfitted once again in her rec-suit. The likelihood of injury for her was fairly slim outside of direct confrontation.

And that was why Redd remained so alert. She'd given herself the task of acting as Ara's bodyguard. If she was being honest with herself, she didn't have the strength for anything else.

The girls approached the crenellations and took in the current state of the battlefield.

Gnarled hunks of burning wood and cherry-red metal heated beyond its breaking point created their own light, throwing a red cast to the knots of fighting surrounding them. The illumination shivered long, strange shadows from alien bodies.

Redd couldn't make heads nor tails of what the burning debris had been, but there were three piles of the stuff that now rose like small mountains from the plains outside of Everdark.

Piles of dead lay everywhere, in such profusion it turned Redd's stomach and brought her mind forcefully back to her nightmares. She had to steel herself to keep her eyes up.

The mechs, out in the distance to keep them away from the infantry (without anything as large as themselves to fight), stomped and kicked to take out huge groups of little bodies. In her near-hysterical state, Redd had a hard time not thinking that was funny.

"Look," Ara whispered, and Redd followed the angel's dark gaze.

She'd seen them earlier, but hadn't had a chance to stick around and observe for long. The two bug-like creatures at non-bug proportions.

A giant centipede and millipede, called a 'centipod' and a 'millipod.'

Unstoppable, slowing for nothing, they made their inexorable way through the goblins and their forces, crushing and grinding anything in their path to jelly.

An orc Berserker leapt on the back of the centipod, hacking ferociously at the thick carapace. Shards flew, and a crack formed, which the Berserker tore into with relish, his muscles straining as he deepened the hole to reach the soft innards.

A shiver went through the centipod. Redd watched in horrified fascination as the segments separated, and each became its own individual. They surrounded and descended on the Berserker, and she had to look away.

When she dared peek back at the carnage, the individual segments were barreling around the battlefield at breakneck speed; no organization, only rage. Several remained to guard the wounded segment, however, and that surprised Redd more than anything she'd seen of the creatures so far.

Enough of the enemy were pushed back from the gates of Everdark that now the infantry entered the battle. The dwarves and drakkan were already in the middle of it; instead of waiting to come through the gate, they'd just sailed over the wall. They attacked in small groups of various configurations. The drakkan fought as one might expect; preternaturally agile, swinging their spears with the deadly grace and efficiency of a species long used to being top of the food chain. There was a kind of meditative nature to them that contrasted sharply with the dwarves, who were all chaos and a laughing frenzy — weapons and beards flying, battle songs and war cries exploding from the depths of stocky chests.

Out of the gates now emerged the elves. Shining in silver or gold armor and carrying shields larger than themselves (which was a wonder considering how slender the elves tended to be; it really spoke of their innate strength), they moved in triangle formations with slow, measured steps.

A group of Brutes broke away and rushed them; silver blades snaked out from between the slats in the shields, and over the shield-bearers' shoulders, spears thrust to keep the enemy at distance. In the center of the formation was a small group of Rangers with ranged weapons. All in total, each of these triangle-shaped formations was made up of about a dozen people.

As more of these emerged, they spread out over the battlefield, further opening the space in front of the wall.

Ranger drop pods pierced the cloud cover to bury into the ground in calculated increments in that cleared-out area, and more vehicles emerged. These were smaller and less armored than the ones Redd had seen earlier, but they were fast and well-armed. As each dropped, they fired up and sped off to the outskirts of the battle.

Finally the elf-and-Ranger wedges ceased their march from inside of Everdark — there was a heartbeat's pause, then a staggered group of figures sauntered onto the field.

Redd's heart skipped to see them.

Chani led the group, literally bristling with weapons. Aside from her normal pistols, two straps crossed her chest, crowded with ammo and grenades. Across her broad shoulders was a rifle, and on her back was a tank from which a tube led into a gun-like nozzle that Chani carried in one hand. In the other hand was a large, unwieldy gun, the size of a rifle but with a barrel capable of loading an apple. The length of it was covered in foreign dials and lighted panels.

Behind her and slightly to her side was Ty, again wearing his armor, whose tension was palpable. While Chani was grinning frighteningly, Ty was more stone-faced than she'd ever seen him. His eyes were fixed on the distant hill, and the orc that waited.

At his side was Pheonix, who never changed in any situation. At least, not that Redd could tell.

Behind them, walking abreast of one another, were Tinkerfist and Stonebreaker. Tinkerfist was much like Pheonix in that his emotions didn't show outwardly, but Stonebreaker was obviously in his element. Uproarious laughter carried over the distance between him and the wall.

The elf-and-Ranger groups continued to clear a path through the enemy for these individuals. Chani, Pheonix, Ty, Tinkerfist, and Stonebreaker took to this path with easy confidence, and as they passed, Redd could just barely hear cheering from the troops. She closed her eyes and opened herself; a wave of energy, like a tangible thing, spread outward in ripples from these heroes into those fighting all around them.

More people came out of the gate — angelic and elven medics and Healers, running like their asses were on fire. As the enemy were pushed further and further back, soldiers would break off from the wedges, sling wounded over their shoulders, and the line of this slow-moving rescue cadre would meet a medic halfway.

Some were left behind, remaining on the ground, unmoving.

Sadness welled up in Redd.

She watched as an angel knelt beside one corpse, deformed by being trampled by many feet. The angel clasped his hands before him and spread his wings protectively over the body, shielding it from her sight. His wings trembled and the feathers took on their own incandescence, and she could *feel* the prayer radiating from him. Astonished, she watched the energy flow back into the body, correcting its wounds, returning life to its tissues — and then, most miraculous of all, the soul (who she realized she could sense waiting nearby), stepped back in to inhabit its former flesh.

Redd was too overwhelmed by all the new information and horror intertwined to know how to react to witnessing a resurrection.

The angel slumped and it was the warrior they'd resurrected who caught them. There was a murmured conversation that Redd could sense without hearing, then another medic ran to help the exhausted angel — while the warrior dug around on the ground and found a sword.

The warrior adjusted their armor, then took off sprinting to the front lines.

Ara was unnaturally silent. Redd could feel her holding herself back.

"You alright?" Redd asked her quietly.

Ara jerked as though startled from a deep sleep, and turned owlish eyes on Redd. "Redd, can you — "

Redd grinned, and the expression interrupted her friend. Ara furrowed her brows, then squeaked as Redd scooped her up.

To take to the sky again was pure exhilaration, but it wasn't long before she was forcibly sobered.

A pair of drakkan, flying slowly and cradling one of their kind between them, approached. The cradled one's leg was severed, spilling green blood. Ara tensed in Redd's arms and she paused midair.

"Do it," Redd murmured, knowing her friend's mind.

Ara nodded and Redd edged closer. The drakkan hovered as the two girls approached, Ara already reaching her hands out towards the dying soldier.

A white glow leapt into life around Ara's hands. Redd's inner sight was blinded by the strength of the Healing, and she watched in wonder.

This was nothing like the Healings Ara had performed on Redd — the little angel was a vortex of prayer and a supernova of light to Redd's inner senses. The drakkan tensed and hissed in pain, but at a comforting word from Ara, calmness waterfalled through them. Her power cocooned the drakkan; they breathed it in, it entered their veins and suffused every cell. Energized and incited, their body pushed into overdrive. Muscle tissue and bone and veins and nerves crawled out of the torn flesh, twining around one another like a den of snakes, fusing. Naked muscle armored itself in natural plating in a wave.

With a final prayer of thanks from Ara that brought tears to Redd's eyes, Ara let the Healing light fade. She looked up, a little dazed, into the eyes of the three drakkan. Snarls showed rows of sharp teeth — it took Redd a moment to realize they were smiling.

The drakkan that had been Healed bowed their head until their bottom jaw touched their chest, and Ara dipped hers in a sheepish response.

The trio separated and performed a graceful pirouette, and, just like the resurrected warrior, returned to battle. Redd shook her head, and it took a nudge from Ara for her to remember their mission.

Redd dropped them at the edge of the nearest skirmish and hesitated, paralyzed by a moment of indecision.

Why did I come down here? she thought in desperation. *Why did I bring Ara into this lion's den?*

Ara, however, was apparently afflicted by no such debate. As soon as her feet touched the ground, she was off and running, her long braid thumping the backs of her calves. Redd stared after her.

Ara skidded to her knees, heedless of the dirt and dust turned to stinking mud by blood and gore, and laced her fingers together before her face. Her one wing stretched upwards towards the sky. A womb of light surrounded her and Redd shivered to hear the cadence of praise and pleading spilling from her lips.

What was happening? Why had Ara changed so?

A silken veil, barely seen and sparkling to the inner eye, settled over the combatants across the entire battlefield. Goblin wrenches and orcish jagged swords rebounded before they contacted flesh, minor wounds healed spontaneously, blood loss halted, power and physical energy were replenished.

Even Redd felt it — the tingling under her skin, butterflies in her stomach, the feeling of lifting up, of love and support.

The next hour was a blur.

The infantry wedges and the centipod and millipod made way for the heroes to take a leisurely walk to their own battles; the drakkan and dwarves had moved to the outskirts of the battle, hemming the enemy in to keep them from fleeing.

All that was left was to clean up remaining goblin forces — though why Chani and the others had to go personally fight the enemy generals, Redd still wasn't sure.

Redd helped by sniping things from a distance with her psyker power — with no training, she felt she'd be a liability in the thick of things — until she was no longer needed. By then, she could feel the strain (though she'd been energy-transferred and had slept and eaten and had more stim pills than she could count, she still wasn't entirely recovered from her joining with the golden light, so she tired out too easily), and had returned herself to the confines of her own mind and the ground.

She searched for Ara in a moment of panic, noticing the lack of her protective prayers — but found the little angel asleep in the arms of an elf, who was carrying her back towards the gates. She shook her head, amazed and awed by her friend. She'd pushed herself beyond her limits to ensure that others wouldn't be hurt.

Ara had the strongest mother-of-all-living complex she'd ever seen.

She cast her gaze over the battlefield — infantry returning, medics picking through the bodies to find their own, flashes of light speaking of resurrections and Healing. The centipod segments were reforming, but several of them remained apart from the whole to drag unknown bulky objects back towards Everdark.

Finally she turned to the hillock, expecting to see bodies there, too.

Instead, there were ten figures, five on each side, regarding each other across the intervening distance with varying reactions.

Something clutched her heart in icy fingers. The final battle hadn't happened yet — what were they waiting for? Her eyes fixed on Ty. He burned. Kser exuded arrogance and triumph. He was savoring Ty's anger, the fact that the Bladesinger was teetering on the edge of losing his cool.

Kser's lips moved, and Redd caught the scent of words forming, though she was too far away to hear them.

***

"Another Bladesinger — am I to be gifted with a second Deimmortalizer?" Kser asked with a laugh in his voice. "But this one is so young, hardly even worth the energy to weave the spell … perhaps I will just bathe in his blood instead."

When Ty showed no reaction, Kser lifted the Deimmortalizer, angling it so that Ty could clearly see the former elf's visage. Ty stiffened, a trembling beginning in his limbs. Kser, the permanent rictus of a smile on his disfigured features stretching wider, ran a long, pointed black tongue over the cheek of his unholy weapon.

Ty exploded.

The song that emerged from Ty's chest through his throat was deep and akin to the bellowing of some enraged beast. His swords were already dive-bombing the laughing orc as they flickered into being, each strike parried by one of Kser's four weapons. Ty was unhinged with rage, but Kser was supernaturally fast.

A whirlwind of hate was growing in Ty. It infected him, gave him power, but stole his concentration. There were no coherent thoughts, only rage. It filled him, spilled over like boiling water splashing over the edge of the pot, to manifest in the air around him. A wind picked up, stirred the dust at their feet as Kser and Ty danced back and forth.

Whatever had almost happened in the training ring of Everdark had Ty in its grip once more.

The others squared off, waiting for someone to make the first move. Tinkerfist and Stonebreaker stood next to one another while the Warboss clone and the Clan-Head took up posts opposite them. The Warboss clone twitched and muttered to himself. Meeting Stonebreaker's gaze, he broke out into unintelligible gibbering and screaming at the top of his lungs. This clearly amused the dwarven General. The Warboss clone's eyes misted over and he waved his hands wildly over his head, the trinkets and statuettes covering his body clicking and clacking loudly. At the same moment, the Clan-Head launched at Tinkerfist — and barely managed to avoid Tinkerfist's shield, thrown like a two-hundred-pound discus.

Power gathered around the Warboss clone. The Clan-Head struck at Tinkerfist, who deflected the blow with an armored forearm, and brought his hammer down, Stonebreaker stood his ground, grinning under his beard, and the infuriated Warboss clone shoved his hands out before him like he was pushing something away, a bolt of lightning cracking into existence. The Clan-Head lifted both his weapons to parry Tinkerfist's hammer, then windmilled his arms to bring them around, turning the parry into a strike. The lightning bolt slammed Stonebreaker full in the chest … and instantly dissipated.

Meanwhile, the Grand Mistress and Pheonix stood motionless. Pheonix: loosely balanced, as patient as a mountain; the Grand Mistress: sizing him up, but visibly nervous.

On the far end of them, Chani, still smiling, bowed and offered an elegant arm to Vathath.

"We may require some space from these brutes — wouldn't want to get dirty, would we?" Chani said with false courtesy.

Vathath sneered and began to walk, Chani paralleling her. Neither woman took her eyes off the other.

By some unspoken consensus, they stopped at the same moment and faced each other. Chani stood with lackadaisical ease, the nozzle of her flamethrower and the barrel of her other weapon both pointed away and to the ground. Vathath simmered with irritation but made no move against the Ranger Commander yet.

"Typical coward-ass orc," Chani lamented, "won't attack first. Fine!"

Lightning-fast, she hefted the gun with the wide barrel, propped it against her shoulder, and fired at an upward angle. Vathath skipped out of the way, but caught the outer radius of the explosion and was showered with chunks of burning rock and smoldering dirt as the grenade went off just where she'd been.

"Let's see you dance!" Chani yelled, and the grenade launcher *thoonked* again.

Vathath stopped moving and threw her hands up, a shield flaring into life. The plasma grenades bursting against her shield set everything around her to flames.

"Coward!" Chani called, and dropped the grenade launcher. "Creator-loving cunt, you gonna hide behind that shield all day? Fine, I got a present for your goblin-fucking ass!"

Chani reached behind her and whipped the rifle out. Vathath's eyes widened. She forced her shield outward, snuffing the flames surrounding her, and called up a quick magical bolt. Chani aimed, not bothering to step out of the way — the bolt fizzled as it hit her personal null-shield. The orcish sorceress, on the other hand, had no choice but to dodge, as energy weapons ignored magical barriers.

Vathath mouthed a few words and threw her arms out, and the ground beneath Chani rolled and opened. Chani swore and jumped to more solid footing.

Vathath laughed and kept the rock underneath Chani's feet from supporting her. "Now who is dancing?" she called mockingly. But her amusement would be short-lived. The orc readied herself to cast another spell … a deadly mistake. Without the constant focus on keeping Chani unbalanced, the rock hardened. Chani knelt down in that moment and aimed steadily. Vathath lifted her hands — and they spattered into bone chips and black blood. The wounds instantly cauterized.

"Go ahead, finish that shit you were about to cast at me!" Chani challenged.

***

The acid stink of fear was so strong coming off of the Warboss clone then that even Stonebreaker could smell it.

"Didnae work, hmm?" he asked, almost gently. The ugly little goblin shook violently, rooted to one place, his beady eyes large with panic. "Never fough' a dwarf face-to-face before? Yeh know we're immune tae the fae-stuff."

The Warboss clone screeched and flailed his arms, calling down lightning, poisonous fogs, gale-force winds, columns of fire — and each time, as soon as the conjuration touched Stonebreaker, it dispelled. The dwarf didn't make a move against the Warboss clone in retaliation, letting him tire himself out in the grip of the dwarf-fear. It wasn't until thick, thorny branches burst from the ground to encircle Stonebreaker that a shadow passed over the jovial General's wide face. Stonebreaker jerked a finger and they, too, popped out of existence.

Stonebreaker raised his weapons threateningly: in his left hand, a power-hammer engraved with runes and scenes of the glory of the Stonebreaker clan, in his right, a giant axe whose blade was also a chainsaw.

"Now, tha' was a mistake," he drawled. "Yeh doan scratch a dwarf's armor."

The dwarves, despite their stocky frames and love of the underground, were also known to, occasionally, fly. Stonebreaker wore power armor — enhanced with hidden pistons and enchanted with dwarven runes — the only magic known to the dwarves. He squatted, those pistons priming and engaging. The pistons fired with the straightening of his legs, propelling him forward a distance many times his own body height.

Sure, it wasn't … exactly flying. But a ton-and-a-half, fully-armored, four foot tall dwarf couldn't jump over a pebble normally. For dwarves, it was like taking to wing.

The Warboss clone squeaked in absolute terror and stumbled backwards to avoid the first downward chop from Stonebreaker's power-hammer. He rolled sideways and pulled something from inside his tattered robes. As Stonebreaker bore down on him, he leveled an ugly pistol with two pressure tanks on either side of it at the dwarf's chest.

Stonebreaker hissed in surprise and threw himself to one side. The last-minute movement saved his life — the infamous goblin bolter loosed its kinetically-driven iridium missile, which punched through the armor just below Stonebreaker's shoulder instead of piercing his heart.

Smiling with shaky relief, the Warboss clone dropped the bolter to the ground as the dwarf fell to one knee, supporting himself partially with his axe.

His ease would prove premature.

Stonebreaker rose like a newly-birthed mountain from the violence of a quake, the war cry "*For Druim Kazak!*" erupting from his throat in a basso boom. He raised the axe, and put a certain pressure on its haft, which fired the chain-blade to spin with a feral growling. The Warboss clone's eyes bugged out and he reached for the bolter, but it was too late.

Stonebreaker's axe dropped like a guillotine and cleaved him in half with a bloody, chunky spray, from the top of his head to his groin — right along the vertical line that separated the two halves of the Warboss clone's armor.

The two halves fell to opposite sides, organs spasming as they ceased to work, blood and bile and shit running down to pool beneath the mutilated corpse in a fetid smoothie of bodily fluids.

Stonebreaker heaved himself to his feet, an angry grimace pulling deep crags into his lined face.

"There. Now yeh're truly two, yeh stupid bugger. Doan say a dwarf never did yeh a favor."

***

The Clan-Head was a brutish, unskilled but very powerful fighter. He'd risen to the top of his clan through cruelty and sheer strength alone — very few goblins knew any form of sophisticated martial art and even less were intelligent or patient enough to overcome their physical limitations in other ways, so he was essentially a pumped-up bully.

Tinkerfist was clan-brother to Stonebreaker through a marriage between the dwarven Regent and Tinkerfist's sister, an unprecedented union that had united the warring clans of the dwarves and the mercenarial gnomes. It was his brilliance that had given the universe the instant portal and the combat techniques for fighting seated in a mech, among other things. He was the Accord's Diplomatic General Extraordinaire — the prime mediator for the Accord — the foremost gnome in the universe, aside from being, in his own right, something that left genius far behind.

His title, Tinkerer of the Third Level, would sound like a misnomer for such a prodigious fellow to someone who was not familiar with gnomish society. Tinkerer of the First and Second Levels was in fact the Master Tinkerer of the Universe — the gnomish name for the Creator. The Creator was so far above any creator inhabiting any other plane that he took up two spots.

Tinkerfist was very old, and unlike in human society, this did not mean he was infirm of mind or body. It meant he'd *survived* to that age, a difficult enough thing to do that it required a fair bit of determination.

His armor was the most technologically advanced to ever exist, made out of the toughest stuff, enchanted with the most fervent devotion.

He was at this battle because he wanted to be, and no one had the right to tell him 'no.'

And he hated bullies.

So, needless to say, this was not a fair fight, but not in the way one might think if one were to come across the two combatants with no prior knowledge of them. The eight-foot-tall Brute — corded muscle straining at every point on his body — versus the aged gnome, who broke perhaps four feet, even taking the mech into account.

The Clan-Head attempted a forward strike with both weapons that overbalanced him and sent him stumbling forward. Tinkerfist boosted the propulsion on his mech and shot upwards, putting himself at the level of the Clan-Head's snarling mug to avoid the attack. He kicked the Brute in the face, breaking several bones.

Roaring, the Clan-Head swung savagely, uncontrolled, momentarily blinded by pain and blood. Tinkerfist's mech could maneuver on every axis, and so as he hovered, he moved neatly, avoiding the swinging weapons.

The Clan-Head recovered and redoubled his efforts, chasing the much-smaller Tinkerfist around like a giant trying to smash a hummingbird, and with as much success. Even when he did manage to land a blow, it rebounded, leaving the mech unscathed.

It dawned on the Clan-Head that he wasn't going to win. Not only that, but even at his strongest and quickest, he'd never been a match for Tinkerfist.

An unfamiliar feeling stole through him: fear.

There was a subtle change in Tinkerfist a moment before it happened; the gnome stopped and lowered his weapon. The Clan-Head, being not very bright, fumbled and paused as well, confused. Tinkerfist's expression didn't change, except perhaps to betray a little pity.

Something slammed into the Clan-Head from behind. He teetered, paralyzed by shock, but felt no pain. He was aware of falling, the world tilting and spinning at crazy angles. As he hit the ground, he saw his own legs and the edged discus Tinkerfist had thrown earlier returning to its master, and knew what had killed him.

***

"Bast-damned bitch," Vathath hissed, her voice distorted through sharpened teeth and lack of lips.

Chani regained the sight picture down the scope of her rifle and went to squeeze the trigger. The rifle became boiling hot in her hands. She yelped and dropped it, sidestepping as

Vathath shot forward and opened her mouth. Flames billowed from the purple depths of her throat, and Chani skipped to the side to avoid the spread. Vathath turned to follow her: Chani angled out of the spell's limited range.

She yanked her energy pistols from their holsters. With a sort of unpleasant-sounding burp, the flames cut off, and Vathath took off running at an angle toward Chani to avoid the barrage.

Chani backed up, but in order to keep the pressure on, she couldn't move very far or fast, so Vathath closed quickly. She narrowed her eyes at the pistols, mouthing a word.

Chani swore vehemently and fluently, dropping the now-frozen pistols. She reached behind her to the small of her back and pulled out a short-barrel kinetic shotgun. Vathath grunted in surprise and threw herself to the side as the shotgun fired — but not in time. The cone of incendiary rounds caught her side, shattering the chitin crystals there and punching burning holes in her flesh, which leaked noxious black blood.

For a heartbeat, Vathath gawked, wide-eyed and uncomprehending, into Chani's cold stare.

Then she made a decision and whipped around, tearing off toward the distant woodline.

"*NO YOU DON'T!*" Chani roared. She snatched a grenade out of her harness and chucked it, which Vathath darted to avoid. Chani let loose another waterfall of invectives and took off after her, hucking grenades with all her strength to try to get them out in front of the fleeing orc.

Vathath was known to the Rangers for being a practitioner of blood magic of a particularly cruel variety. She was an outcast to her own people for said blood magic, but for different reasons than the Rangers were after her — the orcs felt that using anything but orc-made or Pestilence-made was 'betraying' their people. Vathath had been on Chani's list for a long time, and Chani wasn't about to let her escape.

Chani had only one grenade left, but knew that Vathath was not an athlete. Chani sprinted after her with determination and quickly caught up. When she gauged that she was in range, she swung the flamethrower's wand around — the nozzle from which the flames emerged, connected to the tanks by tubing — and let fly with a stream of fire.

Vathath then spun around and raised a hand (*What?!* Thought Chani), directing the flames back at Chani.

Chani skipped backwards and let the trigger go, but the flames, and Vathath's incessant laughter, followed her.

Now she was pissed.

The bitch had been casting a regeneration spell as she ran. She'd only managed to get one hand fully done, but it was enough for the spell she cast next (some spells required audible or kinetic components, especially in maguses who hadn't spent enough time studying the threads of the Weave.)

Chani realized Vathath had *let* Chani close in to be in range for a spell. She thrust her one hand out, and her putrid blood followed the motion, shooting out to grab at Chani's limbs and throat.

The look on her face was one of delirious triumph —

— but the blood-tendrils bounced off of the personal magic null-shield that Chani's Commander's belt generated.

Chani grabbed Vathath's face and threw her down to the ground. The orc flipped onto her stomach, and tried to crawl away over the broken, dusty ground.

Chani had no pity; no hesitation; no mercy.

She pulled one energy dagger, slammed a foot into Vathath's back, and yanked the orc's head back to an angle it was loath to adopt.

In one swift motion, Chani brought the blade in her other hand across the exposed throat — the only weak spot on a Bound; the only spot not completely encased in putrescence chitin. The energy blade bit deeply, sliced without resistance, and a terrible smell rose from the fatal wound.

Chani didn't wait for the death-throes to finish before turning away.

Orcish bodies stunk to high heaven, and she wasn't about to have that smell on her for the rest of the day.

She did, however, toss her final plasma grenade over her shoulder, setting the corpse ablaze.

***

The Grand Mistress had accepted and discarded a thousand plans in the few moments she and Pheonix had been staring at each other.

So this is the one, she thought, studying him.

The child who had made the Obelisk and Chosen screech 'Justice.' Who had — obviously by sheer chance — taken out Ka'Resh and Zu'Resh. But he was deep in both the elves' and Rangers' innermost circles; likely it was only by their aid that he had managed anything at all. The Obelisk and Chosen saw only what they wanted. She wasn't about to rely on anything either of *those* entities yapped about. Yet, it was true that this armored infant was making certain groups … nervous. And here he was alone, and the Grand Mistress had the chance to kill him, remove a thorn in evil's collective side.

As a Grand Mistress, she was only one step beneath Matron, the twelve rulers. She had something in her possession — thanks to that crazy Elysian — that would allow her to challenge one and ascend to her rightful place at the top, and she was damned if she was going to let the opportunity slip between her fingers!

But there was no way to strategize in this situation. Her information sources hadn't mentioned anything about *this* ragged bunch. They must have pulled together the defense of what she'd been told was a battered, weakened city in record time.

Damn the Chosen for agreeing to the duel protocol!

As her anger rose and her eyes finished sweeping across the armored figure across from her, she tensed.

A memory not her own lined up with her inner eye and she growled, freeing her whip from its loop on her belt and snapping it.

"You're the bastard who killed my creature!"

His lack of response inflamed her further. With a shriek of rage, she let the pain-whip fly — one touch would seize up the target's nervous system and cause them extreme pain — which to her incredulity, he didn't bother to dodge.

It wrapped around his neck.

Before she could even laugh, though, she found herself yanked forward and the whip handle flew out of her lax grip. The armored youth slowly, while holding her horrified gaze, unwrapped the whip from around his neck, and snapped its flexible length into pieces with quick lateral yanks. Like it was no more than a child's toy.

He threw the pieces on the ground.

"You have one more chance," he gritted.

Something niggled at the back of the Grand Mistress's mind, but pure fury dominated her thoughts. Growling, she unsheathed her vibro-blade — a sword with tech that allowed it to vibrate at the frequency to easily slice through a variety of materials — and clicked it over to its highest setting. It roared to life and she leapt at him. The male dark elf tied her waist scrambled to follow her, but he was expected to keep up and she would make no allowances for him. He'd risen through the ranks of her harem for his cunning and speed.

Her opening strike was returned with such strength that it knocked her back and she almost lost her balance. In less than the blink of an eye, the youth had weapons in his hands. The niggling doubt became a small worm.

She stared at him in stark shock.

Nothing can turn back the vibro-blade! It can cut through even deutronium! What is this?!

His weapons were not right. One crackled with lightning, the other burned with a red glow. They *watched* her, hungry.

The worm was now a gnawing, many-toothed thing, wending its way through her mind and leaving behind sticky, raw … fear.

The youth lifted his own blades and the Grand Mistress realized her time was up. She gave the signal to her slave — the youth's eyes flicked from him and back to her — but it was too late.

Yanking power from the life-spark of the planet itself, she duplicated herself many times over at the same time as unclipping her slave's chain from her belt. The duplicates surrounded the youth, and she spun on her heel and ran flat-out for the safety of the forest, already fumbling to activate a jump. She just needed to get to her dark energy cache, then she could port out.

Then the youth was in front of her. All decorum gone, she shrieked in fear and tried to dart around him.

A mechanical hand caught her by the throat. Her feet left the ground. As she choked, dismay sparked in her pain-addled brain.

He destroyed all of my doppelgängers and my slave that quickly?!

The youth was furious, and though she'd faced fury more often than she'd faced nearly any other emotion, this wasn't like anything she'd seen before. The Grand Mistress was mesmerized by his gaze — depthless, abyssal.

Is this truly Justice?!

And then — a shock, pain, and wetness. She struggled to look down, but needn't have bothered — the youth withdrew his crackling sword with a vicious yank that made the Grand Mistress scream. It was smeared with the luminous green of dark elf blood and bits of organ.

Then — blessed Bast! — the youth wavered on his feet and lost control of the arm holding the Grand Mistress up. The mortally wounded dark elf met the ground hard.

Her slave must have gotten the Bast-damned brat with the Godslayer-poisoned dagger he carried as a last resort.

After a moment, the dark elf managed to roll over and get to her feet, clutching her stomach to keep everything inside.

With a backwards glance full of grudging hatred, she made for the woodline.

***

Pheonix reached inside his breastplate, into the Ranger armor beneath it, into a pocket. With fingers going numb from the poison coursing through his veins, he took out his communication crystal and said two words into it:

"Help. Now."

The crystal fell from his hand and he fell with it.

***

Just a little farther, The Grand Mistress prayed, and promised, and begged. *Just a few more steps, and I can make it. I can sense the dark energy already. It will save my life.*

Even she wasn't convinced, and the fear pulsed in her with its own heartbeat.

Too much blood; it soaked her from stomach to ankles, a sticky reminder of her own mortality.

I shouldn't be bleeding this much, she thought feverishly. *Why hasn't it stopped?*

The reality was, she couldn't sense the dark energy. She couldn't sense anything. The world around her was as dead as she was going to be in a few scant minutes. The reality was, the dark energy that supported her existence, her abilities, even her healing …

Gone. Stripped by the youth's sword.

For the first time, she regretted.

But that was only the coward's response to impending expiration. Were someone, anyone, to offer her life again at any cost, she would take it and renege on any deathbed promises.

Even praying to her patron God, Bast, got her no response. She couldn't tell that the link had been severed, and her desperate need went unheard.

She didn't even sense the Elysian when she appeared.

The Grand Mistress cried out and fell to her knees, overcome with fear that the shadowed shape (*why is it so dark?*) looming over her was the youth, come to finish her off, that the poison somehow hadn't taken.

There is no resistance to Godslayer poison, she comforted herself, panting. *At least he* ***will*** *die.*

She squinted at the shape. She went cold as the features resolved themselves. No, this was worse than the youth. Worse by far.

"Did you retrieve it?" the Elysian asked, her voice as sharp and thin as the knife slipped between the youth's ribs.

The Grand Mistress had no strength left to talk. The Elysian knelt down, into the breast pocket of the Grand Mistress's suit, and pulled forth a thin silver chain, on which hung a carved stone dragon's head. The Elysian drew in a quick breath, her blood-red eyes glued to it.

The Elysian's eyes met the Grand Mistress's; the dark elf shivered.

In the way Tinkerfist was beyond genius, Ichiryu was beyond rationality.

"We are finished, then," the Elysian whispered.

The Grand Mistress opened her mouth to — to, what, ask for help? She was dying. Even now the edges of her vision greyed, the pain receding into numbness.

But a part of her would rather die than receive any aid such a creature could render.

The Elysian turned away. It shocked the Grand Mistress, and she struggled to raise a hand.

"Wait," the dark elf choked.

The Elysian paused and looked over the bony concave of her back.

" … please … "

The Elysian's expression remained unchanged. "Our transaction has been concluded."

The Grand Mistress gaped and watched the darkness swallow Ichiryu.

The numbness was creeping up her midsection now. It was too hard to keep her hand over her stomach. Slowly she lowered herself to lay flat, her muscles giving out. As her body settled and her hand fell away from the jagged wound the youth's sword had delivered, she saw the purple coils of her own intestines roll out, slick with her blood.

And yet, she had ceased to care.

***

It was easy to claim that they were evenly matched — that Kser was holding back, or that Ty was too angry to utilize his full potential. The reality was that Ty was consumed by his rage, and that Kser hadn't yet attacked, but that was far from meaning that they were even.

Were Kser to attack, he would leave himself open, and the battle would be over.

And he knew it.

He'd tried, and had the broken chitin to show for it. Now he was biding his time, preparing to catch the crybaby with the Deimmortalizer. As soon as it touched any elf, they would cease to exist.

That's all he needed: one moment. One unguarded second — less than a second!

But the kid was infuriatingly fast, and with every motion that might have led to a strike, Kser found a sword in the way.

He'd fought Bladesingers before — duh — and they *did* tire, so all he had to do was wait. But then again, he was four weapons against six, and the sheer pressure the kid radiated was making it hard just to draw breath.

Just — one — shot!

The monotony of *parry, block, deflect, defend* was starting to get to him. He didn't have a very long attention span, and he could feel himself already starting to lose concentration. That made him angry. The kid didn't seem to be tiring at all, and here he was, a Sword-God, getting bored in battle!

Time to hurry things along.

"Do you know what he did when I cut his head off?" he asked in a sibilant undertone to Ty, knowing even through the wind ripping at them that he would hear.

Ty responded with a low growl through the song. Kser grinned maliciously.

Get him angry enough and he'll mess up. I won't have to wait for an opportunity — he'll want to get his hands on me.

"We had him tied down and naked in our temple, in front of all the People," he continued nastily, watching the anger move under Ty's skin. "We tortured him, in every sick way we could think of, for days. Would you like to hear them listed alphabetically or chronologically?"

The wind gained strength. The swords moved faster, just by a hair.

"It was beautiful, his blood, and he made the most delicious noises and faces as we slowly cut his throat. I wanted to make it last. He died so slowly, his agony and fear and despair all woven into the spell, lending it strength." Kser sighed in lascivious remembrance. "It was perfection."

The wind — it was unbearable, as though he were trapped under the weight of a starship.

It was now almost opaque. If he turned his head the right way, in his peripheral vision, he could almost see other blades. They winked in and out of existence, trading between formless and solid in an instant and back again.

It was then he realized he couldn't hear the Song, and that he wasn't seeing things. But by then it was too late.

A sword speared him through the shoulder and disappeared, shattering his chitin and spilling black blood.

What was left of Ty's control was gone.

All Kser saw in his eyes was death.

***

Redd hovered at the edge of the freak windstorm, frenzied in her worry. She couldn't see to its interior, couldn't make out the shapes of Ty and Kser any longer.

With her inner sight, the whole zephyr looked like an outpouring of sick red, with shapes she couldn't quite make out darting in and out of the flow. And Ty was its center.

But his song — it made her physically ill to hear. She wanted to cover her ears, hum, scream as loudly as she could, anything to keep it from invading her. The *wrongness* of it was intolerable. But there was no way to refuse its entry; Ty's anger pumped through her system, his need for vengeance and death weaved into the melody that was now a hideous howling. Merely stoppering her ears wouldn't make it go away.

Redd fluttered her hands and shuffled from foot to foot in her panic. She was gathering her resolve to delve into the storm and save him — *somehow* — when it abruptly vanished.

That was to say, it solidified into thousands upon thousands of blades.

For a split second, she saw Ty and Kser, locked body-to-body in a deadly struggle. Then the swords descended, and she had to look away.

People hurtled past her, from behind, at breakneck speed.

She could feel Kser's death without seeing it, in the change that rippled through the blades. Kser was gone, and yet the swords remained. They hovered, trembled, spun about as though confused — then slowly, as one mass, turned inward.

Toward Ty.

Redd wanted to cry out, but, as if in a nightmare, fear and desperation had closed her throat and robbed her limbs of movement.

Luckily, there were others present not so afflicted. More people rushed past her, heedless of the danger, into the center of the army of weapons.

Ty's horrible song was sparser now, his voice fading and cracking, and a new song took its place — different voices, their song one of sunlight through leaves, the whisper of the wind, the tittering of a sparrow as it darted through clear blue skies. Redd's heart leapt with hope. The elven Rangers.

Woven into the Ranger song was yet another, this with higher-pitched voices. Its rhythm reminded her of … Pheonix, oddly. How safe he made her feel.

Ty was silent, but his emotional turmoil (and the swords), hadn't yet gone entirely. She could sense the singers struggling with him, fighting the rage that wouldn't let him go.

And they were losing.

It was one of those moments that later she couldn't recall correctly, one of those things that the mind buries to protect itself. A reckless decision made at the right time, for the right reasons, the subconscious bypassing the consciousness to take direct control of the body.

She seemed to make a lot of those.

She didn't remember getting across the intervening distance, only seeing his face as her hands cupped his cheeks. He burned like he'd contracted a fatal fever, far hotter than a body should be. His eyes were shut so tightly it contorted his beautiful features into something monstrous. Every muscle in his body was rock-solid.

She whispered his name, ran her fingers across his brow, and, when he didn't respond even to that, gripped him tightly and pressed her forehead to his.

"I'm here," she whispered. "I'm here, it's okay. You can do this, my love. Push it back. You can do this."

When it seemed her words weren't reaching him — a battle she couldn't win but damn if she wouldn't try — she called on the golden light, set it to buzzing under her skin, ready to take on the swords of his rage even if it killed her —

Then something released. The intangible bonds that held him in the stasis of fight or die loosed, and he fell limp against her with an exhalation that might have been a sigh.

She sagged backwards and caught herself at the last moment — he was heavier than he looked, and she hadn't been ready — but other hands were instantly there to take some of the burden. She looked up, and saw only the empty sky above her. The swords were gone.

She hiccuped a relieved laugh and looked to the nearest face — but all that met her was grimness, determination … fear. It sobered her immediately.

They sang to him as they took him away, but she walked with them, holding his hand. She refused to leave and they didn't ask her to. She talked the whole way. She told him about Chaos Earth, about her favorite music and vid shows, her favorite foods. She talked until her voice went hoarse.

Though he didn't respond and didn't open his eyes, he squeezed her hand once, weakly, and she knew he heard.

TWENTY-TWO
Aftermath

"Report," Chani said, her strong voice carrying over the conversations around the table.

The exhausted, drained, but elated leaders hushed and turned their eyes to the Ranger Commander. The first to speak was a high-ranking elven scout, who gave dry but necessary after-action reviews regarding remaining enemy forces (zero), corpses of the enemy leaders (found and burned), no enemy presence detected as far as they could range in a reasonable amount of time, and numbers of civilians returning to the city.

The next to report was Pheonix's corps Commander, in lieu of Pheonix himself. Pheonix himself, the elf said, was recovering well from the Godslayer poison and should return to action shortly, thanks to the concerted efforts of the angels, elves, and his own natural resistance. Murmurs of relief went around the table. Next he covered casualties (a very small list of un-resurrectables, though their gene-seeds had been recovered), the list of recovered items, and finished with a general estimate of enemy forces faced.

Tinkerfist was next. He set something down on the table. There was a sudden thick silence. A goblin bolter — the weapon that shot Stonebreaker. Bolters had been the bane of many a dwarf, who, being made of rock, weren't as susceptible to most other types of weaponry as other, squishier, species. But because of goblin ingenuity and cowardice mixed, the dwarves and allied species had never been able to get their hands on one, and therefore had no effective countermeasure for them.

But now they'd recovered a working bolter, and Tinkerfist, without a trace of pride or arrogance, said that he had the schematics already laid out in his mind for a solution.

Chani's corps Commander took over, relating updates about the pirate dreadnoughts captured and the enslaved preparing for rehabilitation.

A medic spoke up next regarding the state of the Healers' force — how many needed sabbaticals, a return to Availeon, or a purging (elven Healers worked much like traiteurs by taking sickness into themselves, which would build up and poison them over time, thus the need for purging). She also talked about the pirate slave outbound species (the beasts Redd had freed), the number of resurrected, and the number already headed for their homeworlds. Sadly, the drake, who had sustained such wounds that he couldn't be Healed in time, and who was, by nature, an un-resurrectable.

The drakkan Shell-Commander offered to take care of the body until such time when he could be dealt with appropriately.

Chani appointed two Ranger Captains to handle the building of garrisons on-planet, the allocation of supplies, and the recruitment of Rangers for the first two-year tour.

Then she reminded the assembled of the celebration to be taking place shortly, said that the dwarves had damn well better bring beer, and dismissed the meeting.

***

Redd loitered outside the door to Ty's room, alternately raising her fist and letting it drop.

They'd kicked her out a few hours prior and made her rest and eat again, although she was too wound up to do either with much success. Ty had calmed down and was sleeping when she left, and she'd been told he was awake now … but in what state, she was afraid to find out.

Finally she took a deep breath and knocked lightly.

At first, no answer came.

Cold despair welled up — then, he called softly from inside.

Redd pushed the door open to a lightless room. Ty stood by the window, silhouetted by Everdark's gentle phosphorescence. He was still tense — she could sense that without even trying — but he also radiated an intense sorrow and biting regret.

She inhaled to steel herself against the force of his emotions and closed the door behind her, crossing the room towards him.

Silently, she laid her forehead against his back and closed her eyes, willing some of her strength to flow into him — but she was just as conflicted.

He shifted slightly then, putting a minute distance between them, and turned to gather her into his arms. It was a crushing hug, and she ignored the difficulty in breathing to wind her arms tightly about him in return. He needed it.

Hell, they both did.

"What happened?" she asked.

And waited.

"It was a Bladestorm," he said finally, quietly, in a tight voice. "Something that happens when Bladesingers berserk. It is very rare, and … fatal … to the untrained."

"What?" she managed.

"You saw it," he went on, stronger. "It was turning on me — that's what it does, when its target is dead. The rage is so complete, it will destroy the soul that spawned it as well as … anything else in the area."

Tremors ran through him as the reality of what had happened hit him. Redd clung to him, trying to be supportive while her mind whirled.

Slowly he calmed, some of the stiffness running out of his muscles. Sighing, he laid his head on her shoulder.

"It's not all bad," he murmured, a ghost of his usual humor in the words. "I am to be a War-Bladesinger. It is what becomes of those Bladesingers who threaten a Bladestorm, whose emotions run too hot. They are trained to call on it and control it, although I am the first to survive a full Bladestorm conjuration without training."

He paused, and his voice went distant. "It was like being the center of a storm … I had no identity except for the storm, no idea who or where I was. It was … just rage." He sighed tremulously. "It would have killed me that way if by no other means … except for you." His voice took on a subtly different texture — one of memory, of warmth. "I do remember you. I was so devastatingly alone in there, I couldn't even hear the Song. But you brought the Song with you. And I found the strength to fight."

He caressed her chin with gentle fingers. "You saved me."

She shook her head. "I didn't do anything. You're the one who fought it. The most I did was help."

"Shush," he said, and kissed her gently. "Let me be grateful."

He pulled her in for a hug, and for a long time they remained that way, drawing comfort from the shared embrace.

But Redd remained conflicted.

Ty was one of the three people — Ara and Chani being the other two — she'd made a serious and lifelong connection to during these last few months.

And that scared her.

So much of her life felt dull before coming to Haven. Was this connection with him more of that dullness sloughing off? Was this how things were supposed to feel?

Her grip on reality was tenuous at best, if she was being entirely honest. What were emotions but visceral reactions to things perceived as tangible? What even qualified as real —

something too dull or something too bright? Dreams faded after waking, but so did the sense-experienced. The memory muddled all. What decided which held more weight?

For Redd, with every new experience came the uncertainty of, *Am I doing this right? Is this okay?* And she had no one but herself to answer.

Ty pulled away with a sigh, which distracted her from her quickly-spiraling thoughts. He offered a smile; he was worn and tired, but he was trying.

Her heart went out to him.

Looking into his beautiful eyes, she remembered something Chani had said: "*Nothing wrong with having fun and not really worrying about the 'forevers,' yeah?*"

I'm afraid, Redd thought, *but I have to trust myself, and trust these people that I've decided to love. Not everyone is like my parents. Not everyone is out to betray or hurt me. I have to try, just like Ty is.*

"Ready?" Ty asked.

A poignant question. She studied his gaze for a moment more, wondering how much he knew, then nodded.

He draped an arm over her shoulders and they went outside, where Ty immediately halted. He was staring off to the side. She followed his gaze.

Three elves were engaged in some kind of ritual not far from the door to Ty's room. They hadn't been there before. One elf sat, singing, with shards of something in their lap which they gracefully wove their hands over. Following the motions was what looked like glittery clay, melding and reforming into a long, flat shape. An elf stood on either side of them, hands out, eyes closed, chanting in time with the song of the melder.

Ty's eyes were distant again. Redd nudged him. After a moment, he glanced at her.

"They are making the new sheath for my Lawblade. There are two components to controlling a Lawblade — physical and mental. Physical control is represented by the sheath. A Bladesinger can actually die if the mental control is lost during a berserk or a Bladestorm, or if his sheath is forcibly removed or destroyed. The Lawblades will turn on him."

"What makes this new sheath so special?"

"It is stronger, it will protect the Bladesinger from a Bladestorm, and there are two slots. War-Bladesingers wield two weapons."

"Two weapons — two Lawblades?"

"Yes, or a Shadeblade."

"But, wait — you're *chosen* for a Lawblade."

"You can be chosen twice," Ty chuckled.

"And the other?"

"Those chosen for a Shadeblade are, instead of the Altar of Law, drawn to the darkest parts of Spiraea's Wood, where they find a Shadeblade awaiting them. They are ... *wilder*, I suppose, is a good word for it."

"Bladesingers — War-Bladesingers — none of you can use normal weapons?"

Ty shook his head. "We can, but not with the Bladesong. We can pick up a sword and swing it and learn how to use it, but we can't take that same physical sword and suspend it with the Song. The swords spawned by the Lawblade aren't fully real, and the Song isn't meant to interact with the physical in that way."

"What are they saying?"

"Those standing chant the spells of protection and strength that will bind to the new sheath, and thus, to me. The Smith sings the story of Andural, a Bladesinger-Smith, who was killed and made into the first Deimmortalizer. He was later freed and given his body back, an occurrence that had never happened before and has not happened since, so he could continue his work as a Smith."

Ty frowned for a moment, unsure, then went on: "Andural developed this technique, and so, is honored during its use." He squeezed her shoulders lightly. "Let's let them work."

He drew her away down the hall, the ethereal interweaving of voices following behind.

***

The war room was crowded for one last war council.

The Seraphim waited patiently while the leaders and important figures from the defense of Everdark settled. She inclined her head to the crowd and gave her enigmatic half smile.

"Welcome. I trust you all know about the celebration, so we will attempt to make this as fast as possible. The first order of business I'd like to discuss is our guest, Tisaki. She declined to speak to the group but agreed to tell me her story — understandable, considering what she has been through."

The Seraphim lowered her eyes.

"While there is much to it, I will paraphrase. An Elysian named Ichiryu has made a planet on the outskirts of Dark Sector her own. Tisaki is of a species native to that planet; in fact, she and her bonded mate were the leaders of an underground rebellion to overthrow her. Ichiryu got to Tisaki's mate and brought him under her sway, I assume with a spell similar to what was used on Tisaki herself. Weakened by his influence, she eventually allowed Ichiryu to work magic on her. Through this, she and her mate were separated mentally and used against their own people."

The Seraphim paused, waiting for the rumbling of angry murmurs to subside.

"Tisaki confirms," she continued in an unusually harsh voice, "that Ichiryu met with the dark elves, the orcs, and the goblins on separate occasions, and, using wealth stolen from Tisaki's people, bought their services against us. Ichiryu also forced open a large tear to our world, although Tisaki was not privy to the knowledge of how.

"Tisaki's orders upon entering Everdark were to kill someone in particular. She and the dark elven assassins had different missions. She believes they were to be a distraction, and that Tisaki herself was the true assassin for someone that Ichiryu has become utterly fixated on."

The Seraphim met Redd's eyes with silent conviction. Redd thinned her lips but said nothing.

"Moving on. As many of you are rightly concerned, I am pleased to announce that Lord Justice made a full recovery from the effects of the Godslayer poison. The body of the individual responsible was recovered and burned, so the gene-seed is destroyed. Justice has been served."

Mutterings of relief and a few scattered cheers swept the crowd.

The Seraphim then removed the crown from her head and lifted it on her palms. Silence fell once more, reverent to the artifact.

"This is the crown of Ashera, only rightfully worn by the true Queen of the angelic peoples. I am not eligible for such a position, as the Creator's decree is that a Seraphim cannot rule, only serve. Therefore we must choose someone from among us, the few survivors of the angelic species, who is worthy."

A moment of hushed contemplation overtook the assembled.

Then — Ara raised one tiny, pale hand.

"Yes?" the Seraphim said.

"May I make a suggestion?" Ara asked.

The Seraphim nodded once.

"I nominate Arrista Legaia."

Heads turned, voices expressing curiosity, agreement, support. Arrista had nearly killed herself to keep the plague from claiming as many citizens as possible; she had been a source of emotional and spiritual comfort for her people while they were pinned down by the *erukahl* and cut off from the universe.

She'd been a rallying voice when it seemed that there was no hope, helped mediate between the councilors and the people to mitigate disputes and prevent conflict, provided invaluable support for how to best utilize and ration their meager resources.

She had already been a true leader during a time when, without one, Everdark would have collapsed under the weight of tragedy, and was a beloved figure besides.

There was a silent, immediate, overwhelming consensus that no better nomination could be presented.

Those close to Arrista shuffled away, leaving her bewildered in a circle of empty space. Arrista turned large eyes on her twin, who smiled with benevolence and love.

"Are there objections?" the Seraphim asked.

No one spoke.

The Seraphim nodded, and Arrista made her way towards her twin like one dreaming.

"Kneel, Arrista Legaia."

Arrista obeyed.

"Do you swear to serve the angelic peoples with honor and honesty, for as long as we deem you worthy?"

"I do," Arrista said with conviction.

"Do you swear to protect the angelic peoples and hold the life of the lowest above your own, for as long as we deem you worthy?"

"I do."

"Do you swear to subjugate your own personal will for the betterment of the whole of the people, for as long as we deem you worthy?"

"I do."

"Do you swear to hold the Creator's laws above your own, to respect what this crown represents, and … well, do the best you can?"

Arrista grinned through tears. "I do."

"By the authority granted to me in the Creator's name, I give to you, Arrista Legaia, the crown of Ashera and the rightful place as the Queen of the angelic peoples!"

The Seraphim set the crown on Arrista's brow. A flash of light burst outward from the two of them, only to be sucked inward a moment later, gathered into Arrista. It settled into a gentle glow.

Cheering erupted among the viewers as Arrista rose and faced them. She seemed to bear herself differently — in the way she stood, shoulders back and chin up, and the proud, elated smile.

"At that," the Seraphim said over the din, heard without shouting, "go! Celebrate the end of the war, the crowning of a new Queen, and the renewed strength of the angelic species!"

The cheering became the deafening uplifting of dozens of voices, suffused with joy so intense it brought tears to many an eye.

They were free.

***

Redd stopped, in awe of the spread the species had prepared.

In the center of Everdark's main square were six long tables, each boasting a different assortment of goodies.

One had what appeared to be flora of some description although Redd would be hard-pressed to relate any of them to the plants she was familiar with. Scattered around the platters were oddly organic-looking crystal flutes filled with a clear liquid.

The next table was much more familiar to her; it was piled high with steaming meats (from what animals though, again, Redd couldn't begin to guess), oozing in their own juices, fresh breads, and bowls of soups and stews. This was the only table with a centerpiece, which was a many-tiered sculpture of a dwarf in robes and an armored breastplate, wielding a shield and hammer. It was ringed with beautifully crafted, artfully gilded glasses of something fizzy and ranging from blood-red to olive green. Around the centerpiece were caramelized carcasses exuding tantalizing, meaty odors … but also sort of like hot rocks?

The table next to that one was probably the angelic contribution, considering its mushroom content, and the fact that it contained a much less luxurious and extravagant spread than the others around it. Redd felt a stab of sadness — the angels didn't really have much left in their larders, and this was probably a large portion of it. But then, she guessed they hadn't been required or even asked to contribute. And with a portal into Terelath and supplies constantly streaming in, they would be in no danger of starving.

The next table had to be the oddest. In neat little stacks were multi-colored cubes, all completely uniform in size and shape, each accompanied by a sleek metallic decanter.

The second to last table looked a lot like the second, although with a strange lack of beverages and side dishes. Replacing them in accompanying the roasted animal parts were strange pods, each the size of an ostrich egg and in varying shades from green to black.

On the last table, Redd was surprised to find she actually recognized some dishes. Steamed fish laid out by the dozen, bowls of noodles in fatty broth, heaps of mixed vegetables, and small dumpling-like dough balls all rubbed elbows with metallic packs the size of small bricks. An assortment of beverages were laid out on one side.

People of all species were now pouring into this central area. Grinning, Redd made a beeline for the last table, eager to dig into some noodles. She halted as hands took hold of her shoulders and directed her to face the first table. Ty propelled her with gentle but no-nonsense force, even when she dug in her heels.

"Hey hey hey, where are you taking me?"

She couldn't see him, but she heard the smile in his voice. "You must try elven cuisine first."

"I don't wanna," she whined.

She felt him lay his chin on her shoulder. "Training doesn't happen overnight, you know. You'll be stuck in Terelath for years, at least. While there will be replicators, you won't always have access to them. You've got to try other species' foods."

Redd glanced wistfully over her shoulder, craning her head to see around Ty's grinning face. "If I'm going to be there for years, shouldn't I get my fill of food I'm used to now?"

"I want to share this with you," he said, becoming serious. "But I won't force you if you really don't want to."

His arms wound around her and he squeezed gently. Relaxing into the embrace, she thought.

"I guess," she said finally. "But I'm just going to *try* it. Don't expect that I'll like it. And I still want my noodles."

"Thank you. And I'll make sure you get your noodles."

But before she could so much as take one bite from the plate Ty piled high with fruits and vegetables from Availeon, she sensed something that made her pause.

A familiar mental signature — familiar, but … *no, that's impossible…*

And she saw him.

She surged from her seat, mouth open in disbelief, vision blurring with tears.

It couldn't be. I watched him die.

Tygjak.

People respectfully moved out of his way both due to his bulk (he stood easily seven feet at the shoulder) and the part he had played in the war. It was hard to mistake who and what he was; the burn scars around his massive neck from the collar were only barely covered by a different collar, this one with a little box on it. He had similar wrappings and boxes across his bigger wounds. Redd figured they were some kind of healing devices.

Up close he was terrifying, a wall of corded muscle and huge teeth. But Redd wasn't afraid.

She disentangled herself from Ty and ran to him. He bent his head low. She threw her arms around him — carefully, so as not to bump one of his many injuries — and was content to cry.

"How — ?" she finally managed.

A concerted effort from those who love you, came the mental response. With it were a rush of disjointed images.

Somehow, though he'd been dead for hours and well beyond the point of no return, Pheonix and Ara had resurrected him.

I stayed, Tygjak said in her mind. Images came again: a lushly fertile jungle planet with sprawling cities in the massive treetops, others of his kind — his pack — and acceptance. She took a sharp breath as meaning settled, conveyed better through memories and emotions than it could have ever been through words.

She had saved his life, so she was a part of his pack. And he expected her to come visit.

Her first instinct was to downplay. She had freed him, yes, sure, but he'd died anyway, and that was a failure in her mind. But they had a link now, and she already knew what his reaction would be as though they were trading half-formed thoughts.

Yes, he had died, but he had been resurrected. His people were not the type to focus on the past or the circumstances; they valued the thought behind the action (for a telepathic species, this wasn't surprising) and lived in the present.

"I have … obligations … " she waved her hands, trying to find the words.

Tygjak gave a twitch of his long tail and a flick of one rounded ear, apparently meant to brush off her statement.

When you can, he said. *Your pack needs you. But, you are also now my pack. It is ... important that you come with me and be honored. Until then, I will stay with you.*

Redd put her hands up. "No, you don't have to, you've been gone so long already — "

A low growl, not aggressive but negating her protest, cut her off.

He put one large yellow eye up to her face. *I do not abandon my pack. You are now family. I will stay.* He leaned back up. *Unless you truly wish me to leave.*

It was not a threat or trying to coerce; he meant it honestly. Fear, relief, and gratitude overwhelmed her and she put her forehead against his nose.

Don't leave me alone in my own head, her mind whispered.

"Thank you," she said aloud.

He rumbled, a sound she took to mean pleasure or happiness, and butted the side of her head with his. It almost knocked her down, but she recovered her balance and turned to Ty.

She found him standing a few feet away, watching the exchange with the widest eyes she'd yet seen on an elf.

"Ty, this is Tygjak. He was … a slave. They used him on the battlefield. I freed him." She couldn't help the embarrassed pride in her voice.

"Tygjak, this is Lord Tyyrulriathula." Elven wasn't so hard to pronounce when you'd spent enough time around them. "He is a Bladesinger and the Commander of the Phoenix Legions."

Tygjak rumbled again; this had the tenor of being impressed. *A great warrior. I am pleased he is your mate.*

Redd burned. Ty's shocked expression melted into a grin. She didn't even want to know how Tygjak knew they were together.

Transformation rippled through Tygjak's flesh. He shrank, his spine straightened, the bones of his legs and arms shifting. When it settled, he was quite a bit smaller and stood upright, but not that much more had changed. He was still muscular, covered in the short, velvety brown/orange fur and the natural dappling, he still had a tail and yellow eyes, but his features were roughly humanoid. Deep-set, round eyes, a wide nose, thin lips, square jaw. The tufted feline ears remained. He gave a fierce smile, showing fangs.

"It isn't often that I am called to use this form, but it is," he paused to consider his choice of words, "interesting."

Though he was speaking a language Redd understood, there was still something about his manner of speech that reminded her of growling. Even as a humanoid, there was no mistaking what he truly was.

"So you will join us?" Ty asked him.

"Of course."

***

Now several hours into the festivities, most of the gathered folk had eaten their fill and were imbibing the various drinks and partaking in other forms of entertainment.

Knots of trading broke out around the slightly quieter perimeter — it wasn't often that so many different species got together to celebrate, and many saw it as an opportunity to stock up on rare items unavailable on their particular planet. Not everybody liked Terelath or could get there easily.

Elves sought out drakkan and looked to take home some of the egg-like 'dragon-pods' that were considered, by elves, a delicacy.

Gnomes offered their odd trinkets and complicated machinery; dwarves, their precious gems and metals; the Rangers brought the particular conveniences of a military society (the biodegradable tents, the cubed food); and the elves bartered with fine home-grown silks (sung from the silkworms), organic weapons, musical instruments, magical or blessed talismans, and any number of other things manufactured on their massive homeworld.

The trading was dwarfed and drowned out by the various bursts of song, dance, show, and story that had broken out around each table.

The dwarves had a particular style of story-song that involved loud, boisterous singing, many toasts, the stomping of feet, and mock-battles with much uproarious laughter to hint at their content. The elves performed a beautifully choreographed dance with the Ladies providing a subtle light show to imitate the dappling of luminescence and shadow that was apparently pervasive in Terelath. The drakkan, so stoic from a distance, treated their listeners to stories woven with such fluid grace that they had been known to bring the King and Queen of the elves to tears. The gnomes eagerly demonstrated some of their more oddball contraptions. The Rangers and angels were the only two tables without entertainment.

To an outsider, it would seem like a mishmash of pointless noise. But for someone wandering amongst the tables, each performance stood out where it needed to and merged seamlessly in with everything around it in the in-between spaces.

The species were mixed so thoroughly, one was hard-pressed to see two of the same standing side by side. And in the background, out of the portals poured a steady stream of supplies, people, and building materials.

The fortification and expansion of Everdark had begun.

***

Imae took another sip of her beer and turned her eyes to the ground, taking a moment to shut everything out.

When she looked up again, she met a pair of smiling grey eyes. Chani made her way through the crowd — straight for Imae. She was actually content where she was, and wasn't about to let her Commander drag her into that uncomfortably crowded menagerie.

“Hey,” Chani called as she got close enough. Immediately defensive, Imae grunted a greeting. “Nice spot you’ve found yourself.”

Imae eyed the older woman, waiting for the other shoe to drop. Chani just grinned disarmingly.

And here it comes, thought Imae acidly.

“I’ve got someone I want you to meet.”

Bingo.

Imae sighed and looked into her mug, gently swirling the liquid around. “I don’t want to be social right now, Auntie.”

“It isn’t out in *that*, I promise. I know how you feel about crowds.”

Imae hadn’t ever said anything of the sort, but she wasn’t surprised Chani had picked it up. She’d grown up around Chani, since the Commander was good friends with her parents. While not the current *official* head of Abyssterilon, some said Chani should be, so she got around with the other clan heads.

And apparently, according to what Imae had witnessed over the weeks, everywhere else.

Imae’d heard her parents talking enough to see the patterns in the ‘politicking’ within the Rangers. Chani was, essentially, the de facto head of Abyssterilon, given that its official leaders, Taylor and Dwayne Abyssterilon, essentially just took their orders from her behind the scenes. Imae knew about it, but didn’t know why or, really, care to. All of this say-one-thing-and-do-another bullshit was just another reason why she’d skipped ship and ended up in this mess.

Imae went to argue further, but stopped herself. “I’m not going to get out of this, am I?” Imae sighed and raised her glass. “Can I take this with me?”

Chani eyed it. “I wouldn’t.”

“Oh, it’s one of *those* meetings?” Imae asked, lifting a brow.

Chani laughed again and slung an arm over Imae’s shoulders, turning her towards the entrance of the alleyway they were standing in. "You're too smart for your own good. Just shut up and let's go."

***

As soon as Imae rounded the corner, she stopped dead. Chani's arm tightened and the much stronger woman forced her forward.

"You had to talk to them sometime," Chani murmured in her ear.

Tucked in between several buildings was a little hidden courtyard, in the center of which was a dry fountain that had seen better days. And standing in front of that fountain were Imae's parents.

While her feet trudged woodenly along, Imae struggled internally with panic.

Imae looked up and met the eyes of her mother. A small, compact woman, she had a presence about her much like Chani: the confidence and strength of a Ranger officer. Her father stood stonefaced, slightly behind her mother, a walking brick of a man still very physically capable even into his grey years. Her parents were both older; they'd waited to have a child, Imae had always assumed, to fulfill their illustrious military careers, but she'd never thought to ask.

There were a few moments of awkward silence as Chani backed away, leaving Imae stranded to face the people who loved her most. Imae's brain scrabbled for something to say and came up empty. She looked at the ground to try and gather her thoughts — and was caught up in a crushing hug by tiny but muscular arms. Imae's mouth hung open as her mother released her, sniffling. Her father came up behind her mother, smiling, and put a huge hand on his partner's shoulder.

"We came as soon as we could slip away," her mother started in a slightly wavering voice. "You can probably imagine that HQ is in an uproar right now."

“That communications blackout had us completely stonewalled,” her father put in, his voice a deep, cool rumble. “We had to have messengers transport back and forth to even get updates on the battle.”

“What we’re trying to say is, we’re glad to see you safe.” Imae’s mother leaned in and gave her another tight hug.

“I’m … glad to see you guys, too, but why did you come on-planet?” Imae asked when she was free of her mother again. “I’m sure the Commander has a transcomm you could have buzzed.”

Her parents glanced at one another.

Imae’s gut knotted. *Here it comes*, she thought.

“We didn’t want you to be able to cut us off. Imae, honestly, what were you thinking? Why did you sneak away from HQ?” Her mother asked, sounding more confused than angry. “Do you know how much we had to go through to cover up this whole mess? How many careers you put on the line with this childish stunt, including your own? You know the scrutiny we are under after Damien … ”

Imae dropped her eyes to the ground, resentment and rebelliousness welling up. She felt hands on her shoulders, gentle.

“I’m not lecturing — I honestly want to know. This is serious, and you’re old enough now to make responsible decisions. Anyone in charge of soldiers has to realize that the smallest things they say and do affect everyone around them.”

Imae tore away and backed up a few steps. “That’s just it, mom! I don’t want to be like you guys! I don’t *want* to be in charge of soldiers, I don’t *want* to be an officer! But nobody asked me what I wanted! It’s always about the Rivios name, always about taking charge and responsibility and blah blah blah! If I’m old enough to make decisions on behalf of *other people*, in *combat situations*, where people’s *lives* are in danger, then I’m damn well old enough to make decisions on *my own life!*”

There was a tense silence.

"You're right," her mother said, shocking Imae thoroughly. She and her father exchanged meaningful glances. "We discussed it at length before we decided to come down and speak with you in person. And we came to the conclusion that, in our zeal to protect the Rivios name, we put too much pressure on you."

"W — what?" Imae choked.

"If you're positive that you don't want to be an officer," her father said, "then we believe you. Do you know what you *do* want to do?"

Imae blinked too much and couldn't respond at first. Then she blurted: "I want to be an engineer."

Her mother smiled. "A fine choice."

"We will start the process of removing you from cadet training as soon as we get back aboard ship," her father added.

Imae leapt at them and they enfolded her in their arms. Despite herself, tears leaked out of the corners of her eyes. As her parents released her and she pulled back, she rubbed her eyes. The angry tension she'd been carrying around released, and she almost felt for a moment like her legs couldn't support her.

"But for now, enjoy your time here," her mother said gently. "Try not to worry so much. We have heard you; we apologize that we pushed you this far."

Imae nodded, unable to speak.

"But as for us, we need to get back," her father said. "Officers aren't allowed to have fun. You know how it goes."

Imae shook her head, chuckling. She hugged her parents one last time, then watched as they walked away. She turned to Chani once they were gone. The older woman had a forced innocent look on her face and refused to meet Imae's eyes.

"That was a mean trick," Imae said accusingly.

Finally Chani met Imae's gaze with lifted eyebrows. "Who, me?" Laughing, she shoved her hands into her pockets and spun on one heel to face the way they'd come. "I hope there's still some beer left, I'm parched."

"Don't change the subject."

"Hey look, some dirt!"

"Auntie!"

***

Redd watched, fascinated, the two elven women moving with such sinuous synchronicity that they seemed to be one creature, splitting and reforming under the colorful light display provided by a Lady standing behind them.

She sat on the bench at the elven table, cradled in the circle of Ty's arms. A crystalline flute rested forgotten at her elbow. Tygjak squatted on the other side. She'd asked him if he wanted one of the pillows Ty and herself sat on: he'd declined, saying squatting was how his people naturally sat in this 'morphological configuration' (whatever that meant) and putting his butt fully on the ground would be uncomfortable.

It was the third day, and the celebration had lost a good number of its participants. The square was still packed, but it wasn't overflowing as it had been before. Redd could tell things were finally winding down — the general feel and flow of energy was one of sedation, calmness, relief. People's movements were slower, there was less dancing and more relaxing, talking. Even the boisterous dwarves were taking a break from their loud entertainment style and were mostly napping, as quietly as the dwarves ever seemed to do anything.

Redd let her eyes wander from the performance, taking brief moments to watch the goings-on around each table. She felt strangely low-key, herself. Maybe it was just the comfort of having it all over with; maybe she was infected by everyone else. Maybe she was just happy that no one but Ty had paid any attention to her.

Smiling, she tucked her head under his chin and was rewarded with a little hug.

A ripple of silence interrupted things. Redd turned to see a split opening in the crowd and leaned up onto her knees to get a better look.

The Seraphim smiled with motherly affection as she made her way to the elven table. The throngs moved outward around her, creating a space. Bowing her head, the Seraphim slowly spread her wings. It was like watching the petals of a flower unfold. They were pure white, and glowed slightly, leaving an afterimage when they moved. She rose into the air and lifted her arms, tilting her chin up.

"We, the angels, have fallen so far," she began, her voice carrying unnaturally. "The demons split us apart, and the Elysian ruined us. Our planet mutated. We were pinned down and harried by those mutations, and its spawn. We were betrayed and abandoned by one of our own kind who lost the way. We were removed from the Book of Races, mourned or forgotten by the rest of the universe. Forced to watch as our power waned and our people fell, one by one."

She paused and looked around triumphantly. "No more! We endured the tests of the Creator and came out victorious and stronger than ever! In honor of those of us who survived and those who are gone, this is my gift to you."

Redd shuddered as power spiked from the Seraphim; she felt it take form and spread as rapidly as a startled bird took to wing.

A wind picked up, and the sky lightened. Redd, along with everyone else, looked up. The clouds boiled and spun. Urged by the incredible strength of the Seraphim, who floated motionlessly with her arms spread, the clouds were chased away.

A starscape of unparalleled beauty stretched overhead, widening as though seen through an opening door. Redd let out the breath she had been holding and rested her hands on Ty's arms. He pressed his cheek against hers; she could feel his smile. Tygjak rumbled approval.

There was no cheering, no raucous jubilation, only a quiet appreciation for the breathtaking and long-missed sight of the sky. Redd did hear some quiet crying in the crowd. She blinked her own tears away, knowing what this must mean to the angels who had lived tethered to the ground and cut off from the freedom of the air.

It was symbolic, in a way. The angels had been stuck in Everdark for so long, that the parting of the clouds seemed a fitting and final note to — as the Seraphim had said — a long, hard journey.

TWENTY-THREE
New Beginnings

Redd found (with a certain amount of smugness) that she didn't have to sleep very much to feel rested. A few hours and she was ready to go.

Though, no one slept much that night. Redd and Ty ended up standing in the churned fields outside the inner city as morning lightened the horizon to a dull grey, banishing the stars. The remainder of the partygoers and most of the city of Everdark filtered in to fill the space. A sense of eager anticipation permeated the crowd as the minutes ticked by and the sky turned violet, then pink, then orange, and finally blue.

Two Ladies ascended to the topmost part of the wall and raised their hands simultaneously. Redd's eyes instantly adjusted to light they hadn't seen in many weeks, and she realized what the Ladies were doing. With the angels being under cloud-cover for centuries, their eyes would have long become accustomed to the darkness.

There were probably certain younger angels who had never once seen the sky.

***

It wasn't until midmorning that everyone split up and headed back into the city to, finally, begin the process of rebuilding. Redd, Ty, and Tygjak wandered back to the main square, where Redd was surprised to find the detritus of the celebration already cleared away. More portals were set up, and the supply train carried on in true earnest.

"What is all that, anyway?" she asked Ty, gesturing at said supply train.

"Much has changed in Everdark, and on Assisi. It was decided to keep contingents here for now to support the angels. The flora on this planet evolved to a sunless world; now it will die. The elves will help restore the ecology. The dwarves have an innate connection with metallic deposits, and are excellent builders. The drakkan will help the planet heal itself, and aid in smelting. Of course, the Rangers, gnomes, and dozens of other species whom you haven't met will be helping out as well."

Ara and Pheonix entered the square. Pheonix was wearing a new set of armor, this one the most beautiful Redd had seen on him — or, anyone else — thus far. It was black with silver detailing: galaxies and stars seemed to play over its surface.

Ara paused, uncertain, glanced back at Pheonix, then swept her gaze over the open space. She caught sight of Redd, and a smile blossomed on her cherubic face.

Redd started toward her.

"Hi," Redd called as she got close enough.

"Hello!" Ara responded, radiating joy.

"Lord Tyyrulriathula," Pheonix said.

"Still so formal." Ty shook his head in exasperation.

"And Packmaster Tygjak," Pheonix said.

Tygjak flashed his fangs. "Good hunting, Swiftstrike."

Redd looked at Pheonix, yearning to thank him for what he did for Tygjak, but unable to find the words. He seemed to know she was watching him; she averted her gaze quickly as he looked up.

Ara's eyes shone. "There is so much to learn in Terelath, I can't imagine ever wanting to leave! I can't wait."

Redd's stomach knotted. "Yeah … "

"What's wrong?" Ara asked, concerned.

"It's just — new place, uncertainty … " she trailed off and shrugged.

Ara took her hand. "I'm here," she said quietly, full of conviction. "We have gone through hell together, Redd; you are my heart sister. Whatever trials await us in the future — in Terelath or beyond — you will not face them alone. I promise you."

Ty grinned and caught up her other hand. "You know you're not getting away from me. I *live* in Terelath. If anything happens, I'll be the first there, blades bared."

"I do not let harm come to my pack," Tygjak said, feral and forceful.

"I will be returning to Terelath as well," said Pheonix. "You shouldn't worry."

Emotion choked Redd's chest, made it hard to breathe. She blinked back tears, pulled Ara and Ty in for hugs, then nodded. She didn't trust herself to speak. There was nothing left to say.

Ty turned her as she released them, and it filled her vision: a portal, larger than all the others, leading to the green paradise that was the home of the elves.

Tygjak took a deep, sharp breath into his open mouth, like he was scenting the wind. "Availeon," he murmured. "It has been so long."

"Terelath," Redd whispered.

Ty smiled proudly.

"My beloved home. And, at least for now, yours as well."

Epilogue

Ichiryu fingered the dragon pendant hung on a delicate chain around her neck. Things had not gone according to plan, true, but it wasn't entirely a loss — that was what happened when you were smart and made plans within plans within plans. Something was always bound to go right, even if everything went wrong.

Kill two birds with one stone? Ha. Waste.

Kill twenty? Genius.

A smile curled her small mouth. The ancient angels had hidden the pendant well, which had proven to be a nuisance … but no matter.

She closed her eyes and willed a release. The pendant flared hot on her neck for a moment, and then was as dull and lifeless as the piece of stone it resembled.

When she opened her eyes, a woman stood before her. She and the tyrant Elysian met gazes; what Ichiryu encountered was curiosity, and power.

A power that was overwhelming, but as long as Ichiryu had the pendant, there would be no dissent.

Ichiryu said:

"I'd like to propose a deal."

***

Seraphiel's mind wandered far from her corporeal form, enjoying power denied to her for over three hundred years.

Threat gone; celebrations over; clouds removed; they'd now begun the long process of healing Assisi and fixing the damage done not only caused by the Elysian conflict, but the long parting from the rest of the universe.

But for right now, she wasn't needed. The outpouring of help from the other species meant that she needed only advise the new Queen, and that wouldn't often be necessary. Arrista had been the de facto leader of Everdark for quite some time and had fallen into the role seamlessly.

Something pinged on her awareness, and it sent a shock through her system.

The barrier around Godholme was gone! She could feel the other angels — *on their colony*! They'd been encased in the barrier!

We are not the last of the angelic peoples; the Creator's children live on!

A chill followed the thought:

Then why were we removed from the Book of Races?

Glossary

Age/Ages - *Term* - A measure of time. Generally about one-hundred-thousand True Years, though more accurately bookended by major events. The Age in which the events of Everdark take place is the Sixth Age.

Andural (*Ann*-du-rahl) - *Character* - Elven First. Legendary Bladesinger-smith who forged the superstructure of Terelath, the elven garlands, and many elven artifacts. Believed to be long dead.

Angel - *Species* - A species made by a collaboration between the Creator and its consort, Ashera. Angels are one of the most malleable and least physical species, and tend to be fanatically devoted to the Creator. Until Haven was discovered, they were thought to be extinct due to the Elysian campaign against the Creator.

Ara Luschia Invenes (*Ah*-rah Loo-*shee*-yah In-*veen*-ehs) - *Character* - Archangel. Healer. Scholarly, empathetic, and prim.

Arrista Legaia (Arr-*ih*-stah Leh-*Gah*-yah) - *Character* - Angel. Everdark's Master Healer. Perpetually cheery and knowledgeable. Mediator and natural leader.

Arkitekt - *Species* - A mysterious species that, in the distant past, spread gene-seeds and artifacts throughout the metacosm, apparently at the behest of the Creator, then disappeared utterly. No one currently knows why, or what became of them.

Ascended - *Group* - The Creator's direct influencing forces within the metacosm, representing elements and concepts.

Ashera (Ah-*sheh*-ruh) - *Ascended?* - The Creator's consort. Not much is publicly known of her, other than that the angels particularly revere her.

Assisi (Ah-*see*-see) - *Location* - The angelic homeworld. Razed by Elysian 300 years prior to the events of Everdark and The Fractured Balance.

Availeon (Ah-*vay*-lee-uhn) - *Location* - The elven homeworld. Orbited by Ranger HQ.

Bedaestael (Beh-day-*stay*-ell) - *Character* - One of Pheonix's swords. Crackling lightning. Talkative and whiny.

Bladesingers - *Group* - An elven Calling, the chosen of the Ascended of Law who are gifted Lawblades. At present, only male elves can become Bladesingers.

Bladesong - *Phenomena* - A Song (mixture of magic, sound, and quantum) allowing a Lawblade to suspend in the air and spawn multiple other, magical blades. The Bladesong controls the movement of all the blades in a complex composition.

Bladestorm - *Phenomena* - When a Bladesinger's emotions run too hot, he has the chance of losing control of his Lawblade, which will create a feedback loop that spawns thousands upon thousands of blades to destroy his target and anything in the vicinity … including himself.

Chani Abyssterilon (Sha-*nee* Ah-biss-*tear*-ih-lawn) - *Character* - Race of Man. Special Projects Commander for the Rangers. Competent, cunning, parental. Knows far more than she lets on.

Chosen - *Group* - Beings tethered to the Obelisk; a political body meant to communicate the Creator's wishes to the metacosm. They answer to the Obelisk and the balance.

Cira (*See*-rah) - *Character* - A Blackwing Praetorian (a company commander) from Everdark.

Citadel - *Location* - A cluster of five towers in the inner city of Everdark. Houses the war room and Seraphiel's sanctum.

City Center - *Location* - Haven's only town, in which lives angelic survivors.

Corruption - *Phenomena* - The name for the changes that happen after Elysian visitation/interaction. Its mechanism is unknown.

'Creator's Light' - *Term* - A reference either to the literal light of the Creator (meaning the Creator's direct energy/power) or the more euphemistic love or attention from the Creator.

Cybernetic augmentation - *Technology* - Physical technology-based augmentation, a step up from implants. Usually only used to replace a limb or other major body part.

Dark elf - *Species* - A subspecies of elf that split away from the others for wont of power. They are often seen associating with slavers (or are slavers themselves).

Demon - *Species* - An evil species that came from 'the Nether' (though it's not known what/where that is). Grotesque and hungering only for domination and death, it took a sacrifice of unrivaled proportion to stop them during the Great Demon War. The metacosm is constantly on the lookout for demon portals or signs of demon activity.

Deutronium - *Term* - The hardest known ore in the metacosm. An incredibly valuable resource, as only its discovery made long-term spaceflight and space stations possible.

Dragon - *Species* - Similar to fae, they are almost never seen in the metacosm, but proof of them exists in the drakkan and in other places.

Drakkan (Dra-*cahn*) - *Species* - Hominid/dragon mix. Agile, intelligent, withdrawn.

Dwarf - *Species* - A species of rock hominids created by the Forgemaster. Boisterous, aggressive, single-minded about their interests (which mostly include minerals).

Elf - *Species* - A First species; immortal and magically-inclined, tied to nature and the elements. They believe emotions are for the 'lesser species' and that they've risen above them.

Elven Council - *Group* - One of the governmental bodies of Accord space made up of mostly elven Seconds. Based in Terelath, they work closely with the Chosen and, to a lesser extent, the Rangers and Accord.

Elven Seconds through Sevenths - *Groups* - Elven generations based on birth order by Age and, though less important, parentage.

Elysian (Eh-*lee*-see-ann) - *Species* - Space-faring species of 'false Gods' made quickly legendary for their cruelty and power. Unknown provenance.

Errick Tinkerfist - *Character* - Gnome. Master Tinkerer of the Third Level (leader of the gnomes) and Accord Diplomatic General Extraordinaire (prime mediator for the Accord). A mind so complex, they used snapshots of it to model early supercomputers on.

Erukahl (*Eh*-roo-kahl) - *Species* - Psionic hive species mutated into existence on Assisi after the Elysian attacked. Ruled by the *erukahl* Queen.

***Erukahl* Queen** - *Character* - Mysterious hive-mind behind the *erukahl*. Seems to hate the angels, repeatedly attacks Everdark.

Everdark - *Location* - The name Pirroun took on following the Elysian's devastation of Assisi.

Evil - *Group* - Due to 'the balance' being the accepted ethos of much of the upper echelon of political power in the metacosm, evil has claimed legitimacy by way of the Creator's will. Evil people and organizations (such as sapient traffickers, thieves, poachers, raiders, etc.) have no need to hide their activities, as they are openly the 'balancing' factors of the metacosm.

Executioners - *Group* - An organization formed by ancient elven leadership and unleashed onto the metacosm, gifted special garlands that give them authority superseding any other governmental body. Known for their staunch dedication to Justice.

Fae - *Species* - A rarely-seen and rarely-documented species.

Federated Earth/Chaos Earth - *Location* - An uninitiated, technologically-advanced planet, inhabited mostly by humans, located on the edge of Dark Sector.

Firestorm - *Phenomena* - When a psyker loses all control, they infuse the molecules around them with elemental fire, which ignites into a fire-tornado surrounding them. A firestorm is multiplicative and will feed on itself; if the psyker is not calmed, the firestorm will condense to the point of detonation, giving psykers the nickname 'planet-crackers.'

Firsts - *Group* - The initial individuals of a species brought into existence directly by the Creator. They are older than Time itself and are often nearly on-par with Ascended in both knowledge and power. Very few are known of in the Sixth Age, though where they went is a common topic of debate among academics and citizens alike.

Fold-space - *Technology* - Ranger tek allowing an individual to store items within a space that is accessible only by this tek and by certain quantum-minded individuals.

Freija (*Frey*-ah) - *Character* - Archangel. Everdark's high priestess/director of religious matters. Serious and quick-minded.

Fug (Commander Fug) - *Character/Term* - A Ranger Commander whose exploits became so legendary among the Rangers that his name ended up synonymous with bad decisions and is often used as an expletive. (As in: "For Fug's sake.")

Garland (elven) - *Term* - A circlet worn by most elves. Said to be forged en masse as gifts to his people by Andural.

Gnome - *Species* - A diminutive species created by the Forgemaster. The most technologically-savvy species in the known metacosm, who prize the ability to tinker above all things.

Goblin - *Species* - An evil species known for their disregard of life and close-to-gnomelike obsession with technology. Enemies of the dwarves.

Godholme - *Location* - Quantum space at the center of all the multiverses. Said to be where the Creator and Ascended live. Takes on the appearance of a small planet covered in constantly moving, intricately-interlocking, filigreed metal plates.

Grey Mages - Group - The only class of mages that use Will magic, a sect of whom serve Law as peacekeepers on Availeon.

Grand Mistresses - *Group* - High-ranking dark elf females. Grand Mistress is one step below Matron, the highest rank in dark elf society.

Haven - *Location* - A series of mostly-uninhabited islands floating above Assisi's surface.

Healers - *Group* - Individuals with the power to Heal without technological means.

Hominin - *Term* - A species group relating to humans and Race of Man, among others. Many of this group were created by the Creator. Generally characterized by their shorter life-spans and tempestuous natures. Excludes those of primate genetics.

Hop - *Character* - Species unknown. One of Ichiryu's assassins. Seems to care about Tisaki's wellbeing.

Ichiryu (*Itch*-ee-ree-oo) - *Character* - Elysian. Hears voices. Is actively attempting to kill Redd. Rules a planet in Dark Sector.

Imae Rivios (Ih-*may Rih*-vee-ose) - *Character* - Race of Man. Ranger cadet. Immature, stubborn, mechanically gifted. The child of the heads of the Rivios clan.

Implant - *Technology* - Bio-nanotech that bonds with a body's systems to enhance it in some way from the inside (e.g. translation, communication, or access to archived information).

Initiated/uninitiated - *Term* - To be initiated is to be aware that other species exist outside of a society's planet/ current knowledge. Most initiated societies are expected to be contributing to or participating in metacosmic society in some way. Most uninitiated planets are left that way for a reason.

Jewel City - *Location* - The most affluent megacity (a very large city raised above the ground through technological means, though not floating) on Federated Earth.

Kser (Keh-*serr*) - *Character* - Orc Bound Sword-God. Cowardly and cruel.

Ladies (elven) - *Group* - An elven Calling, the chosen of Celestial, Ascended of the Weave, who are gifted with direct access to the Weave. At present, only female elves can become Ladies.

Law - *Ascended* - No name known. The rarely-seen enforcer of Law in the metacosm. Gifts Lawblades to Bladesingers.

Lawblade: A quantum blade given to Bladesingers.

Lazarus (Lah-zah-russ) - *Ascended* - The previous Ascended of Justice. Killed in the Second Age by Bast, evil God of Murder.

Legion - *Group* - The Elysians' only documented sociopolitical structure, though beyond its existence, not much is known. Dissolved with the disappearance of the Elysian 300 years before the events of *Everdark*.

Leonin Stonebreaker (General) - *Character* - Dwarf. Head of the Stonebreaker clan of dwarves and Acting Regent of all the dwarven clans (in lieu of the rightful dwarven king, who is 'cooling his head'). Exactly what you'd expect from a dwarf: loud, loves to fight. But under his boisterous laugh is a cunning mind. Clan-brother to Tinkerfist through a marriage to Tinkerfist's sister.

Life - *Ascended* - The Ascended of Life. No name given. Distant but kind and welcoming.

Life-spark - *Term* - A light within every individual that denotes their species. Can indicate other things too, like health status. Can only be 'read' or seen by certain species/ individuals.

Lucifer Invenes (*Loo*-siff-ur In-*veen*-ehs) - *Character* - Archangel. Ambitious, controlling, arrogant. Runs Haven/City Center with an iron fist. Ara's father; Lutius' brother; Persephone's husband.

Lutius Invenes (*Loo*-shuhs In-*veen*-ehs) - *Character* - Archangel. Dependable, nurturing, observant, jokes a lot. Former Blackwing-in-training. Ara's uncle; Lucifer's brother.

Mana - *Term* - A byproduct of the Weave's interaction with other domains and realms, fuel for the complex quantum calculations that make up the effect known as 'spells.'

Malol (Maa-loll) - *Character* - One of Pheonix's swords. Burning red. Grumpy, quiet, hungry.

Miasma - *Phenomena* - A mysterious toxic fog plaguing most of Federated Earth's surface.

Multiverse/'verse' - *Term* - Separate complete universes next to each other. The barriers between verses can be crossed, but it is a dangerous and highly-controlled thing.

Orc - *Species* - An evil species known for their worship of the God of Pestilence. They drink 'pustulence,' a substance made by their Elders and their God, to prove their devotion — but it also rots them from the inside out.

Paul - *Character* - An incompetent Ranger soldier who seems to show up constantly in places he doesn't belong. Talks to his helmet.

Persephone Invenes (Perr-*seff*-oh-nee In-*veen*-ehs) - *Character* - Archangel. Empathetic, strong, cunning. Ara's mother; Lucifer's wife.

Pheonix Barandor (*Fee*-nix *Bare*-ann-door) - *Character* - (Yes, it is 'PhEOnix,' not 'PhOEnix.') Genetic experiment who was raised by slavers. Has few emotions and an obsession with Justice.

Pirroun (*Pih*-roon) - *Location* - Angelic fortress on Assisi, guardpost against Silencefall.

Prophets (of an Ascended) - *Group* - Similar to how the Ascended directly act on behalf of the Creator, Prophets directly act where even their Ascended may not.

Psykers - *Group* - Short for Psychokinetics Users, humans with a mutation that causes a third brain lobe to form, which allows the psykers to manipulate molecules directly without using the Weave as a filter or conduit. The lobe's placement in the brain saddles psykers with extreme emotional instability.

Ranger HQ - *Location* - The most advanced spacefaring vessel in the metacosm. A planet-sized sphere made up of multi-layered rings surrounding a gravitic core. Most Ranger operations happen out of this location.

Rangers - *Group* - A militarized, space-faring society working closely with the Universal Accord to attempt to keep peace and protect innocents within Accord space. The mitigating factor to 'evil,' and, although not blatantly contemptuous of evil (for the sake of 'the balance'), then subtly so.

Rangers (elven) - *Group* - Personal servants of Spiraea. Known for being able to thrive in the wildest of Nature. Many are bow-users.

Ranger Great clans — Abyssterilon, Rivios, and Akamatsu - *Groups* - The Rangers were formed in the First Age by John Abyssterilon and Damien Rivios, whose families then went on to solidify the resulting political structure around themselves, creating the first two Great clans of Abyssterilon and Rivios. Lesser families (like Barandor and Beowulf) then aligned themselves with a Great clan to vie for political power. Akamatsu was a later addition to the Great clan structure.

Rec-suit - *Technology* - A universal biological recovery suit developed by the Rangers. Worn by nearly every Ranger under their armor. Has multiple iterations, uses, and designs.

Redd (*Red*) - *Character* - Human. Uninitiated psionic from Federated/Chaos Earth. Survivor of medical child abuse. A pile of coping mechanisms in a trenchcoat of sarcasm.

Resurrection - *Phenomena* - When the soul is drawn back into the body shortly after death and the body's systems restarted. Incredibly complex Healing magic.

Ruemilanthrasia (*Roo*-eh-mih-lann-*thray*-see-ya) - *Character* - Elf. Spiraea's Prophet and an elven Ranger. Easily amused, observant, charming. Loves vegan cheese.

Sapient - *Term* - A being with higher thought processes and a soul. (The Accord has an entire checklist to determine whether or not an individual/species is sapient. Note: sapient is different from sentient.)

Seraphiel (Serr-*aa*-fie-ell) - *Character* - Seraphim: Creator's Aegis. Protector of Pirroun/Everdark. Calm, kind, zealous.

Shielding technology - *Technology* - Generally comes in two types: generators and personal belts. Shield generators are massive and massively powerful, but can only produce one kind of shield (kinetic, null, magic, etc). Shield belts closely layer a field over an individual's body and can be tuned to shield the user from multiple sources of affective properties.

Silencefall - *Location* - The place on Assisi to which angels banished their most dangerous threats. Everdark/ Pirroun has protected its only entrance since antiquity.

Slavers - *Group* - Evil merchants focusing on sapient trafficking.

Song - *Term* - Generally used by elves and angels to refer to the Creator's Song, the background music to the metacosm that only certain species and individuals can hear.

Space pirates - *Group* - Evil scavengers made up of a motley assortment of societal rejects from all across the metacosm.

"Specials" - *Group* - Federated Earth term for people born with powers.

Spiraea (Spih-*ray*-uh) - *Ascended* - "Lady of the Woods." Ascended of Nature. Fierce, moody, enigmatic. Patron of the elves and Availeon.

Temperjoke - *Ascended* - Ascended of Chaos. Personality and actions 'dictated by Chaos.'

Terelath (*Teh*-reh-lath) - *Location* - The main city of the elven homeworld of Availeon. Seat of the Chosen.

Terminal - *Technology* - A boxy piece of every-technology, used for anything from creating food to dispensing knowledge.

The balance - *Term* - The belief espoused by those in power (such as the Chosen and the elven Council) that evil was created by the Creator and is meant to remain in balance with non-evil — that finding harmony between the two is the Creator's greatest wish of its creations.

The Creator - *Character* - An omniscient, omnipotent being who is said to have created the metacosm and everything in it.

The Dark Sector - *Location* - The sector of unmapped space (that which is outside of Accord space) known to be controlled by evil interests.

The Federation - *Group* - The ruling body of Federated/Chaos Earth. Fascist in strange ways.

The Forgemaster - *Ascended* - Ascended of makers. Creator and patron of the dwarves. A hermit, obsessed with his work as a smith; unflappable.

"The Golden Light" - *Character/Term* - Power/entity of unknown provenance that exists at Redd's core.

The Metacosm/Creation - *Term/Location* - Everything that was, will be, is, might be, ought to be, and shouldn't have been. A universe and its shadows.

The Obelisk of Time/"The Obelisk": A Creator artifact that claims to be the origination of laws that the sapient species should follow. Speaks through its Chosen.

Thread (of the Weave) - Term - Individual strands of the Weave, each attuned to a different magical element.

Tisaki (Tee-*sah*-kee) - *Character* - Species unknown. One of Ichiryu's assassins, though she doesn't seem to be particularly happy about it. Struggling with something she can't remember.

TKers - *Group* - Short for Telekinetics Users, Race of Men with a mutation that also causes a third lobe to form in the brain, though in a different location, allowing them to emit wavelengths that can directly manipulate objects with mass. This lobe's placement causes crushing depression.

Transport/"bug" - *Technology* - Small non-armored Ranger air vehicle used between ground and upper atmosphere.

Tygjak (*Tig*-jack) - *Character* - Tigrii. Formerly enslaved by the pirates. Wise, confident, tired.

Tyyrulriathula/Ty (Tee-rule-ree-*aath*-you-laa/Tie) - *Character* - Elven Seventh. Bladesinger and apprentice smith. Flippant, honest, emotional. Pheonix's best friend.

Universal Accord ("The Accord") - *Group* - A political entity consisting of every initiated non-evil species. They work closely with the Rangers to keep peace and support civilians of all shapes and origins — not just in Accord space, but beyond it as well.

Unit - *Term* - A base ten measurement system (milliunits, centiunits, units, etc.) primarily used by the Rangers.

Vathath (Vah-*tha*-th) - *Character* - Orc Bound sorceress outcast from her own people. User of blood magic.

Veric (*Veh*-rick) - *Character* - Angel. Everdark's military master. Dedicated and humble.

War-Bladesingers - *Group* - Bladesingers who threaten a Bladestorm. They are specially trained, taught to harness the Bladestorm.

Warboss Clones - *Group* - Clones of the goblins' ultimate leader, the Warboss. One is sent to every major battle the goblins partake in.

War-Ladies - *Group* - Ladies who threaten a Spellstorm (similar to a Bladestorm). They are specially trained, and gifted with phylacteries that absorb the intense excessive mana they exude.

Weave-user - *Group* - A person capable of manipulating the Weave and mana. These people go by many names: magus, Weaver, spell-caster, spell-user, etc.

Weave - *Term* - A mesh of 'threads' that makes up one of the major base supports of the metacosm. These threads and the Weave itself can be called on to use magic in the physical domain.

Wrist-comm - *Technology* - Short for wrist computer.

Zadkiel (*Zahd*-ky-ell) - *Character* - Seraphim: the Creator's Eye.

Zasfioretaeula (Zass-fee-oh-ray-tay-*ee*-uu-lah) - *Character* - Elven First. Prime War-Bladesinger. Cool, unreadable, professional.

About The Prime Speakers

What is a Prime Speaker, you may be asking?

Well, others may refer to our profession as 'author.' We Speak for the Metacosm, and bring its stories to this reality.

A is an opinionated intellectual with a penchant for theology, psychology, politics, hard sciences, and mathematics. They are a combat veteran with severe complex PTSD, bipolar, and ADHD. They've traveled all over the world and enjoy video games. The majority of the Metacosm was crafted by them over several decades, influenced by *Dungeons & Dragons*, real and emerging science, world observations, video games, and books.

N is a neurodivergent (autistic and ADHD) creative magpie. While writing fantastical stories and drawing the characters from them was something she'd done since she was a child, it was discovering anime (specifically, *Pokemon* and *Sailor Moon*) that led N into the arts seriously. Her long list of creative interests include photography, 3D, illustration, videography, fashion design, character design, and, of course, writing. N has the rare genetic connective tissue disorder Ehlers Danlos Syndrome and a myriad of fun comorbidities.

All things Metacosm:

http://metacosmchronicles.com

Printed in the USA
CPSIA information can be obtained
at www.ICGtesting.com
LVHW042326101224
798832LV00036B/549
* 9 7 9 8 9 9 1 1 8 7 4 0 4 *